PENGUIN BOOKS

THE END OF THE WORLD NEWS

Anthony Burgess was born in Manchester in 1917 and is a graduate of the University there. After six years in the Army he worked as an instructor for the Central Advisory Council for Forces Education, as a college lecturer in Speech and Drama and as a grammar-school master. From 1954 to 1960 he was an education officer in the Colonial Service, stationed in Malaya and Borneo.

He became a full-time writer in 1960, though by then he had already published three novels and a history of English literature. A late starter in the art of fiction, he had previously spent much creative energy on music, and has composed many full-scale works for orchestra and other media. His Third Symphony was performed in the U.S.A. in 1975.

Anthony Burgess believes that in the fusion of musical and literary form lies a possible future for the novel. His *Napoleon Symphony* attempts to impose the shape of Beethoven's 'Eroica' on the career of the Corsican conqueror. His other books include *The Long Day Wanes: A Malayan Trilogy*; the Enderby novels (including *The Clockwork Testament*); *Tremor of Intent*; a biography of Shakespeare intended to act as a foil to his Shakespeare novel, *Nothing Like the Sun*; *Honey for the Bears*; *The Doctor is Sick*; *The Wanting Seed*; *MF*; *Urgent Copy*; *Beard's Roman Women*; *ABBA ABBA*; *A Clockwork Orange*, made into a film classic by Stanley Kubrick; *Ernest Hemingway and His World*; *1985*; *Man of Nazareth*, the basis of his successful TV script, *Jesus of Nazareth*, and *Earthly Powers*, voted in France, 1981, the best foreign novel of the year.

Anthony Burgess

The End of the World News

An Entertainment

PENGUIN BOOKS

Penguin Books Ltd, Harmondsworth, Middlesex, England
Penguin Books, 625 Madison Avenue, New York, New York 10022, U.S.A.
Penguin Books Australia Ltd, Ringwood, Victoria, Australia
Penguin Books Canada Ltd, 2801 John Street, Markham, Ontario, Canada L3R 1B4
Penguin Books (N.Z.) Ltd, 182–190 Wairau Road, Auckland 10, New Zealand

First published by Hutchinson & Co. Ltd 1982
Published in Penguin Books 1983
Reprinted 1983

Made and printed in Great Britain
by Richard Clay (The Chaucer Press) Ltd,
Bungay, Suffolk
Set in Linotron Plantin

To Liana

Foreword

by John B. Wilson, BA

In pursuance of my duties as literary executor of the author of whom this, his first published posthumous work, is herewith offered to the delectation of some readers and the undoubted bewilderment of others, duties more arduous than I had anticipated when I assumed the office with no prospect of more than moral recompense, I set out to seek such manuscripts of his as would not, if published, seriously diminish his reputation while at the same time providing a modicum of needed sustenance for the author's relicts who, like the relicts of most authors, were in, and remain in, want.

I discovered a large number of manuscripts, some in a finished state and in fair copy, others, in the foulest of foul copy, clearly unfinished or, indeed, hardly begun. Some of the manuscripts were musical. One consisted of three hundred pages of full orchestral score with vocal and choral lines – an incomplete opera in mock-Puccinian style, its provisional title *The Hamlet of Roaring Gulch* and its libretto a version of Shakespeare's tragedy with a Wild West setting (Claudius the owner of a saloon formerly the property of his dead brother, Hamlet the grieving son back from a law college in the East, Polonius the old doc with nubile daughter, Laertes and Hamlet confronting each other with guns at high noon, and so on). There was a set of twelve stories with the collective title *The Bad-Tempered Clavicle*, seemingly attempts at assimilating fugal to narrative form, or it may be the other way about. Our author, to neither critical nor financial profit, was much concerned with the musicalization of fiction. I distinctly remember his muttering, and occasionally shouting, on more than one occasion the word 'Counterpoint!'

So some of the manuscripts were musico-literary. But by far the greatest number were pseudo-literary or sub-literary. His cultivation of sub-literature, the elimination from narrative composition of what may be termed poetic values, represented a recognition of the ineluctably growing authority of the visual media, particularly television. One bulky typescript, which has been processed into the work you have now before you, I discovered packed in a shopping bag marked boldly UPIM, this being the name of a celebrated Italian chain store with branches all over the peninsula, and the mouth of the bag was closed with abundant adhesive tape. Perusal of this typescript by myself, and by others on whom I called in the hope of enlightenment, my own powers of literary or sub-literary judgment being only moderately developed, was a process fraught with dubiety and puzzlement. There seemed, despite a double unity – that of the typeface (Olivetti STUDIO 45) and that of the typing paper (Gevafax 701) – and the fact of willed collocation, to be not one work here but three. Another possible factor of unification, that of the sub-literary nature of the style, was the only internal indication that this was intended as a single work, though the heterogeneity of the contents militated against that supposition. The sheets were unnumbered.

There appeared to be here arbitrarily assembled a fantastic tale of the end of the world, a brief biography of Sigmund Freud clearly intended, on the evidence of a preponderance of simple dialogue and a minimum of *récit*, as the raw material of a television series, and the libretto of a musical play on the theme of the visit of Leon Trotsky to the city of New York in 1917. (The music for this latter project was later discovered in rough short score and a variety of inks.) The three works, if they may so be called, were, so to speak, shuffled casually together, but very occasionally there appeared to be tentative verbal devices, roughly pencilled, in the nature of loose sub-literary stitching, clearly designed as points of cross-reference between them.

Having, as I did, the responsibility of decision on the advisability or otherwise of offering the work or works for publication, it seemed necessary to seek, in such private papers as the author had not, opposing his periodic tendency, destroyed, some clue as to his intentions. In the cobwebbed corner of the toilet of what I may dignify with the name of the author's final residence, I discovered a pile of books, a library of beguilement, consisting of a volume of Henry James's letters; a book of poems by one Geoffrey Grigson, most of the pages of which had been roughly torn out for presumably a tersive purpose; a work of musicology by a certain Hans Keller, much scrawled with bitter pencil obscenities; and a number of works of paperback fiction, e.g. *Let Her Scream*, by Anthony Powell; *Death in*

Undress, by S. Bellow; *Thrust of the Gun*, by Paul Bayley. Beneath these works was a notebook containing sparse entries in the hand of our author. One page consisted of the following:

algorithm – any method of computation, usu. involv. series of steps as in long div. Also algorism.

fiddler crab – genus uca, found in Amer. coastal regions. Back claw (one only) in males much enlarged. Fiddling move. of this claw attracts females.

The soul may come into existence because of tyranny. The tyrant takes everything from us so we are forced to believe we are left with something. This something we call the soul. Maurice could say this perhaps.

inkle – linen tape used for trimming.

microcosmic salt – white soluble solid from human urine.

Saw photograph of late President Carter and wife in White House late at night eating hamburgers and watching television. Note well – they were watching three screens simultaneously. Question of having something else to watch while commercials are on, late night commercials being the dullest and most frequent. But – this must be future viewing pattern. True visual counterpoint. Is this also possible future for the novel? Consider carefully, mon vieux.

mahewu – fermented mealie-meal porridge, stimul. Bl. Afr. in S. Afr.

magnetic flux density – oh never mind world grows too bloody compl.

You can take your choice of time and space. In matters of history you can't have both, esp. if you're German. Young K, a German, thinks me more capable of Nazi sentiments than himself, because I was brought up in the Nazi period.

Aaron's beard – rose of Sharon.

abelmosk – musk mallow.

abseil – descend by rope (from helicopter).

I have ascertained that, widely published in European picture magazines in the last year of President Carter's tenure, there was indeed a photograph of himself and his lady viewing simultaneously three television programmes. The author's comment on this procedure and its possible application to the craft of the novel provides an evident clue as to his intention in the work you have before you.

A letter, of which he had retained a xerox copy, to a girl whom he addresses as 'Dear Jenny', clearly a student in an American university, gives what I consider to be the clinching clue to that intention:

The three greatest events of all time? My dear child, that's too much. Event, anyway, is too instantaneous, too much of the big bang. Let's say the moment when an animal brain stood for the first time revealed as a human brain, the completion of the invention of writing, the (don't laugh, I mean it) abolition of slavery in the West. Not good enough? Perhaps some of the other 'great men' you're writing to will give you better answers. I have no difficulty in stating what I consider to be the greatest events of the past century – the discovery of the unconscious by Sigmund Freud, the Trotskian doctrine of world socialism, and the invention of the space rocket (physical, as opposed to merely psychological or ideational, transcendence of our dungy origins). Put that in your college magazine if you like. To you my love. XXXXXXXXXXX, old as I am.

It seems clear then, from this documentary evidence, that what you have in your hands is an attempt to incarnate in three selected narrative themes a structural notion derived adventitiously from a visual news item. The themes are linked through the author's own somewhat eccentric (at least in my view) evaluation of human history. There are doubtless other, more hermetic, links whose discovery I leave to the idle and ingenious.

The typescript was left untitled. I suffer from insomnia and spend long mosquito-haunted Mediterranean nights listening to the Overseas Service of the British Broadcasting Corporation. Every hour, on the hour, I hear the bulletin of actualities, which sometimes finishes with the formula: 'That is the end of the World News.' This evocation of the formula in the title I have given to this book by my old friend will, I hope, not displease his shade. He too was an insomniac exile listening to the voice of Britain, much distorted as always by the jamming of the Russians and the Albanians in their efforts to stifle the air's truth. He served the truth through a lying medium. He sleeps well now. Would to God I did.

Villefranche, 1982

A March noon, and the Central European heaven full not only of grey scud but of aircraft of the Third Reich in a menacing dance celebratory of the wholly beneficent ends of the *Anschluss*: tranquillity, order, uniformity, protection from free thought, that sort of thing. As the passenger plane began to land, Dr Jones clicked a picture on his Kodak of the airport building with WIEN on its roof, and also one of a squadron of fighters in formation of exquisite symmetry on the airfield. Then he and five fellow passengers climbed down the shallow steps to meet a blonde greeting ground hostess, a big wind, and the thrum of engines high over. They were led into a terminal, a small building full of the guttural sorrow of refugees loaded with luggage and the oppression of a long time to wait to get out, also the jokes and sneers of uniformed officials. Pennants with the crooked cross hung. Adolf as Parsifal gloomed mystically from the wall near customs and immigration. An official with swastika brassard was assisting the Austrian immigration official to sneer at proffered passports. At Jones's passport he did not sneer. He said with fine politeness:

'*Darf man sich erkundigen warum Sie Wien besuchen wollen?*' Why coming to Vienna?

'*Dies,*' Jones said, '*ist zum ersten Mal, dass ich gefragt werde,* WARUM *ich nach Wien komme. Ich komme nach Wien, weil ich Wien liebe.*' First time ever asked WHY. Come because like the place.

'*Sie sprechen gut deutsch für einen Engländer. Ihr beruf wird hier als Doktor der Medizin angegeben. Was tut ein englischer Doktor hier?*' Speak good for Englander. Passport says doctor. What does English doctor want here?

'*Ich bin,*' Jones said, '*kein Engländer. Ich bin Waliser. Ich bin Berater der Psychiatrie. Wien ist das Zentrum der psychoanalytischen*

Bewegung.' Welsh. Psychiatric consultant. Vienna centre of psychoanalytical movement.

'*Nicht mehr. Sie meinen die Schmutzigkeiten von dem Juden Freud. Sie überraschen mich, Doktor. Die Waliser sind arisch.*' Not any longer. Filth of Jew Freud, you mean. Surprised at you, doctor. Welsh are Aryans.

'*Arisch,*' Jones affirmed, having nearly said *Arsch* or arse, '*ist ein sprachlicher Ausdruck. Ich bin nicht sicher, was Sie unter jüdisch verstehen.*' (Courage: we shall not be using subtitles much longer.) Aryan a linguistic term. Not sure what mean by Jew.

'*Hier,*' the official with great charm said, showing teeth cleaned with Aryan Odol, planting a firm Nazi chop on Jones's passport, '*ist nicht der Platz Sie zu belehren. Vielleicht eines Abends bei einem Bier. Vergnügen Sie sich bei Ihrem kurzen Aufenthalt im Dritten Reich. Heil Hitler.*' This not place to teach. Perhaps some evening over a beer. Enjoy brief visit to 3rd R. H.H. Done.

Jones smiled something filthy in Welsh and then went to look for a telephone. He pushed through guttural sorrow towards one. A loud harangue started from the tannoys. Heils hailed frequently. He got through and spoke. He listened. He spoke. He said *Courage* and hung up. He went outside and picked up a taxi with a swastika flag on it. From the taxi he snapped with his Kodak banners, cheering crowds, tanks, armoured cars, whole streetloads of jubilation and submission. The driver could not well hear his directions because of the noise. Eventually they found the place, the Internationaler Psychoanalytischer Verlag.

Brownshirted boys were bringing out spilling armloads of books and loading them onto a truck. A brown dog scratched itself and yawned. Jones clapped his coke more firmly on his head and grasped his tight-rolled umbrella like a sword. He paid the driver and went in. He entered a room in which brownshirts counted money scooped from a drawer. Others dismantled the book stock. Martin Freud stood helpless, guarded by a dumpy fierce SA man with a pistol. Martin was mild, bewildered, slight, in handsome middle age. Jones said:

'What is this?'

'Under arrest.'

'*Wer sind Sie? Was tun Sie hier?*' the SA man cried.

'I,' Jones said with care, 'am the British representative of the International Psychoanalytical Publishing House. Who you are I neither know nor care. What you are I can smell from here. You are trespassing. This is private international property. Get out and take those dirty little boys with you. *Sofort.*'

Incredulous, then doubtful, then truculent, the SA man pointed his pistol at Jones. 'You too are under arrest,' he cried.

'Fool,' Jones bluffed loudly. 'I am a subject of the British Crown. You can't put me under arrest. Now get out.'

The SA man dithered. 'You will not say fool. You insult the uniform and you insult the Führer.'

'Not my Führer, *Gott sei dank*. Come on, out. *Schnell.*'

'Don't,' Martin whimpered.

'I telephoned Anna. She told me what was going on. It's hopeless, of course. We've got to get you all out, all of you. Meanwhile wait. And bluff.' He turned on the SA lout again. 'I demand to be permitted to telephone His Excellency the Ambassador of His Britannic Majesty. He'll sort you out, my friend.'

The SA thug liked that. He showed teeth not Odol-cleaned. 'He will do you no good. This is the Third Reich. You will learn.'

'So you forbid a foreign national to contact his own embassy? Is this a unilateral declaration of war?'

'War, you will get war. Get in that corner. You're under arrest.'

Jones smiled with great sweetness and told the SA swine what he was in tuneful Welsh and what his Führer was too, and how both had been born out of a dog's arse. A load of books appeared in the arms of a youth with pimples and brassard. One fell to the floor and opened. It showed in bold colour a diagram of the human brain. 'Dirty Jewish filth,' the SA pig said.

'How,' Jones asked Martin, 'are things with your father?'

Martin shrugged and told him.

When the loud thudding sounded on the door of the apartment, Martha Freud herself went to answer it. She was too old either to learn fear or to lose the habits of dignified politeness. So, opening the door and seeing five youths of the Sturmabteilung, on whose pimpled innocence (but she knew there was nothing more dangerous than innocence) scowls sat like pornographic covers on five volumes of the tales of the Grimms, she smiled and said: 'Yes, gentlemen?'

'We're coming in,' their leader said. He had a twitch under his left eye, a sign of grace perhaps. He twitched a pistol at her. The boy in the rear nursed a rifle.

'I'm afraid,' she smiled, 'the Herr Professor sees only one patient at a time. Which one of you seeks a consultation?' They bumbled in and she sighed. 'If you insist. Do please wipe your feet.'

The second of the lads looked about him in the entrance hall, which had its overflow of totems and pictures from the Herr Professor's study and was also rich with daylight. 'Rich dirty Jews,' he offered. Martha Freud said:

'No, we're middle-class *clean* Jews. That is why I ask you to wipe your feet.' The third started to do so on a reflex and was snarled at by his leader with *Dummkopf* and *Vollidiot*. The youth with the rifle prepared to stand by the door as a sentry. Martha Freud said to him: 'Please sit down in that chair. This is not a police station. Nobody stands in this house when there is a place to sit. And please put the butt of that gun thing in the umbrella stand. I will not have my parquet scratched.' The young man, bewildered and hearing the tones of his grandmother, obeyed. 'This way, gentlemen,' Martha said. They followed her into the sitting room.

They saw Viennese bourgeois neatness. They let eyes and open mouths seek dirty pictures in vain. They saw a handsome lady in early middle age sitting on a straight chair and reading a big book. It was too well bound to be dirty. 'I think they want money, Anna,' her mother said. 'Poor boys. You'll find the housekeeping money in its usual place.' Anna put down her book but her eyes seemed to rest on an after-image of the text. She went to a shallow china jug on the mantelpiece. Her mother looked at the boys with pained benevolence. Anna emptied the jug onto the silk runner on the round table. 'Will,' Martha Freud said, 'the gentlemen be so good as to help themselves?'

'We want more than this,' the leader twitched, scooping spilling silver into his shirt pocket.

'Of course.' And Martha herself went over to the effigy of a fierce tribal god which guarded a little cashbox on a corner whatnot. She poured the contents onto the table.

'More.'

'I'm afraid we haven't any more. If,' Martha said, 'you'd care to bring a letter officially stating how much is required by your organization, whatever it is, we would naturally look for more. We should, of course, require a receipt.'

Anna spoke. She spoke somewhat pedagogically. 'You know that the desire for money is infantile? It goes back to a baby's playing with its own mess. Pleasure in handling fecal matter.' She clarified. '*Absonderungstoffe*.' She overclarified. '*Scheisse*.'

That broke a kind of spell. 'Right,' the leader twitched. 'Let's start. A rich Jewish house. Rich dirty Jewish bastards.' And he went over to a cloisonné vase with, in his young innocence, the intention of smashing it. At that moment

At that moment the man himself walked in. He was small, old, neat-bearded, suffering, his mouth strange and lumpy-looking. But the eyes were very fierce. He said nothing. He just looked. The leader yelped as though the loot in his shirt pocket was starting to scorch the nipple beneath. He said:

'We're going now. But we're coming back.' To get out they had to pass the old man's eyes. They didn't like that. 'The Gestapo's coming. They'll beat the shit out of you.' He gulped, flooded fully by those eyes. Nobody saw them to the door. In the hallway something was apparently dislodged from something. The Freuds heard something fall lumpily to the parquet.

'How much?' Freud asked Anna.

'About seven thousand schillings.'

'Just for one visit. More than I ever got paid for just one visit.' Behind his back, like a concealed weapon, he had been holding a cigar. He now put it with pain into his mouth, forcing the jaws to open with an irritable pressure of his free fingers on his bearded chin. The cigar was still alight. He puffed and went out puffing.

Martin and Jones now spoke English. The SA thug listened unhappily. The Führer ought to force the whole world to stop speaking foreign languages. These two could speak good German. They were speaking this other language now so that this loyal servant of the Führer should not understand. He let this dirty Jew speak this other language for a bit. Martin said: 'Things aren't too bad with him. But you'll never get him out of Vienna. He talks about the destruction of the Temple by Titus. Some rabbi, he said – I've forgotten his name – got permission to open a school for the study of the Torah. He thinks it's going to be the same here. He said the Jews are used to persecution. He doesn't seem to understand the first thing about the Nazis.'

Time to cut in. '*Nazi. Nazi. Dass versteh' ich.* Speak German and stop that foreign cackle. You,' he said to Jones, 'are you too one of these filthy Jews?'

'No, I'm not a Jew,' Jones said with clarity and relish. 'But you are, my little friend. You're trying to disguise it. I know Jews. It's been my study for years. I can tell by the shape of your nose and the length of your skull that you're a Jew. I'm going to ask your superior officer for a sample of your blood. I'm a man of learning, a scientist, a doctor. I know you're a Jew, it sticks out a mile. When they find out, you're going to be in big trouble.'

The SA thug went now into a big rage. He clicked off his safety catch and turned on Jones in genuine menace. He seemed to ask Jones if he would like this shitting gun rammed right fucking down his bleeding throat. Jones said, as the gunpoint approached:

'Go on, do it. You'll go down in history as the man who declared war on the British Empire. Your Führer won't like it, of course. He'll hang you. But you'll have your little place in the history books.' The SA thug was not now listening. He was stiffening to attention as his superior officer stamped in, followed by a civilian who smoked a cigarette and dribbled ash down his porridge-coloured overcoat. The SA officer, a lopsided man with an angry wart on his neck which his collar just failed to hide, looked severely at Jones and Martin and asked:

'Your names?'

'I am Dr Jones, a British citizen. Your man here decided to put me under arrest for trying to protect the property of an international publishing house. You really ought to choose your lower ranks with more care. This is the son of Professor Sigmund Freud.'

The officer started to kick his thug. 'Out, dumbhead, you will hear about this, fool, learn to behave, shitbrain.' The pig went off snarling at Jones's grin. '*Servus*,' the officer said. 'This gentleman is the commissar appointed for the liquidation of Viennese Jewish psychoanalysis. He is Dr Sauerwald.' Dr Sauerwald spat out his cork tipped fagbutt and held out a hand to Jones. Jones kept one hand in his overcoat pocket, the other on his umbrella crook. Jones said:

'It's a pity. Psychoanalysis has saved lives. The lives of Gentiles.'

'We've no objection to Aryan psychoanalysis,' Dr Sauerwald said. 'To Dr Jung. It's the Jewish school that has to go.'

'I see,' Jones said. 'Well, you'd better get those guffawing little boys there to do some sifting. There's a lot of Aryan psychoanalysis there being got ready for the bonfire. Writings of mine, for example. What bloody nonsense.'

Dr Sauerwald said to the SA officer, at the same time blindly putting a fresh cigarette on: 'Let me talk to Dr Jones. I'm sure you've other things to do. Beating up the enemies of the State, for instance.'

'Heil Hitler.'

'Hitler,' Dr Sauerwald said, smoking. And to Martin: 'There's no point in your staying. Thank you for your er.' Martin was out of that door before the SA officer. Dr Sauerwald, cigarette tin still in his hands, offered a cigarette to Jones. Jones grinned sadly at the brand-name, which was Wahnfreud. Sauerwald grinned too as sadly. 'Mad joy,' he said in English. Then in German: 'It is what we all feel in this great age of Nazi enlightenment. Mad Freud. He evokes none of that emotion.'

'Not even among the thousands who've been cured of madness by his methods?'

Sauerwald puffed and dripped ash. 'I studied chemistry under Professor Herzig,' he said. 'Do you know the name?'

'An old friend of Freud's. Jewish, of course.'

'Listen,' Sauerwald said with an urgency that made his cigarette coal glow hard. 'I won't conceal from you the extent of my anti-semitism. I believe history will bless Adolf Hitler for quelling the power and influence of the Jews. Your own British Empire is being undermined by them. They're everywhere. Clever, of course. Inventive. And this is one of my troubles. I admire cleverness and inventiveness. The Jews are also great teachers. I admire Professor Herzig as much as I admire any man in the world. But I hate the Jews and I want to see the whole Jewish race destroyed. Can you understand this?'

'No. But I think I can understand what you propose doing. Well, I'm here to disinfect the pure Nazi Viennese scene by trying to persuade Dr Freud to get out. England's ready to have him, I think. He has followers in England.'

'As I said, your Empire's riddled with Jews.'

Jones was angry. 'Oh, for Christ's sake stop this bloody nonsense about the Jews. It's I, a bloody Welshman, who am primarily responsible for the spread of Freud's doctrines in Great Britain. I, a Celt. But if you want to make out that a Celt is a Jew, which your party ethnologists are quite capable of – Sorry sorry sorry. I know you're trying to help a great man. What will happen if he stays?'

'Concentration camp,' Dr Sauerwald said. 'Death in one form or another. But if he dies here, the rest of the world will say he was killed. I don't want that. It's a matter of money. He has to buy his way out. There's a tax called the *Reichsfluchtsteuer* — '

'You have some charming terms.'

' – And other taxes, imposts, fines, voluntary gifts to the State. How much money has he?'

'Not much. But don't worry. Money can be raised.'

'Does he have money abroad?'

Jones did not reply.

'You see, all foreign funds have to be called in before we can issue an *Unbedenklichkeitserklärung*.'

'A what? No, don't repeat it. I see your point. It can take a long time to call foreign money in. Years and years. I hope you realize that Freud is a very sick man. Cancer of the jaw. I think your masters might concede that even a sick Jew should be allowed to die in peace.' His voice thickened. 'No, absurd of me even to suggest it. It's hard for us decadents to take some things in. Like the idea of a total and metaphysical brutality. Sorry sorry sorry. What are you going to do?'

'This,' and Dr Sauerwald spat out the butt. 'I'm going to make a notarized declaration that he has no money abroad. I hope to God they believe it. We'll get him out. As a tribute to that filthy Jewish swine of a professor who was the finest man in the world.'

'God bless you, Sauerwald.'

'Help, you said help?'

'God help you too.'

The Ritz bar in Paris was almost empty. A drunken American sat at the counter complaining to his wife about the absence of Ernest Hemingway. 'Well, where is he, for Christ's sake? Always here, he said. Look me up here, he said, any time, for Christ's sake.'

'Maybe,' his wife applied a deep almost mourning shade of lipstick, 'he's killing bulls some place.' She was beanpole-thin, in beige.

'Any time, he said, for Christ's sake.'

At a table near one of the walls two men sat. One was the United States Ambassador to France, W. C. Bullitt, and the other Graf von Welczeck, to France Ambassador of the Third Reich. Graf von Welczeck said:

'The situation is extremely delicate. Your President wishes to send an official note?'

'Hardly.'

'The Führer is in a state of truculent defiance. Not of sweet reason and conciliation.' The English accent was perfectly patrician. 'The Austrian *Anschluss* has given him great confidence. He will be delighted to snap his fingers at President Roosevelt.' He snapped his own fingers for two more martinis. Bullitt said:

'Roosevelt and I are old friends. I sent him a friendly message, no more. It's not a State matter. We try to think of certain acts of your government as – well, internal matters. Even the sudden silence of – well, certain world-respected Jewish musicians and writers. But there's a scale of values. Some men don't belong to the Third Reich at all. Schoenberg. Einstein. Dissident Gentiles too. Thomas Mann, Paul Hindemith.'

'Those got away.'

'Those got away.' The martinis appeared.

'What am I expected to do?'

'Merely respond to world feeling. My President has already sent a cable to our chargé d'affaires in Vienna. But all we can expect is a possible – well, lenity.'

'From the Gestapo?' The Graf sipped without pleasure. 'My dear Bullitt, Vienna was always antisemitic. The Gestapo is merely a new arm of indigenous intolerance. Your chargé d'affaires will do no good.'

They sipped. 'They make good martinis,' Bullitt said. The American at the bar counter whined:

'Any time, he said. Ask for Ernie Hemingstein, he said, for Christ's sake.'

Bullitt's martini-holding hand shook a little. 'Graf von Welczeck,' he said, 'I take it – you wouldn't know the importance – the earth-shaking importance – '

'Yes?'

'I was under treatment, you know. From him, personally.' He hid his lower face in his martini glass.

'I *didn't* know.'

'It's one of the great discoveries. We were all children before he came along. He's taught the world what the human mind is like.'

The Graf said sourly: 'All that infantile sex.'

'Shocking, yes. Like the sun not really going round the earth. Like men being cousins to monkeys.'

'Oh, we can take all that. But – well, incest and anal eroticism. Wanting to sleep with your own mother. Kill your own father.'

'Isn't it true?' Bullitt said with some ferocity. 'He's healed people, you know. Cured them. Like casting out devils.'

'The National Socialist Party,' Graf von Welczeck said with gravity, 'is altogether opposed to superstition.' He looked Bullitt in the eye without smiling. Bullitt began to smile. The Graf smiled very faintly. 'I'll do what I can,' he said.

'Any time, he said, for Christ's sake.'

There was a Nazi flag high above Berggasse, near Number 19. Jones's rolled umbrella thrust and thrust in the direction of the sound of a band on the march, marching feet, cheers. Very four-square music, like a Calvinist hymn. Like a speeded-up Bread from Evans's. He marched to Number 19 and knocked. A chewing girl, country from her cheeks, let him in. He went straight to a study full of idols and effigies and signed portraits of the safe or dead great. Freud opened his mouth with pain and difficulty to insert a cigar. He winced.

'How is the new prosthesis?'

'As bad as all the others. A great thick door in my mouth.' He lighted up and puffed. 'I'm not going. You see how I am. Old and weak. I couldn't even climb on to a train.'

'You could be lifted.'

'Like an infant. So. I am on a train. Then I go where? No country wants refugees.'

'Marie Bonaparte will look after you in Paris. I'm going back to London to see the Home Secretary. We belong to the same club.'

'Your skating friend?'

'You remembered. You stay in Paris till the permit comes through.'

'With the Princess? I think not.'

'You've a lot of packing to do. All these idols and effigies and signed portraits.'

'A soldier doesn't desert his post. Nor a captain his ship.'

'You remember the *Titanic*?'

'What about the *Titanic*?'

'Lightoller, the second officer. He didn't leave his ship. His ship left him.'

Freud tried to chuckle but winced instead. 'A newborn child in the palace of the Princess. Like Moses. You ask me to consider a rebirth.'

'Start packing tomorrow.'

'I think not.'

This time there was not merely a thudding on the outer door, there was a manic ringing of the bell as well. Martha Freud herself went to open. There were four men in dark crumpled suits. The chief of them said: 'Gestapo.'

'I'm sorry, gentlemen,' Martha said. 'I don't know the word. Are you selling something?'

'The Geheime Staatspolizei.'

'Ah, Secret State Police. That's something new. I don't think we had that before we were liberated.'

'Liberated? May we come in?' But they came in anyway.

'Well, they tell the Austrians they've been liberated from weakness and decadence and the evil influence of the Jews. To think we've been an evil influence all these years without knowing it. Yes, do please come in. But I'm afraid we've no money for you. Those little boys in brown keep taking it all.'

'You talk too much, *gnädige Frau*,' the chief said. He was a decent-looking haunted-looking middle-aged man like a dismissed schoolmaster. 'We are the Gestapo. When we want talk we ask for it.'

'Like my husband, yes, I see. He's cured many people of madness just by letting them talk to him. You're called the Secret Police because you get people's secrets out of them – is that it?'

'This is duty, you understand? It will be no pleasure for us to have to make your house untidy. But we must search for books and papers. Of an anti-Nazi kind, do you understand?'

Martha was now angry. 'You will *not* make my house untidy,' she cried. 'I have heard of you people tearing things up for whatever nonsense it is you're looking for. No. This has always been a tidy house. It has been my duty and pleasure to keep it clean and neat for my husband. There are no anti-Nazi pamphlets here. We'd hardly heard of you people before you came bouncing into our city with your ridiculous little flags. I must ask you gentlemen to leave.'

They did not smile. The chief said: 'Pamphlets, eh? So you know all about pamphlets. Your husband has been a member of some secret Jewish society, hasn't he?'

'He belonged,' Martha said, 'to the B'nai B'rith Verein, if that's what you mean. An association of Jewish gentlemen. He used to give them talks. Now he has cancer of the mouth and cannot talk easily any more.'

'Talks against the Nazi Party?'

'The Nazi Party did not even exist when he gave his talks. He talked about the human mind, which has nothing to do with the Nazi Party.'

The second man, who had the look of a butcher but spoke with a lisp, said: 'You mean that as an insult, *gnädige Frau*?'

'How do you mean, an insult? I don't see any connection between politics and the study of the human mind.' They did not quite know how to take this. They looked at each other. The chief man shrugged and said:

'We will start.'

In the sitting room they checked the titles of books on the shelves, reading the spines aloud, then throwing the books in a heap on the Turkey carpet. Goethe. Schiller. *Three Men in a Boat. Alice in Wonderland*. Schnitzler?

'Dirty. But not anti-Nazi.'

Martha wrung her hands, looking on. Her husband and daughter were out, these horrible men must have known that, oh when would they return? They returned when the Gestapo were debating the Bible. The Bible was Jewish. The issue of the Bible had never been made clear, rather like the works of Shakespeare, though Shakespeare had been established as antisemitic. Luther's translation was apparently in order, Luther being an Aryan German, but this Bible they were looking at now was in English or possibly Dutch. Freud and Anna entered in outdoor clothes. Freud gave the Gestapo a look of Mosaic annoyance but not surprise. The Gestapo men were at once interested in Anna.

'This woman?'

'This lady,' Freud said, 'is Fräulein Anna Freud. My daughter.'

'Speak up, you do not speak clearly.'

'The prosthesis in my mouth renders due apologies.'

'I don't think,' the chief man said, 'it's necessary to search any further. Instead we will take this *lady* to the Hotel Metropol.'

'Gestapo headquarters,' Anna said. Her mother let out a wail. 'This *woman* will go with you, if that's your wish. But please don't speak of taking me. I am not a parcel.'

Freud's speech was terribly distorted. 'Tlake mle,' he said. 'She knows nlothing. I am the grleat slinner aglainst the Nazli ethlic.'

The second man took Anna's left arm, but she shrugged his hand off.

'Whlat dlo ylou wlant? A rleclantation of mly crlimes?'

'I've heard of your headquarters,' Martha wailed. 'You torture people there. Why did you have to come to our city? Why can't you leave decent people alone?'

'Is it a plublic crlucifliction ylou wlant? I dlemand tlo ble tlaken. Leave mly dlaughter alone. Shle wlorks for chlildren. Shle dloes nlothing blut glood.'

'Don't worry,' Anna said. 'Come,' and she made as to leave first.

Freud raised his right hand to heaven. The gesture was jokingly interpreted.

'Heil Hitler.'

They went. Martha sobbed. Freud, shaking, took her in his arms.

The corridor where Anna was made to wait was underground and lighted by dim lamps in little wire cages. There was, she was thinking, a recognizable Jewish physiognomy, though there was room too – intermarriage, Crusader violation – for blond and snub exceptions. All the waiting Jews on the long benches were of the *Stürmer* caricature type. It was a pity. A filing clerk came out of an office, whistling. From the office whose door he briefly opened came the noise of passionate weeping. In the distance three sharp animal howls, then silence. The Jewish man sitting next to her said:

'Three hours already. The thing to do is not to worry. They want you to worry. To be afraid. You know the story of the two Jews before the firing squad? Any last request? asks the captain. Yes, says Isaac, a cigarette. And you? says the captain to the other. Esau just spits in the captain's eye. Oh Esau, cries Isaac, why do you want to make trouble?'

'A good story,' Anna said. 'Encouraging too.' She got up and went to the first door on the corridor. She opened it and went in. Inside there were men in shirtsleeves working on documents. She called clearly: 'I have work to do. How much longer is my time to be wasted?'

There were various vocal responses after the first shock of silence. Out of here get back there yiddess wait your turn bitch you wouldn't be so damned impatient if you knew what they're going to do to you. Anna said:

'If I'm going to be interrogated I demand to be interrogated now. I was brought here to be interrogated. Why then am I not being interrogated? I want to get this time-wasting interrogation over.'

A bulky man smoking a cigarette with a long silky ash came in. The rest shut up; here was a man in authority. He was not in shirtsleeves. He looked on Anna with large insolence and said: 'You are – ?'

'Anna Freud. Brought here to be interrogated.'

'About what?'

'There's only one crime, isn't there? I presume I must be an enemy of the State.'

'Get outside there,' the man said. 'You'll be called when you're wanted.'

'Now. My patients need me. Your department is much too frivolous.'

That term took some taking in. It had never been used of the Gestapo before. *Leichtsinnig*. It got her dragged to an inner office where a very senior official smoked busily, pretending to brood over a file. From above the mantelpiece Adolf seemed to be reacting to a faint but pervasive bad smell. *Leichtsinnig* indeed. 'Anna Freud,' Anna said. 'Brought here for interrogation.' The bulky man who had brought her shook his head as at the world's *Leichtsinnigkeit* and went out. Anna sat on the wooden chair facing the desk.

'You will stand.'

She stood. 'Yes, perhaps you're right. I mustn't make myself at home. Forgive my impatience. I have work to do. May we begin?'

'Freud.' The name had clanged faintly. The Hitler expression over the mantelpiece confirmed its bad odour. 'Daughter of? Wife of? Sister of?'

'Come. He's an old man, that at least you should know. Daughter.'

'You follow him? You do his kind of work?'

'With children, yes.'

'With children.' Hitler confirmed his disgust. 'Tell me some of the things you do.' The official's thin look was lubricious.

'I cure anxiety, maladjustment, hysteria – Do you really wish to know?'

'I know enough. I know that your father's dirty invention is a travesty and an abomination. It's a Jewish attempt to corrupt childhood innocence. Children knowing about sex – falling in love with their mothers and wanting to kill their fathers.'

'The truth,' Anna said, 'is always painful. Until we grow used to it. But the truth has nothing to do with dirt and corruption. I've been brought here presumably to talk sense. Are we to talk it or do you wish to put me to the torture?'

The telephone buzzed. The official gave it a *Ja* and a *Guten Tag*. There was urgent talking at the other end. He kept saying *Ja* to it, his eyes surveying Anna from neat black hair to earrings, brown-cloaked shoulder to shoulder. When he had spoken his last *Ja* and put down the receiver he said to her:

'You need not think, Fräulein, that this kind of foreign interference will do you or your family any good. They speak very bad German also.'

'The Americans?'

'The chargé d'affaires, ridiculous foreign title. They mean the *Geschäftsträger*. Foreign Jews poking their large noses into the affairs of the Third Reich.'

From afar came a sudden scream. It started sharp and tailed off into a wail. The official sucked it in with relish like tobacco smoke. Anna froze. Then she said:

'Affairs of the Third Reich, yes.'

'For the moment you are free to go. But you will come back tomorrow. And the day after. And the day after that. Come very early.'

'For interrogation?'

'You may call it that. Very, very early. Now go.'

She went to a *Bierstube*, unwontedly, and ordered a *Grosser Braunen*. Her thirst was intense. An orchestra played Strauss's *Morgenblätter*. Brownshirts laughed and caroused. A *Stürmer* nose was thrust into a dish of *Schlagobers*. No, no, but it could have happened. As she left she met on the dark street the joke-telling Jew of the underground passage. He limped and was very dirty. 'They let you go,' she said.

'For the time being. They have no sense of humour. I told them the story about Hitler crying out: Who are the enemies of the Reich? and Jakob Bernstein replies: The bicycle-riders. Why the bicycle-riders? cries Hitler. And Jakob says: Why the Jews?'

'One of my father's jokes.'

'They didn't think it was funny.' There was caked blood in his smile. Anna escaped from it home.

The dining room seemed to have been rearranged around a brimming ashtray. Her father was wet-brown with tobacco tar. He embraced Anna, crying over and over: 'Oh my God.'

'How many have you smoked?'

'Eighteen, twenty, I didn't count. Oh my God. What did they do to you?'

'To me nothing, yet. They told me to go back tomorrow.'

'And are you going back?'

'Of course not.'

Her father nodded in grim satisfaction. Her mother came in from the kitchen. She did not embrace Anna. Instead she howled. 'The shame of it. The shame. Your father is smoking himself to death. Never before has he in the dining room. Everything is changing. Supper is nearly ready.'

'To think,' Freud said, 'that I hesitated. To think I was so damnably innocent. I, the specialist in guilt. We're leaving Vienna.'

'Well,' Anna said, 'you always hated Vienna.'

'Yes, I've spent all my life hating it. And now I suppose I'll weep. Who knows anything at all of the heart of man? Will anyone ever resolve even the smallest of the human contradictions?'

'You're in pain, father. I'll take out your prosthesis. It's not been cleaned all day.'

'Yes,' he said in agitation. 'Take it out for ever. Throw it away. What good is it? A soft-boiled egg for supper, dribbling it out through my nose. I neigh like a horse when I try to speak.'

'You've had too many cigars, father. You know it makes you nervous.'

'Turning into a child again. Helpless.'

'Sit down now,' Martha said. 'Put that cigar out. I'm bringing in supper.'

'An ungrateful and treacherous city.'

Birdsong, sunlight and honeysuckle. The study window was open to the Viennese summer. The study itself was bare of its gods and demons. Freud, at his desk, blew cigar smoke at Dr Sauerwald. Sauerwald, in a summer suit, opened his briefcase. He took out a document. He said:

'The delay was none of my responsibility. I have done everything possible to to – '

'Expedite matters, yes. But there was never any hurry for me. It was the others. Most of them, thank God, have already left. I fear there are others of my family who must stay and suffer.' He gave Sauerwald a fierce Mosaic look.

'But you yourself,' Sauerwald said, 'you must admit you have been – well – left in peace – treated with respect – '

'A swastika flag flies above this apartment. I have had visits from thugs – both in uniform and out of it. My son and daughter have been hectored and bullied by the secret police. My books have been burned. The science of the mind has been destroyed. Jews have been humiliated, tortured, sent to labour camps, exterminated. The process of liquidating the Jews has been partially financed with my own expropriated funds. Peace, respect – yes, of course.'

'Jones, I take it, Dr Jones – has successfully concluded – '

'The British are letting me in, yes. They are very vague about Jews, the British. They are not quite sure what a Jew is. One of the strengths of your party is its absolute certainty about race, science, art, the desirable life. Whatever nonsense you have there in your hand – let us have it and get it all over.'

'A mere formality, you understand. The final condition for an exit visa.'

Freud took the document and read it through a veil of smoke. '*Du lieber Gott* – "Have been treated by the German authorities and by the Gestapo in particular with all the respect and consideration due to my scientific and literary – That I could work and live in full freedom – Have not the slightest ground for any complaint –" So you people are at last acquiring a sense of humour.'

They looked at each other expressionlessly. Sauerwald shrugged. He said: 'I cannot, of course, force you to sign. But I have to point out that the issue of –'

'Yes yes yes. Well, as we Jews are expected to be villains and blackguards, it is in character for us to lie.' He picked up his desk pen. He then grinned horribly at Sauerwald. 'May I add something?'

'I regret that you may not. You may not in any way modify what is an official document prepared and ratified at the highest level – '

'I only want to add this,' Freud said, already writing it. ' "I can heartily recommend the Gestapo to anyone." And then my abominable name to sully the Nazi archives.' He had not switched off the grin. Sauerwald grabbed the document and left.

The Freuds took an evening train. The old man had to be hoisted up the steep steps like a heavy item of luggage. A couple of SA boys with rifles laughed. Freud heard the laughter. From the top of the steps he cursed them with his eyes. It was a long curse. Their crests did not fall. The curse of an old man being hoisted onto a train.

It was three in the morning when they reached the French border. The train stopped. They waited. 'Seventy-nine years,' Freud said, not for the first time nor the last. Two young jaunty immigration officers entered the compartment. Freud lighted a cigar.

'*Rauchen verboten*. This is an official examination.' Anna handed the papers over. Freud audibly cursed in English. 'Excuse me, I did not understand what you said.' Freud hawked and spat.

'This damned prosthesis.'

'Sigmund,' Martha said, 'don't make trouble.' Anna grinned sadly.

'*Alles ist in Ordnung. Heil Hitler.*'

'May I smoke now?' But they had gone.

'We're free?' Martha asked. 'No more Nazis?'

'No more Nazis. No more Vienna. Seventy-nine years of it. An ungrateful hypocritical antisemitic obscurantist vicious frivolous stupid brutal detestable city. No more Vienna.' But his eyes brimmed. Anna settled to the reading of a cheap sensational novel in English.

All this happened a long time ago, children, so forgive me if I am vague on detail. But the date and place are sure. The date was 18 December and the last day, evening rather, of the Christmas term. The heat was seasonably intense, and the school nativity play was being held in the open air. Three hundred odd parents and children sat on plastic-backed chairs in the playground of St Bede's Primary, Nowra, New South Wales, and watched Jack Tamworth, Joey Warwick and Bertie Domville as shepherds watching their flocks by night. Their stage was a set of planks on trestles, the sky they sat under a real one. The Southern Cross spoiled things rather: you were not supposed to be able to see the Southern Cross in Palestine. But the three boys sounded like three shepherds. Mr Lithgow, the English master who had written the script, had given them real sheepmen's language.

'Who's that joker there then?' Joey Warwick asked.

'A bloody poddy-dodger,' Bertie Domville said.

Ronald Birchip, one of the older boys, winged and nightshirted as the Archangel Gabriel, was coming towards them, bare feet making the boards creak. 'Hail, O ye fortunate shepherds,' he said, giving the Australian Labour Party salute.

'Sounds like a Pommy bastard,' Jack Tamworth said.

'Have ye not seen that star rising in the east?' Ronald Birchip said, pointing firmly towards San Francisco. 'It is as a sign. A great travail in the heavens has brought to birth a fiery wonder, and this night it shines over a lowly stable, where the Prince of Peace, himself a fiery wonder, shall be brought to birth by a virgin.'

'What's a virgin?' Joey Warwick asked.

The headmaster, Mr Maitland, frowned round at Mr Lithgow. Mr Lithgow had, in the interests of realism, gone too far. This was supposed to be a reverent bloody occasion. But Gerald Bathurst, reporter on the *Wagga Wagga Sentinel*, a small yachtsman and former air navigator, winner of an astronomical quiz on Channel 37, was saying to Lithgow: 'Christ, there's a coincidence.'

'What is?'

'There *is* a new star in the east. Look.'

'I can't see anything.'

'God has a great sense of showbiz, I'll say that for the bugger. Look, man. A bloody new star in the bloody east.' Some of the audience were going shhhhh. 'Can't you see it?'

'Are you sure *you* can?'

'Me tight? On three schooners and a rusty nail? I know the sky. I look at it, remember? I'd be doing an onomy column not an ology one for the rag if anyone was bloody interested.'

Shhhh. Shhhhhhhh.

'Look,' Mr Maitland said, 'this is supposed to be a holy occasion.'

'A scoop,' Bathurst said. 'A skyscoop. I'd better go and.' He trod on the little toe of the right foot of the stout lady next to him. Owww.

Shhhhh.

'I can't see anything,' Lithgow said.

Whether he could or not, boys and girls, it was at last available to his naked eye and to all naked eyes in the southern hemisphere. Lynx. Lynx. It had once been thought to be an asteroid or minor planet. The gap between Mars and Jupiter had long been known to be full of minor planets, scraps of celestial nonsense spinning round the sun. Round, many of them, many of them small. But some not all that small and some not round at all. There was one in the shape of a canister of toilet cleanser, more than a hundred kilometres long. Hector. A lot of them had good old classical names, just like toilet cleansers – Ajax, Hercules, Vesta, Juno. But there were also some of unclassical origin – Victoria, named after an ancient empress of India; Brucia, because the man who discovered it did so with a telescope donated by a lady named Miss Bruce; Marilyn, named after somebody's daughter. After the first Great War of the twentieth century, the American Relief Administration had helped Soviet Russia get over a devastating famine, and Soviet astronomers had responded by discovering a new minor planet and calling it ARA. It was because certain astronomers had their instruments trained on that gap in the sky between Mars and Jupiter that Lynx was at last (I intend no pun) spotted. Asteroids were despised by some starmen: the vermin of the sky they termed them. But others dedicated their lives to those spinning bits of rubbish.

There were two men, one in Florida, CDA, the other in Lilienthal, Europe, Teutphone Province, who laid equal claim to the first sighting of Lynx. The American, whose name was Lynch, wanted the asteroid to be called Lynchia. After all, there was a Pickeringia, a Blenkinsopia, a Piazzia, a Gaussia. The Teutphone invoked the same precedent when he demanded it should be called Marxia. The Global Astronomic Sodality, GAS, bade them compromise and call it Lynx. Marx in vain appealed for March. Lynx seemed, soon, to be rather a fitting name. The radio signals that the heavenly body pulsed out had a certain snuffling intonation, like some great cat on the scent of fodder. Lynx was not, as we now know, an asteroid. It was a major planet, though not of our solar system. It seemed to have been tne satellite of a star unnamed and unlocalized. By some gravitational vagary or other it had become a maverick, a heavenly rogue. That night in Southern Australia brought its first snuffle of tidings of great horror. It was of earth's size but its density was at least ten times greater. It had wandered into the stream of earth's history and, at leisure, proposed bringing that history to a messy close. Astronomers knew about Lynx. They knew the worst, though not all were prepared to admit it, even to themselves.

Gerald Bathurst's blepophone call to Professor Bateman of the Canberra Observatory was the first of several. Bateman's secretary gave unsensational information. A name and a vague destiny. Lynx, a heavenly body in Sector G476, now at the beginning of a period of sharp visibility in the southern heavens. In a few months the northern hemisphere would see it too. It would get into the gravitational pull of the sun and then go haring off again into the immensity. A flash in the heavenly pan, so to speak. Bateman and his guest, Professor Hubert Frame of the University of Westchester, knew more and better, or worse.

They had finished dinner, which for Frame had been mostly Australian burgundy and cigarettes. Frame was sixty, of a dangerous thinness, a man worn down to intellectual brilliance and a pathological appetite for tobacco. He was an ouranologist, and his official title at the university was Coordinator of Space Travel Studies. He had come to Canberra to deliver the Israel Goodman Memorial Lecture on Early Ideas Concerning Magnetospheric Storms and Electron Activity Relations. During the talk he had not coughed at all, an act of will

Bateman supposed, but he was coughing enough now. The talk, which had seemed to some to be delivered in cartoon balloons of cigarette smoke, had been well received. Bateman said, as so often before:

'You ought really to give them up, you know. How many a day is it now?'

'Eighty, ninety. A bit late to talk about giving up, wouldn't you say?'

They were in Bateman's study, a pleasant room full of russet leather, medieval astrolabes, small highly coloured fish of the South Pacific in dim-lighted rhombic glass tanks, group photographs, deep-diving trophies. 'That cough must be a nuisance.'

'I take these,' Frame said, showing Bateman a packet of Rasps Extra Strong. It bore a picture of an ancient genius coughing his heart up. Frame fed himself three pastilles and lighted a fresh Cataract from the stub of the old. 'The two go well together,' he suck-puffed, breathing out eucalyptus like a koala bear. And then: 'The Responsibility of the Scientist. We've all been asked to give talks with some such title at one time or another. I've always refused. The question is: what do we tell them?'

'We tell them, if by *them* you mean the so-called Fourth Estate, that Lynx, when he gets close enough, will exert a palpable gravitational pull on the earth. They'll want to know what that means, so we tell them. Tidal waves, earthquakes, seaquakes. Then Lynx snuffles off.'

'But,' Frame said, coughing, 'comes roaring back.'

'I like to believe that none of us is really sure about that, Hubie.'

'We're sure. We're damned sure. We're sure all right.'

'One thing at a time,' Bateman said. 'Sufficient unto the day, and so forth. The first job is to convince the heads of our respective governments that they'll have to declare a state of emergency.' He looked out at the summer heavens beyond the open french windows as he went over to the little bar to fetch cognac. The term *emergency* had led him to cognac.

'A national matter, then.' Frame coughed it out. 'In the long run it will have to be a national matter. What they nowadays call a provincial matter.' Bateman nodded as he poured cognac for them both. It was Australian cognac. *Beware of French imitations*, the commercials said. They both knew in what way it was a national, or provincial, matter. Bateman said, handing over a gold-swilling balloon:

'Politicians are a nuisance. They won't be able to blame this on anybody. They can't make party issues out of it. Coalition governments. They don't like those.'

'You'll speak to your PM tomorrow?'

'Who am I to speak to the PM? That thing up there will get bigger, then somebody will want to know what it is, and then a question will be asked in the House, then they'll get on to the Minister of Science and finally they'll get on to me. That question, of course, may never be asked. No time for frivolities with so much party legislation to go through. Politicians make me sick. *Bloody* sick.'

'They're the frivolous ones.' Frame coughed. 'My poor dead wife's first cousin married our President's sister. It's an involuted mode of getting into the White House. God works in a mysterious way. It so happens that our President's son Jimmy is to marry shortly – the assistant woman counsellor at West Point. There will be junketings in the nation's capital. I shall be there, as a marginal relative. Jack Skilling will hear about Lynx amid flowers and California champagne. Ten days' time.'

'Of course,' Bateman said, 'we reckon without Legrand. For all we know Legrand may be telling them about the End of the World already. Headlines in *L'Univers* and *Figaro* and so on.'

'The French are an excitable lot,' Frame said in a new gust of smoke and eucalyptus. 'Nobody will believe him. But I shouldn't be surprised if Burgos is preaching doom in Valparaiso. After all, they'll have seen Lynx there by now. Look, like a damned idiot I find myself out of cigarettes. I could have sworn I had another pack. You don't by any chance –'

Bateman smiled. It was a good smile on a sixty-five-year-old retired army kind of face, seawindsuntanned. A fit man, strong and paunchless, a non-smoker all his life, he took from his jacket pocket a twenty-pack of tipped Robotti and handed it to his friend. His friend, in manic eagerness to tear the pack open with his nails, nearly shredded the contents. 'Bless you, Joe,' he said, a Robotti wagging from his lips.

'How will you get on?' Bateman smiled. 'There'll be no tobacco up there.'

Frame frowned a second, as though he thought Bateman meant heaven. Then he smiled and said, coughing: 'I shan't be going. I'll be lucky if I see the thing completed. If it ever is completed. If it's ever even damned started. Politics again,' he smoke-sighed. 'Big words. The survival of the race through its most valuable representatives. The trouble is we've inflated language to the limit. We need to get an epic poem written just to show the bastards the awesomeness of what they're up against. The responsibility of those who rule our race in the face of it. Milton, thou shouldst be living at this hour.'

'Has your doctor been saying something?' Bateman frowned.

'I don't need a doctor to tell me. I *know*. I'm thin, I'm tired, I coughed something up the other day. Tired, yes. Very tired. Ready for sleep.'

'You can sleep on the plane.'

'I meant in a bigger sense.'

'I know damn well what you meant. Is your bag packed?'

'Yes, except for those films. The evidence, the ineluctable, the incontrovertible.' Bateman handed over the envelope that had been lying on a small fretwork Indian table. Frame weighed it in his hand. 'We were always talking about working for the future. And this is what the future is.'

'Man will survive.'

'Why the hell *should* he survive? For the sake of whom or what?'

'For the sake of the future.'

'The future.' Frame gave out the word in two brief bitter coughs. Then he drank off his cognac and went to the bedroom with the envelope. He packed it between his dirty shirts and his other suit. The ineluctable, incontrovertible. He was glad that he had smoked himself to death. When he came out coughing to the central living space into which all the rooms of the bungalow disembogued, he found Bateman ready to take him to the airport. He was looking glumly at the huge wall telescreen, on which a giant newsreader rainbowed out the end of the news. The new star in the east was a godsent bit of froth to end on, after all the weighty items about terrorists, politicians, the end of oil, the impending end of peace, as the long truce had been cynically termed. Nativity play at the school in Nowra, Christmas star, the real thing, no tinselled stage prop. Gerald Bathurst the first to phone in. Here he is. Bathurst quipped about no virgin births having yet been reported in New South Wales and the unlikelihood of three wise men coming from the east, namely New Zealand, the New Zealanders being traditionally known as Poms without brynes. Bathurst smirked off and then the newsreader, shuffling his papers together in complacency, and Bateman switched off a Manegloss commercial. He led his coughing friend to the car. It was a gorgeous antipodean night. Their trained eyes saw Lynx well above the horizon.

They travelled silently for a time towards the southern tip of the metropolitan Commonwealth Territory. 'A future,' Bateman then said, 'for Vanessa. You want that, surely?'

'Vanessa wandering through space, generating generators and genetrices of generations. It sounds pretty dull, doesn't it?'

'There'll be generations who've never known anything else. Born in a spaceship of someone born in a spaceship of someone born in a. Give Vanessa my fondest regards. God, what a pity, what a bloody damnable – '

'Yes yes yes.' Brian, Bateman's police technical supervisor son, was to have married Vanessa Frame, but Brian had been killed by rioters in Ballarat, Victoria. Vanessa had been doing research at the Ouranological Institute in Melbourne at the time. All of five years ago. 'And when I consider the son-in-law who's been wished on me instead – half-assed dilettante, not even good in bed so far as I can put two and two together. There'll have to be an end to that pseudo-marriage. Candidates chosen singly, not in tandem. He may, of course, die in a bar brawl. He may have a sudden accession of self-denying nobility. Val as Sidney Carton. Most damned unlikely.' He went into a fit of coughing. They saw the lights of the airport. They slid soon into Traflane F. 'Whatever she says, I stand on that single nomination. Not because she's my daughter but because she is what she is. She doesn't have to be fed into VOX or PIT or UNY or whatever damned ordinator it's going to be. She's the only one who can take over. And if she starts insisting on damned Val going with her – '

'Women are strange.'

'Strange? Daisy and I were married for thirty-five years and I never knew the first thing about her. And here's Vanessa saying she loves that half-assed no-good. Strange is not the – '

Bateman let him cough and then said: 'When you say *take over*, you don't mean totally in charge?' He was now steering towards the ANSWER terminal (Air New South Wales Eastern Runs).

'No. Just my aspect of the venture. As for overman or overwoman, that'll be up to VOX or PIT or UNY.' He got out of the car. 'No need to see me off. Parking's too much of a problem. Will you be at GAS in February?'

Bateman had got out of the car too. 'Yes. Bring Vanessa if you can. Thanks for coming. You gave them all something to think about. Watch that – ' And then, awkwardly, they embraced. A crowd of football-team supporters just back from Christchurch saw this, guffawed, and cried: 'Poofters.'

Frame dozed in his first-class couchette speeding east towards the Commonwealth of the Democratic Americas. His cough shook him into waking, so he injected a miniamp of S9 into his wrist. That would quieten the cough for an hour or so, but he didn't like the aftereffects – nausea, shivering, constipation. He wished he could sleep, but the hiss of the name Lynx Lynx Lynx through his auditory caverns kept him in full wakefulness. Strange that the terror of the thing could so attach itself to the name, since words, as Saussure had taught, were mere arbitrary collocations of phonemes. Lynx was for Lynch and Marx. But the name would not have been possible if the constellation Lynx, between Ursa Major and Cancer, had not been renamed in honour of the Russians who had clarified its structure and photographed its essence. The experts were satisfied with personal anonymity but had insisted on Babushka – the pet name of their electronic telescope – as the homely new nomenclature of that uselessly distant stardust.

A whirring noise below told him that the capsule containing passengers for San Francisco was being released. He whirred back the curtain that had hidden his gaze from the stars to find daylight outside and, below, the city. Then down hurtled the capsule. He rang for the stewardess to bring him orange juice, coffee and a pack of Lombard cigarettes. While waiting to be served, he began to cough and felt something slimy and sickening come up into his mouth. He spat it into a tissue and then ceased to cough. Dissolution.

Soon Manhattan lay below and, children, Professor Frame had a terrible vision. The city was washed in huge swirling seas of ochre and greenish eggyolk, mounting in regular rhythms ever higher and higher, till they broke in spray from the pinnacles of the Newman Tower, the Patmore Center, the Scotus Complex, the Outride Building, Paternoster Convention City, the two-hundred-storey Tractarian Folly. And then the island split down the middle and from the wound thus made fire leapt and smoke billowed. The fire was lashed out by the waves but came back again, snarling. The towers crumbled and went down into momentarily gaping holes in the ocean, and then all was covered in dun hell smoke, puffing and bellying. Then, boys and girls, ladies and gentlemen, the city was what it was, proud, the skyscrapers thrusting like saluting swordsmen sprung from dragons' teeth, lovely in sunlight, and Frame and his fellow passengers were told to prepare for landing.

At that moment Valentine Brodie, husband of Vanessa *née* Frame, was delivering his last lecture before the Christmas break. He was a handsome man of thirty-eight, with a well-trimmed black beard and rather unhappy hazel eyes, a strong nose at variance with the weakish chin hidden by the beard, a fine forehead and the beginning of a beer-drinker's paunch. Val and Van, he and his wife were known as, or Lentine and Nessa. The VA their names held in common was a motif woven into the curtains, cushions and bedspreads of their apartment, and all the books on their shelves belonged, so the bookplate proclaimed, to VA BRODIE. This assertion of a common initial syllable was somehow pathetic, since their marriage was evidently failing and could not be salvaged by a coincidence of letters. They had in fact first met at a party where pairing was effected through an identity of first-name initials, had gone about together thereafter, considered that they had fallen in love, married in spite of their father's opposition. Or, of course, because of it.

Val was an instructor in science fiction, and he was himself moderately well known as a practitioner of the form. Paperbacks of his well-made but trivial fantasies were to be found in college bookstores, but also in airports, tobacconists, and pornoshops, and they existed also in cassette adaptations and microfiches. The best known were *Desirable Sight*, *Eyelid and Eyelid*, *Cuspclasp and Flukefang*, *Maenefa the Mountain* and *The White and the Walk of the Morning*. But he was too modest to deal with his own work in the two courses he ran: he began with Cyrano de Bergerac and ended with Bissell, Hale and Galindez. He was now addressing a group of graduate students in the Englit Complex of the University of Westchester and was recapitulating the point on which he had begun three months before.

'One book I have not mentioned,' he said, 'since it doesn't seem to come into the scifi or futfic category, nevertheless seems to me to be the true progenitor of the genre. I mean Daniel Defoe's *Journal of the Plague Year*. This is an imaginative reconstruction of London, England, in 1665, at the time when the bubonic plague was brought into the port by rats from ships plying the Eastern trade. The plague spread rapidly and disposed painfully and horribly of a large proportion of the population, but the city survived and gained a new moral strength from its ordeal. This, I think, is what our genre is about – the ways in which ordinary human beings respond to exceptional circumstances imposed unexpectedly upon them. The bubonic plague, a Martian invasion, global dehydration, the end of the world – '

'That's what you said when we started,' said Dan French, a lanky student with a slow bray. 'And what some of us said was that that killed the whole idea of the genre. And there you are, you see – this plague book you talk about gets right away from it. You might as well say that old Anglo-American guy, Harry no Henry James, was an SF writer because he wrote about how people responded to surprises. I mean, that's what the novel *qua* novel is about. Right? People responding to surprises. Right?'

'Exceptional things is what I said. And on a large scale. Would you accept that a book about the end of the world and how it affected people, in say, Cincinnati or Columbus, Ohio, would be scifi?'

The class began to wrangle unprofitably, as it usually did. A bright boy named Juke Harris tried to put everybody right. 'Science fiction,' he said, 'has to have scientists in it. I mean, even this plague book thing of Doc Brodie's has a thing in it which can only be dealt with by scientists, doctors of medicine being kind of scientists. If the book is based on some big unexpected thing that scientists are concerned with, then it's science fiction.'

Judd Gray said that the job of scifi, futfic really, was to prophesy. To get us ready for things going to happen in the future, right? No, said Penny Dreiser, it was to give us the future in the present, because none of us would get the real future future. Then, to Val's slight embarrassment, they started asking about one of his own books – *Cuspclasp and Flukefang* – which was about people in a state of neurosis induced by a headache pill which had unforeseen side effects, and this neurosis made them believe the end of the world was coming any day now, and they were all most ingenious in their suppositions as to how it was going to come – a great explosion at the centre of the earth, a world epidemic what wiped out whole populations in minutes, a war with nerve gases and poisoned water, air pollution, invasion by fierce warriors from outer space. Then a cure was found for the neurosis, people began to live again, and the end of the world came in a form that nobody had expected. What they wanted to know was why Val had just ended his book like that, with those words 'in a form that nobody had expected', without saying what the form was.

Val said: 'You're always saying that scifi should open up the imagination. Well, the book ended with everybody's imagination wide open. They'd had all the kinds of end of the world that anybody could think of, so what was left? That's the job of the reader's imagination to find out.' Cheating, cried some of his class. The writer had certain obligations to his readers. Life put the riddles, the writer's job was to try and answer them, and so on. 'Science fiction is, let's be honest, ultimately a triviality,' Val said. 'It's brain-tickling, no more. The American cult of mediocrity, which rejects Shakespeare, Milton, Harrison and Abramovitz, has led us to this nonsense – a university course in, let's face it, trash. Christ, we should be studying Blake and Gerard Manley Hopkins.' This was indiscreet. He was surprised at the vehemence with which he condemned the very thing he was being paid to promote. Cunningly, a dark musky girl with the top buttons of her shirt undone, Tamsen Disney, cut into the shouts with:

'How does Dr *Vanessa* Brodie think the world is going to end?'

There was an interested silence then. Everybody knew Vanessa Brodie, if not with more than a superficial acquaintance with her professional brilliance, certainly with a total awe at her beauty. Some of the men students thought more highly of Valentine Brodie for his being the consort of a goddess than they did of him as a writer and teacher. He slept with her, handled her divinity in the flesh, and then came down to earth to teach science fiction. Everybody now listened closely to Val's words: it was almost, but not quite, like creeping into their bedroom and watching invisibly, by courtesy of an old SF guy called H. G. Wells.

'My wife,' Val said – a mild thrill of concupiscence went through some of them – 'well, she has little time for that kind of speculation. She leaves that to us humbler children of fancy. Anyway, her eyes are on outer space – ' (ice-blue eyes, some of the students knew, saw them now, on outer space) ' – and any danger from there, apparently, is so ineffably remote that it's not worth considering. Some asteroid, for instance, hurtling in and perhaps smashing Greater New York. Or Moscow. The Martians are *not* coming. The earth will die when the sun dies. Man may starve himself to death by his stupidity, or cease to breed. Nothing apocalyptic, anyway. Leave all that nonsense to the SF men.'

'How about Lynx?' asked Margaret Hammerstein.

'What about Lynx?' asked Val.

'Well, there was this news item on TV this morning. They showed this thing in Australia, a film that is, and said that it was an intruder from outer space, Lynx that is. What does Dr Vanessa say about that?'

Was there a touch of insolence in it – *Dr Vanessa?* No, just verbal economy. 'You're not to worry about Lynx,' Val said soothingly. 'I read the *New York Times* this morning, as some of you probably did. Correction: improbably. It's going to spin round the sun and then spin away again into space. Plenty for the scientists to be interested in, very little for the science fiction writer.'

'But,' said Margaret Hammerstein, 'there's this scientist in South America – Caracas or Rio or some place – who says it's going to spin towards the earth and cause trouble.'

'My concern,' Val smiled, 'is science fiction, a very minor compartment of literature. And now – a happy Christmas and do some serious reading during the brief break. Try *Paradise Lost*. In the sense that the material of the poem is theological, it can be called a kind of science fiction.' As the class shambled out, he called Tamsen Disney. 'Your essay,' he said. 'The one on Otis L. Grosso and Parachronic Fantasy.' He spoke the title with mock pomposity, smiling. 'It's in my office.'

Her lips smiled back, but her eyes were hot. 'I want an A.'

'It's not worth more than a C.'

'I want an A. I've got to have an A.'

'We'll see about that.'

They took the shabby elevator together to the top floor. Though they were not the only ones in the cabin, she boldly put her hot hand in his cold one. When they had entered the office and he had locked the door, she was in his arms and had her mouth on his at once. He trembled as he undid the buttons of her shirt that were still buttoned and fondled her pert firm breasts. Her flesh was brown with fine black flue. Paradisiacal fruit, lovely in waning but lustreless. 'Wait,' she said, and peeled off her tight trousers. This was the prized, the desirable sight, unsought, presented so easily, parted me leaf from leaf. He kissed the fire at the coynte. He took her on the broadloom carpet, groaning. Afterwards she said:

'An A. I want an A.'

'You've got an A.'

'Now.'

Naked, he crawled to the desk and her essay and a red pencil and gave her a great big undoubted A. 'There.'

Dressing, she said: 'Why are you so *hungry*?'

'Hungry?' He took a bottle of Komitet vodka and two plastic cups from his filing cabinet. He poured. 'There, take this in your right hand and say after me.' Then, not jocular but sad: 'All right, hungry is right.'

'She doesn't want you, won't let you?'

'Rather the opposite. I don't want her. I want to want her. It would make things so much easier all round. But I can't want her.'

'She's one of the ten most beautiful women in America.' Tamsen was referring to the results of a poll in *Wesches*, one of the student magazines. Grace Flagg, singer; Doris Cosby, movie star; Vanessa Brodie, scientist. Third, not bad.

'Perfection,' Val said, as though he were giving a lecture, 'is lovable by definition.' Sitting gloomily, tousled, in shirt and pants and bare feet, he gave himself more vodka. 'To perfection,' he gloomily toasted.

'You mean,' she said, thrusting her own cup forward, 'she puts you down all the time.'

'She doesn't mean to do anything except be loving and a good wife. She has the most brilliant scientific brain in the world, after her poor coughing father. Her body is a wonder. She loves sex. She knows all about it too. She's read all the books. *Let's try Hamsun Three,* she says, and then she shows me. Then I lose whatever erection I have. I shouldn't be telling you all this. You're only a student.'

'A good student. I just got an A.'

'You see what she's done to me,' he groaned. 'She's made me corrupt.'

'She looks to me like an iceberg,' Tamsen said. 'If I were a man I'd prefer something a bit warmer. Someone like me.' She smiled. 'I don't suppose you're in a hurry to get home. I'm going to the Gropius rally tonight. We still have two hours if you want them.'

'It's not tonight yet.'

'Right, but first I'm going to Hart Rebell's poetry shout and then I'm at the movie club committee meeting. Two hours, like I said. Why don't you get a mattress in here? Or cushions or something soft anyway.'

'I don't intend to make a habit of this,' he said primly.

'That sounds like the voice of post-satisfaction. I could soon get you into a pre-satisfaction state again. Look,' and she undid her shirt all the way.

'I have some shopping to do. People for dinner. She'll cook a superb dinner. White wines chilled to perfection. Red wines *chambrés*. Her father will be back from Australia by now.' He kissed her breasts.

'Something to do with that Lynx thing?'

'Oh, the hell with that Lynx thing.' The prized, the desirable. When they had finished, and then finished the raw vodka, she said:

'There ought to be an A plus.'

'That would be going too far. That would be perfection.'

'I'll be writing other essays.'

'Over which I shall be quite dispassionate.'

'Post-satisfaction. We'll see, we'll see.' And then: 'I'm going to the Gropius rally.'

'You said that already. I suppose you want me to ask why. Why?'

'It's the best entertainment in the world. Beats all your science fiction. He scares me so that I wet my pants.'

'Ah.'

'All that thunder about hell and damnation. Miserable sinners writhing in the unquenchable fire. I get excited.'

'And what do you do afterwards?'

'Writhe. With Maureen and Edwin and Archie and Minnie and Benny Goodhue.'

'Women are insatiable.'

'I'll be thinking about you. Or perhaps not. That paunch of yours turns me off.'

'It's a gesture in the direction,' he said, 'of human imperfection.'

'Quite a nice little poem. I must remember that.'

'How is the book?' Freud asked his daughter.

'So so. I think I'll sleep a little.' Her mother was already snoring faintly. *Ungrateful bastards* was in the rhythm of the train. Obscurantist, ignorant. He thought back. The lecture had been given on a winter's night and the heating was in a state of dysfunction. How many in the audience? Not many, but those that were there were uniformly hostile. He remembered saying:

'The close observation and detailed study I have made in Paris of Professor Charcot's methods leads me to an inelectable conclusion – that, through hypnosis, a subject can simulate any disease without possessing that disease; that neuroses need have no somatic aetiology, that hysteria is not malingering but a morbid condition applicable to men as well as to women. Or, to put it briefly, we are only at the beginning of the most important study since the science of medicine began – the study of the human mind, which is not the same as the study of the human brain.'

They started the shouting down before he had properly completed that last statement. Distinguished neurologists all, shouting vulgarly. Gauss:

'It seems necessary to remind Dr Freud that hysteria is a female condition, despite what his precious French mountebanks are teaching. *Hystera* – it is the Greek word for the womb. Men, so my thirty-five years of clinical observation tell me, do not possess wombs.'

Laughter. Oscheit:

'All diseases are physical. Every disease discloses a physical cause. If a patient shows the symptoms of paralysis and has no corresponding lesion, how can his condition be described except as one of pretence, or malingering?'

Shouts of approval. Haussmann:

'Dr Freud is acquiring a reputation for dangerous meddling with marginal aspects of medicine which, when not mere stage trickery like hypnotism, are revealed as ill thought out and, in proof, highly perilous adventures with drugs that are addictive and ultimately lethal. We have not forgotten that Dr Freud endeavoured to introduce cocaine to the medical world – with what results we know, alas, all too well.'

Murmurs. Cocaine cocaine.

Fleischl's thumb reduced to a hideous stump of dead flesh and yet the pain intense and continuous. Fleischl lay on the sofa in his lodgings, writhing. Freud said with young eagerness:

'Listen, Fleischl. I've found the answer. I've found the way to get you off morphia. Cocaine. A product of the South American coca plant – incredible. It kills pain, promotes energy, wellbeing. I've tried it. I did ten hours' work and needed only two hours' sleep. It kills hunger as well as pain. It's miraculous. Here – '

He tendered a glass: cocaine with a little water. Fleischl croaked in extreme weariness:

'No more morphia? I've reached the limit. It's ceased to have any – Will this really work?'

'You'll see.'

Fleischl drank. He grimaced. 'It – it – dulls the lips. It dulls the mouth. Will it – dull this?' And he held out the agonizing thumb stump.

'Wait.'

'Non-addictive? Not like morphia?'

'My dear Fleischl, I've been my own guinea pig. I can take it when I need it – leave it off when I don't – '

'God – do I imagine – is it working already?'

'It's dramatic. The effect's almost instantaneous.'

Fleischl's eyes were bright. He got up from his sofa. 'My God, it's – I don't believe it – I have to believe it. I can work again? Get back to my research?'

'Better than ever before.'

It was time for a definitive article. Freud was writing it in his rooms when Josef Breuer came in. Shock was in his face; he looked all of his twelve years of seniority to his scribbling friend. But Freud misread the expression. Strain on the heart, too many stairs to climb. 'Listen, Josef. "The ancient Mexicans regarded it as an incarnation of the sun god, a sacred gift from heaven that sanctified every aspect of their lives." Too literary for a medical article?'

'I can't,' Breuer said, 'get into Fleischl's apartment.'

'Anything wrong?'

'Noises. You'd better come and lend me a shoulder – '

Freud grabbed his hat.

They broke down the door. They found Fleischl moaning and frothing on the carpet. On the table Freud saw – 'Good God, he's been shovelling it down.'

'Help me get him into a warm bath.'

Help me get him into a warm coffin. Reproachful eyes at the funeral on a cold day. Remorse remorse. Still in mourning, Freud and Breuer drank morosely in a tavern. Cold beer. Make it hot toddies. Breuer said:

'We've been friends a long time, Sigmund. You won't mind my saying something – '

'Whatever it is, I suppose I deserve it. Rushing at things – insufficient experiment, superficial research. I didn't see what cocaine was really meant for – an external anaesthetic. Ophthalmic surgeons are being blessed for using it now. I'm still being cursed – '

'No more reproaches. I can't reproach you with being made the way you are – '

'What do you mean?' He paused, puzzled, before raising the hot brew to his mouth.

'You were never meant to be a scientist. A poet, a man of the imagination – that's more like it. You see, you make assumptions – what's true for you must be true for others. You didn't find cocaine addictive, and you took it for granted that nobody else would either. You proceed by introspection. That's not the scientific way, Sigmund. That's why – forgive me – that's why I fear – well, you're fascinated by what you call the mind, not the brain, not the nervous system – this formless invisible thing that theologians call the soul. There's only one soul you can know about, and that's your own. I fear you'll assume that other minds are the same as yours. The scientific way is the way of objective observation. You can observe behaviour. But you can't observe what causes the behaviour. Don't try. Leave well alone.'

Meynert's words too, after that lecture. Meynert, looking like a cleaner and less untidy Beethoven, on his feet, saying, long gnawed-looking index finger extended: 'Leave well alone. This is not merely *my* advice. This is an injunction that comes from a lifetime of experience of the human brain. And, if Dr Freud will forgive the reminder, from the man who taught him and tried to put him on the right road.'

Meynert and Freud walking the male mental ward, full of beds with labels, like autumn-bottled fruits: PARANOIA, MANIC DEPRESSION, GENERAL PARALYSIS OF THE INSANE. A man far gone in emaciation railed manically at Freud:

'You're a Jew, I can tell, a filthy Jewish bastard. It's you Jews that have been poisoning the water supply. That's why I'm dying of thirst, you Jewish bastard.'

'Antisemitism,' Freud said to Meynert. 'Is that also a classifiable mental disease?' Meynert smiled sourly. Two tough male nurses sweated over the restraining of a man standing on his bed, screaming:

'Snakes coming from the ceiling, get them out of my bed. Red and yellow and green. Snakes wriggling down. Argggh.'

'Forgive me, Professor Meynert,' Freud said, 'but how are they to be cured?'

'They can't be cured – only classified. We don't have the information to cure them with – not yet. When I've been able to examine at least ten thousand human brains – then I'll have the first glimmering of an understanding of the roots of insanity.'

'So – these just have to die?'

'The sooner the better. I want to get at their brains.'

'Die,' said a patient confidentially to them both. 'I heard that word – die. Like Jesus Christ. They said he had to die, but he didn't die. You know why he didn't die? Because he didn't exist. Jesuschrist was the name the Romans gave to two bits of wood nailed together. A jesuschristus, that's what it was called. And they built a whole religion on two bits of wood. Fools fools idiots.'

That first patient was still railing. 'Jew, Jew, filthy Jew, you make me drink my own piss.'

Deeply disturbed, Freud said to Meynert: 'Classification as a substitute for treatment. It's not good enough.'

Deeply offended, Meynert replied: 'This is insolence, sir – damned Jewish insolence.' It was enough for Freud to smile and cock an ostentatious ear to the railer ('Make me eat my own'). Meynert's grin was acid. He had the grace to say: 'Infection.'

'Agonizing,' the lady said. Freud saw himself in the cheap mirror and was discouraged. Middle-aged, shabby, he must get his beard trimmed. The consulting room shabby too, though at least it had a couch in it. He was yet to use that couch for clinical purposes. Etymologically right: *kline* was Greek for a couch. He and the lady sat on either side of the desk. Freud said:

'The odontological report says your teeth are in perfect condition, Frau Neurath. Does that make you feel better?'

'Agonizing. The neuralgia is spreading up into my brain. I can't go on, doctor. You'll have to give me something.' A fine fat lady with a fine set of gnashers and crushers. He said:

'With your permission, *gnädige Frau,* I'm going to send you to sleep for a little while.'

'You mean – hypnotize me?'

'There's nothing in it. No magic, no mystery. Lie down on this couch. You'll find it comfortable enough. Please. You want to be cured. I know I can cure you.' For she was reluctant. 'Please.' She lay on it primly. 'Now.' He knew how to do it, not even his worst enemy could deny that. Good subjects anyway, these Viennese bourgeoises. Why? Boredom, a new thrill. And then, my dear, he *hypnotized* me. No! Yes. Tell me more, Lise. 'You're getting drowsy. You try to lift your left arm but you can't. You're so tired, so weary – '

And so she was. Her lids were down. He began to count from twenty backwards.

'Can you hear me? We're back at the time when the pain first started. You're a child again. How did it start? Who made it start? Who hurt you?'

She made childish noises of distress. 'I wasn't doing any harm. I wasn't doing anything. Don't, mother. Don't.' The distress was real and loud. 'Owwww.' Tears started. 'I'll kill you, mother. I will. I'll wait till you're asleep and then I'll – Owwww.' So that was it. Her hands were clutching her silk dress near the crotch. He could lift her out of it now. He began to count from one on.

She sat at the desk.

'Less pain, yes?'

'Yes, a little less. How did you – ? It was the deep sleep, wasn't it? I haven't been sleeping well, doctor.'

'As a child,' he said carefully, 'you did what all children do. Exploration of your own body. Curiosity. Masturbation – do you know the word?' She knew it. She didn't like knowing it.

'This is an outrage.' But not very loudly.

'Come, Frau Neurath. We're talking of an innocent childish activity. Your mother hit you when she found you doing it. The neuralgia you think you have – '

'I do have it, I do.'

'It's a self-inflicted punishment. You feel guilty. You convert your mother's slap into – '

'It's still there, it still hurts.'

'But it's not as bad as it was.'

'Not quite so bad. But it'll be back, I know it will. You said you'd give me something.'

'I've given it you. The beginnings of an understanding. It's not a real pain. There's no organic cause. You're punishing yourself for – '

'What you said is dirty, wicked.'

'Nonsense. There's nothing to feel guilty about. There's no reason for you to torture yourself. Come and see me again this time next week. I think we can cure that neuralgia for ever.'

But she sadly shook her head.

At dinner he talked to Martha. 'It always goes back to sex. Sexual guilt of some kind or another.'

'Shhh. Not before the children, Sigmund.'

'They don't understand – Besides, what if they did? Why should sex be a thing to hide and cloak and smother? It's fundamental, so fundamental that we're frightened of it – like some dark barbaric god. We have to bring it into the light.'

'Do that in your consulting room,' she said firmly. 'Not here. Do you hear me, Sigmund? I won't have the children hearing that sort of thing in *my* house.'

'Sorry, dear,' he said meekly. He smiled at the children as he chewed a mouthful of veal. They looked back at him with dark serious adult eyes.

And so to Frau Ohler. She lay on the couch, quite relaxed. But she would not submit. 'Your eyes grow heavier and heavier. You're so tired. You must sleep – you must – ' She looked at him with the bright eyes of a rested child. He sighed. 'I'm afraid you're not a very good hypnotic subject.'

'With respect, doctor,' Frau Ohler said, 'perhaps you're not a very good hypnotist.'

This hit him hard. But he recovered. He smiled ruefully and nodded. 'You may be right, Frau Ohler. So we just talk, yes?'

'No,' she said. '*I* just talk. You listen.'

Something of a revelation. He said humbly: 'I listen. I do more. I efface myself.' And he got off his wooden straight-backed chair, took it to the not well-dusted corner behind the head of the couch, then sat again. Invisible. Like, God help us, a father confessor. 'Now,' most humbly, 'Frau Ohler?'

'Let me try to understand. I'm happy. I have the finest husband in the world. I have an adorable baby girl. I have a beautiful home. And yet – why am I so depressed? Why do I want to kill myself? Why?'

Tentatively: 'Because you're – '

'Because I'm not really happy. And then this thing keeps trying to get under my skirt – '

'What thing?'

'It's wrong, it's wicked, I shouldn't have such feelings. I deserve to die. I *must* die.'

'Sex,' Freud said, humbly. 'Your husband doesn't want it any more. But *you* want it. And you see attractive men in the street and you think of them – imagine them – '

'How do you know this? I didn't tell you – '

'You feel guilty about having these desires. Guilty. You have to be punished. You have to kill yourself.'

She began bitterly to weep. He got up and went round to her and, tentatively, humbly, put his fingers on her arm. She twitched them off, gasping. 'I'm so wicked, terribly wicked. I don't need to make love, I shouldn't want to. My sister Ursula, she's a nun, she doesn't need to – '

'You're not a nun. You're a healthy young married woman. You want to make love. Why shouldn't you? It's natural enough, God knows. And if your husband doesn't want to, then – well, it's natural for you to think of doing it with others. That's not wicked. That's good and wholesome and right.'

She wiped her wet cheeks with her cambric. 'What can I do? What can *you* – '

'I can't tell your husband that he's driving you into these suicidal fits. He's not my patient. But *you* can tell him. You must find a way to show him – that it's his neglect that's making you – '

'So,' she said, the brighter-eyed for her shed tears, 'it's *not* wicked.'

'Not at all wi – '

Wein Weib und Gesang was the Strauss waltz the fiddlers discoursed while Freud argued animatedly with Breuer and others at their wonted table. 'Notions of wickedness,' he was saying, knuckles white as he grasped his beermug, 'are hypocritical emanations from the parents, the elders, the State. Why is sex wicked? Because it is a mode of pleasure which sneers at the repressions of the elders. It is, as we know, not at all wi – '

'Dr Freud?' It was a tall, overimpeccably dressed, fierce and upright man in prosperous early middle age. Freud felt his shabbiness. He stood.

'Dr Freud, yes. Good evening. You are – '

'My name is Ohler. Herr Ohler.'

'Ah. And how is Frau Ohler?'

'Never mind how Frau Ohler is.' He struck Freud viciously on the left cheek with a stiff leather glove. He struck. Freud was. *Struck*. Astonished. 'If you were a gentleman and not a cheap Jewish quack you'd challenge me for that. How dare you. *How dare you*. Trying to turn my wife into a whore.' And he struck again. Freud's friends did not interfere. They looked open-eyed. The man stalked off. Freud rubbed his cheek. Not at all wi –

He rubbed his cheek, unseen of the young man who lay on the couch. He listened.

'And I can't. I can't.'

'You're a lawyer,' Freud said. 'You know as well as I do that there's no law forbidding it. The Church may frown on it, of course. The Old Testament tells us of the sin of Onan. But there is no commandment which says Thou Shalt Not Masturbate. The interdiction and the punishment are left to nature.'

'You mean – they're right? It's physically harmful? It can make you blind – mad?'

'Superstitions,' Freud smiled. 'No, I mean that nature intended semen to be discharged in the healthful, life-giving, loving, normal way of companionate congress. A man and a woman. Continue in this manner and you'll end up like Narcissus in the old legend – loving yourself, incapable of loving a woman. Do you understand me?'

'But I do – I mean, when I – that is, I imagine women – one at a time, that is – a different one every time.'

'Some people would say: why limit yourself to one when there's so much choice?'

'But I always come back to – her.' He tried to twist his neck round, scared, to look at eyes surely ready to strike him down. But Freud was unperturbed.

'Your mother?'

'How could you know that – how could you guess?'

'I'll let you into a professional secret. In the last few years I've compiled a dossier of cases of anxiety neurosis. About one hundred. Every single one is sexual. You understand me? You moan about sexual guilt, but there's hardly a man or a woman in Vienna who's not in your position – one way or another. When it's bad, it's a neurosis. When it's just a nagging ache, it's normality. We all have our sexual problems.'

'But not like this one – not like – '

'Yes, each of us wants to be the great exception. Do you ever go to the theatre?'

'Sometimes. What does the theatre have to do with it?'

'Go tonight. I'm going.'

'What's the play?'

Freud smiled and then lighted a cigar.

It was an adaptation rather than a straight translation. The Freuds shared a box with the Breuers. Oedipus cried in his agony:

'Let him be cursed, the man who sought
To do good to a dying child, the life-bringer.
I should have died innocent Here he is,
Sons and daughters of Thebes, your shame,
The author of your pestilence – Oedipus,
Killer of his father, defiler of his mother – now
Let me be hidden from all eyes. Let me go hence.
I am unworthy of death. Let me wander
And keep my hell alive. Cast me out.
Or do worse. Or better.'

Creon said:

'The gods must instruct me. I await the word.'
'You were given the word.
The god pronounced death on the defiler.'
'We must await more guidance. A king is a king.
Come, let us go in.'
'One prayer at this shrine
That saw so often a united family
Give praise and thanks. Let me go.
A man can do no harm there.'

And the armed palace guard let him move downstage. In his closed fists he held the brooches of the dead Jocasta. He raised the brooches to his eyes and pierced his eyes. The chorus screamed:

'Horror. Horror of horrors.'

Oedipus said faintly:

'Dark dark. The sun has burst there
For the last time.'

The chorus yelled:

'The eyes of the world are out.
The gods scream,
Finding poison in the wine cup.
The mountains are molten,
The sea blood.

The mounting moon
Turns her face away.
Day will never return.'

Oedipus, his face a mask of blood, was led tottering off.

They ate pastries and drank coffee afterwards. The fiddlers played the *Kaisermarsch*. Scents of pomade and cologne and more exquisite distillations. Furs and feathers. All bourgeois Vienna seemed to be here. Freud had to raise his voice to be heard.

'Of course, he doesn't really put out his eyes. The eyes are a kind of upward displacement of the testicles – '

'Please, Sigmund,' Martha said, faintly as Oedipus.

'His guilt can be expiated only by self-castration.' People began to look curiously at him. He was no whit abashed. 'The guilt is terrible because the crime is terrible. But why is the crime terrible?'

'Killing your own father,' Breuer said. 'Surely one doesn't have to ask why.'

'Oh, I don't mean that crime. I mean copulating with his own mother.'

'Please, Sigmund.'

'Look,' he said urgently. 'Sex is the most important subject in the world. I'm becoming tired of having to speak about it in a hushed voice.'

'Most important to you, perhaps, Sigmund,' Breuer said. 'Not to everybody.'

'I know. You told me a long time ago that I mustn't extrapolate my own priorities on the rest of the world. But my work's convinced me that more brain space and living time are filled up with sex than the world's ready to admit. Guilt about sex. Taboos on sex. Thinking and dreaming and brooding about sex sex sex – '

'People are looking at us, Sigmund.'

'Sex is at the bottom of everything.' A couple of whispering men stopped whispering and looked at Freud with shocked interest. 'Take that case of yours, Josef – the case of Anna O. as we have to call her, though why not come out with it and say Bertha Pappenheim – '

'Don't,' gritted Breuer. 'She may be here.'

'That's finished,' Frau Breuer said urgently. 'He doesn't want to talk about it. Finished – isn't it, Josef?'

Breuer flushed. 'I don't want to talk about it.'

'Exactly. It's embarrassing. A clinical case, a matter of sober medicine, but embarrassing. Because she had this hysterical pregnancy and blamed it on you. "I'm having Dr Breuer's baby," she said.'

'Stop, Sigmund,' Breuer went, 'do you hear me?'

'A case of simple psychological transference. It's happening to me all the time.'

'Sigmund,' said Martha, 'you never said – '

'Oh, there's nothing in it, nothing personal, anyway. All that pouring out of hysterical emotion – it has to attach to somebody. So it has to attach to the nearest object – the doctor himself. The other day one of my women patients threw her arms round my neck and started kissing me. Then, thank God, Grete came in with the coffee – '

'She never said anything to me – Nor did you – '

'A sensible girl. A pure clinical matter, of no personal significance whatsoever.'

'I see,' Martha said. Frau Breuer changed the subject. She said:

'I thought they did very well tonight.'

'Who?' Martha asked thankfully. 'Oh yes, the company. A bit too much shouting and screaming, I thought.'

'Exactly,' Freud said. 'Hysteria. Guilt not well understood. And I return to my former question – why the guilt? All right, we'll accept without question – for the moment anyway – that incest with your mother is the most powerfully tabooed notion in the world, but why the hysteria of the play, a hysteria that the actor has to match with hysteria of his own – '

'As I said,' said Breuer, 'murder of his father – '

'As *I* said, sleeping with his mother – *Why* is it wrong?'

'You mean it's right?'

'I didn't say that. I want to know the rationale behind the taboo.'

'Oh, Sigmund, why bother?' Frau Breuer said. 'It's just a fantastic old fairy tale, a horror story – '

'No, *Oedipus* is more than that. It has a profound and, shall I say, immediate appeal. As terrible and moving tonight as it was two thousand five hundred years ago. Why do we become so *involved* in the plight of Oedipus? Because he's ourselves.'

'*Herr Ober*,' Breuer called. '*Rechnung, bitte*.'

'A fundamental and mysterious problem, but one that the modern age forbids us to discuss. The ancient Greeks weren't so squeamish. They knew the ghastly desirability of incest. The things most thoroughly prohibited are the things most deeply desired. I must write something about it – '

'You do that, dear,' Martha said with great eagerness. 'Write about it.'

'I will, I will. But we ought to discuss it first. Dialectic – the interplay of ideas. You know what my mother said to me, Martha, when I said I wanted to get married? She said: "When a man marries, he divorces his mother." An old Jewish saying.'

'The waiter's slow,' Frau Breuer said. 'Perhaps we could pay at the desk.'

'At the desk, yes,' Breuer said, rising. And they got up, three of them eagerly, one reluctantly.

'Incest, incest, incest.'

'Please, Sigmund – '

Sigmund saw in the new mirror a forty-year-old practitioner with a neat if greying beard. Not prosperous, not yet. The luxury of the room was all reserved to the new couch and its cushions. There was a young and handsome woman lying on it, in great distress.

'And where, Fräulein Ilse, was your mother at the time?'

'I can't remember.'

'You mean you don't want to remember. Try and see the house, the room. It was a summer's day, the sun was shining – '

'It was raining. Rain came in through the roof.'

'You saw the rain? Where did you see the rain?'

'It was coming into the bedroom. There was a little pool of rain on the floor. In the corner.'

'And your mother?'

'She was lying down, I think. On the sofa in the living room. Reading. She was lying down when I went upstairs.'

'Why did you go upstairs?'

'I don't know.'

'And when you got into your room this man was waiting for you. How did he get in?'

'I don't know.'

'Why didn't you run away? You could have run downstairs and called your mother.'

'I was frightened.'

'So you let this man do what you said – in your hand – this hand – the hand you can't move.'

'In my hand. He made me.' Tearfully. 'I had to take it.'

'And what did this man do then?'

'I can't remember.' Hysterically. 'I can't.'

'Listen carefully, Ilse. I know who this man was. It was your father, wasn't it?'

'No no no no no – '

'It was your father. Try and see his face now. It was your father, wasn't it?'

She sobbed and sobbed.

'There's nothing to be guilty about. And there's nothing wrong with your hand. The hand's perfectly all right. You'll see. When you accept what happened you'll see, when you stop fighting it. Listen, Ilse, it's one of the oldest things in the world – the love of a father for a daughter, a daughter for a father. And sometimes the love becomes that sort of love. You didn't shout, you didn't struggle – because you wanted it – try to accept that. It's happened to thousands and thousands of girls. There's no crime, no dirtiness. You've been trying to punish the hand that held him – by paralysing it. The power of the unconscious mind is huge – it can do anything. Do you understand me? Look – your hand is moving. Look at the fingers – '

There were eight at table that evening, eating the usual Viennese cold supper. Five children and their parents, Minna, Martha's sister, a tall and gaunt and sharp woman. Martha said:

'A certain gentleman was asking about you today, Minna.'

'You say that every day,' Minna barked. 'It's kind of you to want to make me think I'm still wanted. But I don't particularly want to be wanted. Thank you all the same. Who was the gentleman?'

'Ah,' Freud went.

'I ask merely out of politeness. If my sister takes the trouble to invent a gentleman for me, I can at least take the trouble to persuade her that her invention wasn't altogether in vain. More coffee, Sigmund?'

'Please. No, I think I must open another bottle of Riesling. I ought to celebrate my hundredth case of – paternal molestation.'

'Please, Sigmund – the children.'

'You mean,' Minna said, 'the acquisition of a new case or the attainment of a cure?'

'Oh,' Freud said indifferently, 'she's cured. Paralysis of the right hand. The offending member. Member – interesting.'

'Sigmund – '

'What I find interesting,' Minna said, 'is that you seem to take the cures for granted. It's the diseases you enjoy.'

'Not the diseases. Just this huge mysterious terrain where the diseases germinate. I think my book's nearly ready.'

'You insist on publishing?'

'Oh yes, of course. I must spread the gospel.'

'They'll throw stones.'

Martha, troubled, said: 'Sigmund, I hope you're not going to – '

'Make myself more unpopular than I am already? It's a small price to pay for the privilege of disseminating the truth.'

'I saw Frau Doktor Schlimmbein in the market this morning,' Martha said. 'She looked right through me. As though I were glass.'

'I'm sorry that you have to suffer as well, Martha. But would you want me to be smug and stuffy and stupid like Herr Doktor Schlimmbein?'

'Oh no, I don't care. Not really. But still – '

'Still,' Minna said, 'you wish your husband weren't so uncompromising. I too had an uncompromising – fiancé.'

'But,' Martha said, 'he was only uncompromising about Sanskrit. Nobody worries about Sanskrit.'

'You'd be surprised,' Minna said. 'There are some very erotic books waiting to be translated out of Sanskrit.'

'Please, Minna, the children – '

Minna addressed young Martin. 'Erotic, sexual – do you know those words, young man?'

'Minna!'

'Sexual,' Martin said, 'is what father and mother do. But not much these days.'

'Martin!' Even Freud blushed. Minna smiled.

'The other word I don't know. But I'll find out.'

Not now nearly ready but altogether ready. The thick manuscript lay on Dr Krafft-Ebing's desk. There was a coffee tray on top of it, and spilt coffee part hid the fylfot design of the tray. Dr Krafft-Ebing however, a handsome man in his fifties, had no slipshod look about him. His suit was stiff and new. He combined in his welcoming smile tolerance and caution.

'I see you have finished reading it.' Freud removed some papers from a stuffed chair and sat.

'Dr Freud – you know my work – my published work. You would not regard it as the work of a man in love with the repression of, ah, dangerous ideas?'

'You wrote it in Latin, sir. That was a kind of repression.'

'Be reasonable, man. To tell the world of sexual perversions in a living language – coprophily, necrophily, sodomy – why, I was lucky to see it out in Latin. And, even in Latin, it's had its effect. Our stupid magistrates are beginning to realize that what they called a sexual crime is really a sexual disease. The mental ward, Dr Freud, not the prison – '

'Where's the difference? There seems to be no cure available in either.'

'Wait. It may be a long wait. When we understand the structure of the human brain we'll be able to cure any mental disorder. But mental disorders will never be cured *your* way.'

'That book, Professor Krafft-Ebing, is a record of cures. Some total, some provisional, but all cures.'

'Cured hysteria, which is not a disease anyway.'

Freud spoke warmly. 'A woman comes to me with incurable migraine, another with paralysis of the limbs, another with suicidal impulses. Men too – with persecution mania, with disabling and unintelligible guilt, with crippling anxieties – these I have cured. To say that they're hysterical, mere imagination or malingering is as much as to say that the pain isn't real, that the paralytic can really walk, that the blind man could see if he tried. And all because there's no physical aetiology. Yet the truth about so many diseases is diametrically opposed to the half-truth of tradition. You say that the body affects the mind. I say that the mind can very horribly afflict the body. The secret of neuroses lies deep in the patient's memory, in the vast uncharted tract of the unconscious. This I am probing. I am digging out the suppressed mental causes of disease. In showing the patient the cause of his ailment I cure the ailment. Or rather, under my guidance, the patient cures himself.'

'Very eloquent. Look at all this spilt coffee, very clumsy. You have a certain gift of rhetoric. Your writing there sometimes attains a force and elegance more often associated with poetry or fiction than with scientific investigation. Please, please, listen to me – it is lucid, closely argued, clearly presented – but there's something to which my instinct says no, no, and no again.'

'What is this something?'

'Once you get into the patient's unconscious mind you find a forgotten memory, the memory of some suppressed and terrible event which causes the lesion – '

'No lesion. We're dealing with the mind, not the body.'

'Very well, the event which seems to instigate the hysteria, the neurosis, the – psychosomatic ailment – may I use that term?'

Freud smiled faintly. 'If I may use it too. Psychosomatic is a fine term.'

'Now you push memory back to the limit. There's a regressive process, yes?'

'The root of the ailment lies far back in the patient's childhood. I suppose we can call that the limit.'

'And it's here that my instincts say no, no, and no. You would have it that the causative event of the neurosis is always sexual – '

'Always. I did not wish to find it so, but I did. I was led to it reluctantly.'

'But – I wish someone would take this coffee tray away. Dr Freud, children have no sexual life. Sexual life does not begin till puberty.'

'That too I used to believe. Reluctantly, again reluctantly, I was forced to accept that sexuality begins almost at birth. That it's not confined to the genitals or the erogenous zones. That it begins when the infant puts its lips to the breast of its mother.'

'You have stated it succinctly. And my powerful negative is reserved to an amazing, shocking, terrible, totally inadmissible theory – '

'I have no theories in that book. Only facts.'

'Facts? *Fact?* You wish the medical world and indeed the world outside to accept that children, mere babies, have sexual relations with their own parents? You present that as a fact? The boy gets into bed with his mother and copulates? The father physically assaults his own daughter? *Fact?*'

'These terrible truths stem from the unconscious minds of the patients themselves. I did not invent them.'

Krafft-Ebing sighed profoundly. 'We have few illusions left in this modern age. Still, I'd assumed we could hold fast to one truth – the innocence of children. Their cleanliness. Their little minds and bodies unspotted by lust – that of their parents or their own. Nothing in your manuscript accords with the facts of childhood as we know them – '

'But now, from my testimony, you know something new about childhood. Or rather something very old that the world has rejected because it could not bear to discard the myth of childish innocence. Children are sexual beings. It is our myth of their innocence that represses that truth and causes neuroses. That is one of the themes I shall be writing about soon.'

'You may write, Dr Freud,' Krafft-Ebing said with care, 'you may write all you wish of these – barbarous odes to the depravity of infancy. But you may not publish.'

'*May not?*'

'May not under the auspices of our university press. May not so long as you belong to the brotherhood of the neurologists of Vienna. The medical school of Vienna is the greatest in the world – the world acknowledges this. We're respected from New York to Tokyo, from Stockholm to the antipodes. But what would the world think if it ever read this?' He jabbed a finger under the coffee tray. Freud took several deep breaths. He said:

'With respect, Professor Krafft-Ebing, you cannot forbid me to publish. Not, true, under the aegis of the medical department of the University of Vienna, but there are other means of dissemination – publishers less concerned with the respect of the hidebound and the obscurantist.'

'Think. I beg you, think. Not only of our reputation but your own. You'll be cutting your own throat.'

Freud got up from his chair. With care he removed his manuscript from beneath the defiled coffee tray. 'I've heard that before. This book is my latest razor. It will cut away a good deal of the gangrene of wilful ignorance, the cancer of torpid conservatism.'

'There you go again with your rhetoric. You should take to politics, Dr Freud. You should certainly give up neurology. Good day.'

Freud bowed stiffly and left. Krafft-Ebing picked up his model of the human brain and looked at it as for assurance of certain truths. Then he rang for the coffee tray to be removed.

Freud lay in bed and dreamed. He was in a vague and shadowy place, quite naked. Fully clothed colleagues surrounded him and screamed in the manner of the *Oedipus* chorus:

'Filth, scum, corrupter, defiler, Jew,
Let him be cast out into the desert, the beast marked with the mark of the beast,
The despoiler of innocence, the incestuous one – '

He was dreaming he was back in bed again. Martha tried to embrace him but he rejected her.

'He despises the flesh of the wife of his bosom,
He lusts after his own daughters and sons – '

He left his bed and, naked, padded to the door of another room. He entered the room. His daughter lay there awake. She screamed when she saw the naked man approaching.

He woke with alarm to find himself in an innocent cotton nightshirt, innocent in bed. Martha snored faintly beside him. Not yet 6.30. Birdsong from the Viennese eaves. He lighted a cigar. He picked up from the bedside table a copy of his book, *not* published by the University Press. Martha began to cough. He stubbed out his cigar hastily. He put down his book. Martha, who had wakened herself with her cough, looked at him with unfocused morning eyes. '*Liebchen*,' he said. He kissed her lightly on the lips and she drew back from the taint of tobacco. He tried to take her in his arms. 'Tired,' she said, then turned away. He sighed. He relighted his cigar. He opened his book again, this time at random, and groaned at two gross typographical errors. A churchbell started, distant, forlorn. Of course. It was Sunday.

A priest in the Marienkirche spoke fire during his sermon. 'You are aware,' he said, 'of how in your daily lives you suffer not only from the deprivations that have been brought upon us in these hard times – a lack of work, the raising of prices – but also by the sight of them that prosper while you do not. There is one race, as you know, brethren, that may be accounted blest of Mammon but curst of God. I sometimes become convinced that that race is permitted to live among us that we may be reminded of the existence of the diabolic principle which God, in his inscrutable wisdom, permits to harry us and test our faith. But must not God's patience be sorely tried at times by the sight of the excesses of greed of those he once led out of the house of bondage? And will he not forgive the loss of our own patience, the rising of our righteous anger?'

Going out with Martha that fine Sunday morning, he found in his letter box a rolled copy of the medical journal to which he subscribed. Seated outside the coffee house, taking coffee with *Schlagobers* in the sun, he read to her, in a comic pompous voice, the review of his book which it contained. ' "It is not perhaps seemly to make racial divisions in the field of human knowledge, but it is difficult to know how to classify Dr Freud's contribution – I am deliberately being charitable – without relating it to a particular endowment – that of the dispossessed Hebrews, with their fantastic belief that the only viable society is the family, with their matriarchy and their tolerance of incest. To an Aryan mind this disgusting compilation of case histories will strike with a sense of the exotic and alien. The disease is not in Dr Freud's patients but in his own mind. Still, as the long history of the Jewish race teaches us, what is health to them is sickness to those brought up in a different dispensation – " '

'I told you,' Martha said. 'I know it's very unfair, but I did tell you not to publish.'

'And that,' Freud said, 'is the only review. Good morning, Schultz.' The Dr Schultz he addressed walked into the coffee house without even raising his hat to Martha. 'To hell with you, Schultz,' to his back.

'I warned you, Sigmund.' Freud threw money on the table and rose. Martha rose, sighing. They walked slowly down the street.

'Exotic,' he muttered. 'Alien.'

A man in a top hat, walking the other way, hesitated on seeing them. Then he perfunctorily raised that hat to Martha and addressed Freud bitterly. 'I read your book,' he said. 'As much of it as I could stomach. I never in my life read such filth. If you expect me to refer any more patients to you you're mistaken. And I'll do my damnedest to have you boycotted by the rest of the fraternity. You polluter of innocence,' he said. 'You defiler. Forgive me, madam, these things must be said. You have the right and duty to know these things. You defiler. You pornological blackguard. Expect ostracism, for you're damned well going to get it.'

'Thank you, Professor Burkheim,' Freud said. And then he saw. 'In for a penny,' he growled. He saw a group of lower-class Viennese citizens turn themselves into a mob. A brick in the window of Susskind the pawnbroker. A lout with few teeth leered as he pulled out a watch on a chain from the now defenceless window display. Two of the mob grabbed with joy the lamenting skullcapped Susskind. 'Wait, Martha,' Freud said, and he brandished his stick like a brand. He waded in, hitting.

'Oh, Sigmund, Sigmund.'

She sat, snoring faintly, in the corner of the railway compartment. Anna yawned and picked up her novel. 'Vienna,' Freud said, his eyes full of tears. 'Thank God we're done with it.'

* * *

'More chocolate mousse?' Vanessa Brodie said, all in gold with a scooped décolletage. Her father shook his head without smiling and lighted a tipped Frick Giant. 'Australia's done your cough,' said his daughter, 'a lot of good. Unpolluted air.' It was a kindly game she played; she knew the worst but she saw no reason for facing it, not just yet. 'You, Muriel?' she said to Professor Pollock. Muriel Pollock nodded greedily and scooped to her mouth the bit that was left from her second helping. She said tactlessly:

'I ought to start smoking, I suppose. It kills the appetite.'

'More than the appetite,' Frame said brutally. Vanessa looked at him reproachfully and said:

'Val?' Val shook his head, smiling with his mouth.

Nobody could deny the charm of this living room with its dining alcove set in a wall-and-ceiling silver scallop shell. VA monograms on russet curtains, chunky coarse-textured grey armchairs from Bonicelli, Milan, that were masterpieces of comfort. On the lime-green walls were paintings by Paxton, Loewy, Treboux and Voorhees. On a teak plinth was a bronze bust of Vanessa by Hebald, queenly neck exaggerated as to length, breasts brazenly or bronzely offered. A stereotelescreen was discreetly covered by a different kind of screen – tapestried nymphs and centaurs by Piers Widener. Cassette-disc-tape-machine in a Whitney-Stanford cabinet. Drinks bar by Franchot Tilyou. Perfection. Val took out a five pack of cheap cigars called Fidel, lighted up and saw Vanessa's nose wrinkle. Vanessa pressed a gold lozenge on a bank of such lozenges on the wall and almost at once a gleaming steel coffee cart came purring aromatically out of the kitchen. Val went over to the bar and brought back Untermeyer New York cognac (*beware of French imitations*).

'I suppose,' said Muriel Pollock, tactlessly again, 'I might as well start eating myself to death.' She was very fat, though not primarily through gluttony. Being fat, she had decided to use her condition to justify gluttony.

Frame looked coldly at his son-in-law, not attempting, even for his daughter's sake, to conceal his dislike. 'I take it,' he said, 'you will understand what er Dr Pollock refers to?'

'Muriel,' Val said, looking coldly back through his rank smoke, 'is responding jocularly to a certain foreknowledge possessed by the Science Department of our great university. Something to do with a certain heavenly body.'

Frame grunted. 'You write fantastic little books,' he said. 'I've read none of them, but I should imagine the situation she and I and my daughter have to think about might well come into your er fantastic province.'

'You mean,' Val said harshly, resentful of the alienating term *my daughter*, 'I am unfortunately in the family and have to be informed, since I am bound to find out sooner or later in some other way, probably from *your daughter*, about something I am professionally unworthy to be informed about directly. Sir,' he added.

'Please, Val,' his wife said, squirming her heavenly body in discomfort.

'Sorry, Van. Sorry, sir. The rumour's right, then – the one from South America? About Lynx?'

'Lynx,' Vanessa said, in the somewhat pedantic tone she sometimes employed, especially when most femininely dressed, 'is, according to all the calculations, preparing to approach the earth and exert a gravitational pull which will have a devastating effect on its structure – '

'And also its inhabitants,' Val finished for her. 'And then?'

'Then it will go away,' Muriel said in a childish little voice, as though referring to the rain that had started to beat at the window.

'Supposing,' Frame said, 'the world should come to an end – '

'Ah,' Val said. 'When is it going to happen?' He drank off his coffee with relish and pushed his cup to the machine for more.

'Nobody,' snapped his father-in-law, 'said anything about it going to happen. The sort of thing that Lynx will do to the earth will not necessarily mean an end to it.'

'It will go away, will it?' Val said to Muriel. 'For ever and ever? Or will it come back again and be even more devastating the second time?' The scientists looked at each other covertly as to say: never underestimate the insights of a lay brain. Frame said:

'We put it to you as a hypothesis. In a science fiction situation – ridiculous idea, ridiculous phrase – what would you do about the end of the world?'

Val relighted his rank Fidel. He said: 'The situation's not uncommon in science fiction. Indeed, it's rather a banal situation. If the work of fiction isn't to end with everybody dead, then somebody builds a sort of Noah's Ark and a selected few, the cream of mankind, get into it, and, by the grace of God or somebody, they find a new and highly habitable planet after a short cruise in space.'

'The cream of mankind,' Frame repeated, then drank a mixture of coffee and cigarette smoke. 'And who's to decide who the cream of mankind is?'

'It's easy,' Val said. 'A combination of high intelligence and high physical fitness, beauty too I suppose, with probably a longish family record of these qualities well attested.' He saw Muriel nodding dumbly. What he was saying was, of course, very cruel. 'One might,' he said in palliation, 'regard high intelligence and special scientific attainments as outweighing the physical qualification. But if you wanted to breed, as presumably you would, you couldn't afford to perpetuate too much unfitness.' He grinned sadly. 'As I see it, looking round this table, only one of our present company qualifies. She, of course, qualifies shiningly.'

'You admit,' Frame said, 'that you don't qualify? Hypothesis, remember, no more. We're talking about a book. A character made in your image wouldn't qualify, you admit that?'

'I'm moderately healthy,' Val said, 'though there's a history of cardiac weakness in the family. Also a tendency to bronchitis. As far as intelligence goes, who am I to judge? If specialist scientific knowledge is a prime desideratum, then I'm out. I'm a dabbler, a literary man, a sort of poet even. My book would probably end with a poet-hero, made in my image more or less, composing an ode as the world collapses. A useless thing to do, but my breed is probably useless.'

'This man,' Frame said, 'would be married. Married to – '

Val again showed his quickness. 'To someone like Vanessa. He would see the spaceship smalling in the heavens, with this Vanessa character tearfully but bravely and invisibly but dutifully waving goodbye. Is,' he said, 'that what is going to happen?'

'No.' This was Vanessa, her face and neck flushed.

'Not science fiction then,' Val said. 'I knew it wasn't. Funny, I've written fictional accounts of people responding with shock and horror and disbelief and so on to these words of ultimate terror, and here I am – here you are too – well, wanting more coffee.' The coffee machine chuckled.

'A hypothesis,' Frame said. 'That's all.' He was showing flight fatigue. He began to cough. 'As they say, we'll cross our bridges when we – ' He coughed.

'I know what you think of me,' Val said hotly. 'I'm a bit of shit compared with that policeman son of your Australian buddy – '

'Not before Dr Pollock,' Frame said. 'Will you give me a lift home, Muriel? A delightful dinner, Vanessa. May we have many more.'

'Next Wednesday,' Vanessa said. 'Christmas dinner.'

'Will there be Christmases in outer space?' Val asked. 'Or is Christ too unscientific a figure?'

'*Please*, Val,' Vanessa said. Muriel Pollock got her bag and coat in a swift waddle to the master bedroom and back. Frame coughed good night. Vanessa kissed his cheek, also Muriel's. They left. The host and hostess heard a cough receding down the corridor outside the apartment. Val gave himself more brandy. He flopped down with it on the Bonicelli settee.

'I never loved him,' Vanessa said, standing, superb in her gold, before him as he frowned hopelessly. 'You've always known that. It was just father's idea. It's you I love, now and always.'

'Why, Van, why why why?' The frown had changed to a scowl of sheer weariness.

'That's not a question anyone asks. You know I love you. Why can't you love me a little?'

'Take it,' Val said, 'that I'm not worthy of you. I mean it. My not being worthy of you gets into bed between us.'

'There was a time when you didn't talk of worthiness. Love doesn't say that sort of thing.'

'Knowledge is no friend of love. Knowing you better made me change. Knowing that you contain me as you contain Frobisher's Hypothesis and the Deuteroastral Anomaly and – oh, all the rest of it.' She was down on her knees before him. He could see the twin swell of her breasts, naked, hugged by gold, and should have felt desire prick but didn't. He knew it would be easier if he could feel desire. Many a marriage sustained itself on desire and nothing else, and there were simple secret devices for promoting desire.

'Put that glass down,' she ordered, and was on the settee beside him, warm and gold. He closed his eyes, trying to evoke an image of the body of Tamsen, or one of the others, all the same one really – dark, musky, hot, ignorant. He dealt cruelty coldly, hating himself, hearing himself say:

'Today, after my class, I had a girl in my office. A student. A little slut of a girl. Not worthy to dust your desk computer. She remarked on what she called my hunger. Hunger. I was hungry.' She drew away from him, as he'd expected. He looked at her eyes, arctic blue, not quite knowing what he wanted them to register – disgust, hurt, puzzlement. It looked, he thought, like puzzlement. Or was it pity? He had not put down his cognac glass. He drank, looking at her over the rim.

'Quite a number of men are like that,' she said calmly. 'There's that old book by Montrachet, *Nostalgie de la Boue*. They can't take sex as a communion between equals. They want sex as dirt, as possession. I don't blame them, you. But I'm a little disappointed. I thought you were learning. I'm not as good a teacher as I thought. Perhaps you ought to read Montrachet. There's also that thing by Peter Nichols – '

'If,' he said, 'or when – tomorrow morning I shall wonder if I dreamt it, this Lynx thing. Then I shall ask, and it will have been no dream. But if this happens, happened, and you had this science fiction thing, the cream of which you are the cream, and – Oh what am I talking about?'

'I'd never go without you,' she said firmly.

'After what I've told you, and the other things I could tell but haven't?'

'I refuse to have it, the failure of love, of a marriage. We'd go together, we'd learn somewhere, *you'd* learn – '

'And if I refused to go? Granted, of course, that they let me go?'

'That would have to be one of the conditions,' she said. 'I know I won't admit it to myself, not yet, but I'll have to soon. Father's going to die. What I know he taught me. I've a duty to science, which means to the race. But I'm not having this cold impersonal choosing by computer. If father claims the right to a nomination, without the intermediacy of computerized *fairness*, I claim the right too.'

'What good am I to the race? I've a brain like a garage sale. I'm a moral rubbish dump. My sex life, as you so kindly tell me, is just snuffling in the dirt.'

'Don't think about the race. Think about *me*.'

'You fall short of perfection, then. There's human virtue in you, meaning corruption.' She said nothing, she examined her golden nails. 'Your father's in charge, is he, or will be?'

'I told you about last month's meeting of Natsci. He was re-elected president.'

'I didn't take it in, not in this new context. You've all known about this for some time, have you?' She nodded, eyes on him. She said:

'You'll know all about it soon enough. There's time to take it in, time to get ready. Time to get all we can out of – ' She made a limp but graceful gesture which seemed to signify the room they sat in, culture, marriage, perhaps sex, and also nature outside, candyfloss, beer in low bars – no, probably not those. 'We'd better go to bed.'

'No.' He did a vigorous headshake. 'Christmas is coming. When, by the way, is the other thing coming, the final thing?'

'The fall,' she said. 'Highly appropriate you'd say.'

'So this is our last Christmas.' He stood up. 'I'm going downtown. I must drink in as much of imperfect humanity as I can while I can.'

'I'll come with you.'

'No, Van. You don't like that sort of thing. Besides, the simple pleasures of the poor and lowly would collapse in face of your frightful perfection. I shan't be all that long. Moreover, I have some thinking to do, don't I? I find low bars conducive to high thought.'

The nuclear-powered hangline from Roelantsen Station got Val to 57th and Third, Manhattan, in a little over twenty minutes. The streets and bars in Basso were lively. The rain had thickened to the first light snow. Christmas was very much in the air. There were drunks, there was violence. Underprivileged Teutprot youth picked quarrels with privileged blacks and browns and blackbrowns, jeering and provoking in their underprivileged argot: 'A sniff in the kortevar, that what you cry for, yeled? A prert up the cull, a prang on the dumpendebat?' Val drank his way from bar to bar – GNYs straight up with four olives, plain Manhattans – and found the stores on Fifth Avenue doing a great late-evening trade. Outside Yamasaki's, all lights and evergreens, a Santa Claus twice as fat as Muriel Pollock, and God knew she was fat, was having trouble with a gang of rowdy Teutprots. They were telling him to jall his little bell up his yahma. But he was having no nonsense. 'Scum,' he cried. 'Droppings.' He was lunging out with a great glove that was probably loaded with shot, for it caught one boy on the ear and sent him scudding to the gutter. 'Witless turds,' he told them. An undermanager looked on uneasily from the nearest store entrance. Five boys set snarling on Santa Claus and ripped at his red robe very rudely. Underneath he was wearing old grey patched slacks. They ripped at those too. Santa Claus cried unsaintly language and hit out viciously. To the undermanager he called: 'Why don't you help, you snotnosed bastard?' The undermanager responded with a look that boded no good to the name-caller but with nothing more helpful. Val himself now stepped in. He was speedy on his feet despite his little paunch, and he had tricks with his fingers that he had learnt when, many years before, he had been a schoolteacher in the Astoria district of Queens. He and Santa Claus quickly sent the young louts flying. Then two policemen came from around the corner, and the thugs did not feel like renewing their assault. The undermanager said:

'What did you call me then, Willett?'

'A snotnosed bastard, I think. Also, now I have leisure and breath, I might add that you are a slabberdegullion druggel, a doddipol jolthead, a blockish grutnol, and a turdgut. Also, of course, a coward.'

'You're fired, Willett. Give me that outfit.'

Willett tore what was still untorn, so that he now stood in normal sinner's clothes, with a red fur-trimmed Santa cap on. This latter he thrust onto the undermanager's head, dousing him like a candle, and draped him with the ripped mass of red cloak, enough for a yacht sail. 'In the classic phrase,' he said, 'I quit. You shitabed and lousy rascal.' To Val he said: 'Thank you, my galliard friend, let's go and drink.'

They entered a bar on West 53rd Street, full of red lights and tinsel for Yule, also of cheerful drunks who seemed to know Willett well, for they hailed him with 'Hi, fat Jack' and 'Well, if it ain't old Hohoho himself' and, more soberly, 'Behold the great Courtland Willett in poison'. Val learnt from this that Willett was probably an out-of-work actor who had surely, with that bulk, once played Falstaff. Courtland Willett: the sort of phony name an actor might take on. Willett, having ordered beer in litre tankards and quadruple scotches to go with them, must have seen this onomastic scepticism in Val's eye, for he said:

'To give you the full version – Robert Courtland van Caulaert Willett, Dutch and English ancestry freely commingled.' He took from an inner pocket a cigar in an aluminium sheath, the longest Val had ever seen, withdrew the brown fumable tenderly, struck a match from a kitchen box on his trouser seat, and lighted up with relish. 'A gift,' he said through ample smoke, 'from a passer-by who had seen me on the boards in better days and well remembered. I played Gargantua once in a stage adaptation of Rabelais's bawdy and erudite masterwork. That he had seen, also my Falstaff. My Hamlet, alas, was not a success. Too fat, they said, too scant of breath – precisely, I pointed out, the words of the Queen in the fencing climax. Who, by the way, is to pay for these potations? I suffer from a disease which used to be called shortage of money.'

'I have money,' Val said. 'I received my professorial salary this afternoon.'

'Then,' Willett said contentedly, 'we have no worries.' There was a talk programme on the stereotel conducted by a thin sly man and his fat jackal. A raddled actress with a perky tomboy manner and hoisted bosom well on show was saying: 'Yah, I guess so, yah, that's about it, I guess.' Willett at once inveighed against the silly stereoscopic faces:

'Sycophant varlets, drawlatch hoydens, brattling gabblers, ninnyhammer flycatchers, woodcock slangams, bemerded lobcocks. Not,' he said in an aside to Val, 'that I have anything against the medium in itself. Years and years and years ago I made a slight but now forgotten name in a couple of things. One was a musical. I sang, I danced. The other was about the Viennese soulquack. I played a small part, I forget which. I have tapes still. You must watch them with me some time.' And then: 'Off with it, absurd pillocky nonsense.'

As if aware of unfavourable comment, the talkshowmaster said that that would be all for tonight folks, tune in tomorrow, and commercials for Roundy Kupkakes, Kingfisher Kingfish in Eggbatter, Beadbonny Mock Caviar came on, all of which products Willett denounced as filth and poison. Val felt a great sadness. He saw clearly, as in a film version of one of his own novels, a great spaceship looking a thousand years for landfall, full of men and women with thin exact minds who would not know who Sir John Falstaff was or ever dream of using a term like 'woodcock slangam'. The dirty delightful world, full of rogues and whores and bad language, was going to come to an end. He ordered more drink and found that Willett was now thundering against the Calvin Gropius rally that was being broadcast from Westchester's own stadium. Gropius's exhortations to repent were thoroughly drowned by Willett's 'Codshead loobies, flutch calf-lollies, idle lusks' and so on, but one of the searching cameras picked up members of the congregation, and among these was Tamsen Disney, her lubberly student companion with a hand on her left breast. Well, let them all get on with it – dirt, life, juice, panting.

Gropius's exhortatory organ was a gnat-squeak compared with Willett's poetic thunder. He was giving the bar Shakespeare, Milton, Dylan Thomas and Gerard Manley Hopkins:

'. . . Heart, you round me right
With: our evening is over us; our night whelms, whelms and will
end us . . .'

The poets had always had words ready for the end of the world. It had been expected from the very beginning: the generation of Noah was not far ahead from Adam. The man sitting nearest the telescreen made a change to another channel, and even Willett was quiet as they all looked at a blown-up image of Lynx, all the way from Australia. It was a mere blob of light, no more. A parsonical voice-over was saying with unction: 'Lynx in the heavens greets Christ the tiger.' And then the choir of the Mormon Tabernacle of Salt Lake City was singing an old American carol:

'Star of wonder, star of light,
Star with royal beauty bright,
Westward leading, still proceeding,
Guide us with thy perfect light.'

Willett, a man as ready for big globular tears as for drink, poetry and invective, started to weep, weeping: 'My childhood. Turkeys as big as sheep and Christmas puddings like cannonballs, and the flaming sauce reeking like arson in a brandy cellar. Gone, gone, for evermore gone.'

'Gone for everybody,' Val said. 'No more Christmases. Let's make the best of this.' And he ordered another round. Those who heard him took his words to mean that the great past was dead and the endless future would be thin and mean and unloving. A young whore was also, encouraged by Willett's huge tears, weeping for lost innocence back in Auburn in the state of Washington. Willett had his arm around her and was soon kissing and fumbling her heartily. An old man took his false teeth out and did a comic caper about the barroom to the accompaniment of somebody's harmonica. The bartender sang about working on the railroad. A girl called Elsie did a drunken tapdance on the counter. A man came in with snow on his shoulders. Christmas was coming. At the end of the night Val could not make it to Westchester. He was taken home by Willett – a wretched single room which fitted its lessee like a pair of roomy trousers. The two snored amicably till morning.

What Val Brodie and Courtland Willett saw on the telescreen in that lively Christmassy bar was, between the talk show and the star of wonder, the final phase of Calvin Gropius's Christmas rally in the Westchester University Stadium. His live congregation alone was about fifteen thousand and his teleauditors must have amounted to some hundred million. It was chilly on the stadium benches, but the chill was mitigated by the chance to sing stirring march-style hymns and stamp and gesture to them, under the direction of a white-sweatered athlete, Zwingli Gilroy, DD. Some of the less devout members of the congregation fought the cold with hip flasks. But the subject matter of Calvin Gropius's address was considerately chosen. In earlier days he would have been called a hot gospeller.

'Fireballs blazing in the intestines,' he told the microphones. 'The body a furnace compounded of many furnaces, and all stoked to blue heat by the diabolic agents of divine punishment. Ah yes, you students, you professors, you men and women of intellectual learning, you rationalists disposed to scoff at the plain words of the Lord, consider this – that because you have cast off the troublesome burden of inconvenient belief in eternal and condign punishment you have not thereby changed the divinely ordained reality. Why should your visions necessarily be the counterparts of God's truth? God is made not in your image but in his own. Sin, you say, is a mere clouding of reason. But sin, as the word of the Lord howls into ears that will hear not, is a stinking reality, an eternal and terrible violation of celestial purity. I too have had my visions, and they have been visions God-given, not products of erring reason. I have seen, have smelt, tasted, heard, touched the endless endless endless terror of the fiery pit. Yes, the Lord has been good to me in order, so I am bold to believe, that I may transmit his goodness to you here assembled, you, my wider audience unseen. Take warning, then – drunkards, fornicators, scoffers, blasphemers, adulterers, liars. Hell exists, hell waits.'

After the thunder of his catalogue and chilling or warming affirmation, Calvin Gropius spoke more softly. 'A star in the east,' he said. 'We have been told of a new star in the east. The folks down under,' he said folkily, 'have been vouchsafed a glimpse of its pinpoint of fire. It has come at Christmas, as a star came for the first Christmas two thousand years ago. A prodigy in the heavens signifying a prodigy on earth – so it was then. And may it not be so a second time? Our Lord Jesus Christ promised the faithful, warned the sinful, of his second coming. And his second coming would serve not the sowing of the divine word but the gathering in of the harvest. Yes, the harvest – which signifies not only the garnering of the wheat but the burning of the chaff. The burning, the burning, the consigning to the furious flames of the pit of doom. May not the time be coming? May not the star be a herald of his approach? The star whose image we have observed on our television screens will rise for eyes unaided by science in our own hemisphere – in God's good time. Nature's good time, one may say – the time of the burgeoning of life after the long winter. In the spring we shall see it. May our hearts be pure and ready. For if it is the harbinger of Christ's second coming, as I believe it to be, may we be purged and clean and have no fear of the judgement.'

The augmented notes of an organ swelled and rose into the crystalline air, and the congregation too rose rustling like the rising of a wind. They sang a hymn composed by one of Calvin Gropius's henchmen, the poet and musician Wyclif Wilock:

'We fear thy anger, Lord,
Less than we hate our sin.
O may we soon begin
To cut the devil's cord
And let thy goodness in.'

Among the members of the congregation who were not singing was Edwina Duffy, a young colleague of Val Brodie's. She ran a course in devotional poetry, more popular with the devotional than with the poetic. She was interested in the nexus between religion and sex, adept at picking sexual imagery out of holy poets like Watts and Wesley. She had even written a well-regarded article for the *Sewanee Review* on the true meaning of the sticking of the lance into Christ's side when he was dying on the cross. Out of his side, the Bible said, came blood and water. Really, she alleged, his final emission was of semen, and the blood–water–lance collocation was obliquely expressive of this. She was not singing because she was too moved to sing. Gropius had an effect on her nerves and glands that was wholly sexual. The voice itself, despite or because of the grotesque magnification by microphones, was like a shot of some powerful aphrodisiac, and the broad handsomeness of the evangelist, undiminished by distance since he was projected stereoscopically onto a great silver screen, set up shivers in her that could not be confused with the effects of winter-night cold. Her boyfriend, Nat Goya, had refused to come with her to the rally. 'Orgy porgy,' he had said, 'superstition, nasty nonsense.' She had accused him of ingratitude. He did not understand the accusation. He soon would, she told herself, as she made her way out through Mouth D, a mousy girl disregarded by most males, a thin creature demure and nunlike. Her ardour was hidden: not for her, or for men who glanced incuriously at her, the flaunting of breasts in a sweater or wagging crupper in tight pants.

It was but a brief walk to the brilliantly lighted staff car park, where her yellow Goodhue Seven awaited her animating key. There was much activity there tonight, the moving out of many cars. The atmosphere was devotional, meaning sexual. Hell, she was thinking, hell. Hot dark hell, raging. A nether cavern. The sexual significance must always have been evident.

She drove down Gottlieb Way, turned right on to Tucci Avenue, left onto Nesbitt Street, and stopped outside Pell House, an apartment block where many of the young single professors lived. The doorman who let her in nodded knowingly. She rose in the elevator to the nineteenth floor. 'In,' cried the voice of Nat Goya. She went in. He was a thin hard young man with very little hair. He sat at his desk in underpants only for the central heat, marking papers. He was in the Department of Microagronomy and was reputed to be moving towards brilliance. He looked at her unsmiling, as if she were another paper to mark. She smiled, and her demure face was transformed to that of a courtesan. She put off her dowdiness with her clothes. So far the one word spoken had been 'In'. Soon it became the second word, this time spoken by her. Microagronomy was far. To delay his ejaculation he repeated over and over to himself the chemical formula for monosodium glutamate: $HOOC\ (CH_2)\ _2CH\ (NH_2)\ COONa$. But this was soon transformed into meaningless vocables – *hook chacha coona hook chacha coona* – which matched the rhythm of his thrust. She, at the moment of their joint climax, felt herself being impregnated by Calvin Gropius who, for a reason she could not at first comprehend, wore a bright star on his brow. 'The second coming,' she said.

'What?'

'A poem by Yeats.'

'What's a poem by Yeats got to do with it?'

' "And what rough beast, its hour come round at last, slouches toward Bethlehem to be born?" '

'I don't see what in hell's name that has to do with – '

'Never mind,' she said. 'Rhythms get into your head when you – The mystical state,' she added. He frowned. But soon enough he could see a point in that business about the second coming. Later, while they drank instant coffee from mugs, she said: 'Gropius is remarkable.'

'In what way remarkable?' he growled jealously.

'The energy. He goes on about God and Christ but it could just as well be about Belial and Beelzebub. Great big blind crashing sexual energy. Bethlehem and the rough beast. There were three beasts in that manger and one of them was wild wild wild.' She put down her hardly touched mug. 'Come on,' she said. 'Time is so short.'

'What do you mean – time is so – '

'Oh, come on.'

'Let me finish my – '

'*Come on.*'

Calvin Gropius was not aware, in a particular sense, of the effect his rally, personality, words were having on Edwina Duffy and others like her. In a general sense, of course, he was well aware of the sexual impact that was in a manner a secondary articulation of the evangelical impulse. It was all in the Holy Bible, like everything else. Salome and John the Baptist, for instance. That pouting little sexpot, surrounded by drooling lechers of the Galilean court, fell not for one of them but for an emaciated burning-eyed incarnation of the primal force of the universe. God, devil, demiurge – words words. Gropius, taking fruit punch with the committee of the Student Christian Body of Westchester, could see how the wide eyes of the girl members were devouring him. He was neither gratified nor repelled. Religion and sex spoke equally of life; they met in the agricultural myths out of which the most sophisticated faiths had been generated. But he never, on these social occasions, tried to take advantage of his charisma. He was a family man of fifty-five, with three grown-up sons. He was four times a grandfather. He kept himself physically fit, chemically subdued the timely greyness of his hair, visited his dentist every three months, not that he should be attractive to women but that the Lord's truth should be attractive to them. And to men, of course, also.

Despite his worldly appearance, he was not what is called a worldly man. He had a small ranch in Arizona, which he now had no time to run, and a penthouse apartment in DeWitt Towers, East 35th Street, Manhattan. He had ten million dollars in the bank, no colossal sum at that time, and few worries about the material future. But about the future of his soul, and the souls of his fellow men and women, he was sincerely concerned. He believed in holiness, a loving but just God, the redemptive powers of Christ's blood. He believed that man had done all that he was predestined to do through sheer ingenuity and intelligence, and that now man must look, more than ever before, to the needs of the spirit. He saw self-indulgence all about him, too much wallowing in the ecstasies of the flesh, too much violence and cruelty and unkindness and selfishness, and he desperately wished to play some part in the spreading of the regenerative word. He was always delighted to be able to talk and pray with the young, and the ingenuous and ingenious spiritual inquiries of the young he took most seriously and endeavoured to answer with earnest and candid appeals to divine reason as presented in the Holy Bible. The future, he considered, not unreasonably, lay with the young.

'The Second Coming,' one lank-haired girl of Korean extraction was saying. 'Does that mean that Christ has to be born again, like that first time, or will he just step out of heaven at the age he was when he died, all ready for the Last Judgement?'

'The Bible says nothing of a second birth,' Calvin Gropius told her. 'One birth was enough, as reason must tell you. Christ exists, as man and God, waiting in heaven for the day. The day may be soon.'

'You say that,' said a young man who was enduring a phase of devout scepticism, 'because we've come to the end of the second millennium. They were saying that sort of thing in the year one thousand, but the world didn't come to an end. Why should there be a sort of magic in the number 2000? And why, for that matter, should you have to bring a star into it? It all sounds like a lot of superstition to me.'

'Right,' said his quadroon girlfriend. 'You really believe the end of the world's coming? Now?'

'We have to be careful,' Gropius said, 'in interpreting Holy Scripture. There's a rhetorical level of meaning and a literal one. I don't seriously believe that this whole structure of the earth, and the spatial annexes around it, are going to collapse in smoke and flame and the sky is going to be filled with the sort of scene Michelangelo painted on that wall in the Sistine Chapel. I believe rather that men and women will become more aware than ever before in the history of the world of the nature of good and evil and that they'll finally take sides. Some will be on the side of Christ and some on the side of the devil. Then there'll come the final conflict and the end of man as history has known him. Man will have to start again, as after the Flood.'

'The fire next time,' a white youth said.

'Yes, the fire of human conflict. That fire will be the judgement.

The righteous will survive it, but the righteous will be few. I speak Christ's word to millions, but do not in my heart believe that more than a wretched little percentage will be among the saved.'

'So it's going to happen but not just yet,' said the Korean girl. 'Not *now*. We're just going to start getting ready for it now. You mean there's plenty of time really?'

'Never plenty of time,' Gropius sternly said. 'To make our souls ready requires all the time that life can give. But do not think that you can stop the great conflict coming about by refusing to be involved in it. It was predestined to happen before time itself began. The forces of darkness have rejected Christ – the secularists, I mean, the totalitarian rulers and their subjects. They have defined their good and know it is not Christ's good. An underfed and overpopulated world, united under Antichrist, will beat at the doors of us all before this coming year is out –'

'That you prophesy?' the sceptical youth said, deep down the profoundest believer of all there present. 'That you know?'

'Armageddon,' Gropius said. 'The last great war, fought by Christ's followers against the forces of Antichrist. The Judgement is contained in the very notion of Armageddon. The righteous who die will sit at his right hand. The righteous who survive will build the kingdom of righteousness on earth. It's all in the Bible.'

'Another glass of fruit punch, Dr Gropius?' asked the wide-eyed girl secretary of the SCB, who had, Gropius noted dispassionately, as nice a little Christian body as he had ever seen.

$HOOC\ (CH_2)\ _2CH\ (NH_2)\ COONa$

Hook chacha coona hook chacha coona.

A rhythm which, though somewhat anachronistic, will do well enough on the orchestra before the chorus raises its collective voice. The skyscrapers of New York are seen against a leaden morning sky. Young men and women in the dress of the period they sing about sing, as they wait at a street crossing:

1917:
The scene: Manhattan.
Four years have flown

Since Wilson first sat in
The White House.

A hop and skip and jump as they cross. The long skirts of the girls are split, for dancing comfort, to the thigh. And now more young men and women in a subway train, the vehicle's rocking inducing stylized body movements.

Europe's burning hot
But not this nation.
She shines alone,
A bright isolation-
ist lighthouse.

Men shovel snow in Central Park, balletically swinging their spades.

There's a glow in the January
Snow though.
Is something going to happen?
Is the European war
Going to rap on
America's door?

Men and women come up out of the subway, jostling with others going down into it. The jostle is dancelike.

1917:
We've seen the warning.
Something's in store
This perishing morning.
Is it peace or war coming on?
We'll know much more before
1917
Has been and gone.

The entire chorus sings over newsreel images.

The stormy grey Atlantic
Is afire with U-boats.
The Brooklyn yards are frantic-
ally building new boats,
Red white and blue boats,
Just in case.
The army camps are filling

With the stern and steady.
You can hear the sergeants drilling
And the high and heady
Trumpets already
Every place.

The chorus walks to work in marchtime.

We'll fight all right if we must.
In God, meaning us, meaning US us,
We kind of trust.

Dance dance dance across busy streets, in and out of stores, on to and off streetcars. Two opposed mob orators try to detain the dancing hurryers.

PACIFIST ORATOR: Keep out of it, America. It's Europe's war.
Let *them* batter themselves to bits.
Let *us* leave them to it.
We'll sell them the arms to do it.
To both sides, impartial. It's
What neutrality's for.

WARMONGERING ORATOR: The Huns are sinking our ships.
If that's not an act of war,
What is, I'd like to know.
Kaiser Wilhelm's Empire
Flaps its wings like a vampire
Ready to suck our blood. So
What are we waiting for?

PACIFIST: Keep out of it, keep out of it,
Non-imperialistic democratic America.

WARMONGER: Get into it, get into it,
Non-imperialistic democratic America.

PACIFIST: Do you want our boys to go over there
And catch syphilis and poverty
From the British and French?

WARMONGER: Do you want our world markets to be ruined?
Do you want a poverty-stricken Europe
Unable to buy American goods?

PACIFIST: Let's make it peace.
WARMONGER: Let's make it war.
PACIFIST: Peace.
WARMONGER: War.
PACIFIST: Peace.
WARMONGER: War.

This antiphony is caught up by a section of the chorus as an accompaniment to the following by the rest:

There's a glow on our faces
Though they're wind-skinned.
Perhaps the fire of battle.
Are the trumpets' martial tones
Going to rattle
Our indolent bones?

A WORKING-CLASS DEMAGOGUE: Comrades! We want peace, and we want war.
The workers want to be left in peace to wage war against the bosses.
Forget German and Allied victories and losses.
We want to fight here, not there.
American workers have their own heavy crosses
To bear.

Olga, a very pretty dark-haired New York girl, tries to make her way through the crowd. She has a rectangular piece of wood under her right arm. Behind her, shambling, tripping, is a small ugly member of the proletariat who calls himself Sasha. The chorus resumes singing and dancing:

1917 –
We've seen it coming,
Hearing its roar
And ominous humming.
Is the god of war on his way?
We'll know much more,
We'll be able to say,
Before
1917

Has seen
Another day!

The scene changes. The piece of wood that was under Olga's arm is revealed as a plaque on which, in fine Cyrillic script, is printed the following:

НОВЫЙ МИР

Under Olga's direction, Sasha affixes this to the door of a shopfront. She opens the door with a heavy key. From a waiting van pieces of office furniture are removed by surly removers. These move the pieces indoors. People stand around, curious. A man says: 'What's that – Chinese?'

'No, comrade,' Olga says.

'What's it say?' says nailing Sasha.

'You're Russian and you don't know Russian?'

'My old man knows it. Us kids just kind of let it drop.'

'It says,' says Olga, '*Noviy Mir*. It means New World. It can also mean New Peace.'

'Yeah, that's kind of nice,' Sasha says, 'I guess. America. The New World. Hard as the old. Cold as the old.'

'*Not* America,' Olga says. 'Listen.' And she sings:

The new world hasn't been built yet,
For its builders don't have much luck.
The capitalistic flowers
Have not begun to wilt yet,
The proletarian hour's
Not struck.
Though our world's coming tomorrow,
Who knows when tomorrow will come?
We're going to make things hum
Some day somehow,
But that some day isn't now.

The chorus, which has transferred itself hither, moves for two measures.

The new world isn't a thing yet,
Just an idea born in your head.
The workers like uncaged birds
Have not begun to sing yet,

They're learning to say the words
Instead.
You don't bring
Change with a hatchet
Or punching the boss on the snout.
We have to work it out,
Doubt not we can,
And plan
The United States of Man.

The chorus vocalizes in wailing background.

The kids hack coal in the bosses' mines,
And the nightsticks crack at the picket lines,
And the girls sew shirts for a dime a day,
And the cops are all in the bosses' pay,
But it's going to change,
Strange as it seems.
What we're dreaming isn't dreams.

'You mean revolution?' says Sasha. 'Don't let the cops hear you.'

'This country,' says Olga, 'was born out of a revolution. Besides, the cops are workers like everybody else.'

'The cops is just cops,' says Sasha. 'If you build this you talk of, they'll still be cops. Revolution cops. More revolting than the ones we got now.'

'One revolution's enough for any country,' says Olga. 'What I want is evolution – gradual change under the existing system, the workers' society growing like a flower, the international society of the world's workers. The world's here in New York. All the nations, all the races. This is where it has to start.'

'Yeah,' says Sasha. 'Very nice, them words about work. Me, I just work.' And, having finished the affixing of the plaque, he follows the removers in. Olga finishes her song:

The new world's only on paper,
The new words have to come first.
Then look for the flaming flag
On hovel and skyscraper,
Informing you that the bag
Has burst.
The new world's coming tomorrow:

I'll yell it again and again.
But if you ask me when
Then hear me say:
It's the day after
The day after
The day after
Today.

The working-class demagogue has reappeared. He shouts: 'Workers of the world, u –' Seeing a couple of policemen come round the corner, interested, swinging their truncheons, he converts that last word into 'You have my profoundest sympathy.' Buzzers buzz, sirens hoot, clocks chime. The chorus sing and then dance off. Olga takes one more look at the name plaque, then goes inside. The chorus:

Time to go to work,
An irksome burden.
Freedom's absurd,
Another big word, an–
other puff of wind in the ear.
We work till we bust for we must and
1917
Will be seen to have been
Just
Another year!

The scene changes to the interior of the *Noviy Mir* premises. Olga is arranging papers and her typewriter table. Sasha sweeps his way to the door. He opens it to continue his sweeping and Bokharin, Volodarsky and Chudnorsky come in, dressed in a very bourgeois manner. Bokharin has a strong look of a younger Courtland Willett. They see Sasha and raise their fists to him in a Communist salute. He halfheartedly responds, but converts the gesture into a nosewipe. Then he sweeps his way out. The three men approach Olga.

'As from today, comrade,' says Bokharin, 'in these new and commodious premises, things change. I'm no longer your editor. One man in charge – it smacks of imperialistic dictatorship.'

'No, Comrade Bokharin. Or yes, Comrade Bokharin.'

'We have an editorial committee instead. Meet my colleagues and yours, exiles from the homeland like myself, like yourself. Comrade Volodarsky. Comrade Chudnorsky.'

'Kak vui pozhovarnyetye?'

'Kak vui pozhovarnyetye?'

'Ochin khorosho,' Olga says. 'Olga Alexandrovna Lunacharskaya. But I get called Olga Mooney.'

'Luna – moon,' says Volodarsky. *'Da da.'*

'No,' Olga says. 'My mother's second husband's called Mooney. He's a policeman.'

'Is it,' says Chudnorsky, 'perhaps not the best time to rehearse for tonight?'

'Madness,' Volodarsky says. 'A political meeting of paramount importance, and we have to sing songs.'

'The American way,' says Bokharin. 'A frivolous people. We must learn how to introduce ourselves to them. You see, most of the Russian names have their ends chopped off on Ellis Island. The Americans can't stand anything that goes on too long.'

They nod gloomily and begin to sing from rumpled manuscript parts:

Bokharin,
Volodarsky,
Chudnorsky.
Bok and Vol and Chud,
Sounding like the thud
Of a baseball bat on a ball.
Chudnorsky,
Volodarsky,
Bokharin.
Chud and Bok and Vol,
Sounding like the fall
Of a garbage can in the mud.
We have to tolerate
These bourgeois deformations
Of our true appellations,
But wait.
Volodarsky,
Chudnorsky,
Bokharin,
Vol and Chud and Bok,
Sounding like the talk
Of a man whose mouth's full of gum.

Come the day when our exile's ended,
Our names will be splendid as before:
Volodarsky,
Bokharin,
Chudnorsky,
Once more.

'Once more?' says Volodarsky.

'We do the dance now,' says Bokharin.

'A dance yet.'

Gloomily they perform an arthritic gopak or trepak, then go into a breathless coda:

Come the day when our exile's finished
They won't be diminished any more.
Volodarsky,
Chudnorsky,
Bokharin,
As before.

'Enough of this bourgeois nonsense,' says Bokharin. 'Work hard, Comrade Olga. Work for the cause. A good thing you have no union. Whatever the union rate, we couldn't pay it.' The clock strikes nine. 'He's late.'

'No,' says Chudnorsky, 'the clock must be fast.'

And so the door at once opens and in strides

They sped towards Paris. Freud said: 'What time did we arrive at the station, Martha?'

'You know perfectly well, Sigmund. Two hours before we had to. As always.'

'I promise,' Freud said, 'that when we take the train from Paris to London-I'll arrive at the very last minute.'

'And if we miss it?'

'We won't miss it.'

'We won't miss it, father,' Anna said, looking up from her English novel, 'because you'll be at the station two hours before.'

Freud thought about that. 'I know,' he said, 'I know. But it will be for the last time. England. I shall die there.'

'You'll live there first,' Anna said.

'Well – the ritual of a two hours' wait for the last journey – I don't think you'll begrudge it me. Strange, though, strange – was I right about the aetiology?' And he brooded.

A younger Freud and a younger Martha and their six children sat waiting for a train. Their luggage surrounded them. Martha said: 'Sigmund – I don't want to complain – but this is madness.'

'What's madness, my dear?'

'We know perfectly well what time the train leaves, yet you get us here at least two hours before. You can't sleep all night, and I can't sleep either. You keep checking on whether the train's actually running. You worry about losing the tickets. And then we go without breakfast to get here ridiculously early. It's madness.'

'Madness is a very vague term. Unscientific. Call it a neurosis.'

'Well, if it's a neurosis you ought to try to cure it.'

'I only cure *harmful* neuroses.'

'This harms *me*. It makes me a nervous wreck.'

'Nonsense. Waiting for trains is part of the joy of travel. The children *love* waiting.' The children, bored, dejected, played a languid spitting game behind the shelter of the piled luggage.

'And then,' Martha said, 'when the train actually arrives, you don't seem to want to get on it. You remember you need cigars or a newspaper. It will be the same today. In fifteen minutes,' checking by the station clock. 'You'll see.'

'A *harmless* neurosis. When I have time I'll look into it.'

'Meanwhile we wait.'

'Father,' the children called. 'Dad. Daddy.' They were on the train now and the train was ready to move off. Martha sat in a corner seat, grim and silent. Freud opened the door and got aboard while the train was actually moving.

'It came over me,' panting. 'I couldn't –'

'You *could* have. You know there's a toilet on the train.'

'It was a matter of –'

Soon he lighted a cigar and said: 'Vacation by courtesy of – I've forgotten the patient's name.'

'Herr Boecklin.'

'Of course. Why did I forget?'

'You always forget when it's convenient to forget.'

'That's not true. I'm grateful to Herr Boecklin. Grateful to a grateful patient.'

'But you don't want to be grateful really. You think you should be getting what you're worth. Not relying on gifts.'

'I wonder. Why do I always forget Anna's birthday?'

'Perhaps you didn't want her to be born.'

'Such nonsense.' He smiled across at Anna, who did not smile back. He rumbled something and opened his newspaper.

Alpine air like chilled *Sekt*. He drew it in by the lungful from the open second-floor window that faced the great jagged panorama. Martha unpacked. 'Away from it all,' he beamed. 'Dirty Vienna. Dirty work.'

From the corridor outside their bedroom there suddenly struck up a woman's hysterical crying.

'You spoke too soon, Sigmund.'

An elderly woman with long wavy filaments growing out of her sharp chin, ajangle with a big bunch of chatelaine keys adangle from her waist, was sternly comforting a pretty blonde chambermaid. 'I'm a doctor,' Freud said. 'Can I help?' The girl screamed at that and then fell into mere sobbing. The elderly woman, evidently the housekeeper of the inn, said:

'Nobody can help. Nothing except time. *It's* her mother.'

'Poor girl.'

'We've been saying *poor girl* for the last six months. Come on, Gretel, we've work to do.'

'So it was six months ago that she that her – '

'Come on, girl,' the housekeeper said. 'Nobody's mother can live for ever.'

' "Thou know'st 'tis common?" ' Freud stupidly quoted. ' "All that lives must die, passing through nature to eternity." '

Gretel caught that *Ewigkeit* and started to whimper in terror. 'I'll go to hell,' she whimpered. 'I know I will.'

'Gretel,' the housekeeper said, 'I tell you for the millionth time that you've nothing to be guilty about. It's not your fault she died. You were a good daughter, do you hear me?' And then: 'Sorry for the disturbance, Herr Doktor.' She led distressed Gretel away. Freud shook his head sadly and then remembered he was on vacation.

The green Alpine slope, air of preternatural cleanness he flawed with cigar smoke. Martha was knitting. The children chased each other towards the wooded valley. 'Remember our courting days?'

Freud tenderly said. 'The trips to Grinzing, the Wienerwald – No money, no prospects. Not much more now, I suppose. The monument I dreamed of – Freud the great man – "he who unravelled the riddle of the Sphinx" – ah well, enough to be rearing a family, to be only a little in debt.'

'But you're disappointed, Sigmund, true?'

'Disappointed that those who say they're dedicated to the truth don't want the truth. My colleagues. Even Breuer. They're frightened of sex. Why are they frightened?'

'They're not frightened, they're just embarrassed. You talk about it too much. There are some things nobody wants to be hearing about all the time – like, you know – '

'Like bowels and bottoms and faeces.'

'Please, Sigmund – '

'It's no accident. The organs of generation, the organs of elimination – all within a handspan of each other when they're not actually identical – all conveniently tucked away – '

'We came here for a holiday, dear.'

'There's never any holiday from these things.'

He leaned over and kissed Martha. Martha's fingers went on with their knitting. He prolonged the kiss while his cigar smouldered in his own fingers.

'No – people will see – '

'Only the children – '

'*No.*'

Freud broke away and somewhat gloomily said: 'Ironical. Sex is for the consulting room. Late to bed, early to rise. Are we settling down into being – well, an unpassionate pair of companions?'

'We have our family.'

'There speaks the voice of biology. And man hasn't properly learned how to separate the act from its biological consequences. Not yet. Perhaps nature doesn't want him to.'

'I don't understand you. But then, I hardly ever do these days.'

'Anxiety,' Freud said. 'The number of cases of sexual anxiety I have. Coitus interruptus. Condoms that split. Perhaps the Emperor ought to forbid sex by imperial fiat. Vienna without sex. An interesting situation. Less glamour, less anxiety. No work for Dr Freud.' The luncheon bell rang shrilly from the inn.

There rang shrilly from the kitchen during luncheon the scream of, it had to be, the girl Gretel. Guests looked up from their fish or veal. Martha nodded resignedly at Freud. Freud went into the kitchen.

Gretel was being restrained by the innkeeper and his wife. The cook held a knife he had, it appeared, wrested from the hands of Gretel. Gretel screamed. Sedatives were upstairs in his bag. There was, however, a bottle of culinary brandy on that sideboard over there. 'Give her some of that,' Freud said. 'Quieten her down. Get her to bed.' The innkeeper, a thin man, cluckclucked as the brandy mostly glugglugged over Gretel's kitchen apron. Gretel gagged and went ugh. 'I'll see her in her bedroom,' Freud said.

She was quieter after her brief alcoholic passing out. He said: 'How did your mother die?'

'She choked. Couldn't breathe. They said a fishbone.'

'Fish for dinner, then. Did you cook the fish?'

'My sister.'

'So you *didn't* kill your mother. I want you to try to remember something. I want you to go back in time. I want you to think of your father. When you were very very small.'

'I can't remember.'

'Yes, you can. We never forget anything. You loved your father, didn't you?'

She started to whimper, but there was no hysterical demon ready to rise. What rose instead was a memory. 'They were in bed,' she said. 'I saw them in bed.'

'Ah,' Freud said.

Flawed crystalline air with cigar smoke. Children played in valley. Martha knitted. 'It will take time,' Freud said. 'God help me, have I to take it all on myself – the ailments of the world? There's nobody here. If I went to the local sawbones and told him, he'd denounce me to priest and police. A ceremony of exorcism in the cell of a village lockup. But you can *see* she's better. Everybody can.'

'Everybody can see how she feels about *you*, Sigmund.' The needles clacked in hopeless reproach.

'Simple transference. It means nothing. The important thing is no more hysteria. No more trying to stab herself with a kitchen knife.'

'For the moment. She won't do it while *you're* around.'

'But don't you see, Martha – she *understands*. Her father made a sexual advance to her when she was a child. She accepted the advance and then her mother became a rival. She wanted her mother out of the way. And now that she's dead she feels it's all her fault. Her long-suppressed wish has been fulfilled. Now she begins to understand the irrational source of the guilt. Understanding is everything.'

'What,' and Martha gave up knitting for a minute, 'can a girl like that *understand*? An ignorant uneducated country girl. Besides, there's another thing. If she only imagines she killed her mother, why can't she imagine that horrible disgusting business with her father?' She looked at her husband with sudden concern. 'Are you all right, Sigmund?'

'What,' Freud said in a little voice, 'do you mean?'

'I mean she may have made it all up, about her father getting into bed with her, and, well, all the rest of it. She may have *wanted* it, silly ignorant girl, and that ought to make her feel guilty enough. But as for *doing* it – Well, look at *our* children. Do they ever think of killing me – and the other thing?'

Freud choked on a mouthful of smoke. He looked at the cigar with grave distaste. He held it in a hand that trembled slightly. 'I must,' he said, 'get them, I mean, observe, analyse. I've neglected them, I can see that. The cobbler's children are the worst shod.' Then, defiantly: 'It *must* be so. She was so definite about it – like all my patients.'

'Sigmund,' Martha said sternly, 'you will leave our children alone, do you hear? I will not have our children meddled with. Never let me have to tell you that again. Our children must preserve their innocence.'

'Oh Martha,' Freud moaned, 'how little you know. But – it *must* have happened. Childhood education. I wrote a whole book about it.'

'A book,' Martha said with grim lips, 'which has done us no good. I've no friends now. Not one.'

Freud frowned at the prospect of coming torment. A whole book, all wrong. The assertions, all wrong. It was not possible. He saw the real truth approaching from afar in mockery. The retraction, the bowed head. He looked up and saw a man in blue uniform coming down the grassy slope. 'A policeman,' he said faintly. 'What does he want?' And what could he plead but guilty?

'You know what he wants,' Martha said. 'That girl's been talking.' She looked at her husband with no love.

The policeman was upon them. Freud rose from the grass. He very nearly put out his hands for the cuffs. The policeman saluted. He had a paper in his hands, but it seemed too small for a summons. 'Dr Freud? We had this telegram at the station. Urgent, they said.'

'Thank you, yes yes.' He searched his pockets clumsily for small change. Martha, grimly efficient, handed over a couple of coins from her bag. The policeman saluted again and went off. Freud unfolded the folded message. 'Oh my God. Father.'

'I felt it right from the start. I knew it in my bones. I *knew* we shouldn't have a proper holiday.'

Packed, paid, they waited in great heat at the station. The circumambient Alps had become somehow uselessly gorgeous.

'Two hours. The stationmaster laughed. I saw him.'

'I can't help it. Oh, why doesn't it come?'

'At least there's nothing to make you rush away just as it comes in. You have cigars?'

'Yes yes yes.'

'You'll make yourself ill, Sigmund. I counted twelve this morning. Like a big baby, sucking away.'

He ignored the Freudianism of the image.

'Father. Dad. Daddy.' They were all aboard except him. The train was already moving off. He ran to mount. He fell into the compartment panting. 'Ridiculous,' Martha said.

'She had to see me, she said. Privately. She gave me this.' Wrapped in newspaper, a huge homebaked cake.

'Ridiculous.' And she glowered at Gretel smiling and waving from behind the ticket collector. The girl rode off with the entire Alpine resort into the past. Martha irritably took out her knitting. 'The thirteenth,' she said as Freud lighted up.

Later he said: 'I don't think I have anything to feel guilty about. And yet it nags all the time and will go on nagging. Was I kind enough, generous enough? I despised him for one thing. I still despise him. I was right. I still am.'

'You mean about the hat?'

'To do that. A swine of a Christian knocks his hat into the middle of the road – '

'I know, dear. You've told me many times.'

'He just smiles and smiles and smiles. And then he meekly picks up his hat from among the horse turds – '

'Sigmund – the children – '

' – And puts it on again. He failed me there. He failed us all. He begot a big family and couldn't support it. Poor mother. A heroine, a saint – '

'What you mean is a mother. A Jewish one. She doesn't like me. I shan't go to the funeral.'

'It's just that old saying of hers. It means nothing.'

'It meant a lot. "When a boy marries he divorces his – " '

'Yes yes yes.'

'The look in her eye.'

'Yes yes. Poor poor mother.'

The very hallway of the house was crammed with family. Aunts, uncles, sisters. His mother, upright and vigorous though old, embraced him fiercely. Alexander, his younger brother, shook his hand sadly while the embrace prolonged itself.

'You'll be hungry, Siggy. I have a big dinner ready.'

'I've already eaten, mother.'

'Eaten? But you knew you were coming to your mother's house!'

'Martha made me eat something. I didn't want to, but – well, she'd already cooked dinner – '

'Women from Hamburg – what do they know about cooking?'

That was rhetorical. Freud asked if it was sudden.

'How could it be sudden when we were all expecting it? Come and see him, then we eat.'

He saw him alone, stretched out on a table, lighted with votive candles. 'If there's anything I did that offended you, father,' he said aloud but not loudly, 'I'm sorry. I've done things that you weren't able to do – become a doctor – published a book. I'm sorry.' The analyst pricked the mourner. Why must he be sorry for things that gave his father pride? 'You go nowhere now – into the earth. I take on your burdens – the son becomes the father. If I could pray, I would. But there's nobody to pray to.'

'Dinner's ready,' his mother's voice called. 'Come on, Siggy, it will get cold.' Cold, yes. he thought. He improvised a gesture of farewell.

Round the table were the busy mother, the sisters and brothers – Pauline, Anna, Rose, Mitzi, Dolfi, Alexander, silent relatives. Roast chickens, vegetables, wine. Freud could eat little. The others had keen appetites. 'Like a bird,' his mother said. 'I've seen you get thinner and thinner. You can't afford to lose weight, Siggy. You'll have nothing to lose when you're ill. Eat, child, eat.'

'They made you a professor yet?' Alexander asked.

'It will be a long time, Alex. I'm the bad boy of the Vienna Medical School.'

'Bad boy,' cried his mother. 'I'd give them bad boy. But what can you expect from a lot of *schmutzige goyim*?'

'I'm the *schmutzige* one, mamma. Dirty Freud they call me.'

'Why?' she asked with bird-eyed suspicion. 'What have you been doing, Siggy?'

'Treating neuroses, mamma. Opening up the depths of the human mind. There are a lot of strange things down there. My colleagues say I ought to leave well alone.'

'The Jewish ones too?'

'I'm the odd man out, mamma. Not a friend in the world.'

'Not a friend? You got your family. You got me. Your father had a look at your book, Siggy. You know that?'

'He wouldn't have understood, mamma. It's a book for medical men.'

'Right. A lot of big words, he said. He was proud of you knowing so many big words. More words than you and me know, Amalie, he says. But he understood a lot. Rich patients he must have, he said to me.'

'Rich?' He said it sadly.

'Rich and idle, right. Who could afford to have troubles like that if they were poor? Time on their hands, inventing diseases. And dreaming about their fathers and mothers. A lot of nonsense. Girls in love with their father. Who ever heard of that?'

Rosa started to cry.

'There there, Röschen. I know you loved your father. But this is different love, what Siggy here calls a disease of the brain.'

'*Not* dreams, mamma,' Freud said. 'That's the whole point. Neuroses don't come from dreams. Dreams are nothing. Neuroses come from things that actually happen.' He said it stoutly but felt hollow within.

'Dreams? What else could they be but dreams? A lot of dreaming up things for idle minds. As though a girl would get into bed with her father.'

Rosa wiped her nose and sniffed.

'Well, if you cure them of dreaming that sort of nonsense you're doing good work, Siggy. *Schmutzig*, indeed. It's these idle rich that are *schmutzig*.'

She ate. They all ate. Freud picked.

'A boy in bed with his mother, that's different. A boy needs his mother. Needs her warmth and love and protection. Don't let me hear anyone call that *schmutzig*. Eat, Siggy. Let me cut you a nice piece of the breast.'

Such innocence. Or was the innocence his?

Older, thinner, greyer. He saw himself in the consulting-room mirror and caught a first sketch of his dead father. The rain beat on winter Vienna. A shrewd wind searched for cracks and found them. Martha came in with coffee. He gave her a wan smile. He took the cup and sat on his couch. Martha sat at his desk, looking at him with a doctor's scrutiny.

'It's absurd,' she said, 'me asking you to go and see a – I mean you ought to be able to – '

'It's guilt,' he said. 'It's an unreal sort of guilt. It started off as the guilt that any son feels on the death of his father. But now it's become pathological. It grows. Six months since he died and it still grows.'

'You ought to take a holiday. A change of scene.'

'We can't take a holiday till summer. And even that depends on whether we'll have saved enough by then.'

'I don't understand this. You have a lot of patients now.'

'Some of them don't pay. It's an aspect of a process I should have expected. They think they've cured themselves – which in a way they have. Or they think they were never really ill.'

'Minna,' Martha said, 'wants to go to Italy. She's saved enough. She doesn't think it's right for a maiden lady to travel alone.'

'She wants me to go with her? At her expense? That breaks too many taboos. To be the paid companion of my own sister-in-law. Besides, we take our holidays as a family – you, me and the children, Martha.'

'*Me* and the children, Sigmund. A holiday with you is like not having a holiday at all. It's true, dear, you know it's true.'

'I regret it's true. I'll change, I promise. I'll forget about – I nearly said – you know what I nearly said.'

'About sex, dear, yes. Sex is just part of your work now. I know. I don't mind.'

'Married friends, with six visible proofs of burning passion. Sex sublimated into six.'

'I don't know that word.'

'It's a new one.' He looked at his watch. 'I have a difficult patient coming. Frau Kleist.' He stood and drew Martha to him. She pushed away and gave him a friendly peck. She picked up the coffee tray and said:

'Don't be late for supper.'

'It is not true,' he said firmly and tenderly, 'about Hamburg women. They *can* cook.'

'Ah,' she said, nodding, going out. 'I see.'

And then there was Frau Kleist, a luscious blonde lady of some forty years or so, lying relaxed on the couch and pouring forth about her father. 'He made love to me,' she said, 'every day. Sometimes it was difficult. My brothers used to come in and watch. And my mother too, once or twice. But he always called her foul names and sent her away. Then we used to go to a hotel. I was supposed to be at my music lessons. He was supposed to be visiting clients. But we were in a hotel bedroom. Together.'

'Did,' he said with deep disquiet, 'all this really happen, Frau Kleist?'

'Of course. Many many times.'

'Or did you just want it to happen?'

'I wanted it to happen. And so it happened.'

He could not hold back a profound groan. She noticed. She said: 'What is it, doctor? Have I done – Have I said – '

'Nothing wrong, Frau Kleist. Continue, please. About your father.'

'He had the strangest fancies. He insisted on doing the most amazing things. What others would call dirty. May I say? You promise to tell no one?'

'Everything,' he said heavily. 'Tell me everything, Frau Kleist.' And he listened in gloom as she told him everything.

Trotsky. Handsome, in his late thirties, over-energetic. He greets his comrades: 'Vol. Bok. Chud.'

'Two days in the country,' Chudnorsky says, 'and he's an American already.'

Trotsky, attracted, goes at once to Olga, hand held out. 'Lev Davidovich Bronstein. But call me Trotsky.'

'Leon Trotsky?' She is fluttered. 'The great Trotsky?'

'And your new colleague, comrade. Great? There are no great men in the revolutionary movement. Greatness is a bourgeois concept.' But then he has a vague cloudy image of a statue of somebody and adds: 'Oh, I don't know though – '

'You're not tired, after your rounds of Newyorkskiy gaiety?' asks Bokharin.

'You mean the New York Public Library? Fascinating. I learned some unbelievable facts about American exports. I was drunk with statistics.'

'Vodka?' says Bokharin, and he produces a bottle from a desk drawer.

'Russian vodka?'

'Stroganoff's vodka. All the way from Brooklyn. The real McCoy.'

Chudnorsky finds cloudy glasses. They drink, with hearty *zdorovyes*. They do not offer Olga any. 'You settled in all right?' asks Chudnorsky. 'Natalia's all right? Your two sons are all right?'

'Okay, I guess,' Trotsky says. 'My sons taught me that already. Quick to learn, kids. Russian, German, Polish, French, Spanish. Yidglish. But quick to be seduced too. My wife too. Seduced already.'

'Already?'

'Already. Has visions of a New York ballet, crazy notion. Gone off today in the automobile of a certain Dr Goldstein. To see his estate in New Jersey. The man calls himself a socialist. And he has a chauffeur. It won't do, comrades.'

'What won't do?'

'Decadent American capitalism. Bloomingdale's. Avenue Number Five. Hamburgers. With onions and relish yet. Macey's. The IRT. It worries me. We got this worker's apartment on Street Number One Hundred Sixty-Five. West. Eighteen dollars a month. And things provided. Incredible. Luxury. That's not right for a worker.'

'You want,' says Volodarsky, 'they should have none of these things?'

'Deprivation means oppression, comrades. Oppression means revolution. How can the worker revolt when he's got electric light and a gas cooker and garbage disposal and a telephone? A telephone yet. We got those, and now the kids are revolting.'

'Against what revolting?'

'Against me revolting. The kids say no need for a revolution in Russia. Just send the Russians to New York. The American worker – ach.' He sings:

Amenities, amenities,
He's got too many amenities.
Obscene. It is

Unclean. It is
Not right.
Facilities, facilities,
It's loaded down with facilities,
His billet. His
Docility's
A fright-
ful nightmare.
Phonographs and photographs
In fine gilt frames.
If you protest he only laughs
And calls you names.
How *can* the revolution come
When he is stuffed up with chewing gum?
His belly aches
But it's with steaks
And candy bars.
Amenities, facilities,
Are killing all his abilities
To reach up to the stars.
We have a telephone.

BOKHARIN: That's bad?

TROTSKY: I never saw one in Petrograd,
And what a revolutionary device
For sending vital messages,
While here this modern marvel is
For finding out the latest Wall Street price,
For ordering a double chocolate ice.
My children treat it as a pet
And play the numbers like roulette.
Last night –

CHUDNORSKY: Yes?

TROTSKY: You should hear the calls they made.
A Mrs Elmore Schlitz who's deaf,
The Rockefellers' under-chef,
The chief of the Long Island fire brigade,
A girl who panders to men's lust,
The chairman of the Morgan Trust,
The Council for Industrial Expansion,
And then they had a cosy chat

With some big bug who's living at
A feudal palace known as Gracey Mansion.

Ah, luxuries, oh, luxuries,
New York's awallow in luxuries,
Its cocksure busy buck sure is
The king.
Commodities, commodities,
Baked beans and similar oddities
They worship like a god. It is
A thing
To bring one
To a state of palpitat-
ing wrath and rage,
Just seeing how they venerate
A living wage.
Each worker I've been looking at
Is just an overfed pussycat,
His only dream
Is double cream
And motor cars.
In every single facet he
Is thwarting his capacity

(he orates)

to end the domination of the capitalistic monopolistic oppressors with their governmental lackeys and by erecting the classless society on a broad basis of economic equality to

(he sings)

Grab the new moon as a sickle
And hammer out a new cosmos
Whose sparks shall be the stars.

Trotsky's three male colleagues, though not Olga, are inclined to applause, but there is the noise of disturbance outside in the street and Trotsky rushes to the window with great eagerness. The others shrug and get on with work – examining mail, correcting proofs.

'It's beginning,' Trotsky cries. 'Here in the richest city of the world. The revolution. Who would have thought it?' He opens the window and lets in a blast of east wind. 'Women – well-dressed women too – smashing shop windows.'

'Ach,' Bokharin says, 'it's nothing. Military supplies being rushed to the ports. Blocking the railways. America's getting ready for war. The American answer to German unrestricted submarine activity. The goods aren't getting in. The prices are going up. The people protest at the rise in prices. Simple as that, comrade.'

Trotsky shuts the window and comes away somewhat dejected. Olga has been plucking up courage to say something. She says it now.

'Comrade Trotsky – '

'Yes?' He goes over to her as to a little girl and takes her hand in his. She snatches her hand away.

'You spoke of revolution.'

'Yes, little comrade.'

'Is it to be the policy of this newspaper to preach revolution?'

'But of course, little comrade.'

'It wasn't like that before. We preached socialism without violence. The slow and gradual and gentle and imperceptible taking over of the State by the worker.'

'You did, did you?' And he looks frowning at Bokharin, who merely shrugs.

'I,' Olga says, 'am a socialist who doesn't believe in violence.'

'Then,' says Trotsky, 'you're not a true socialist. Have you read your Karl Marx?'

'Yes. Karl Marx knew my father. In London. My father was in London before he was in New York. He was a great man for the ladies, Karl Marx, so said my father. Always sniffing at skirts, like a dog. Those are my father's words.'

'That, comrade, is just the kind of irrelevance that would appeal to a frivolous mind.'

'Irrelevance? My father said that if Karl Marx had spent more time on his prose style and less time on women his book on capital would have been easier to read.'

'Hm,' goes Trotsky, as if conceding a point. 'Comrade, dear sweet pretty little comrade, you have been infected by British so-called socialism, I can see that. Bernard Shaw, H. G. Wells, Sidney Webb, Beatrice Webb. Fabianism, they call it. Going nice and slow, like a tortoise. Well, comrade, we want no tortoises in the movement. We want speed, action, violence, the teeth of the tiger, the trumpeting of the elephant, the rage of the lion.' He is instinctively moving into oratory; his male comrades instinctively prepare to applaud. He quells them with a look.

'I see,' Olga says. '*Your* way. You're in charge.'

'No one's in charge, comrade. History is in charge, the ineluctable movement of social forces outside any man's control.'

'So there's nothing for us to do except wait?'

'No. We must help history along. History walks slowly. We must give history a ride in a fast automobile.'

'And you're the driver?'

Sasha comes in, admitting a uniformed chauffeur, tall, elegant, self-assured. The chauffeur says:

'A message for Mr Trotsky. From Mrs Trotsky.'

Trotsky goes up to him with some truculence. Uniforms, he does not like uniforms. 'What are you, comrade? A general in the United States imperialist army?'

'I'm a chauffeur, sir. In the employment of Dr Goldstein.'

'You see, comrades,' Trotsky tells his colleagues in bitter triumph. 'That's the big American *socialist* I told you about. What's your message, comrade?'

'Excuse me, sir,' the chauffeur says, 'I am not addressed as comrade.'

'So. You're not a capitalist. And you're not a worker. What are you?'

'Something better than either. I'm a man who understands the internal combustion engine.'

'Something worse than either. You're a slave.'

'Of the internal combustion engine.'

'Just,' Olga says, 'as we're the slaves of history. The big thing is to be able to drive, isn't it, Comrade Trotsky?'

Trotsky doesn't like this. To the chauffeur he says: 'You believe all men are equal?'

'No. Some men know more about the internal combustion engine than others. When you get equality nobody knows anything about the internal combustion engine. If I were not a gentleman I would spit on your equality. The message, sir. Mrs Trotsky and the two young Master Trotskys will be staying some little time on Dr Goldstein's country estate. Mrs Trotsky is proposing to prepare the choreography for a ballet. She says she wants a rest from revolutions.'

'No need,' says Trotsky, 'to ask you what *you* think about revolutions.'

'No, sir. The internal combustion engine gives me all the revolutions I require. And those revolutions are genuinely progressive. They get people from one place to another. Good morning.' And he goes, leaving Trotsky a little angry and a little puzzled. But he turns with a show of sweetness back to Olga.

'Pretty sweet little comrade, you will learn while I am here in exile,' he says. 'You will take down from my mouth my utterances. I have a speech to give tonight to the Workers' Rally. To work. Then you can translate it and sell it to the *Jewish Record*. A hundred thousand circulation a day. Ha. Fabianism. Ha.' They go into a quintet.

TROTSKY: You can't make an omelette
Unless you break some eggs.
OLGA: I don't want an omelette.
TROTSKY (*fiercely*): You have to have an omelette.
BOK (*gently*): Comrade Trotsky begs
You *please* to have an omelette.
OLGA: You don't mean eggs.
You mean heads and arms and legs.
THE MEN: Good.
OLGA: Gently does it.
TROTSKY: Gently doesn't do it,
Gently never could.
CHUD: Who is this Comrade Gently?
TROTSKY: You don't expect those swine to be persuaded by a song
Like a lady on a balcony at night.
We have to fight.
Am I right, comrades?
BOK: Right.
VOL: Right.
CHUD: Right.
OLGA: *Wrong*.
TROTSKY: You can't play Prince Hamlet
Unless you kill the king.
OLGA: But I'm not Prince Hamlet.
TROTSKY (*fiercely*): You have to be Prince Hamlet.
VOL (*gently*): Such a little thing:
So *please* be Princess Hamlet.

OLGA: You don't mean act.
You mean beastly bloody fact.
THE MEN: Good.
OLGA: Gently does it.
TROTSKY: Gently doesn't do it,
Gently never would.
VOL: Let's liquidate this Gently.
TROTSKY: You can't expect the ruling class to pack their bags and go
Having smilingly consented to confess
Their wickedness.
Am I right, comrades?
BOK: Yes.
VOL: Yes.
CHUD: Yes.
OLGA: *No.*
TROTSKY (*sighing*): It's like this, you see,
Pretty little comrade –
OLGA: Please don't you call me
Pretty little comrade.

Trotsky sighs again and points to Volodarsky.

VOL: The State is an engine of capitalist cunning
For pushing down the workers, is it not?
BOK: Full Marx.
CHUD: The workers need to use it till the bright new order's running
Smoothly – then the State will rust and rot.
TROTSKY: How are we going to grab this most essential apparatus,
This stainless steel executive machine?
By pelting the exploiters with rotten ripe tomatoes?
By telling them what naughty boys they've been?
OLGA: No.
TROTSKY: Well, how?
OLGA: Change from inside.
TROTSKY: That's been tried –
It's an old hat now.
OLGA: Spreading the word.
TROTSKY: Absurd.
ALL THE MEN (*on a long-held chord*): Absurd.

TROTSKY: Caviar with blinis
Means slaughtering a fish.
OLGA: I'd rather feed on wienies.
TROTSKY (*fiercely*): *Chilled* caviar. *Hot* blinis.
BOK (*persuasively*): It's Comrade Trotsky's wish
You taste it.
VOL: Without blinis.
OLGA: You don't mean fish
But a bloodier sort of dish.
VOL: So?
OLGA: Gently does it.
TROTSKY: Gently doesn't do it,
Gently doesn't know.
CHUD: I thought we'd buried Gently long ago.
TROTSKY: Hamlet couldn't move, but we have legs.
We're going to make an omelette by breaking more eggs
Than you'll find in a ton of caviar,
So we are.
We'll reach as far as man can get.
Will we fight, comrades?
Am I right, comrades?
VOL: *Da.*
BOK: *Da.*
CHUD: *Da.*
OLGA: *NYET!*

Trotsky sighs yet again and says to Olga: 'Sweet pretty little comrade – sorry sorry sorry. Listen to me, saying sorry. Why am I saying sorry? Russian women like to be called sweet and little and pretty, and we all know why. Sweet – comrade. Will you learn? Will you try to learn?'

'Will you learn too, comrade?' says Olga, sweetly, prettily.

Trotsky mumbles something and then says: 'Get your pencil and paper, comrade, and take down a speech.'

She equips herself for stenography and waits. Trotsky shambles over to the window and looks down on the avenue.

* * *

Freud looked out of Minna's window on to a view of rainy Vienna. She listened, sharp-eyed, bright. Freud said, misting her window with cigar smoke: 'A point I never realized, never could realize – the unconscious mind doesn't know the difference between lying and telling the truth. All it's concerned with is libido, energy, desire – it distorts facts to make its points. All I've listened to, all I've written – all fantasy, all of it, none of it ever happened.'

'None of it?'

'Who can say now? I must confess there were limits of plausibility. Frau Kleist, for instance – an incredible confession of paternal debauchery. I had my doubts, but I drove the doubts away. I didn't want them. I was too eager to believe I'd made an astonishing discovery.'

'Factuality was never the point – is that what you mean?'

'You've hit it. I affirmed to Krafft-Ebing that child seduction was common – was, indeed, the invariable basis of all sexual neuroses – and now I find it's the wish, the desire, that matters, and the truth means nothing. How could I have been such a fool?'

'It requires wisdom to be a fool.'

'None of your cheap paradoxes, Minna, please. Another thing, a thing I'm beginning to see – oh my God, is there no end to the work to be done – Dreams, dreams. A lot of their memories put day-dream, night-dream, fantasy, fact on the same footing. That girl who told me she had a box – How big was the box, I asked. Oh, sometimes big, sometimes small, she said, and her father put logs of wood in it. She was telling me a dream. Do you see the meaning of the dream?'

'Staid spinster that I am, I see it. What do you do now – burn all your writings? Issue a recantation?'

'I publish the truth when I've had time to digest the truth – '

'And how much time will your colleagues need to digest it? They'll have to grow new stomachs first.'

'Meanwhile, I cure myself – if I can – '

'Of what?'

'Of my own neurosis. A neurosis is for treatment only when it's harmful. This guilt about my father's death is affecting my work, sleep, appetite, wellbeing. I begin to feel the first stirring of an understanding of the guilt, but I have to be sure. And if I'm right – if I'm right, Minna – the world will come to an end and then start all over again – a new world. Men and women will know themselves for what they are, for the first time. It will be a terrible terrible shock to the world. And to me – '

He left her with no valediction. She shook her head in pity.

Cigar smoke was a nimbus about him as he furiously wrote in his study. And then he had the impression of the slow formation of an image in the swirl of smoke about his desk lamp. He looked at it. It solidified into the projection of a buried memory. He recognized the small boy in the striped nightshirt who toddled out of his bedroom and along the corridor to a locked door. Locked? No, not locked – merely closed. He listened as he reached up to the doorknob. The noise of harsh rhythmical panting. He turned the knob and went in. Dawn light was coming from the wide uncurtained window. A man and a woman on the bed. They were doing things to each other he could not explain. The woman was his mother and this man, who was his father but not the father he saw every day, was doing something that made her keep crying out. He looked, wide-eyed. They had to be stopped. He knew what to do. He urinated on the carpet. The couple on the bed, mouths open, looked aghast.

'Siggy!'

'Look,' the man said, 'at the dirty little brat – ' He began to get off the bed. The boy put his hands protectively round the part of his body that was offending and avenging.

'Dirty little – He'll never come to anything. I've a good mind to cut it off – '

'No,' Freud said to the smoke. 'You didn't say that. You couldn't – ' His cigar had gone out. Tremblingly he relighted it. He saw something new in the flame of the match.

A railway line. Night. Workmen were repairing a sleeper, their labour lighted by harsh flares. There was a small boy in the train, looking out at them. He was in a sleeping compartment. The flares illuminated his mother. She had stripped herself quite naked. Naked, she searched in a case for her nightdress. She put it on and turned to the small boy, smiling. He had closed his eyes, feigning sleep. She kissed him. Then she climbed into the overhead bunk.

Freud blew out the match. He sucked a lightly burned thumb. He must get confirmation of that memory. It explained something.

'Fancy you remembering that, Siggy,' his mother smiled, piling vegetables on top of his roast chicken. 'And you such a little boy. Yes, we were going to see your grandmother, and they were doing work on the line. We were two hours late, imagine. Yes, I can see all those fires now. All along the line.'

'Two hours early.'

'Late, Siggy – two hours late.'

'Sorry, mamma – I was thinking of something else.'

'Eat, eat, child. Mustn't say that now, must I? No child, head of the family. Taking your father's place. Your poor poor father.'

Freud looked from her bright unremorseful eyes to the eyes of the others round the family table. No remorse anywhere. They ate heartily. Remorse was reserved to the eldest son. He pecked at his food.

He lay on his couch and talked to himself. 'No one to transfer to. Must I imagine myself listening to a self converted into a father confessor? Another Dr Freud sitting behind my head, listening? Well, digest this, Dr Freud – I'm anxious not to miss the train. And then when it arrives – I'm frightened of getting on it. Now we know why, don't we, Dr Freud? My mother. Desire of my mother. Fear of desire for my mother. Why fear? Because my father will come along and – no, no, that goes too far – '

But his hands had gone instinctively to his crotch. The door opened with no noise, and Martha came in with the coffee tray. She saw. Shamefacedly he removed his hands. Wearily he got up from his couch.

'How,' Martha asked jocularly, 'is the patient today?'

'Cured of one thing, I hope. Next time we travel, Martha, we shall be at the railway station five minutes before the train leaves – no more, no less.'

'Oh, you please yourself now, dear. We shan't be travelling together any more. But Minna will be pleased. You're taking her to Rome, remember – '

'Italy, but not Rome.'

'Why not Rome?'

'Because – oh, it's too hot in summer – there's the danger of malaria, typhoid, Roman fever – '

'Only in Rome. I see. Not in Naples. And yet they say "See Naples and die." I'll be back for your coffee cup. I've a pie in the oven.'

'No, you haven't. You can't, we've not – Sorry. Symbolism, I'm bursting with symbolism.'

'So long as it's not catching.' She smiled with affection, leaving. He sat at his desk, sipping the hot Vienna brew. He caught another – was it a memory? A memory of someone else's memory? Of someone else's memory of someone else's story? A dream? The feeling was dreamlike. A small boy in a huge hall full of mirrors. Desperate to micturate, the boy examined all the doors. One of them was inlaid with mother-of-pearl. He rushed to it, bursting. He opened it. He was micturating there with relief when the Emperor Franz Josef entered with a chamberlain. They caught him at it. The Emperor cried:

'Off with his head!'

The order echoed and echoed and re-echoed.

Freud frowned over that, coffee drunk, smoking. When did he dream that? For it was certainly his own dream, it had the feel of something inside his own head. A room. *Ein Zimmer*. But there was also *Frauenzimmer*. A woman a room, a room a woman. He started writing furious notes. Mother-of-pearl. The room was his mother. He was not urinating, he was – disguising the sexual act, the act of emission – into his mother, oh my God. Off with his head. Not his head, his penis. Not the Emperor – a figure in authority, a father, his father –

'Take this in if you can, Dr Freud,' he told himself. 'The child desires his mother – every son desires his mother. The father is the rival. But he's strong, powerful, a man in authority. He seeks to avenge the impious act of transgression. There's only one revenge – castration. It's true, true for everyone – there are no exceptions – '

He was back in the theatre. 'Here he is,' Oedipus cried,

> 'Sons and daughters of Thebes, your shame,
> The author of your pestilence – Oedipus,
> Killer of his father, defiler of
> His mother. Now let me be
> Hidden from all eyes.'

He watched the memory intently. Oedipus put out his eyes. The chorus screamed.

> 'Dark dark. The sun has burst there
> For the last time.'

Horror, horror of horrors. Freud paced, puffing hard. 'No wonder. I wanted him dead without knowing it. I must – Who can I tell? Who?'

Some time later he was in a different theatre, one for medical instruction, empty save for five listeners. He said:

'Our course has been a – traditional course in neurology. What I am about to say on this last occasion of our meeting may seem irrelevant to your studies. I merely place before you the findings of prolonged research on the neuroses – not dogmatically – merely as hypotheses for your consideration.'

He looked at them. They wanted to go. They didn't want hypotheses.

'The sexual instinct is, I repeat, present almost from birth. It is fixed on the parent of the sex opposed to that of the child. The girl child is sexually attached to the father, the boy child to the mother. To the boy the father is an avenging rival. To the girl, the mother. The emotions are repressed but find their outlet in neuroses. The neuroses are characterized by a sense of guilt – guilt at a fancied desire to kill the parent who is a sexual rival – '

One student looked at his neighbour and nodded. Both began quietly to leave.

'We may use the term Oedipus complex, after the Greek myth of the man who kills his own father and marries his mother. It is present in all of us, this condition. There is no exception. It is one of the mainsprings of the human psyche. We are all, every one of us, male or female, a reincarnation of the guilty Oedipus. Our task as analysts of the sick soul – as, may I say, psychoanalysts – is to extirpate the guilt, to allay the plague that has stricken the suffering kingdom of the soul. We at last stand face to face with the excitatory cause of the neuroses.'

The three remaining students looked at him and then at each other. They said nothing.

Wearily he finished. Lamely. 'At least think about it.' And then, 'Thank you for your attention. You may go.'

A middle-aged Viennese, paunched with prosperity, lay on the couch. He listened incredulously to Freud. Freud said:

'At last I think I've uncovered the seat of your neurosis. Hatred of your father, a sexual fixation on your mother – it's what I call an Oedipal situation. Have you heard of Oedipus?' The man said nothing. 'Don't be shocked. It's universal. It's in all of us. It's in myself.'

'This I cannot. This is. I never.'

Freud soothed. 'I know. The shock of discovery can be very painful.'

'Painful!' The patient got up heavily from the couch, sending a white pillow to the carpet. 'The filth of it. I admired my father, I never dreamed of – '

'You did dream. You told me your dreams.'

'Dreams! Are you sure you're not – What I mean is, in need of a rest, doctor? I was gaining benefit, I know I was – but this – If you'll prepare your bill – This is, of course, the end of – '

'Not the end, Herr Hofbrau. You'll be back. Who else can you turn to?' The patient looked at his doctor with distaste. He got out quickly. Freud sighed.

He was asleep in bed with Martha. He suddenly awoke, looked at his bedside clock, tore out of bed. He pulled off his nightshirt and dragged open a drawer, searching for –

'Sigmund, Sigmund,' Martha cried. 'It's late!'

He was asleep in bed with Martha. Martha shook him awake. 'Sigmund, Sigmund, you've overslept, it's late – '

'But I'm already up,' he said sleepily. 'Can't you see? I'm dressing.' But he wasn't. He was in his nightshirt, in bed. He came fully awake. 'Dreams,' he said, 'remarkable. You know why they're there? To protect the sleeper – to persuade him to go on sleeping.'

'Oh, you and your dreams,' getting up, dressing.

At breakfast he said to Anna: 'Any interesting dreams last night, *Liebchen*?'

'I'm sick of you and your dreams,' Martha said, pouring coffee. 'If it's not one thing it's another. First it's Oedipus. Now it's dreams.'

'Dreams are important. Dreams are wishful thinking. To convince the sleeper that everything's all right. To make him go on – '

'Sleeping. I know, you've already said that. Go now, your first patient's waiting.'

He gulped his coffee. But he still delayed. 'You know that slight inflammation I have down here, Martha?'

'On your – what you call your perineum. Better, is it?'

'Oh, it's all right. Kept me awake a little, though. So when I dropped off again I dreamed I was riding a horse. That made everything all right. That explained the slight irritation. Dreams – remarkable.'

'Go on, go.'

So he went to listen to a young woman who affirmed that everybody hated her, everybody.

'Everybody?'

'All my sisters and aunts and brothers and cousins. The whole family.' She started to whimper.

'Shall we go back to your dream?'

'It's only a dream.'

'That's right, only a dream. Let me hear it.'

'But I was only four.'

'Come on.'

'Well, there was this dog walking on the roof, and then something fell off the roof, a slate I think it was. And then they carried my mother out of the house. Dead. Wait, there's something more. There was a boy who said *bitch bitch* at me in the street. And when I was three, it must have been three, a tile fell off the roof onto my mother, and it made her head bleed.'

'Now let me try to explain it to you. The dog is a bitch. It's also you. You make something fall from the roof. It kills your mother. The dream expresses a wish. You wanted your mother to be dead.'

'No no no no no – '

'Oh, not consciously. Besides, you were a very young child. All young girls love their fathers, and they want their mothers out of the way. All girls – it's universal. Listen to me,' for she was whimpering again. 'Nobody thinks you're bad, nobody hates you. Everybody goes through this state when they're children. We call it the – never mind. You're lucky. You've come to realize it. Most people haven't.'

'You mean that's the reason?'

'Guilt. Something deep down making you feel guilty. And you punish yourself for the guilt by thinking that everybody hates you. Go home now. Think about it. Come and see me at this time next week.'

While she was getting doubtfully up from the couch the door was unceremoniously opened and a sour burly man with a folded note came in.

'Please,' Freud frowned, 'wait in the waiting room.'

'But the Professor said it was urgent. It's all in this note.'

The girl left, not whimpering. Freud looked at the note. 'Professor Nothnagel? Impossible. Professor Nothnagel sent you to *me*?'

'Degeneration of the spinal cord. That's what it says. He said you could cure it. Doesn't it say that there?'

'It says you have the symptoms. You'd better lie down on that couch.'

'Why?'

'I want you to relax. I want you to tell me a few things.'

'Aren't you going to examine me?'

'Yes, but not your spinal cord.'

'Oh, all right then.' And he lay down with an ill grace.

That afternoon Freud dressed formally, complete with tall hat, and knocked on the door of Professor Nothnagel. He found Professor Nothnagel, a craggy elderly much bewhiskered man, writing with a show of great concentration. Freud said without preamble:

'You sent me a patient.'

'Ah yes. Dr Freud, isn't it? Yes. How's he getting on? Symptoms of degeneration of the spinal cord. It has to be a neurosis. You're the man for neuroses.'

'But,' and Freud took a deep breath, 'you were one of the first to deride my theory of the aetiology of the neuroses. You scorned my view of their sexual origin.'

'Did, did I? Never mind that for now. How's the man getting on?'

'A failure. I can't begin to approach him. He won't talk. He won't free associate. When I mention sex he threatens to hit me. I'm discontinuing treatment. I take it that your only aim was to demonstrate the futility of my methods.'

'No. Persevere. Good day to you.'

And he went back to his show of writing concentration. Freud jammed his tall hat on his head and, baffled, left.

'What, for instance, did you dream last night?'

The patient lay dogged on the couch. 'I don't dream. Never have. Dreams are a lot of nonsense.'

Freud sighed and got up. He confronted the sullenness, sullen beefy hands folded on belly. 'Herr Feldschuh,' he said, 'I'm sorry. I've done my best, but it's apparently not good enough. Only one kind of doctor can function without the cooperation of the patient, and that's a veterinary surgeon. Get up, go. I don't want to see you again.'

The effect was dramatic. The man grew pale. 'No, no,' he said in fear, 'please don't say that. I've been too ashamed to talk. I did terrible things when I was young – sexual things. I'm ready to tell. I want to be cured. Please.'

Freud nodded grimly. 'You're ready to start?'

'Yes doctor please doctor.'

Freud sat alone at a coffee-house table. He was usually alone. He read the evening paper, sipped at coffee and a glass of water. Professor Nothnagel came up and sat down without invitation. He said:

'He came in to see me.'

'Who? Ah. Well?'

'I knew it was a neurosis. Keep on with your treatment. Nonsense, of course. If you think you have a convert in me, you're gravely mistaken. I think your so-called psychoanalysis is a lot of trickery. I think this business of the sexual aetiology of the neuroses is a sham and a dirty sham. I think you're a freud, Doctor Fraud. Sorry.'

'And yet I cured a patient nobody else could cure.'

'Oh, I've seen warts cured by rubbing a raw potato over them. I've seen a lot of trickery in my time. Because you effect a cure it doesn't mean it's medical science. Still, carry on.' And he got up. 'Give me thirty years,' he said, 'thirty years that I haven't got. Give the world at large a hundred. Then your trickery may turn into medical science. Meanwhile, good luck with your dream book.'

'How did you know about my dream book?'

'Word gets around. It won't do you any good. *Grüss Gott.*'

There they were – copies of *Die Traumdeutung* by Sigmund Freud on a table. Freud said to the bookshop proprietor: 'How is it going?'

'I'm surprised, really.' He was a weasel. He brought to Freud a faint odour of lunchtime sour cabbage. 'There's a good market for this sort of thing usually, especially before Christmas. *Napoleon's Book of Fate*, *Cleopatra's Dream Manual*. Your book seems, if I may say so, to be rather heavy going.'

Freud nodded sickly.

'A pity. My first failure in this line. I've always done a steady trade in dream books.'

'You've read it, of course?'

'Oh, I don't read books. I only sell them.'

'That's not quite the way I would put it. *Grüss Gott.*' And he went out into the cold street.

On the cold street Trotsky sees something which gives him an idea. He starts to dictate: 'This morning as I looked out of my window in Manhattan I saw an old man, ragged and diseased, searching for something in a garbage can. The weather was freezing, the wind

Siberian, his broken boots showed naked frozen toes. At last he found what he was looking for – a stale and rancid bit of bread.'

'A thing,' says Olga, looking up from her dictation book, 'can't be rancid and stale at the same time.'

'You are telling *me*?'

'And I'd like to – Pardon me.' She gets up and looks out of the window. Trotsky's right hand can hardly be prevented from going round her delectable waist, but he sternly resists temptation. 'Yes, he's there all right.' And she goes back to her chair, where she sits, pencil poised.

'You think I would lie?'

'Continue, comrade.'

'In the midst,' Trotsky grunts, 'of wealth, the most abject poverty. Here we have a country prepared to waste millions of dollars on a useless war and totally unwilling to rescue its destitute from from from – '

Sasha opens the door and says: 'Some socialist gentlemen to see Mr Trotsky.'

'There is no such animal as a *socialist gentleman* – ' And they come in, well-dressed, prosperous, accompanied by an Episcopalian bishop. Their spokesman is Mr Krumpacker. Mr Krumpacker says:

'Mr Trotsky, we ask you to say nothing about your joy and satisfaction in being here after your tribulations, deprivations, incarcerations in the land of your birth. The joy and satisfaction we may take as already expressed. But the true joy and satisfaction are ours. Welcome to the greatest city in the world. May I first introduce His Grace Bishop Smith – '

'A *bishop* yet?'

'A *socialist* bishop, Mr Trotsky.' With extreme unction.

Trotsky is incensed. 'A sanctimonious magnate with a knout under his surplice – '

'Please,' sternly, 'do not confuse the American episcopate with your own bloodsoaked ecclesiastical princes, fat on the blood of the mujiks, dripping with gold and silver, fawning on your godless Tsar and Tsarina, a shame and a disgrace to what was once Holy Russia.'

'What,' more incensed, 'do you know of Russia, holy or unholy, you purveyor of superstitious claptrap?'

The bishop gives out a note on a pitchpipe. The socialist gentlemen sing:

God save the workers,
Bless the workers' cause,
God keep the workers
From the bosses' claws.

'God. God. They sing of God. Oh, God help me.'

Christ was a worker
And was crucified
With two more workers,
One on either side.

'Who asked you to come here, blasphemous capitalistic hypocrites? Shut that caterwauling row, do you hear me? Out out out – '

Fight them and smite them,
Devils out of hell,
Bankers and brokers,
All with goods to sell.

God, be our comrade,
And thy heavenly son,
And the Holy Spirit,
Comrades three in one.

During the above Trotsky raves. 'Corrupted by the fleshpots of America, riding round in your limousines, flashing the gold in your teeth, have you forgotten what God is? God is a creation of the exploitative classes, the feudal lords and their successors the capitalists. Religion is no more than a tranquillizer doled out by the bloodsucking parasitic capitalists to keep the suffering workers quiet. The free society of free workers doesn't need this bogeyman God, it scorns God, spits on his image. Down with God, away with God, kill God stone dead.'

And at that point the socialist gentlemen sing Amen. But also a voice is raised among them, near the back, and it says:

'You didn't say that in Yanovka.'

Trotsky is near petrified. He knows this voice. 'Who's that? Who's speaking? Who here knows anything about Yanovka?'

'I.' A rabbi, greybearded, shrunken. 'Rabbi Yehonda. You remember the *schul* in the wooden hut near Yanovka? It remembers you.'

'What are you doing here? Who told you to come? Did I reach the New World only to have the Old World thrown in my face? It's all over, Yanovka. Yanovka doesn't exist any more. Go away, Rabbi Yehonda. You're not here. You're a ghost conjured by my confusion – '

'Confusion? I'm glad to hear of your confusion. A human condition, not a political one. Yanovka existed. Your father's little estate. The old way wasn't a bad way, Lev Davidovich. The working week and the peace of the Sabbath. God blessed Yanovka.'

Dark and then a confusion of lights. Green and the endless steppes. A fir tree in the wind. It is the inner voice of Lev Davidovich that sings:

> Yanovka, Yanovka,
> Where we fed the stove with straw,
> And the samovar sang all day,
> And as far as the eye saw
> The steppes lay.
> Yanovka, Yanovka,
> With the brown eggs fresh and warm,
> And the rollicking in the hay,
> And the smell of the spring storm,
> The spring day.
> My brothers and I
> Played at old maid in the winter,
> Saw the light splinter
> The lake in the summer,
> The drama in the fire,
> The drama in the sky,
> Learned to sing, to sigh.
> Yanovka, Yanovka,
> Where the hunter wound his horn
> And the owls would go mousing by,
> And the undulant gold corn
> Was house high.

And now brass and drums and strings agitato.

> No! No!
> It wasn't so idyllic –
> Those orders in Cyrillic
> Script
> Forcing the peasants to fight for the Tsar

Some place far away.
No! No!
We knew of peasants fleeing
And saw them caught and being
Whipped.
'That is the pattern of things as they are,'
I heard father say.
And sometimes we couldn't sell the harvest –
Foreign dumping was the cause.
And the churchbells sang: 'O man, thou starvest
Because of immutable market laws.'
No! No!
There wasn't any learning
To satisfy my burning
Need.
The books that were written by Engels and Marx
Hugged the dark some place.
No! No!
There wasn't any justice,
The law was just a dusty
Screed.
The sea of the steppe was infested with sharks,
God's eyes were sparks in space.
Nightmare! Nightmare!
Dream . . .

And the noise is stilled, the tempo softened.

Yanovka, Yanovka,
Where I loved both sun and shade
And was happy and very young
And I heard the violins played,
The songs sung.
Yanovka, Yanovka,
Where I drank my morning milk
And I played round my mother's chair,
And the night was the dusky silk
Of her hair.
No! No! No more of the past,
I've drunk the last of its wine.
The future is what I call mine.

All too clearly I see
My memory lies because
Yanovka never was,
Never could be.

In a daze he looks about him. He is entirely alone except for Olga, who sits patiently with her pencil and pad.

'Where,' he says, 'is everybody? What's happening round here?'

'You seemed to have something on your mind. So everybody left. Are you ready to resume – dictation?'

He bangs his brow to clear his brain of green, blue, milk, memory, fancy. 'Read me back what I've already said.'

' "In the midst of wealth, the most abject poverty. Here we have a country prepared to spend millions of dollars on a war and totally unwilling – " '

'I didn't say that. I said: "*Waste* millions of dollars on a *useless* war." Your task, comrade, is not to edit but to transcribe.'

'But I can't transcribe what I don't believe.'

'What you believe or disbelieve is not relevant. You are at this moment merely the instrument of my thoughts.'

'High-handed, comrade, wouldn't you say? Employer and operative, master and slave.'

'No,' with force. 'Comrades, comrade. Colleagues, comrade. Operative and cooperative, comrade.'

'Let me cooperate by saying that what you say is stupid. How do you know it's a waste of dollars? How do you know it's useless?'

'Stupid?' aghast. 'You dare to say *stupid*?'

'Dare? Why shouldn't I dare? You've dared to say that a lot of things are stupid. Christianity, idealism, parliamentary democracy. I'm merely saying that Trotsky is stupid.'

He breathes deeply, then he paces. He says: 'Listen, comrade. All war is wasteful, useless, wicked, unless it's the class war. All other war is war between rival capitalistic systems. Such wars use the proletariat for capitalistic ends. The proletariat must refuse to be involved. Is that clear?'

'Go on,' Olga says, 'comrade.'

* * *

Jimmy Skilling, younger son of the widower President of the Commonwealth of the Democratic Americas, was duly married to Flavia Rowley, a social counsellor of the West Point Military Academy, where Jimmy had graduated some years back with high honours, at the White House in Washington on the Feast of Childermass or Holy Innocents. Professor Hubert Frame, by virtue of his dead wife's marital kinship with the First Family, was, as he had foretold, among the wedding guests. Having, on the Feast of St Stephen, coughed up another grey gobbet of lung, he was not disposed to cough much now. Still, in view of the gravity of the discussion he proposed with the President and the need to hold it without hacking interruptions, he had received two special injections – one to inhibit the cough reflex, the other of a nicotine surrogate, so that his tobacco-starved body would not fidget. It was thus as a cigaretteless man that he faced Jack Skilling in the holy of holies of the home of the head of the executive. The President, hands folded, inclined his head in a listening pose, the furled flag of the Commonwealth behind him.

Jack Skilling was the first Canadian to assume the highest honour that America, or the Democratic Americas, could accord one of its citizens. The addition of the Canadian provinces, along with the single province of Mexico, to the existing fifty-three states, had been seen as inevitable as early as 1985, beginning as an act of defensive unification against the increasing threat of Soviet Russia and her Third World satellites, a single military command begetting a centralized executive control in Washington. The British Commonwealth had gone into liquidation, save for sundry pockets faithful to the old sentimental ideal – chiefly Gibraltar, New Zealand's southern island, and the Falklands. Jack Skilling had been born a member of that Commonwealth in Toronto, but had come early to New York City, there to be elected mayor three times running on an independent ticket. His candidacy for the presidency was inevitably supported by the majority of Anglophone Canadians, and many citizens of the old Union had had hopes that the Canadian tradition of comparative incorruptibility in politics might regenerate the White House. This was in spite of Skilling's far from immaculate record in City Hall, but it was recognized that New York could corrupt even the incorruptible. The general faith in Skilling as President had not, in the last four years, in fact been misplaced. The first New York mayor and the first Canadian to achieve the supreme office, he was also destined to be the last. But there was probably no better man around to preside over his country's final dissolution.

'Lynx,' Frame said. At once Skilling took from a side table a copy of that morning's *Pravda*. He showed the headline without saying a word:

АМЕРИК

'So,' Frame said. 'We might have expected that. The American beast in the sky. Single-minded, the Russians, I'll say that for them. How about the Chinese?'

'It ties up,' said Skilling, 'with the Year of the Cat. They just seem to regard it as an occasion for louder fireworks. As for the Soviet Presidium, it's already acting on the er astronomical data and making its salvatory preparations.'

'What kind of preparations? What kind of salvation?'

'A spaceship.'

'Ah.' Frame nodded. 'So you already know what I want to talk about.'

'Two things, isn't it? The need to plan a national evacuation to the centre of the American land mass. The need to prepare our own spatial salvation. Or is that second project too previous?'

'The position is,' Frame said, 'that Lynx will, after its devastating perigee – '

'How devastating?'

Frame, somewhat surprised at himself but realizing the inadequacy of words to the situation, impulsively picked up the presidential paperknife and walked a metre and a half to the large terrestrial globe which, with its inset lights that marked capitals and strategic areas, shone like a Christmas tree in the afternoon gloom. Frame, gritting his teeth, sliced all the way down Africa, the plastic yielding easily. He jabbed and ripped at all the coastlines of the world, then stopped, breathless. 'Earthquakes,' he said, 'seaquakes, reawakened volcanoes. That's the gravitational pull. Sorry about that, by the way. I'll have another globe sent to you tomorrow.'

'No,' the President said, 'it's as well to have a true picture. I see that you've put some of the lights out – London, Paris. There goes New York. There goes Washington.'

'Lynx,' Frame said, 'after this devastating prologue, will go away. It will circle the sun, joining our planetary system. Then it will return, having, on the other side of the sun, come to some complicated conclusion as regards the solar pull and its own rotation. All our calculations point to its colliding with the earth. Whether it will be a glancing blow, a head-on crash, or an irresistible tug is not yet established. Its mass, as you will know, is considerable.'

'Thank you,' Skilling said. 'I've already heard all this, of course. I won't look elsewhere for denial or confirmation. Your word will do for me. So,' he said, 'doomsday. Catday. Day of the Big Cat, the Final Catastrophe or Cataclysm. Politics,' he said, 'being the art of the possible, all the possibilities I can see relate to – well, putting off the end. Mass evacuation from the coasts. The possible. How much of the final truth is it possible to tell the people?'

'It's easier for the big totalitarian collectives,' Frame said gloomily. 'It's taken for granted there that nobody must know the truth. I'm no politician, but I can see no way out of the telling of the half-truth.'

Skilling smiled sadly. 'Mankind cannot bear very much reality. The Blessed Thomas Eliot said that. A ruler's job is to promote the bearability of life. This is the half-truth the people will be told – that a *temporary* quitting of the danger areas will be necessary. And after that – '

'Temporary? The danger areas will be just nothing. The total destruction of the great coastal cities. As for the little island nations – no hope, no waiting for the Day of the Cat. My people,' Frame said, 'like yours, came from England. No more England.'

'After that,' said Skilling, 'we get beyond the art of the possible. The presidential voice speaks soothing words over what's left of the communication media. And the Presidium will wave at us from space.'

'The request I make,' Frame said briskly, 'is that America be permitted to save something better than its mere rulers.'

The President grinned sourly. 'You mean its mere scientists?'

'No no no.' Frame was impatient. He longed for a cigarette, that injection having begun to wear off, and had none. The President was a non-smoker. 'There are people, politicians among them, who would face with equanimity the idea of floating for ever in space, round the sun, a new minuscule planet, or one of the tinier moons of Jupiter. Like going on a kind of endless cruise, complete with fornication and old movies on TV. An ark with no Ararat at the end of the voyage. My proposal is not one to appeal to politicians, or to the man in the street. I want to see our civilization preserved. I envisage a spaceship voyaging for centuries, millennia if need be, fraughted with our achievements – books on microfilm, stereoscopic records of our cities and their architecture, our music, technology, metaphysics. I envisage it manned by fine bodies housing great brains, breeding a new generation, teaching it – the process going on for thousands of years. And then, some day, landfall. A remote galaxy, a habitable planet. A fresh start for humanity, but not from scratch. This, I may say, is no mere dream. My daughter and I have long worked on the theoretical logistics of the scheme – '

'Ever since you knew about Lynx?'

'Long before, long long before. You understand the intricacies, the problems of coordination of the various specializations involved. A ship to be totally self-sufficient, indefinitely, eternally – producing its own food, manufacturing its own tools – a city, a country in miniature, a civilization in microcosm – ' He coughed with embarrassment at the incipient swell of rhetoric. The politician brought him down to earth.

'What do you want from me?'

'I want,' Frame frowned, 'a government grant without limit. Money will soon cease to mean very much. I suppose really what I'm asking is the resources you'd grant an army. I want a square mile in central Kansas, fenced round – it could be called, perhaps, a Center of Advanced Technology. CAT.' He grinned without mirth and waited for the inevitable question.

'Why Kansas?'

'An area which is, according to the seismologists, less likely to be disturbed by earth tremors than any other in the Commonwealth '

'The obvious choice, then, for a centre of government.'

'Keep government away,' warned Frame. 'We need isolation. Our project will be unpopular, will be totally misunderstood. It will be regarded as privileged self-salvation, not what it really is – '

'And yet,' said Skilling, 'it is precisely that. A lucky few who are going to survive, who are not going to face disaster. You, your daughter, your scientific friends – '

'My daughter, yes. Me, no. I'll not last out the year. As for the others – a matter of cybernetic choice. Leave it to the blind-eyed computers. We know the specializations needed. We look for the best parameters. Men and women in equal numbers, for evident reasons. But no married couples. Perfection doesn't go in pairs, not in a world given over to imperfection. Mating in space, the creation of a new race that's never known earth.'

'The Space Race,' the President said. 'Your daughter's married, isn't she? To this science fiction man – very popular with my poor wife, incidentally. Eased her last – Never mind.' It had been only a year before.

Frame cut in growling. 'There has to be a divorce. Or something. There's a problem there, but it can be solved. We can't afford the dead wood of paunchy fantasists. Fifty. I had in mind fifty. And room for the doubling of that population. Then comes enforced zero growth.'

'And what do they populate?'

'*Tallis*,' Frame said promptly. 'The bare hull of *Tallis*. The CAT team, if I may call them that, will fit out *Tallis* to what I term the Frame specifications.'

'Fill the frame with Frame,' said the President, a quick man with slogans. 'Who, by the way, told you you won't last the year?'

'Never mind,' said Frame. 'It's true. Can we have *Tallis*?'

'*Tallis*,' frowned the President. *Tallis* was the latest of the moonliners, very large, its propulsion mechanism already installed, due for launching six months hence. 'You talk,' he said slowly, 'in terms of a single venture. May there not be others?'

'Of course there may be others. There will be. And, if you'll permit a prophecy, there'll be a great deal of quiet talk soon, or perhaps not so quiet, about the saving of national cultures. Russia and her satellites have been regarding themselves as mere provincial aspects of a single ideological entity, but you say that the Russian Presidium is thinking of its own skin – not the black and brown skins of its African and South American comrades. The Teutphones and the Francophones – why the hell can't they be called what they used to be called? – the Germans will want a German space colony and the French –' He grinned. 'How is Canada going to feel about it all?'

'Nobody's going to feel anything about anything,' this Canadian said, 'because nobody will be officially told what to feel. There are going to be no plebiscites, no newspaper campaigns, no flags waving. There's going to be a host of *Mayflower*s and *Speedwell*s and *Santa Maria*s set up not by States but by free associations of experts. Is that what you and your colleagues – and I don't mean just American colleagues – have in mind?'

'It's a bit of a contradiction. Free associations, yes, but it's the State's task to provide what only the State can provide – the resources of an army. Now how about *Tallis*?'

'It's fortunate in a way,' Skilling said, 'that the Russian bloc's compelling us to set up a state of emergency. I can see no problem with a *carte blanche* emergency budget. Yes, you shall have *Tallis*. What, by the way, is going to happen to Lunamerica?'

'Thank you for *Tallis*,' Frame said. 'As for our Moon State – you realize that Lynx may gain a satellite at our expense? That the moon may follow heavy Lynx and desert frail little Terra? I refer, of course, to mass not to size. The moon is a woman.'

'What do we do about our Lunamericans? And our Spacestaters?'

'Leave them all there. They'll have their troubles, but they'll be smaller than ours.'

'State of emergency,' brooded the President. 'Congress will respond more readily to talk of commie threats than to something much more – palpable. I can hardly believe it. End of our historic cities. Of the America of our founding fathers. And yet I feel no particular depression. A lot of problems are going to be solved.'

'Such as?'

'A world overpopulated and underfed. Lynx at least saves the world from Armageddon. And at the end of it all there's no justice. The overfed save civilization.'

'Try to save it. Try to.'

'Where will *Tallis* make for?'

'Jupiter,' Frame said promptly. 'And, just beyond Jupiter, turn left for outer space. I think, by the way, *Tallis* must be renamed. Poor dead Tom Tallis won't mind. The spaceship *America*. *America I*. No reason why there shouldn't be other salvatory programmes – *America II*, *III*, *IV*. The more the better. As for Europe, I fear the sole hope lies in a spaceship *Europa*, but there'll be failed attempts at a *France*, a *Germany*, an *Italy* instead. Best not think of the rest of the world.'

'Another question,' Skilling said. 'How much do you know of the er composition of Lynx?'

'I know what's in your mind,' said Frame. 'Is God destroying the earth in order to supplant it with a nice new fresh clean one? Will Lynx be the new earth? No. Lynx has no atmosphere. Frozen hydrogen ready to melt and vaporize when it gets close enough to solar heat. No, kill that hope in yourself, Mr President, kill it in others. We're facing the end of the world.'

VOX, the cybernetic monster which was the pride of Westchester University, was not clever enough to know the end of the world was coming, but, once fed with the necessary data, it had no difficulty in disgorging fifty choice names in a microsecond or so. If the presence of the name Vanessa Brodie – demaritalized to Vanessa Mary Frame – was foreknown, this could not be attributed to nepotic cheating. A female specialist in ouranology, specifically trained by Professor Hubert Frame, healthy and of impeccable genetic antecedents, was required, and there was only one candidate, poor Muriel Pollock being too old and morbidly obese to qualify. But surely, boys and girls, ladies and gentlemen, if single status was a condition for membership of the ultimate elite, there was sharp practice proceeding? Was not Vanessa, despite the anagraphic fiction just alluded to, still married to Valentine Brodie, formerly lecturer in science fiction but now, at his urgent request, transferred to the Department of Drama? The answer must be yes and no.

During dinner one evening in early March, while they were engaged on the main course, Val choked on a mouthful of chicken Marengo when his wife, without preamble, said:

'Tomorrow morning I cease to be Mrs Brodie and revert to my *nom de jeune fille*, as the Francophones so delicately put it.'

Val spent six seconds on the dislodgement of a small bone from his throat. He eventually, gasping, said: 'This is very sudden.'

'Oh, come, you know it's only a formality. No marrieds on the CAT team. So now we're both perfectly qualified.'

Val stared wide-eyed. She had fed him two incredible hunks of information at the same time, as well as this chicken Marengo. He did not know what to say first. He said: 'But – is this – I mean – is it *legally* possible?'

'The filing of a divorce petition is being taken as the equivalent of a resumption of unmarried status. The divorce petition will be filed tomorrow morning. I take it you're not going to oppose it.'

'What,' he gasped, 'are the grounds?'

She smiled sweetly, carving delicately at the fried egg that rested on a golden crouton. 'The Muslims have a useful short word – *nusus*. It means the unwillingness of one of the marital partners to cohabit with the other.'

Val had nothing to say to that, but he was surprised to find his penis twitching. Perverse, how perverse the human instincts. He said: 'You said *we're* qualified, *we*. You mean I was fed into that computer? On what possible basis could I possibly be considered to be –'

'You're Number Fifty-One. A supernumerary. Archivist, historian, diarist, documentarian. Do you consider yourself unqualified?'

'But this sounds like cheating. There must be hundreds, thousands – I mean, how did you work it?'

'Totally against father's wishes, I may say. And it wasn't *worked*, as you term it. Consider the qualifications required. Writer – not enough. Writer with style well regarded by the critics – great narrowing of the field. Writer with smattering of science. Writer under forty. Writer healthy and – '

'I'm not all that healthy.'

' – Writer with Celtic blood. We have to watch the racial distribution. Your family comes from Dundee, Scotland.'

'Sounds like cheating to me.' He brooded, brooding Brodie.

'Writer acquainted with aspects of Framean ouranologistics.'

'Cheating, cheating.' He shoved his plate away. 'I'm not going, you know. It's not fair.'

'Finally, writer opposed to elitism of any kind. You're going, my boy. It's not going to be a matter of choice. You'll be under quasi-military orders.'

'And if I disobey?' He grinned. 'Am I sentenced to death?'

'I don't think the thought of anybody's actually disobeying has as yet been entertained,' she said in her prim way. 'I should imagine you would be put into the work force.'

'What work force?'

'The CAT work force. The hewers and hammerers. The camp builders.'

'Will they know what they're building?' He took a sauced cooling fowl bone between thumb and index and nibbled.

'No,' she said, laying her knife and fork neatly together on her emptied plate. 'They won't exactly. The story is that *Tallis* will be the last word in space labs.'

'*Tallis*?'

'The new moonliner. Taken over by CAT and renamed *America*. *Tallis* the selenologist is being accorded the ultimate honour.'

'An ignorant mob,' Val said, 'that doesn't know it's working its guts out to save a select fifty. I wouldn't mind working as one of the mob. I'd preach revolt.'

She looked steadily at him, elbows on table, hands delicately enlaced. 'Yes, you would, wouldn't you? This – democratic spirit of yours was something required by the programme. Anti-elitist, the common touch. But you mustn't let it go too far. You'd probably be shot. And don't start saying that everybody's going to die anyway – nearly everybody. There's still precious time ahead, more precious than time has ever been. Life can be good, you know, and life certainly isn't going to be dull. You won't want to be shot, believe me.'

Her cold blood chilled him. When the coffee machine waltzed in, it dispensed a beverage that seemed hotter than usual. He warmed his hands on his cup.

'Think,' she said, 'what the project means. It's nothing to do with the saving of a few select lives. It's concerned with the salvage of a civilization.'

He tasted the words with his coffee. 'Where did that idea come from? What committee worked it out? It doesn't sound like your father, God proleptically rest him and his finished lungs. He's always been a great growler against what man's made of the world. Is it you? What, may I inquire, do you know of civilization?'

'If,' she said, 'by civilization you mean the flea-bitten French and Florentines and British who produced rags of poetry and cynical amorous caterwaulings and big stone wedding cakes to the glory of what they called God – well, yes, it doesn't interest me much. But I believe in knowledge and the transmission of knowledge and the dream of setting that knowledge to work again – some day, somewhere.'

'Is there a somewhere?'

She looked down at her hands and then up, fiercely, at Val. 'Yes,' she said. 'Yes. Yes.'

That identical vocable was being breathed by Edwina Duffy as, at that very moment, she lay naked in the naked arms of young Professor Nat Goya in the tumbled bed of his apartment. It was an injunction to him to thrust home seed which, she prayed, would make her pregnant. This evening's lovemaking was not, to either of them, a mere casual appeasement of appetite breaking into the labour of paper marking. It was an anticipation of the consummatory act. It was sacramental. They now knew they loved each other, and tomorrow they proposed being married before a magistrate in Trenton, New Jersey. Secretly. A secret. Their secret. For the moment, anyway. Edwina's parents in Hawaii did not approve of Nat Goya. Nat Goya was still supposed to be affianced to a girl in Charlottesville, Virginia. Unpleasantnesses were always best put off. They would get down, they had decided, to announcing their happy state during the Easter vacation. All the time in the world. Nat now smiled, kissed Edwina, and went naked to the kitchen to make instant coffee.

'No. No. No.'

That vocable was now being uttered very sharply by Vanessa Brodie, Frame as she would be again tomorrow. The coffee, not instant, that her handsome modern machine had served, was serving as a prelude, not postlude, to an amorous impulse. Not the fulfilment, the attempt. Val was surprised at himself. The cognac he had taken with his second and third cups might have had something to do with it. But his impending liberation from matrimony's bonds, the restoration of what, children, had once been termed existential freedom, might have fired his glands more effectually than alcohol. He was, yes, surprised and yet not surprised. He was a sort of novelist, he was empirically interested in human nature, he was given to observation and introspection. Still, he gaped at himself as he tried to take his still-lawful wife in his arms, lewdly, as it appeared to himself (lewdly? Because love, or at least decent ordinary human affection, wasn't coming into it?), and was not really surprised when his wife fended him off with her triple no.

'Our last night together as a married couple.' Hands now limp by his sides. 'It seemed to call for, you know –'

'You're beastly. But you'll learn. There'll be all the time in the world to learn.'

'Yes,' Val said. 'No.' And he went out to get the hangtrain and find his fat friend in Manhattan.

'Yes. Yes. Yes.'

The word was being spoken in colourless clinical confirmation by Dr Emile Fouilhoux, carcinomologist and personal friend of Professor Hubert Frame. He gave a yes to each röntgen image of Frame's pulmonary economy, as the two sat together – long after office hours – in Fouilhoux's surgery. 'So,' Frame said. 'How long do I have?'

'Strictly speaking,' Fouilhoux said, 'you shouldn't be with us at all. Why did you do this to yourself?'

'I've always enjoyed cigarettes,' Frame said. 'Perhaps because both my parents were violent antismokers. They both died, incidentally, of lung cancer.'

'Six months ago,' Fouilhoux said, 'pneumometaphyeusis might have been possible – you know, lung transplant. All I can suggest now is that you enter the Bodenheim. You'll need looking after.'

'I've work to do,' Frame said.

'You'll do no more work.'

'I must. Important things are happening.'

'You're functioning on a minute area of lung. I can give you a supply of DCT3. It won't help all that much, I'm afraid. You ought to be connected to a pneumosurrog. That means the Bodenheim '

'I need six months. No more than six months.'

'You'll be lucky to get that,' Fouilhoux said gravely. 'Very lucky.'

Meanwhile Val and his huge friend Courtland Willett were coming out of one bar off Broadway and making their way to another. There was a bright light in the sky, not the moon, the moon had still to rise. The air this night was remarkably clear. 'Look,' cried Willett, 'Venus.'

'No,' Val said softly.

'Venus,' affirmed Willett, 'the planet of love. My God, you can feel it snuffling around you tonight – love, the burgeoning of green life, the spring.' He began to recite loudly, with round gestures:

> 'Tomorrow will be love for the loveless, and for the lover love.
> The day of the primal marriage, the copulation
> Of the irreducible particles, the day when Venus
> Sprang fully armed from the wedding blossoms of spray
> And the green dance of the surge, while the flying horses
> Neighed and whinnied about her, the monstrous conchs
> Blasted their intolerable joy!'

People in the street paused, open-mouthed or derisive. A cop said: 'Okay okay, break it up.'

'Love,' Willett cried, ignoring the cop. 'The next transit of Venus was due in 2004, so I read or thought I read, but things must have gotten speeded up. How much money have you?'

'About thirty-five dollars. And my credit cards.'

'Good. We'll go to Madame Aphrodite's. Appropriate, highly. That's Venus up there,' he said to a young flashy black.

Madame Aphrodite's was a house of pleasure on East 44th Street. The titular owner was as much a myth as her divine namesake, and the place was run by a certain Mrs Simona de Lancey, a black lady of fifty and startling handsomeness. 'No trouble,' she said to Willett. 'I want no trouble tonight, nor no poetry neither.'

'Love,' Willett said, gesturing so widely that he hit from a flower table in the vestibule a plaster statuette of love's goddess (armed). 'We come for love.'

'You can have that, baby.'

Val was both surprised and not surprised when he chose, from the bevy presented in the sitting-and-drinking room, a girl of lissom and chill blue-eyed beauty with whom, in her patchouli-scented cubicle, he made love sobbingly. No dark musky creature of swamp and jungle tonight. 'It seemed like you needed that, baby,' she said afterwards. They both lay, smoking, sipping whisky, listening to Willett declaiming from another room of love:

> 'People in the streets are dancing, kissing each other,
> Cats are wailing in most melodious counterpoint,
> Bitches have had a miraculous accession of heat.
> In the Bronx Zoo there must be amorous pandemonium,
> Probosces wantonly wreathing, capillary erections
> Of leopards and panthers. Probably even the tortoise
> Moves with a sort of leisurely impetuosity,
> And the air is full of the headiest distillation,
> Chiming madly like bells. It's like a
> Gratuitous Christmas, an antipodean Christmas –'

'Nuts,' said Val's companion, whose name was Stella. 'He's nuts.'

'An antipodean Christmas,' Val muttered. 'That's when the world began to change.'

'What's that you're grumbling about, honey?'

'Never mind,' Val said. 'My friend Courtland Willett is not nuts. Far from it.'

Nor was he. Although he mistook the identity of that bright planet, he was not wrong in supposing that its gravitational pull would induce certain glandular and psychic changes. Another three weeks and people would be driven to impulses they would at first be aware of as quite uncharacteristic. Love, yes, but also jealousy, rage bred of no clear motive, religious mania, dementias of various kinds. A radio was now turned up in another cubicle, in order that Willett's rhapsody be drowned. But he had already finished and was audibly at work on some act ecstatic but subpoetic. The radio sang:

> 'The whole world stinks
> Worse than anyone thinks
> So leap on it Lynx
> Tonight.'

* * *

Summer in Vienna, and the bourgeoisie departing for sea and mountains. Freud and his sister-in-law Minna sat waiting on a railway platform. Minna complained:

'But *why* two hours too early? I thought you'd got over that particular neurosis.'

'Oh, I have. But I like to get here early.'

She shook her head and studied the map. 'Here's our itinerary, then. Turin. Milan. Siena. Rome.'

'*Not* Rome.'

'But I thought we'd agreed – '

'Rome will be too hot. There's a terrible burning wind. You go. I'll stay by the lake.'

'Which lake?'

'Trasimeno.'

Trasimeno glorious in sunlight. They strolled, both in white, Freud in neat panama, smoking, for a holiday change, a slim panatella. Minna had an open guidebook. She said:

'The papers say it's unseasonably cool in Rome.'

'I don't believe it. It's a dangerous climate.'

'Do you want to know the *true* reason why you won't visit Rome?'

'*True* reason?' He nearly choked on his smoke. 'There are a number of *true* reasons, and you know them all.'

Minna spoke quickly. 'There was a prophecy made by the oracle to the Tarquins – that the conquest of Rome would fall to the first man who kissed his mother.'

'Mother earth, we know, we know – and – ?'

'Doesn't that contradict your Oedipus theory? Kiss your mother first and conquer your enemy after. The enemy being the great paternal city. According to the Oedipus pattern you kill your father first and kiss your mother after.'

'But Rome is the great mother city. Rome isn't a big hulking dangerous castrating father – '

'Are you sure? Sit down comfortably on this bench, Dr Freud, and hear what the guidebook says.'

They sat. Freud looked at an oleander uneasily. 'Well?'

'What figure in ancient history do you admire most?'

'Hannibal.'

'He was a man of Semitic race, it says here, who vowed eternal hatred for the Romans. He swore to his father Hamilcar that he'd conquer Rome – '

Freud quavered at the dawn of new knowledge. 'My God, it was here – at Lake Trasimeno – that he defeated the Roman forces.'

'But he never got to Rome. Fifteen years the armies of Carthage under Hannibal stayed in Italy, ravaged Italy, but Hannibal never got more than five miles away from Rome. You're fifty miles from Rome. You're a little more cautious than Hannibal. Now, Herr Doktor, do you see the connection?'

He saw it all right. He was fluent in his exegesis. 'Rome – the symbol of my ambitions. I'm a Semite like Hannibal. My father had his hat knocked into the mud. By a Christian, a Catholic, a son of Rome. Hannibal tried to avenge his father. He failed. *I've* failed. No. Not yet. Minna, I must conquer Rome.'

She smiled. 'Meaning that we pack our bags and buy a couple of railway tickets. You don't need the Carthaginian army. And I think you'll find that Rome will conquer *you* – '

Well, yes, an aesthetic conquest. All those baroque musculatures, the sun allayed by fountains. Fountains. He was completing the act of micturition in the hotel toilet. The man next to him at the stones looked curiously at him. Handsome, bearded, probably Anglo-Saxon. In the hotel lobby the concierge called him.

'*Dottore, scusi – i biglietti* – Dottor Freud – '

'*Ah, bene, tante grazie.*' Tickets for the opera. Bellini. The bearded Anglo-Saxon from the toilet had heard his name. He came up, said:

'Dr Sigmund Freud? Of Vienna?'

'*Servus.*'

'My name is Havelock Ellis.' His German was bad. 'You may recall that I reviewed your book on the aetiology of the neuroses.'

'Of course.' Freud spoke English. 'Vienna reviled me but England raised her voice in my cause. How can I thank you enough?'

'Not England's voice – only mine.' He spoke his own tongue with an intonation of relief. 'And it was raised to no avail. I have published books as well as reviews. You may know my *Studies in the Psychology of Sex* – '

'I fear – '

'No, no, of course you can't know it. It caused a brief but intense flame of protest before it was banned. You and I, Dr Freud, are ahead of our time.'

'A drink?'

'A drink.'

They sat outside Da Trescalini in the Piazza Navona, facing the

Bernini fountain, writhing nakedness, a glorification of libido. They shared a fiasco of Frascati. 'When and how did it start,' asked rhetorically Ellis, 'this fear of the greatest pleasure known to men? The sculptors of Renaissance Italy didn't fear it.'

'The pleasure that young lovers find together,' Freud sadly said. A Roman girl and boy were frankly embracing in the sight of Bernini's giants. 'An affront to the old men, the fathers of State and Church. An affront to their senile impotence. They seek a power in recompense for the sexual power they have lost. The power of rule, the rigour of the law.'

'Oedipus met an old man on the road,' Ellis said. 'He wouldn't have killed that old man if the old man hadn't tried to knock him out of his path with a heavy rod. Isn't the enmity of the young and the old more than a matter of – desire for the love of the mother?'

Freud shook his head in a kind of proleptic old man's dogmatism. 'No. No. No. It's as I've written. Look – '

They both looked at a small boy, whom rougher boys in rags had been trying to belabour in scorn of his sailor suit. He ran crying to his mother who, in voluble Roman, comforted him, holding him to her bosom. He held on to her weeping, as if he would never let her go.

'That's the basis of it. Look – '

The boy's father had appeared, a heavily moustached Roman. He tried to persuade his weeping son to tear himself from his mother and confront the young louts, fight it out with them even, one to four. The mother protested. The father tried to break the embrace, but the son hit the father off, bold in his transport.

'It's as I've written. All my cases confirm it. The Oedipus complex is at the deep root of our drives, our dreams, our very society.'

'Beware,' said Ellis, 'if I may say so, of the pontifical. You feel you've reached the final secret after long striving. Behind the secret may lie other secrets, and others, and others. There's no limit to the unconscious. The human mind will never be fully charted.'

'No. No.' Freud was firm about it. 'We have the key.'

The noontime bells of Rome clashed out. Ellis had to speak up. 'The Church too thinks it has the keys of the kingdom. What are the names of your sons?'

'Oliver. Martin.'

'Oliver Cromwell? Martin Luther? True or not, the associations will serve. Those men were rebels. Admit the virtue of rebellion, Dr

Freud. Rebellion against even yourself. Don't turn yourself into the Pope.'

Freud said nothing. He tried to hold back his frown. He drank up and placed coins on the table. 'I must go.'

'And I can guess where you're going.'

Freud shrugged. He shook Ellis's hand perfunctorily and went off without another word. Ellis smiled and shook his head a little.

Saint Peter's. Freud and Minna gazed up at the horned effigy, the frozen music. 'He's brought down the tablets of the law into the wilderness,' Freud said. 'His people have turned against him to worship a golden calf. They will turn against him again and again. And yet he and he only can bring them to the Promised Land.'

'Will you,' Minna teased, 'ever see the Promised Land? Will you, Herr Doktor Moses Freud?'

Freud thought about it and then firmly shook his head.

'Any member of the working class,' Trotsky says, 'who allows himself to be slaughtered in a capitalistic war shows ignorance, ignorance of his rights as a worker, ignorance of the historical process – '

Olga says bitterly: 'All dead men are ignorant, aren't they?'

Trotsky detects the bitterness in her tone. He speaks more sympathetically. 'I mean that a man is a fool to enlist in a capitalistic struggle. Would you not accept that, comrade?'

'Yes,' she says, 'it's so easy, isn't it? Capitalistic systems warring against each other, one called X and the other Y, and one's as bad as the other. Try calling Pierre back from the dead and telling him that. I'm sure he'd be interested.'

'Pierre?' Trotsky speaks kindly. 'I gathered, I guessed, that you had, shall I say, a shall I say personal concern.'

'Very personal. We were going to be married.'

'Ah.' He waits. He always knows when to wait.

'His name was Pierre Godard. Born in Montreal, Canada. Worked in New York because there weren't many jobs up there. He had no special skills. He'd read, though – French writers – Flaubert, Balzac, Verlaine. He loved the wine of his French ancestors. He loved me, I think. I know I loved him. Then 1914 came. Europe's war, the

Americans said. The Canadians weren't so sure. Pierre was *quite* sure what he wanted to do.' She sings:

He wanted to fight
For the fields of France,
Though he'd never seen
Their purple and green.
Like a latterday knight
Without shield or lance
He went.
His very first sight
Of the fields of France
Was the green of mud
And purple of blood,
For the music and light
And the song and dance
Were spent.
French was the tongue his fathers spoke,
French was the land they had tilled.
Why should a fierce and foreign folk
Wreck what they'd striven to build?
He wanted to fight
For the fields of France,
And they let him fight
A day and a night.
In a hopeless advance
He was given one chance to show
What he felt for the fields of France,
And now the fields of France
Won't let him go.

'Sentimental?' she says. 'Foolish? He should have waited for Leon Trotsky to come along and enlighten him. But he might not have listened. You see – to some people the working class is only a kind of abstraction. It doesn't mean Tom with the warts and Dick with one eye bigger than the other and Harry with the wooden leg. It's a kind of big shapeless grey marching ghost.'

'And France and Canada and America aren't just big splashes on a world map, is that it?' Trotsky says. 'Fight for France, for Russia, for Germany – what does that mean? Fight for *me*, that's what it means, and who is *me*? Me, the man with the golden empire who wants to make that empire bigger still and more and more golden, and if a few million misguided men fall in the mud, slithering in their own blood, what does that matter? There'll always be more.'

'No,' Olga says. 'France is Racine and Voltaire and Debussy and fresh crusty bread and filtered coffee. Just as America is – why should I bother? You don't care a damn about America – except its export figures and the strength of its unions. You don't care a damn about people.'

'I understand,' says Trotsky, 'your talking the way you do, Olga, but – '

'Ah, *Olga*. I'm no longer one of the grey abstractions, no longer just a nameless comrade. Who told you my name, anyway? I didn't tell you. We weren't even introduced – '

'I knew your name. I knew of the pretty girl who was – Never mind. I tell you I understand. You've suffered and you're still suffering. Love – one set of physical atoms drawn to another set. Spiritual, whatever spiritual means, like God. You were in love, and now love is over. Tell me, when did you join the movement?'

'What does it matter? If you must know, about three months after he was killed. Why?'

'I see. Your life was empty and you needed to fill it up again. So you chose the socialist cause. As a substitute for love. Not very flattering to the socialist cause – a mere substitute for something else.'

'A very inadequate substitute.'

'So it must seem to you. So inadequate that you can't give your whole being to it, you can't go to the limit and cry revolution. Sentimental pseudo-socialism. *Love*. Your motives, comrade, are impure motives.'

Olga speaks with dangerous softness. 'And *your* motives, comrade?'

'I know my motives and I have always known them. Disinterested. A submission to the march of history. A selfless concern with the building of the just society. Selfless, yes. As a person I am nothing. A mere discardable cell in the organism of the party which, sooner than anyone thinks, shall be coextensive with the world. Let the movement discard me when it wishes. I'm ready to be discarded. If I can be more useful dead than alive, then so be it. I obey. I did not make myself a cornerstone of the socialist structure as a substitute for failed talent or lost love, whatever love is. I did it out of a pure motive of service for the cause that I believe in and that all men, sooner than anyone thinks, will believe in.' He pants.

'Wrong,' says Olga. 'You have a vision of the name Trotsky shining some day in the fabulous hierarchy of the party. Trotsky Trotsky Trotsky – one of the great names, if not the greatest of all. Lenin, Stalin, Trotsky, but the greatest of these is Trotsky. Trotsky carved in imperishable stone. Why, you even chose the name Trotsky as Lenin chose Lenin and Stalin Stalin. Bronstein wasn't good enough, was it? – too much the name of a Jewish tailor on Second Avenue. Bronstein carved in marble, no, that won't do. But Trotsky – that's different. A hero choosing his own heroic name. Motive, you talked of your motive. You don't know the first thing about your motive. Shall I tell you what it is and what it will be, comrade? Power. Not virtue, not knowledge, but power. Just like the Tsar and Rasputin and J. Pierpont Morgan and John D. Rockefeller. Oh, we know the proletariat is going to rule itself some day, but that some day is a long way off. In the meantime the proletariat has to be led, and who shall be its leader? Trotsky perhaps – why not? And certain party members will deviate from the party line, and they'll have to be taught the error of their ways. How? Well, the apparatus of the State will still be there, won't it, including the police force. Punishment, comrade, oh how I regret it, it breaks my heart, observe the flow of my tears. But you have to be punished, do you not? Alas, all we have are stinking capitalist jails at the moment, but we'll work out good wholesome socialist methods of punishment, in time, all in good time. Not just punishment, but rehabilitation, comrade. Not just the whip to your body but the burning fire of rehabilitation in your skull. Only when a leader is dealing out punishment, comrade, does he know the real ecstasy of power. Power – what a delightful prospect. And tonight you're going to relish the little power, the hors d'oeuvre of power not the banquet of power, of swaying good-hearted American workers to whom you're already a name of power. We should be getting your speech together, shouldn't we? Well, get it ready yourself. I'm going. And I shall not be there tonight. *Do svidanya, tovarishch.*' And she makes a clenched fist which has more of menace than of camaraderie in it. Then she slams the door, leaving. Trotsky, nonplussed, admiring, resentful, puffing, growling, paces the office. Then he goes to the typewriter and tries to type his speech. He is very unhandy and tears out the sheet with quiet obscenities. He gets up and, in a *parlando* style, monologuizes:

All through history
Mind limps after reality.
And what is reality? What's damned well there.
There's no mystery
In physical causality.
Life is simple. Desperately so. Beware
Of making it complex.
Sex, for instance, sex.
The need to breed, cell calling to cell.
Any set of cells will do as well
As any other set. And yet
This word *love*, *lyubof*, *Liebe*, *amore*
Sticks its ugly snout into the story.

All through history
Mind limps after reality.
And what is mind? A burst of electric sparks
Out of the clashing consistory
Of physical actuality.
Love's in the mind, but it isn't in Karl Marx.
Love's in William S.,
In Tolstoy, more or less,
And certainly in Dante Alighieri.
Pushkin? *Lyubof* flows like cream in a dairy.
Those poets aren't to blame. They came
Too soon to recognize their own confusion.
Love, we all know now, is a bourgeois illusion.

That girl now, Olga, Comrade Olga? Olga, cut out the comrade. She says she was in love. Intelligent enough, misguided, but we could soon put that right. But she says she was in love. Meaning that she considered one sexual partner was more suitable than another. A common delusion. Did I ever suffer from it? Of course not. Natalia – a talented dancer, practitioner of a bourgeois art which the revolution will not require, a good party member, an adequate worker for the cause. Suitable, yes. More suitable than the others? I didn't know all the others. Marriage? Bourgeois, but the children have to be looked after. Love of children? Natural, biological, the race has to go on. I think I can say in all honesty that I have never – Lain awake at night. For love. Written bad poems. For love. Gone without my dinner. For love. Good. Love – a thing in the mind, and the mind hardly exists. We're nerve, muscle, sinew, atoms, a stage for the enactment of the dialectical process. Material material. Solid solidity. Mind? Insubstantial, a ghost. And if I say I fear I shall have this girl Olga on my mind?

All through history
Minds limps after reality.
And what is reality? Good solid stuff.
There's no mystery
In physical causality.
Atoms, cells and bones and brains – enough.
The shape of a girl's face,
The thought of an embrace –
Irrelevant nugacities, totally and absolutely supererogatory –
So say Engels, Marx *et al.*,
No *die Liebe* in *Das Kapital.*
But today I find it necessary to say:
Keep away, girl, keep away, girl, keep away!

These, for the record, were the names and specializations disgorged by VOX. They are names you will know, names still living among you. Some of them.

Abramovitz, David T., bibliothecologist
Adams, Maude Quincy, ouranoclinician
Audelan, Vincent, hydroponist
Belluschi, Robert F., microbiologist
Bogardus, Sara, engineer
Boudinot, Louise, engineer
Cézanne, Miguel S., electronologist
Christian, Katherine, heliergonomist
Cornwallis, Douglas C., physicist
Da Verranzano, Gianna, microbibliothecologist
DeWitt, Felicia, biochemist
Durante, John R., engineer
Eastman, K.O., diastemoploionologist
Eidlitz, Mackenzie, energiologist
Ewing, Georges Auguste, diastemiconographer

Farragut, Minnie, physicist
Forster, Sylvia, hupologistics engineer
Frame, Vanessa Mary, coordinating ouranologist
Fried, Sophie Haas, ouranoclinician
Goya, Nathan, microagronomist
Greeley, William, diastemopsychologist
Harrison, Belle, cybernetologist
Hazard, Ebenezer, supplies coordinator
Herodotus, Alger, physicist
Irving, Guinevere, atomospherologist
Jumel, Lilian, engineer
Kopple, Grayson, mellonologist
La Farge, Gertrude, maieutist/general secretary
Lopez, Fred K., engineer
Markelius, Sven Maximilian Josiah, oicodomicologist
Moshowitz, Israel, morphoticist
McGregor, Herman A., ploiarch 1
McEntegart, Angus, ploiarch 2
Nesbit, Florence, mageirist
O'Farrell, Terence, rapticologist
O'Grady, Lee Harvey, astunomicologist
Opisso, Rosalba, diaitologist
Parkhurst, Ethel Armand, engineer
Piccirilli, Attilla, electronologist
Prometeo, Susanna, anacoinotic engineer
Reiser, Deborah, physicist
Roelantsen, Julius C.C., electrical engineer
Sennacherib, Betsy, morphoticist
Skidmore, Owings Merrill, expert in domestic scediastics
Thackeray, Jessica Laura, biochemist
Untermeyer, Fernando S., ouranoclinician
Velasquez, Wouter van Twiller, diastemographer
Wolheim, Fernando Alexander, petrologist
Yamasaki, Minoru, botanical engineer.

Note the pitiful lack of Mexican names, the very slight preponderance of males, the absence of the name Valentine Brodie, which came after the above list had been completed, and the fact that there are, to my computation, forty-nine names only instead of the fifty scheduled. The fiftieth name, or fourth taking it alphabetically, was Paul

Maxwell Bartlett, whose official title eschewed Greekish pretension and was simply Head of Enterprise or, in the eventual colloquial of the team, Boss Cat. His importance requires that we take a closer look at him than can be accorded to the others, except, of course, those in the human foreground of our narrative. *Who's Who in the Universe*, 1999, gives the following curriculum vitae:

BARTLETT, Paul Maxwell: Coordinating Principal, Combined Space Research Projects of Columbia, Princeton, MIT and Univ. of Pennsylvania; Bronze Star 1989; Legion of Merit 1990; Presidential Unit Citation 1991; DSM 1992 (US Navy Special Attachment with temp. rank of Rear-Admiral); PhD (Harvard), DSc (Cantab.), hon. PhD Univs. of Toronto, California, Washington State, etc.; *b*. 17 Dec. 1958; *s*. of Maxwell Everard Bartlett, DD and Dorothy Aline Goodhew; unmarried. *Educ.:* Choate School; Harvard; Trinity Coll., Cambridge; Sorbonne. Professor of Astrophysics, Univ. of Delaware, 1985–86; Member, US Federal Satellite Commission, 1986–87; Adviser, US Defense Project Achilles, 1987; Commander, Mission Philoctetes, 1988–92; Professor of Ouranology, MIT, 1992–95; Delegate, Global Diastemic Organization, 1995–96; Visiting Distinguished Professor, Univ. of Manchester, 1996–98. *Publications: Into Space*, 1988; *An Inquiry into Anti-Matter* (with L.B. Moran), 1990; *The Future of Spaceman*, 1992; *Critique of the Hopkinsian Radiation Belt Doctrine*, 1993; *What We Have Still to Learn*, 1995; *Scenarios Relating to Project Discipline*, 1998. *Recreations:* Athletics, biography, political philosophy. *Address:* 10A, 366 West End Avenue, New York City. Tel: (212) 6894–4400.

A skeletal summary, no more, mere logarithms of ability. No one, meeting the man even casually, could be unaware of the intelligence, the scientific hunger, the dynamic of intuition, the great gift of leadership. Further inquiries into his life and personality would disclose a total lack of vice – he ate sparingly, drank only on social occasions, had no notable sexual life – and a balanced sanity of mind and body very rare outside epic fiction.

Large, handsome and vital, ox-strong, steel-supple, he was a flame on the tennis court, a fish in the swimming pool, a thudding menace in the amateur boxing ring. But he was urbane, eloquent and lucid in conference, and he even wrote well. Those books of his which had a 'popular' pseudo-philosophical theme – as opposed to the uncompromisingly technical works which had made his name in the inner circles of science and scientific strategy – showed that he thought deeply about man's place in the universe. He had read widely outside his own fields, and his *The Future of Spaceman*, for example, was heavily footnoted with citations from Heidegger, Reich, Jung and Teilhard de Chardin.

Most of his non-scientific reading, however, was, as his entry in *Who's Who in the Universe* indicates, in the lives of great people, and the great people who chiefly interested him were subsumed under the vague concept of the 'man of destiny'. He believed that some human beings were better or certainly cleverer, than others, and that these were destined to lead. His favourite biographical subjects were Metternich, Napoleon Bonaparte, Cromwell, Winston Churchill and, alas, Adolf Hitler. All these men had risen to power and fallen from it. He was concerned with tracing the course of the human parabola in each story, probing for the weaknesses but at the same time analysing the strengths. His interest in political philosophy was narrower than was appropriate to an American democrat. He read and reread the *Republic* of Plato, Hobbes's *Leviathan,* Machiavelli's *Il Principe* and Prauschnitz's *Doctrine of the Elite.* From his study of Aristotle he remembered that the term democracy denoted a perversion of government, not a wholesome ideal to be propagated among nations unlucky or stupid enough not to have discovered its beauties for themselves. *Demos,* after all, meant 'the mob'.

One recreation he must have regarded as too trivial to be recorded. As a temporary high-ranking officer of the US Navy, he had disclosed not merely a powerful physical bravery, an ability to get on exceptionally well with superiors and inferiors alike, but also a martinettish temper that served marvellously when quick decisions had to be enforced. He was, it was quietly recognized, a natural leader. His professional colleagues in the navy were glad to see him return to civilian life. He himself was eager to get on with research unhampered by considerations of national defence, but he did not forget the simple joys of command. Often in his apartment, behind locked doors, he would put on his naval uniform, which he kept clean and pressed, and enact, all alone, a tense moment on the quarterdeck, using a vocabulary derived from old movies like *Mutiny on the Bounty*. He never troubled about anachronism and would order keelhauling, would even lash out occasionally at the furniture with a cat-o'-nine-tails normally kept locked in his documents safe. All this represented a harmless diversion which, to one in his high-strung position, was sweetly cathartic.

When the letter conferring the highest power of his career arrived, Paul Bartlett was dressed as a civilian, ready to set off for the weekly inter-university conference in Dalrymple Hall on the Columbia campus – within walking distance of his apartment. The letter was headed with the presidential seal, a note stated that the paper was so chemically treated that it would destroy itself one hour after the opening of the envelope, the letter itself informed him that he was appointed head of a most secret enterprise and that he was to report at Lindsay Airport, Concourse D, Green Lounge, at 0400 hours on 2 April. There was another letter, inviting him to dinner at the home of Professor Vanessa Frame the following evening and would he please blepophone if he was unable to come. Bartlett smiled to himself: he thought he knew what all this was about.

Next evening, as he got into his car for the drive to Westchester, he noticed that Lynx was well above the horizon and now about half the size of the moon (both were just starting their first quarter). The citizens of Manhattan, not easily moved by anything, were nevertheless fascinated by Lynx. Some stood in the streets gawping up at it, some, contemplating the Russian allegation, swore it was a Soviet device for observing American ballistic installations, others had become religious and spoke of the Day of Judgement, yet others – chiefly the idle young – were making a cult of it and spanking drums and shrilling pipes and swinging asses and hips nightly at it. On some highly impressionable psyches it was inducing an instability manifested in various bizarre forms – sudden bad temper, often of a murderous kind, in normally placid temperaments; placidity in the normally violent; incursions of poetic inspiration among stolid bank managers and insurance brokers; satyriasis; sadism; a longing, as in pregnancy, for strange foods. Bartlett knew from one of his medical colleagues that the menstrual cycle, especially in girls under twenty, was being disrupted. He himself had been aware of incipient bouts of light-headedness. Coming, a couple of days before, out of his office in Dalrymple Hall, he had felt impelled to embrace a not very personable secretary of the department. Shocked at himself, he had laughed off the aberration. 'A touch of the Lynxes, Sybil, sorry.' Librium seemed to help some.

At the house of Professor Vanessa Frame, he found his hostess lovely in black silk, a science fiction writer called Brodie slightly drunk, and Professor Hubert Frame in shocking condition. He was encased from waist to shoulders in a noisy respirator plugged into a power point on the wall, equipped also with batteries for travelling between point and point, on wall or elsewhere. Bartlett had not seen

Frame since the Natsci conference, when he had been smoking and coughing much but seemed vigorous enough. Now he was clearly a dying man. Vanessa he had met at some great science convocation or other; the SF man he did not know at all. The genre he practised Bartlett certainly despised as having little to do with science; he wondered what the grinning soak was doing here.

The dinner was one of Vanessa's finest – watercress soup with croutons; roast duck with orange and braised celery; English sherry trifle. But Bartlett was not given to the refinements of the senses, Frame was too ill and Brodie too bleary with booze to eat much. Vanessa said, as if to excuse a meal she had foreknown nobody would eat, something about the days of the *haute cuisine* being numbered. 'We're joining the army,' she said.

'*Your* army,' Frame said to Bartlett. Bartlett frowned slightly. It was as if he were an appointee of the Frames, a puppet general. The Frames spoke too freely of the project in the presence of this SF soak. Bartlett put it to the soak bluntly:

'Where do you come into all this?'

'Some day,' Brodie grinned, 'on a distant planet in an unfathomably far galaxy, schoolchildren will read a book with some such title as *Annals of the Star Trek* or *How Civilization was Saved*. I shall have written that book.' Bartlett grunted. He said to Frame:

'Where is the place?'

'Classified information,' Frame gasped. 'We'll all know when we get there.'

'But somebody knows.'

'The President knows. I know.'

'But I'm not permitted to know,' Bartlett said. 'Interesting.'

'We have to watch security,' Frame wheezed, his respirator wheezing with him.

'We? Who's we?'

'The project,' Vanessa said, 'had to start somewhere. It started with my father.'

'And presumably with you?'

'Well, yes. My father trained me.'

'Back to this *we*,' Bartlett said to Frame. 'You yourself are going to Station X or Y or whatever it's called?' Frame wheezed yes. 'In what capacity?'

'Adviser. Adviser as to what? As to the implementation of the project.'

'Look,' Bartlett said. 'How far am I really in charge?'

'Oh, all the way,' Vanessa said. 'As soon as you know what you're in charge of. Do you have a Z class decodifier? At home?'

'Of course.'

'Well, then – ' And as if she were fetching a cold dessert from the sideboard she went to the sideboard and fetched a bulky bound typescript with RPT (3a) printed on the blancmange-coloured cover. She gave it to Bartlett. Brodie grinned faintly and Bartlett caught the grin. He looked the grinner in the eye while he addressed the other two. He said:

'I'm not particularly sure that I shall require advice.'

'You'll get it just the same,' Frame said.

'You don't look particularly healthy to me.'

'That's my concern.'

'It's the concern of the project. Do we travel together on 2 April? I take it for granted you know everything.'

'You have a camp to set up,' Frame panted. 'A work force will have been dispatched to erect the basic living and working units. Army, of course. You're an ex-serviceman, you'll know the kind of discipline needed.'

'I'm navy.'

'I know. The army knows more about setting up things on dry land than the navy. That's just the way things are. The personnel of the project will be travelling in separate small groups. Staggered. Security again. My daughter and I will arrive at CAT on 12 April.'

'And this er gentleman?'

'Dr Brodie,' Vanessa said, 'must be in on things from the beginning.' The coffee had arrived. Val brought cognac from the bar, zigzagging slightly. He said to Bartlett:

'You haven't touched your claret, I notice. Perhaps you're a hard-stuff man, like me. Let's drink to the salvaging of civilization.'

'I don't drink,' said Bartlett.

'None of us will drink,' Val said with sudden gloom. 'An end to drinking. But what sort of civilization will it be without drink? Or,' he grinned at Frame, 'without tobacco?' Frame grunted. Bartlett waved the typescript grimly. He said:

'I'd better start reading this now. So, if you'll excuse me – '

'That's right,' Val said. 'You start reading it now.'

'Were you ever in the service?' Bartlett asked him, getting up.

'Alas, no. Always a free civilian.' Bartlett nodded, as to indicate that all that was going to change. Then he left, without thanking his hostess for the dinner. 'Friendly sort of bastard,' Val said.

'He's what's needed,' wheezed Frame.

'By me, no.' Val shuddered.

'*You* are *not* needed.'

'Let's not start that again,' cried Vanessa. 'Shall I put you to bed, father?' For now there were three bedrooms in use in the Brodie–Frame apartment.

'Let's hear the President first. Ten o'clock.'

They caught the end of the 9.30 telenewsummary. Disaster in Portugal, devastating tides overwhelming Aveiro, Odemiro and Comporta. It was a long way away. The culprit filled the screen: Lynx, very flushed, in high colour. The President of the CDA came on, easy, smiling, unpanicky. His words, he said, were addressed to the entire Commonwealth. He would use English first, Spanish and French after. What he had to tell them was a very simple matter of elementary science, a question of gravity – that strange thing they would all have learned about at school: Newton and the apple and so forth. Everybody knew how the moon pulled tides just as the earth pulled apples. Well, the moon, our old friend and neighbour, was being temporarily joined by the planet Lynx, not quite a friend but tolerable as a temporary lodger, in exerting a gravitational pull on the tides of a force hardly known before in man's history. *Hardly*: there was a politician's lie. Coastal dwellers would be in some danger. Accordingly, the Commonwealth government was joining provincial governments in establishing certain emergency facilities to be employed during the period of greatest hazard. All coastal dwellers who had (a) their own transport and (b) friends or relatives in Nebraska, Colorado, the Dakotas, Oklahoma and other central states were advised to make their own arrangements to effect temporary – temporary only – evacuation within the next three weeks. Coastal dwellers without one or the other or both of those advantages would be transported free, where necessary, to special emergency camps or hostels, where necessary, in the scheduled safety zones. There was nothing, the President said, to worry about. The Communists were not coming with bombs and gases. Nature, neutral Nature, nobody's enemy, was making things a little difficult for us, no more. In a month or so, when Lynx's transit took him away from the earth, things would be as they were before though perhaps a little wetter. He smiled, wished everybody good night, and then began in Toronto Spanish. A typical politician's performance. When he had done, the local station gave another such show, this time with the Mayor of New York, a jovial black with waved hair, who spoke of reporting times, places, the need to keep cool. Business would be back to normal after a brief exciting interim, in which the central government was making itself responsible for the basic amenities of evacuated life. He repeated this in Spanish and Kuo-Yü.

When Hubert Frame had been put to bed, Val disclosed himself as sober enough. The irresponsible artist act had been chiefly for the benefit of their cold masterful guest. He put his arms gently about the cool body of Vanessa and kissed her gently on her cool lips. 'Shall we,' he proposed gently, 'commit an act that is technically fornication? An act which, I fear, will not be officially approved of when the great work begins?'

She smiled, and, there on the living-room floor, she collaborated in the exordia of the act – the baring of her arms and shoulders and breasts, a delicacy of caressing which grew ever more ardent, and soon the two of them lying naked together, and his tenderness modulating to a fire, and then:

'Not like that,' she scolded. 'Not that way at all. Let me show you.'

'Oh my God,' he groaned.

'You know it. It's Plate Number 4 in *Hamsun*. I showed it you, you knew it.'

'Oh Jesus Christ.' He was up, dancing into his pants, quite flaccid.

'You don't love me,' she cried from the floor. 'That's the trouble, you just don't know what love means – '

'Has everything to be science? Every fucking thing? I know now that I don't want your kind of civilization to be saved. Is there no room for for for clumsiness and humanity and imperfection and drunkenness and and – '

'And whores,' she sobbed. 'Filthy whores. Dogs. Goats and monkeys.'

He grinned sourly. 'That's from *Othello*,' he said. 'There's hope for you, I see. Poor unscientific Shakespeare.' And then he slammed out to get drunk in Lynx-crazed Manhattan.

* * *

'I wonder sometimes – '

The night fields of France. Martha yawned. 'What, Sigmund?'

'Did I fight hard enough for the Jews?'

Anna put her book down. 'You had enough to fight. And to fight for.'

'And yet – I took Vienna's antisemitism for granted. And Germany's. Assumed it was a fact of nature. Not a neurosis capable of cure.'

'It can't be cured,' Anna said.

'It will have to be. It will get worse before it gets better. It sounds like the pattern of a disease. Did I use properly – what – gifts I had?'

'Don't, father, please – '

But consider that evening at the meeting of the B'nai B'rith Verein, with Bernstein accusing him, Freud, who, at the request of the organization, had discoursed on the more entertaining aspects of deep psychology, of frivolity, play, a lack of due seriousness. 'I commend,' Bernstein cried through the cigar smoke, 'Dr Freud's originality, his intellectual range, his eloquence. But I would say this – to play with what he calls complexes, to explain trivialities like errors in everyday speech – the psychopathology of everyday life he calls it – is not the kind of work which a Jewish intellectual should be concerning himself with at the present time – '

There was, surely, the odd murmur of agreement as well as the louder protest that this was no occasion for, that Dr Freud had been specifically invited to, time and place for everything.

'Dr Freud would be better engaged in explaining the roots of antisemitism, which is manifestly on the increase in our society, showing the misguided Gentiles of our city the origins of the disease that smites them – for it *is* a disease, who can doubt it? Is not this, Dr Freud, the ravaging ailment which a Jewish intellectual, especially a Jewish doctor of the mind, should be concerned with extirpating?'

And himself getting up, taking a mouthful of smoke, pronouncing through it: 'I'm not a politician, Herr Bernstein, not a demagogue. I deal with such ailments as are brought to me. Here, at the B'nai B'rith, I take advantage of the kindness you show me in allowing me to talk of matters which my Gentile colleagues regard as distastefully revolutionary, and, indeed, some of my Jewish colleagues also. But my concern is with individual ailments, not the ills of society – '

'Then, Dr Freud,' cried Bernstein, 'you are not the man I took you for. Without the help of its intellectuals, how can our race hope to achieve dignity in its long Austrian exile, wipe out the blight of ostracism, avenge the wrongs done by the Gentile? Every day I repeat to myself a line from Virgil – *Exoriare nostris ex ossibus ultor* – '

'Yes, yes – let someone arise from our bones as an avenger. I'm impressed by your Latinity, but more impressed by the fact that you missed out a word from that line – the word *aliquis*.'

'This is frivolous. Yes, *aliquis* – I forgot it – it only means *some* – *aliquis ultor* – '

'May I pursue my frivolous preoccupation and explain, if I can, why you missed out that unimportant word?'

'Frivolity, irrelevance – ' But Bernstein was cried down. 'Well, if you wish,' he said sulkily, 'I can give you the explanation myself. For some reason I saw the word as two words – *a* and *liquis* – and the words seemed irrelevant to the idea of revenge.'

'Good. *Liquis* – liquid – liquefying – fluidity – *Reliquien* – relics – Does that take you anywhere?'

'No, not irrelevant, after all. Relics – saints – I've been reading a book about – Wait – there was something in the newspapers about the Jews and ritual blood sacrifice – the usual nonsense that comes up during waves of antisemitism – The book? What was the book? Yes, Kleinpaul's stupid book says that the victims of Jewish ritual sacrifice are incarnations of Christ. Saints – yes, I see the connection – saints and relics.'

'Saints – blood – liquid – Where do we go now?'

'Naples.' Bernstein had forgotten his earlier injunction: he was into the game now. 'In Naples they keep the blood of St Januarius in a phial. On his feast day it's supposed to liquefy. Ridiculous superstition. If the blood is late in flowing, the stupid Neapolitans become very agitated – '

'If,' Freud repeated, 'the blood is late in flowing.'

Bernstein was appalled. 'Oh my God.'

'Let us present as a hypothesis this possibility. That a man could omit the world *aliquis* from a common Virgilian citation because of his fear that blood will not flow. The blood of an Italian lady met in Naples, for example. Just a hypothesis.' Everybody looked with interest at Bernstein. Bernstein cried:

'Wasting your talents, Dr Freud. Concern yourself with the major wrongs of society. The wrongs done to the Jews. All this fiddling about with minor deliquescences, I mean delinquencies, peccadillos, miscalcul – ' He went out stumbling.

But Bernstein was fundamentally healthy enough, that was clear. Not like the young man who lay exhausted on the couch among the growing collection of jujus.

'You came to me in a deeply suicidal state. Accused of erotic conduct most reprehensible, cut off from the world. Suffering from cardiac tremors, palpitations, mysterious physical pains. Because of your homosexuality. Instead of loving your mother, you wished to *be* your mother. You believed that children came out of the anus. You wanted anal penetration – a fantastic fertilizing. You didn't want to replace your father – you wanted to punish him for being a weak man, dominated by your powerfully aggressive mother. Is that a just summary?'

The young man's exhaustion seemed a healthy symptom now, the signal of a desire to sleep after long insomnia. 'Oh, that doesn't matter now, does it?' he said. 'The point is that I accept myself. I'm a homosexual. I mustn't look for a woman but for a man – a kind of husband, different, totally, from my mother. And now it's for society to accept me – '

'Society will learn – though very slowly. A sane society could accept the homosexuality of Socrates, of Michelangelo, even Shakespeare. You and I may not live to see the burgeoning of this sanity. For the moment, society is sick. But you are cured.'

'Yes,' the patient said slyly. 'But was it the kind of cure you wanted?'

Certainly not the kind of cure his father wanted. This strong-nosed aristocrat faced Freud in his study. He would not sit. He raged at Freud, unmoved among his books and pictures and trophies of travel, puffing away. 'What have you done to my son?' he cried. 'He's singing around the house, rejoicing in his depravity, crying aloud that he's glad he's a homosexual. You, sir, sitting there smug with your cigar – you call this a cure? You've merely justified his criminality. I've a good mind to take proceedings – I've never – I can't – I – '

'He threatened suicide, didn't he?'

'Yes, he did. And better if he'd carried out the threat.'

'Better that he lie dead at your feet,' Freud said in melodramatic singsong, 'than that he should be a homosexual. I've heard that before, baron. I've heard more than that. I've heard parents weeping because of actual suicides, not mere threats.'

'You, sir, would not appreciate the feelings of the head of an old and noble family of the Austro-Hungarian aristocracy.' Freud grinned slightly: this too was melodramatic. He said:

'I'm no aristocrat, if that's what you mean. I'm a middle-class Jew. My responsibility is not the dignity of the few but the happiness of the many. You resent your son's new-found happiness. You would prefer him to be dead. You make yourself very clear, baron.'

The baron, who did not really have anything to say except what could best be expressed in noises and even an act of violence to some of the exotic objects on this Jew doctor's desk, was saved by the entrance of his wife. The baroness knocked and at once entered. A woman of great beauty and distinction, her clothes and perfume from Paris. Freud stood. She said:

'I heard your voice, Franz. And yours too, Dr Freud. I felt – I think a mother has a right to say something about what is proper for her son. And what is proper is not torment, misery, guilt, screams about the desirability of death.'

'I cannot – ' the baron began. And then: 'I'll wait outside.'

'Good, Franz, wait outside. Dr Freud and I shall not be very long.' So the baron left, somewhat shakily, and the baroness with grace sat, saying: 'My son has talked to me. About what you said. Unfortunately he also talked to his father.'

'Unfortunately? I see nothing unfortunate in the telling of the truth.'

'Perhaps women are more ready for your brand of truth than are men, Dr Freud. If homosexuality is a fact of human existence – so be it. The world has lived with it long enough. Men, unfortunately, wish to see in their sons a kind of sculpture of themselves.'

'Of what they think are themselves.'

'That too is an unfortunate truth. Men carry an image like a banner. They see in mirrors only what they wish to see. Women are more realistic. I am content, Dr Freud, to see my son content. To be homosexual in Vienna is perhaps no worse than – I beg your pardon – '

He had seen it coming. 'Than being a Jew. The important thing, baroness, is to find out what you are and accept it.'

'Which, if I may say so, you yourself have done – against opposition – I mean you recognized your mission and you have not shrunk from its implications. You see, I know you, Dr Freud. I've heard of you – why else did I persuade my son to see you? – I've even read you – *The Interpretation of Dreams*, *The Psychopathology of Everyday Life*.

I read you with pleasure and was surprised. One ought not to read textbooks of psychology with the sort of delight that is proper to a novel.'

'My readability – if I may say so – is another of my faults, according to my colleagues. You do not object to my lighting a fresh cigar?'

'Not at all. It may seem pretentious of a mere laywoman to wonder how long the neglect can go on – '

'Hardly neglect, baroness. Every day brings some new attack.'

'Neglect of your achievement in your adopted city. In your own university. In New York I heard your name spoken with cautious reverence.'

'Indeed? New York? I didn't know.'

'Here, I note, lesser men have their professorships. You remain plain Dr Freud. If you will permit me, I must do something about changing this. I must speak to the Minister of Education – He owes me several favours – '

'The baroness is too kind.'

'Too kind? When you have done this for my son?'

'Not even the baroness's rank, beauty and distinction are likely to prevail against Viennese antisemitism. Dr Freud is a swine, baroness, and he is also a Jewish swine.'

'I detect a certain bitterness. You have waited too long. Your life is to be sweetened, Dr Freud.'

She rose, and Freud rose with her. She tripped to the door and opened it, calling:

'Franz!'

The baron came in, somewhat hangdog. He said: 'Perhaps I was wrong. Our family is surely great enough to ride over the conventions of the herd. And – as you say – Socrates, Michelangelo. I seem to be in your debt.'

'I think not, baron. At least, I hope not.'

He and the baroness smiled at each other. He bowed them both out.

At the *Stammtisch* they greeted him. 'Good evening, Herr Professor, you're looking well, Your Excellency, what will you have, Herr Professor?' Even the waiter bowed. He sat and spoke with some irony:

'Thank you, gentlemen. The role of sexuality has been recognized by His Imperial Majesty. The interpretation of dreams has been duly ratified by the Ministerial Council. The need for the psychoanalytic therapy of neuroses has been passed by a ninety per cent majority in parliament. I'm deeply gratified. I think I can afford a *large* coffee. Black, of course.'

The waiter bowed off. A man at the next table came over. He was fattish, voluble, plausible. He had the look of a younger Willett. He said:

'Excellency, as I should call you – Herr Professor, as I *will* call you – you will not know me or of me. I am Alfred Adler, a practising physician. I have – against opposition, I may say – used your methods. May I join you?'

'Delighted.'

Adler spoke confidentially and drew Freud away from the confraternity of the *Stammtisch*. He planted his chair between tables. Freud had to squeak his own chair nearer in order to hear him. He said:

'The technique of free association – regression – admirable. I cannot altogether accept the overriding role you give to sexuality. I feel there are deeper elements, best explained in terms of society rather than family.'

Freud showed shock. 'Deeper? Deeper than sex? My dear doctor, you appear to have been dabbling. You seem to be picking from my books the morsels acceptable by a limited taste, rejecting the whole banquet, if I may call it that – '

'You invite us to. You write, and your books are hard to obtain. You do not teach. Should you not be teaching?'

'You know our saying – three men make a college. On previous attempts to teach the whole doctrine of psychoanalysis I've had a maximum of two enrolments. No – no teaching.'

'I can guarantee you a minimum enrolment of four – all practising physicians. And one other, a young man, artistic, given to aesthetic theories based on what he has read of yours. He goes astray, I think. I feel you have a duty to put him right.'

'Duty. So now I have a duty to spread the word. Well – things have certainly changed.'

But when he arrived at the university building one day he found a number of loud young men carrying banners. KEIN VERBINDLICHES DEUTSCH and WIR VERWEIGERN DEUTSCH and so on. 'They're picketing, as you can see,' Adler said, coming up. 'They object to the imposition of the German language on all the educational establishments of the Empire. May I introduce you to your students – Dr Stekel, Dr Reitler, Dr Kahane. And this is young Otto Rank.'

'So,' young Rank gangled, almost drooled. 'It's you at last, really you.' The doctors grinned indulgently. They were thick solid men, young Rank was not. Freud said:

'Delighted, gentlemen. Perhaps this enforced exclusion comes as a blessing. Informality is forced upon us. I suggest you come to my apartment. A seminar, shall we call it? Perhaps we're well out of the lecture theatre – too many overtones of dogma, imperiousness, Mosaic authority. Come, it's a short walk.' And so they left the bannered noise. Freud went briskly ahead. Panting, Otto Rank caught up with him. Freud said:

'You're not a medical man, Herr er – '

'Rank, Rank. No, Excellency. I've become fascinated by the possibility of applying your discoveries – to art, literature, music – '

'But my discoveries are essentially of a therapeutic nature. I'm not here to inspire new schools of art and literary criticism, Herr er – '

'Rank, Rank, Otto Rank. But things are capable of explanation now that weren't before, Excellency. *Hamlet*, for instance – '

'*Hamlet*, what about *Hamlet*? No, don't tell me – not now. Rather tell me how you make a living.'

'I don't. I live on dry bread. There are rats in the attic. But things will improve – as the world learns to accept your philosophy.' He beamed in worship. Freud did not like that.

'*Philosophy*? I'm a doctor, not a philosopher. A doctor teaching other doctors.' He looked behind him to confirm this. To his astonishment –

The old man in the railway compartment frowned. 'How far can we trust memory? Was it really like that?'

'What, Sigmund, what's the matter?'

'Nothing, Martha, nothing. Go back to sleep.'

To his astonishment the four had swollen to eight and the number was still growing. Something to do with the picketing, university lecturers shut out. He stopped and waited for them to come up to him. 'I lack space at home,' he said. 'But I think I know where we can find it.'

It was in the park – which park? – in fine clear weather, the spring sun pleasantly warm on his neck. A group of about twenty mature students seated on the grass. Odd people came to look in amusement or surprise. ' – A hypothesis,' he said, 'which the highly materialistic nineteenth century – at last, thank God, over – forced upon us, made us accept as a truth. No disease without a physical cause – none – and so the varieties of madness had to await the postmortal classification of the pathologist, who would search for a cause in the dead nervous tissue and, of course, fail to find it. The profoundest mental disturbances were termed hysteria, and hysteria was not classifiable – it was an aberration suffered by women, to be alleviated by giving a dose of valerian to the womb, the *hystera*, which traditionally loathed the smell of valerian. Or else it was fancy, imagination, no true disease. My own researches led me to suspect that the mind is an entity as capable of affecting the body as the body is capable of affecting the mind – '

A child sucked a caramel on the periphery.

Indoors, later. Lecture theatre, Medical School. The group had grown, though not much.

' – I did not deliberately choose, out of the prurient predisposition of which I have been publicly accused, to find that the excitatory cause of most neuroses is sexual. The technique of free association, of allowing the patient to talk, to delve into his or her forgotten history, consistently brought to the surface sexual frustrations. Eventually it was evident to me that the aetiology lay far back, in early childhood, and was invariably of a sexual nature – '

Halfway through that one of the doctors raised his hand. Freud ignored the signal as long as he could. 'Yes?'

'Is it permitted to ask a question?'

'If you could wait till I've finished my discourse – '

'But there's never time. We need not only answers to specific questions but also discussion. Why can't we have discussion?' There was a quiet susurrus of agreement. Freud frowned. He said, though with reluctance:

'We need a different ambience – less formal.'

'We need a kind of club,' Adler said.

'The Vienna Psychoanalytic Club – a bizarre notion. It puts our science on the same level as chess, billiards and stamp collecting. Nevertheless. But first let me get back to my subject.' He was surprised by an unwonted irritability. 'Where was I? What was I saying?'

'The sexual aetiology of the neuroses,' Stekel said.

'I hate,' he was surprised at his anger, 'to be interrupted. I hate the disruption of my train of thought. It's painful – positively traumatic. Ah. Some event in early childhood. Of a sexual nature, shocking, bundled away into the dark cellar of the unconscious, had, I discovered, to be brought back to the consciousness of the patient – always painfully, always with difficulty – '

Imperious, Mosaic. Adler and Stekel caught each other's eye and faintly smiled.

Otto Rank. He ate ravenously. Martha, not eating, Freud, merely drinking coffee, looked indulgently on. 'More potatoes, Martha,' Freud said.

'No no no no no no, Frau Professor, Excellency. I'm already – You're much too good – much too – '

'Eat, eat, child,' Martha said.

'You make me – so much – one of the family – '

'Yes, interesting,' Freud said. 'What are you? Son? Brother? Sons revolt against their fathers. Young as you are, I think you must be a brother – a younger brother – ' But did not Rank himself, and perhaps Martha too, catch in their nostrils, over the scent of the herbed veal, a whiff of prophecy? The promise of a revolt, a minute crack in the ceiling plaster?

'Was it adequate,' Freud asked, 'what you found in your pay packet?'

'You shouldn't really – I should be more than honoured to serve unpaid – to be secretary is, really – '

'Take what you can while you can, Otto. I foresee no immediate great future for our science. None of us will become rich. At the moment we ride on a temporary ripple of success. At fifty I expected to be settled, comfortable – '

'Aren't we comfortable, Sigmund?'

'Thanks to you, my dear, very. But settled? A discreditable movement with a few followers, in a town that considers itself to be one of the pillars of Western civilization but is really no more than a hidebound gossipy malicious ignorant concatenation of dribbling yokels.'

'You say this after fifty years? This town has become your mother, Sigmund.'

'No, no, my father. A father I'd dearly love to – Never mind.'

'On what day,' replete Rank asked, 'is your birthday, Excellency?'

'Saturday.'

'Ah, I wasn't sure. The other members thought that – well, on the day of the meeting nearest your birthday, they ought – I was asked to give you this before the meeting.' Freud had wondered what the flat parcel was that Rank had placed under his chair. Rank reached for it and handed it over. Touched, uneasy, Freud opened it. He stood, nearer the corner lamp, the better to see what it was. It was a carved medallion of Oedipus. There was a legend in Greek. He translated it aloud. 'He who unravelled the riddle of the Sphinx – ' He gulped. 'And was a man most mighty.' His eyes filmed. 'You remember?' he said to Martha.

'I remember that you told me as a young man – '

'I dreamed it. In this form. This is. I had better sit down. The tribute to – ' He sat; he had a faint sense of trauma. ' – A greatness I had no hope of achieving. I'm – overwhelmed.'

'Dr Adler thought you might be,' Rank beamed.

Adler did, did he? 'The time?' Freud asked.

'Eight twenty.'

'Ten minutes to recompose myself. To prepare calm words of thanks. To appear – less overwhelmed.'

Ten of them in the consulting room. Round an oval table. Kahane, Adler, Stekel, Reitler, Federn, Hitschmann, Meisl, Frey, Rank as secretary, Oedipus himself. Adler spoke eloquently:

' – Hence it seems logical to regard the family as a mere microcosm of the bigger group called society and consider how far the psychoanalytical method can be applied to its problems. The neuroses of society, as we observe, seem to derive more from the struggle for power than from sexual repression. The time has not perhaps quite come for a reorientation of our view of the primary cause of all human neuroses, whether manifested on the analyst's couch or on the battlefield of the class struggle, but increasingly one suspects that behind sex lies power, that the struggle for possession of the mother is a small figure of the power struggle in society. We need more evidence. With more evidence a theory can doubtless be constructed.'

Freud did not like this. He was surprised at the phlegmy resonance of his reply. He sounded truculent. 'It seems to me, Dr Adler, that you propose so radical a reorientation that you cut at the very roots of the whole science – '

'May it yet be called a science?' Adler said.

'In so far as it is a consistent body of knowledge with what may be termed demonstrable laws of cause and effect – but this is a matter of mere terminology. What is incontrovertible is the Oedipus element.' Oedipus, man most mighty, gleamed from a side table.

'Nothing,' Adler said, 'is incontrovertible. I claim, as you yourself once claimed, the right to look deeper. My instinct tells me that in man, and in woman, the two sexes coexist and fight with each other. It is possible, just possible, that some of our neuroses derive from overdevelopment of the female element, in both sexes, *both* – when it is the masculine element that enables the individual soul to prevail in society.'

'You are excessively concerned with society, Dr Adler. Our primary duty as therapists is to the individual – '

'And you are not concerned *enough* with society, Herr Professor. You express impatience when I mention the political movements of the day. You refuse to read Friedrich Engels, Karl Marx – '

'Dr Adler, I can't take on the class war. It will take me my whole life to win the sex war.'

'I cannot,' Stekel began, 'go with Dr Adler all the way – '

'Of course not. He has no way. He wanders through a forest and thinks he is on the highroad.'

' – Nevertheless, I feel that, outside our consulting rooms, where we attempt to look into the narrow tract of the individual human mind – '

'Narrow? You call it narrow?'

' – Outside, as I say, there is a big world which we studiously ignore. We are surely equipped with a technique for analysing the ills of society. At these weekly meetings of our club I become – shall I say, oppressed – with the sense of a certain narrowness.'

'That word again. You're obsessed with it.'

'We're bourgeois Viennese Jews,' Stekel said, 'with bourgeois Viennese patients – '

'I,' Reitler said, 'happen to be a bourgeois Viennese Catholic.'

'The only one,' Stekel said. 'The only one in our midst who seeks his patients from among the working class is Alfred Adler – '

'Picking up Dr Stekel's term *narrow*,' Kahane said, 'I think the true narrowness of our movement lies in the fact that it seems to lack the power, or authority, to cross frontiers. There is an incestuous quality about it – perhaps inevitably, as it is founded on incest. It was inaugurated by a Semite, it is followed by Semites – '

'Viennese bourgeois Semites,' Stekel said.

'One Viennese bourgeois Catholic.'

'It needs,' Kahane said, 'the big blowing wind of the world outside.' Freud said nothing but was aware of a disturbing inner motion like colliding waves of stomach gas. 'Moses was not concerned solely with teaching the word to the twelve tribes of Israel. He was overjoyed when the doctrine of the one eternal God spread to Balaam, an unbelieving sorcerer to whom God spoke through a donkey – '

'And which donkey,' Freud said, 'will God use to speak the truth about our *science* to this world of the big blowing wind? You have heard the words of one great man of this world outside – Professor Aschaffenburg at the Baden-Baden Congress said – said what, Otto?'

Before Rank could find the cutting, Adler spoke the words verbatim, with, Freud thought, relish: ' "Freud's method is wrong in most cases, objectionable in many, and superfluous in all." '

Freud glared at him, saying: 'You see that the bigness of this world outside, its non-Jewishness, its non-Vienneseness, does not predispose it to the speaking of sense, or even charity. The donkeys will go on braying. They won't convey the word of the Lord. Not for a long long time. Better we explore in depth – however narrowly, Dr Stekel.'

There was a knock at the consulting-room door. Reitler showed no surprise, but the others did. Rank got up to answer it. A young man entered. 'It was agreed, you will all remember,' said Reitler, 'that Dr Eitingon – ' A handsome young man, of the world, unshabby, rather different from – 'My friend, Dr Max Eitingon, from Zürich.'

Eitingon had the look of a man who felt he ought to get on his knees to the great Oedipus. 'You must forggggive – My ttttrain was – At last at last I have the – ' He could not get the word *honour* out, but the glottal spasm showed it was in his throat. 'I have already ppp followed your mmmmethods in Zzzzzz – '

'In Zürich?' smiled Freud. 'In the big blowing world of Swiss medicine? You are heartily welcome, Dr Eitingon. Join us.' And the smile, mixed with a scruple of malice, was turned on the others. 'It seems, gentlemen, that we're an international body at last.'

'I bbbbring ggggreetings from Dr Jjjjj – '

'Who?'

With a great effort, 'Jung.'

'I regret,' Freud said, 'that I've never heard of him.'

'Oh, you will, Dr Ffff, you will.'

Meanwhile, the work went on. The plump male patient on the couch spoke of death. 'Blessed release, doctor. If only I weren't such a coward – '

'You don't want to die. You've no reason to wish to die. The death wish is a disguised form of something different and deeper.'

'I want to die.'

'I wish to go back with you to a time when you were very small. Don't be afraid to talk about it. Something to do with your mother. You were very young. You were perhaps in bed with your mother.'

The patient was agitated. 'I knew I shouldn't – I shouldn't – I put my hand – it was really only my fingers – one finger – '

Freud was ruthless. 'You entered where you had come out. Do you understand me?'

'Oh God, it was wrong, I deserve to – '

'How could you know it was wrong? You were only a child. Now let me revert to one of your dreams – the one that you're always dreaming – in which you enter a new house but one you're sure you've been in before –'

'Oh my God – it's not possible – '

'It *is* possible. I think you've hit on the meaning. You dream of entering a house you shouldn't know but *do* know. And, according to what you told me before, you want to stay in the new house for ever. And yet it's not a new house.'

'It can't be – '

'*It is*. Your mother's womb. That's where you want to return. Darkness, silence, unconsciousness, loss of identity. The state before birth. The state after death. You don't want to die, you want to get back into your mother. You need a mother substitute – a wife. That will put the thought of dying out of your head.'

'You're,' he gulpgroaned, 'sure?'

'You may want to kill, of course. That depends on the wife you choose. Or who chooses you. But you won't want to die.' Then Freud lighted a cigar. He was still smoking that cigar when he went in to lunch. He was also waving a letter which had come by the noon courier. He cried:

'Here's a strange thing, Martha. This man this other man mentioned – I'd heard nothing of him before – well, he's sent me this cutting – also a letter – '

'Yes, dear. Put out that cigar, dear. Sit down. Eat.'

He put his cigar down on a plate. Martha tutted and whisked it away to the kitchen. He read the cutting aloud to the children, who were not interested and certainly did not understand.

' – I give Herr Professor Doktor Freud the highest possible credit for originality of approach and unique achievement in the field. I challenge Professor Aschaffenburg to state truthfully the extent of his knowledge of Freud's work. I believe it to be non-existent. His impudent attack at the Baden-Baden Congress of Neurologists and Psychiatrists – '

Martha came in with a hot dish – veal cutlets, noodles. She started to serve.

'And a most effusive letter. He wants to visit me. Well – the Gentiles have at last heard the word of the Lord. Carl Jung. A good strong name. No nonsense about it – '

'Eat, Sigmund.'

'Going to drop in, he says. Take a chance. Blow in like a wind of admiration and, if he may say so, affection. Martha, I'm not very hungry.'

'Eat, Sigmund, do you hear me? Eat.'

The children gratefully joined in. Eat eat eat. So humbly he obeyed. 'Eat,' said Anna.

'I *am* eating. But there are some things more important than food.' Nobody took any notice. He ate.

The lecture he gave shortly after, which was on the psychology of humour, got a number of guffawing music-hall responses. Any serious soul doctor coming in unwarned would deplore the apparent frivolity. If this Carl Jung, for instance, came from straitlaced Zürich.

'Another example. The Jews are so often referred to as the children of Israel that one day a little boy said to his rabbi: "Didn't the grown-ups ever do anything?" The shock there is the shock of discovering a truth – the truth being that the basic meaning of a word has been forgotten and the secondary meaning has lost its metaphorical power. In stories about the traditional mad town of Chelm, some forty miles east of Lublin, the shock is the shock of relief that there are people stupider than ourselves. For example – the rabbi of Chelm visited a prison, and there he heard all but one of the inmates insist on their innocence. So he came back, held a council of wise men, and recommended that Chelm have *two* prisons – one for the guilty, the other for the innocent. Again – the wise men of Chelm began to argue about which was more important to the world – the moon or the sun. The heated dissension was quelled only by the chief wise man's ruling: "The *moon* must be more important than the sun, because without the light of the moon our nights would be so dark that we could not see anything. The sun, on the other hand, shines only by day – when we don't need it." Or again – A farmer, riding home in his wagon, picked up a pedlar who was carrying a heavy burden on his shoulder. The pedlar sat next to the farmer, but he still kept the heavy burden on his shoulder. "Why don't you put your bundle in the back of the cart?" the farmer asked. "It's nice enough your horse is schlepping me," said the pedlar, "without me adding my bundle to his burden." '

An immensely tall man, soldierly of carriage, had entered at the back. He heard Jewish humour and smiled with his mouth. Freud knew who it was. He brought his discourse to an end:

'You can see how jokes like these cleansed, during the long tribulations of the Jews, feelings of aggression – of which laughter is the best solvent. The act of laughter induces a sense of philosophical balance. Laughter is shock, but always salutary shock. Thank you.' They applauded. That again was not right. It would give altogether the wrong impression to –

'His Excellency Herr Professor Doktor Sigmund Freud?'

'So, at last, Dr Jung.' Freud's warm paw clasped the chilly Swiss one. 'Well. Well. Do you walk?'

'Oh yes, I walk.'

'Let us then walk.'

They walked.

The hall hired for the rally of workers is still hung with Christmas streamers. Bok, Chud and Vol, as they have already announced themselves to be in song, have sunk their hot faces into steins of Milwaukee beer. A little band plays. The workers, men and women, dance and sing:

We're having a socialist party,
With non-ideological song too.
A joke and a game
Will be always the same
Whatever the group you belong to.
We're having a socialist party
With just a small measure of drinking.
The taste of a dram
Isn't altered a damn
By your mode of political thinking.
The effect of a whisky or brandy or gin
Depends on the mood not the movement you're in.
If you are a broker
Or if you're broke,
A Coca–
Cola's a Coke.

We don't need a party directive
To render our party effective.
Some esculent stuff
And a glass are enough
To make merry and jolly and bright.
So we're having the heartiest socialist party
Tonight!

Where have these simple workers learned such acrobatic skills? Some, we see, are in the costumes of their national origin. This would appear to contradict the doctrine of proletarian uniformity. They should all be in drab grey but they are not.

We don't need a Stalin or Lenin
To get working women and men in
A mood to rejoice
And raise rafters and voice
In uproarious glorious row.
We are having the heartiest socialist party
Right now!

And here is Trotsky. He mounts the platform where the band plays. The band stops playing at Bok's signal. Bok raises his arms.

'Comrades! Exiled from his native land to the hospitable shores of this most monstrous of capitalistic monsters, Comrade Trotsky is among us!' There are cheers. Trotsky prepares to orate, but his words are drowned at once by a song in his honour:

Trotsky's in New York!
Let his name be hurled
Higher than the Wool-
Worth Building.
Trotsky's in New York,
Stronger than a bull,
Showing us a world
Worth building.
Spilling out his wisdom like a corn-
ucopia,
Fiercer than a hurricane,
Preaching an American-born
Utopia.
Everybody walk

With his head up high
To the sky the dawn
Is gilding.
For Trotsky's in New York!

'Comrades,' cries Trotsky, 'time is short – '

But 'The Finns!' cry the Finns, and the Finns dance with much stamping.

'Comrades, as I said, the time is short – '

'The Russians!' And the Russians hammer the floor with wild cries of the steppes. Trotsky sits down, exasperated. The dance ends and he rises.

'Comrades, dear comrades, let us waste no more time – '

'The Turks!' And the Turks whirl like dervishes, banging belltrees. Wearily, at the end, Trotsky once more rises, but the song in his honour is resumed. Everybody walk COMRADES With his head up high OUR TIME to the sky the dawn IS SHORT is gilding SO LET US NOT WASTE ANY MORE OF IT For Trotsky's in New York!

And now the crowd is ready for Trotsky, but Trotsky does not know whether it is ready for him or not. Still, he tries again.

'Comrades – '

But a lone Mexican appears in shabby shirt, torn trousers, moth-eaten sombrero, with a battered guitar. He sings:

Mexico Mexico
A good place to die
Is Mexico,
Under a harsh blue sky
Where the condors fly.
Mexico Mexico
Oppression is rife
In Mexico,
Rifle and whip and knife
Are a fact of life.
Life is a bed of cacti
Sweetened by sour tequila,
A rancid enchilada,
And cucarachas as friends.
Everything ends
In Mexico Mexico,
An excellent place to die.

Come some day and try
Mexico.

Trotsky is, for some reason he cannot understand, transfixed by this song. Yet nobody else seems to have heard it, and its singer has faded on the last ill-tuned chord of his guitar. Chud says:

'They're waiting, comrade.'

'You said time was short,' Vol says. 'Why waste it?'

'I was waiting till he'd finished his song.'

'Who?'

'The Mexican.'

'We have no Mexicans.'

'Are you mad?' says Trotsky.

'Speak, man.' So he gets up, puzzled and shaken, and tries again.

'Comrades – '

'Get back to Moscow,' cries a heckler.

'I would if I could and I will yet. I am an unwilling exile from my native land.'

'So are we all.' Another heckler. 'What's so special about you?'

'Comrades, this is no time for levity. America stands on the brink of a terrible catastrophe. Your unenlightened leaders propose to plunge you into a wasteful war, to spill the blood of the workers to the greater glory of the American dollar. 1917 – a year of projected infamy can be a year of proletarian victory if the American workers stand firm and cry "No war!" ' And he orchestrates those two last words with a double crash on the speaker's table with the copy of Marx's *Capital* that, like a church Bible, lies there.

'No war!' cry many.

'War!' cry many.

'Those of you who shriek "War!" – do you know what the word means?'

'Sure,' shouts another heckler. 'Blood and slaughter. Bang bang bang.'

'You are deliberately shutting your eyes to the true nature of war as conceived by the capitalists. They posit an enemy who is no enemy. They themselves are the enemy, wherever they are – in New York, London, Berlin, Paris. They ask you, they entreat you, finally they force you to kill your own brothers. German workers, American workers, French, Austrian, British workers – does it matter that they speak different languages? Do they not possess the common tongue of common oppression? The German workers are your brothers. Do you wish to kill them?'

'Nooooooo!'

'Yeeeeees! Down with the Heinies!'

'Peace. Peace. Peace. I, Leon Trotsky, demand of you workers, in the name of the international solidarity of labour, that you workers demand peace.'

'Peace!'

'War!'

A formidable woman gets up from her chair and motions that the female workers rise too. There are jeers from the warmongers in the assembly. She silences them with a single bark. Then she leads the pure sweet women's voices in an *a cappella* plea:

Peace, perfect peace.
Keep our boys at home.
Don't let's have them roam-
ing away.
Peace, perfect peace.
Though the drums may beat,
Loving hearts entreat
Them to stay.
Whirr your wings like a silver dove,
Cooooooooooo about love.
Peace, perfect peace –
All the workers beg,
And a job with reg-
ular pay.
Peace to earn
Dollars to burn:
Peace for the USA.

But Trotsky breaks in on the last chord and yells: 'No! Not that kind of peace, comrades. The peace that means sabotage of American war plans, yes, the peace that means refusal to fight in a capitalistic war, yes. But the class war must continue, be intensified, the war that recognizes no national boundaries, that is not fought on foreign fields but here here HERE. America – what is it but a word, a noise, an abstraction? There are two nations only, the nation of labour and the nation of capital. Prepare for the first and last battle between them. But first – keep out of the capitalist war!'

The greater number of the workers cheer, but a big burly labour leader gets up and speaks:

'Brothers, you know me – Chuck Brown. I salute Brother Trotsky as a sincere and energetic worker for the cause of labour. But he knows nothing of the needs of American labour.'

'Labour,' Trotsky thrusts in, 'is international. American labour is a terminological contradiction.'

'American labour, I say. The American working class is not prepared to tolerate foreign aggression.' Cheers and counter-cheers, *war* versus *peace*. 'I and my colleagues in the munitions factories of these United States know where our duty lies – '

'Know which side your bread's buttered, you mean.' A thin hard penetrating voice.

'Throw that man out. Duty, I repeat, duty. Our duty is to provide the supplies and weapons for the fine flower of American youth to hurl against the German aggressor.' Cheers and counter-cheers, *war* versus *peace*. 'The German aggressor, fellow workers. The German workers are solidly behind their blood-soaked Emperor and his blood-soaked Imperial General Staff – '

'That is not true,' Trotsky cries. 'The worker's revolution is already fomenting in Germany – '

A man like a whippet whips into the hall, breathless. He carries a sheet of paper. He hands it to Brown. Brown reads it with well-simulated horror.

'Brothers,' he cries, 'I have just received a most terrifying piece of news. The submarines of the Imperial German Navy, armed with torpedoes of a new and diabolically ingenious design, have sunk in the North Atlantic the United States merchant vessel *John Hancock*. All hands lost, brothers. Our brothers sent to a watery grave. Millions of dollars' worth of United States manufactured goods at the bottomless depths of the Atlantic. Are we going to tolerate that, fellow workers?'

Desperately Trotsky carves into the loud indignation. 'I saw that paper. That paper is blank. I have studied the shipping lists in the New York Public Library. There is no such ship – '

'Smash the windows of the German Consulate!'

'Hang the consular staff!'

But another worker goes up to Brown and says, loud and clear: 'We know you, friend. In the pay of the bosses. Agent provocateur –'

'What's your name, friend?' Brown asks.

'Ernst Schnitzler.'

'Where were you born, friend?'

'Trenton, New Jersey.'

'Where was your old man born?'

'That's his business.'

'Where was he born?'

'Frankfurt.'

'Deutschland?'

'*Ja.*'

At Brown's violent instigation the warmonger workers, and many who were, but three minutes ago, all for peace, attack Schnitzler. Brown deputes three toughs to look after Trotsky and his colleagues. These three merely have to look viciously at Bok, Vol and Chud for them to retreat with dignity. Trotsky is a different proposition. Trotsky stays and looks truculent. The workers go out singing brutally, bearing Schnitzler as if to hang him, while the pacific ladies beat them with tiny or not so tiny fists, also singing.

MEN

We don't want just war
We want a *just* war
Let the trumpets roar
But for a *just* war
Smite the Germans
Fight the Germans
Show them more and more
What a bloody war is for.
Let your voices roar
But for a *just* war
As we said before
We want a *just* war.
What is justice?
That's a musty s-
ort of thing to ask.
The task in store
Is fighting in a just just war,
Just war
Just war
Just

WOMEN

Peace perfect peace
Keep our boys at home
Don't let's have them roam-
ing away.
Peace perfect peace
Though the drums may beat
Loving hearts entreat
Them to stay.
Whirr your wings
Like a silver dove
Cooooooooo
About love.
Peace perfect peace
All the workers beg
And a job with reg-
ular pay.
Peace to earn
Dollars to burn
Peace for the
USA.

* * *

The first floods did not seem so very terrible. On 3 April, the day after Paul Bartlett's departure for a place unnamed, water came swirling in over the Battery, the Hudson roared and swiped at the quays, the East River sloggered at the United Free Nations Building and dislodged its bas-relief emblem on the riverside wall (a bronze pregnant female figure with arms raised towards a solar cornucopia). The waters were quick to recede in the normal tidal rhythm, leaving streets no dirtier than usual, but the timider citizens began their exodus. On 11 April there were earth tremors in the Bedford–Stuyvesant district of Brooklyn, an area of the borough habituated to calamity. There was also water at waist height on Fifth Avenue, swift however to go gurgling down the gutters. Bad things were happening abroad but, in the interests of maintaining American tranquillity, few of these were being divulged through the regular channels of communication. Still, stories of the entire destruction of Auckland, New Zealand, were leaking in, as well as the deaths of several coastal towns on the Malay archipelago. As for San Francisco, already totally evacuated, there was as yet no report of unusual seismic activity. This, to many, seemed more ominous than tranquillizing. Nature was dabbling, yawning, taking her time.

At eleven o'clock on the evening of 12 April, Vanessa and Val and Professor Frame were packed and ready. Their plane did not leave till four in the morning, but Vanessa, the cool, the careful, never liked leaving things till the last moment. Besides, there was the task of recharging Frame's batteries for the car journey to Lindsay Airport. On the aircraft he would be able to plug into one of the galley points; at CAT he would be permanently set up in his own bedroom–office. Permanently? He gave himself four months. The machine strapped to his body was an ingenious device which, with the aid of the catalyst DCT3, converted oxides to oxygen which rhythmically flooded his bloodstream but enabled him to expire the wastes orally, so that he had a normal supply of breathed-out gases for the speech process. But his heart, he knew, was not going to last much longer. He was on the blepophone now, saying goodbye to Muriel Pollock, whose fat face was clearly tear-streaked on the bleposcreen. Meanwhile Val bit his nails.

'What time do we leave here?' he asked.

'About two thirty,' Vanessa answered. 'Why?'

'I think I'll go into town. A last look. A last drink with, you know, friends.'

'You'll do nothing of the kind.'

'Let him,' glared Frame, putting down the handset and automatically switching off poor Muriel's image. 'Let him. Let him be late if he wishes. We shan't wait. We have our orders.'

'I shan't be late.' Val glared back. 'You old bastard.'

'Father,' Vanessa cried in distress. 'Val. Oh, why can't you both – '

Val stamped out. Frame said: 'As the word bastard has been used, let it be used again. Why do you say you love that bastard?'

'I don't know. Love isn't a thing you analyse.'

'I'll tell you why. You love him as a chunk of raw material you think you can mould. Pygmalion and Galatea in reverse.'

'Who? Never heard of them. Oh, I don't know – I think it's because he's – well, so chaotic – '

'Exactly. You want to do something with that chaos.'

'No, no, not that. There's something in me that – responds to chaos. To imagination, indiscipline, call it what you like. Or perhaps to a different kind of organization than science can provide. You know what I mean.'

'Poetry. Verbal narcotics.'

'It's not altogether sincere of you,' she said primly, 'to sneer at narcotics.'

'I hope he gets drowned.'

'The tides are quiet tonight. Because of the winds or something.'

'Beaten up, then. Knifed.'

'You *are* an old bastard,' Vanessa said. The word sounded terrible on her cool tongue. 'You like him really. You're more alike than you'll admit.'

'There was only one man for you.'

'I never liked him.'

'Never mind, never mind.' Frame closed his eyes, very weary. 'I'll sleep a little.'

So Vanessa, troubled greatly in one part of her mind but coldly organized in another, completed the packing of her hand luggage. Some book to read on the journey, a book totally unconnected with the project, a book chaotic or submissive to a different kind of organization than science could provide? She looked at the hundreds of books they were leaving behind. She picked out one – a volume of poems by Val, his first publication, a private printing done in Iowa City at the state university's Windhover Press. The little collection was called *Scarfskin*. 'Not my flesh,' he had told her, 'not even my skin. The parings of my skin. I was getting small things out of the way in preparation for the big things.' But the big things had never been written – only pitiable romances based on hypotheses scientifically untenable. She read a poem at random:

Why would you not yield
As the field to the plough
As the cow to the milking
As the silk to the weaving
As the leaves to the wind
As the skin to the peeling
The bell to the pealing
Pealing pealing
Our lives away?

She wept a little. She had no great capacity for tears, but she wept a little. And she packed the little book in her little bag.

Lynx was bright and bloody tonight, seeming to stand like an ornamental artefact on the pinnacle of the Outride Building, balanced, if you looked from one particular angle, like a blood orange on the tip of a finger. Val stood and looked an instant from Fifth Avenue. A group of yellow-robed monks, hair shaven, gave exotic song to the heavenly body, banging little drums and tinkling antique cymbals. In St Patrick's Cathedral, interdenominational or panchristian since the Fourth Vatican Council had dissolved Roman Catholicism in favour of a kind of Hookerian faith (the *Laws of Ecclesiastical Polity* man, children. Never heard of him? Never mind) which, in the face of the menace of oil-rich Islam, might reconcile all Christian sects, a night service was in progress and crammed to the doors. Val, unseduced by religion, went to Jack's Tavern on West 46th Street, there to find his friend Willett in Falstaffian flood. Willett, who had recently completed a small acting stint for ABC television (he had played Orson Welles in a dramatization – somewhat indiscreet, seeing the need to keep public panic down – of the creation of that ancient radio adaptation of the other Wells's *War of the Worlds*, and its devastating effect on a public whose naiveté the present American public had long outgrown) and was in funds, was drinking away and inveighing against a Calvin Gropius rally that was being televised:

'Shitabed scoundrel, slapsauce druggel, jobbernol gnatsnapper, codshead looby, turdgut.' But many of the customers told him to hold it, shut it, pipe down, quiet friend, they were interested. The point of interest was that Gropius's congregation was restive, shouting back, not willing to accept his slavery to the Bible and his attempts to impose that slavery on his auditors. To Val, what words of Gropius got through seemed not unreasonable, granted his theological premise:

'There are times when God warns – and if you will not have it that it is God directly sending us these prodigies in the sky and on the earth, at least admit that times of fear have come upon us – warns, I say, each and every one of us to take stock of our lives, examine our faults, consider that mankind approaches a judgement – ' He tapped his Bible vigorously and tried to recite from the Book of Revelations, but his voice was overcome by the collective yell of a huge block of opponents that, well drilled, was on its feet, shouting slogans, waving banners. LIVEDOG, said the banners, LIVEDOG LIVEDOG, and the slogans took up the name – 'Live for Livedog, kill for Livedog.' Val saw that the name was compounded of God and Devil backwards. He nodded to himself – a science fiction situation. Evil? That didn't perhaps come into it. The new god was beyond morality, the ultimate supernatural to be appeased. Lynx was his body.

'Where's this?' he asked the bartender.

'Sacramento.'

California, seedbed of crank faiths. He watched the screen intently, and even Willett, despite odd grumbles about calfshead boggergulls, had eyes of interest now on it. The meeting was being disrupted by the Livedog body, but a purely secular element had crept into the proceedings – young men and women stripping naked and engaging in bacchanalian acts; frotting, mock or real sodomy, fellation, to the tune of 'Leap on me, Lynx'. The scene was cut off rapidly, and commercials supervened, the sanity of salesmanship – cars, carboats, boatcars, travelboxes, realtors seeking to buy not sell. 'Out of here,' Willett said.

'You know I'm off tonight?' said Val.

'Off? Where?' Val saw two Lynxes in Willett's great bloodshot eyes.

'CAT. Center of Advanced Technology. Where I don't know. Highly secret.'

'Off, then.' Willett nodded. They were walking towards Sixth Avenue, which had once been called the Avenue of the Americas. 'The wind,' he said. 'It's changing. There'll be trouble before the night's out. Man is born to trouble, yes yes. In my fifty-five years I've seen as much as any man. I can smell something on that wind. Lynx, cat, catastrophe. Is there going to be an end of trouble?'

'I don't know,' Val lied, loyal to something – her? 'I'm wanted as a kind of literary recorder of this moon project.'

'What's this? People escaping to the moon?'

'Not escaping exactly. The moon, I understand, may leave earth's orbit and become a satellite of Lynx. Think of what this means to scientists. Science fictionists, too. Lynx snuffles off, its moon with it, scientists observing, busy as hell. Me with them.'

'You should sound excited.'

'Oh hell, I don't want to go. I'm an earthman, like you.'

Willett grunted. 'Let's go and eat. Something gross and sustaining. Beef pudding and sausages and stewed tripe and jam roll. Great grumbling spuds roast in their overcoats. Beer by the quart.'

'Quart?'

'You won't have heard of quarts. Too young.' He quoted loudly to the crowded street:

> 'Oh I have been to Ludlow fair
> And left my necktie God knows where
> And carried halfway home or near
> Pints and quarts of Ludlow beer.'

A young Teutprot did a lip fart at him. 'Lob-dotterel,' said Willett evenly. 'Noddypeak simpleton. Idle lusk. Saucy coxcomb. Look,' he said to Val, 'I don't like that at all.'

'Christ,' Val said, 'I know her.' An alley off West 46th Street, full of upturned garbage cans, torn garbage bags, refuse blowing on the growing wind, was also full of fighting youth, girls as well as boys. One of the girls was Tamsen Disney, scanty clothes near torn off her, not alone in that. 'I won't,' she was screeching, 'I won't.' One of the boys, a leering Teutprot, was dressed in a jersey that said LIVEDOG. Who the hell made those, wondered Val in a segment of his mind. Christ, was commerce behind everything, even the end of the world? There were one or two opposing sweatshirts marked LYNX worn by blacks. 'Sacrifice,' panted and grinned a Livedogger, 'sacrifice, baby. The loving Lord demands it.' Willett picked up a rolling empty whisky flagon by its single finger ear. 'We can't do a damned thing,' said Val, fearful. Willett said nothing; he waded in; hit. 'Wrong side,' panted Val as Willett hit out at a black. Tamsen seemed to be on the black side. 'Any side will do,' roared Willett. A point in the struggle, in which language had been reduced to pinpoint monosyllables of outrage and pain, came in which Tamsen was clutched quite naked in Val's arms and clutched back at by dithering fingers. Tamsen did not seem to recognize her temporary saviour, for she hit out at him with teeny fists. 'It's me, idiot,' expired Val. 'Val Brodie.' She screamed, for some reason, all the more for that. Willett was doing well, roaring Shakespeare or somebody. Then approaching whistles pierced like toothache. 'Jesus Lynx,' somebody tried to yell. 'It's the fucking millies.'

There were grey uniforms as well as blue. The militia, the minutemen, the emergies, the specials, some fucking thing. Val and Willett were quick to be grabbed, Willett, whisky flagon brandished in air, bashed ouch ouch on the shin with a nightstick. The sticktrick ready for Val Val opposed with desperate arms, crying: 'We tried to stop it. Look at us. Christ. We're not. Kids.' Kids streaking off, torn and limping, were frankly shot at, gun raised, eye closed. 'O Jesus, let them live,' moaned Val. A black van had drawn up. Tamsen, naked, well mauled by cops' hands, was one of the first in. 'In in, God damn it, in, bastards.' Val followed Willett, hopping, crying feebly now about fucking blasted shitabed scrotflogs or something.

It was black as hell inside the van, full of noises, including the odd cry from, presumably, Tamsen: 'Hands off, fucking pig,' and so on. Then she, or some other girl, seemed to throw a fit, all threshing legs and dangerous fingernails. Some boy or other howled high-pitched like a woman. 'Dark dark dark,' quoted Willett, 'we all go into the dark.' Somebody opposite responded urbanely: 'The vacant interstellar spaces, the vacant into the vacant.' Others, angered, shouted to the quoters to shut their asses. 'Thou toilest not,' said Willett for some reason. 'Few others of like eminence go backwards. Throw sdrow. No, it won't work. Notlim. No. Still, try it. Intellectual sustenance for our long road.' He seemed crazed, delirious, but calmly so. They couldn't at first tell whether they were going downtown or up.

Downtown, well downtown, they knew when the van stopped and the door was pulled open. City Hall area, place of courts and lockups. 'Out out, you little beauties,' sneered a one-eyed red-haired sergeant, cap back to look like a black halo. Val knew sudden panic. He shouldn't be here, he had a plane to catch, it was all a mistake. 'Look, sergeant,' he said desperately. 'I'm looking, me boyo,' and he stamped a black boot on Val's aesthete's sandal. Val limped in, howling. In, he found a great hydraulic hoist without door which rose creaking.

'Tide time,' said Willett with nodding satisfaction, sort of, looking out at the East River. The water was rising, wind-lashed. 'Wait for no man.' Tamsen was shivering. Val took off his jacket and draped it about her. 'Why,' she said, 'it's Professor Brodie. He gave me an A plus,' she told the others. Nobody was interested. The hoist stopped at the third floor, brightly lighted. 'Out,' cried the accompanying sergeant. 'Look,' Val said, 'I demand to see the lieutenant, the captain. I've urgent business, I've a plane to catch. A letter with the presidential seal. Here, somewhere.' He reached towards his inside jacket pocket, meaning Tamsen's right breast. 'Okay, feller,' said the sergeant, 'we'll bleep the President right away.' Then Val remembered that Vanessa, the faultlessly efficient, had both their letters of authorization in her leather carrying file. 'Let me at least – ' And then he let it go, arms dropping, body drooping. Bleep my wife. My wife? The clever woman, Dr Frame.

They were not formally charged. That, they were told, would come in the morning. They were shoved ten in a cell, white walls, open clogged toilet, ineradicable zoo smell, men together, Tamsen off somewhere with his jacket and his pack of five cheap cigars. Willett took out a long silver torpedo and released a cigar, not at all cheap, of aromatic gooseturd colour. He also produced a nailfile and sawed the monster in half. He gave Val the half with the round end. He struck a kitchen match on his behind. They smoked. Their eight fellows snarled or moaned, black and Teutprot together, LIVEDOG confronting LYNX. 'Go, devil,' Willett said. And then, laughing, 'Toilest.'

'What am I to do?' Val near-sobbed. 'What the hell am I to do? They'll go without me.'

'And without me, for that matter,' Willett said evenly. 'Don't worry. There's much of interest still in the world. *I* won't go without you.'

Soon they slept. Later, Vanessa, up in the air, was going through the sounds and motions of sobbing but gave out few tears. Dry ducts, deficient ducts, no room for tears in her trade, but her distress was genuine. Her father, seat turned into a bed, respirator wheezing away, put a dry mottled hand on her lily one and said softly:

'Nothing could be done. He was terribly knocked about. Unconscious. They gave him an hour to live.' He looked at the clock above the cabin curtains. 'He's dead now. Rest his soul, such as it was.'

'You're. So. Heartless.'

'You were always telling him not to go out and get drunk the way he did.' There was a little too much satisfaction in his voice. She looked at him, dry-eyed but all grief, and said:

'How do I know you're telling me the truth?'

A good question, he thought. 'I'm your father. You heard me speak to the Commissioner.'

'You didn't have the bleposcreen on. How do I know who you were. Speaking. To?'

'He was carrying his identity card. No doubt about who it was. A tavern in the Village. The Minetta or some such name.' Not too bad at the fictional art or craft of lying, Frame told himself. Not too bad at all. 'Believe me, dear, it's for the best. In these times. These aren't Norman times, as my poor grandfather used to say.' Strange, he'd even invented that grandfather.

'I. Loved.'

'There was only one man for you.'

'How can you be. So.'

A glockenspiel-surrogate high A came from a megalal, and then a synthetic voice gave news. 'Strong tail winds may reduce our flying time and our ETA may be brought considerably forward. The highest tides yet recorded during the present tidal phase are at this time ravaging the eastern seaboard. Land evacuation schemes are in full process of implementation.' The artificial Standard Yankee twanged off.

'He's better off,' said Frame, 'as he is. Dead, I mean. A badly wounded man trying to cope with all that panic. New York City. A very undisciplined place.'

'You're so.'

'Sure sure sure sure. You'll get over it, think of the future, your work.'

'I don't want to. Live without him.'

'Duty. Think of your duty.'

Few in the cabin seemed to be thinking of their duty. The windows being blacked out, none knew precisely whither the totally automatically piloted plane was bound, though they all had a fair idea of general direction. Westward, but not too much so. There was a subdued atmosphere of hilarity, as on a holiday magical mystery tour, abetted by bottles passed round by hearty men like Skidmore the scediastist and O'Grady the astunomicologist. Deborah Reiser the physicist was agiggle, as were also Florence Nesbit the mageirist and Gertie La Farge the secretary-maieutist. Young Nat Goya was not hilarious. He brooded. He was in love, married, and his wife was pregnant. He thanked God that she had already left Westchester – four days ago, in fact, not too much time really – and, that very evening, while he was completing his packing, he had received her call from her aunt's house in Fort Worth, Texas, where she was already installed and safe. She had by telephone told her parents of their marriage, prematurely true, but the times asked for prematurity. They were not, apparently, unhappy about it. He had longed to match her sweet voice with her sweet face, but her aunt was old-fashioned and did not believe in blepophones, new-fangled nonsense which made people brazen-faced and give too much away with their expressions. As soon as he got to this place where they were going he would call Edwina. He would call her every hour of the day until married quarters were arranged or, perhaps before that, furlough. It was, after all, only like the army all over again, and this time he seemed to be, though still a civilian, a kind of high-ranking officer. Married quarters, with a servant. A Korean houseboy in a white coat. Besides, the project would not last long. The money would be good apparently. They needed money to put a home together. Real estate prices had, inevitably, gone dramatically down in Westchester County, but with the passing of the bad weather, they would rise again. If only he'd been able to put down a deposit now. He heard old Frame say to his daughter: 'Duty. Think of your duty.' He had only one duty, and that was to the best girl in the world. Dearest, sexiest, sweetest Edwina.

Duty. Back in jail in downtown Manhattan, Val awoke from an uneasy sleep to hear Willett's voice singing something about duty. 'All intrepid captains and mates,' he trolled, 'and those who went down doing their duty.' He la-la-lahed a few measures of presumable orchestral fill-in, bowing strenuously a fiddle of air, and said: 'Walt Whitman's words. Vaughan Williams's music. That sounds like a regular sea symphony outside. Jesus. Cacophony rather.' Val came fully awake to hear swishing and roaring, the tumble of what sounded like a tonne of bricks not far off, their own cell shaking like a brig on the high seas. Their cellmates were coming alive like a slowish scale, *accel. molto* at the end, a note of astonishment for each, progressively successively rising. 'Jesus, Jesus,' a black prayed, 'ah meant no harm, man, there's only you.' Somebody started as though struck by taut leather – a water knout had lashed him. Christ, this was the third floor. Willett, on tiptoe, was looking through the bars. 'We're at sea,' he said. Val, looking too, saw marine night sky, most bitter waters, a sickly yellow high wall, flickering floodlights enlemoning it, going down from a wave strike, moon and Lynx peekabooing through thick clotted cloud.

'An eighteenth-century sailor's life,' Willett said. 'A jail sentence with the risk of drowning added. We'd better get out of here.' This seemed to be the view of many, not only in this cell but, from the noise, the neighbouring ones. Willett strode to the corridor bars and yelled louder than most. The religious black with LYNX on his vest called on Jesus. A flurried officer appeared in waterproofs and shining wellington boots. He had keys. 'You birds better swim for it,' he confided. 'No room on our choppers.' He ground metal and conferred freedom. His fellows had done likewise with the other birds. The corridor was full of panicky freed. The liberators, dressed ready for water but destined for the air, were getting into the hoist. Lights were raw and bright but they flickered. Some of the liberated tried to join them, but guns pointed. The red-haired sergeant of their welcoming committee of all those hours back said, pointing a heavy black Politian .65: 'Heavy waters, heavy, heavy. Swim good.' The hoist rose.

'That,' Willett said, 'will not come back again.' Some of their fellows, following an old reflex, were ready to take the stairs down, but a thin Slav cried: 'Water. The fucking sea's gotten in. There.' He jabbed a shaking index. A tentatively lapping tongue of wet green, dirty-flowery with foam, carrying like a silly gift an empty Gelasem pack, protruded from the stairwell. Then came vivid lightning, blueing everything an instant, and, a second or so after, clumsy thudding hoofing blunderbussing thunder. 'Don't like this, man,' said the black for Jesus, ostensibly Lynx. 'Don't like this one little bit.' A white with a punched-in eye sneered: 'This is what your fucking Lynx has done to us.' Willett said: 'It has to be up, gentlemen, and risk the bullets.' They waded and ploshed to the stairs.

It was a long climb – seven more storeys. Willett cursed out of Rabelais with what breath he had left. Val's head was first to peer out of the roof door, obligingly open. He saw helicopters gyrating off into murderous squalls. One roared inaudibly with frightened policemen fearful of being pitched out by the craft's yawing. The waves were good creamed mid-Atlantic, the rain hissed diarrhoeally, moon and Lynx coyly peered, arcs flicked and flickered and then went out.

Manhattan's street lighting all went out. There was an infernal red glow from somewhere in New Jersey. Val came in again and, with the aid of three heavy-shouldered louts, shut the door against the chaos. Lightning blued out a brief message; thunder, at great length, confirmed it. 'No good,' Val cried. 'We'll have to wait till the tide goes down.'

'It's coming up, fuck it,' dithered a weedy Teutprot, one of Livedog's boys, pointing. Water, not much slower than they had been, was dancing up step by step, that empty Gelasem pack still being pathetically proffered, a full Forgier six-pack making heavier weather of the ascent. A cool black slopped down, grabbed a can from the sodden cardboard harness, popped it open and drank. 'Thirsty,' he then gasped. 'You coulda waited,' said the thin Slav. 'They're being delivered to the fucking door.' There was a shove past Val and Willett by some dozen cursing, better be drowned in the open fucking air, and Willett gravely nodded assent to their act, seeing the swift rise, tread by tread, of the flood. The roof had amenities not previously noticed – a kind of tough metal bus stop shelter, probably for the use of roof guards, if there had been such things, people, too late to bother about that now, in wet weather; a twenty-foot radio tower. Some men were in one, others considering, if the water should farther rise, the salvatory value of the other, which swayed terribly in the wind but was toughly hawsered. Moon and Lynx obligingly, with the sporadic aid of lightning, fitfully illumined these. They also showed Willett, who was peering out from the parapet at something he was gravely interested to see – a vast torn wood and metal advertising hoarding, raft-like nudging the parapet corner as if impatient for someone's embarking. The sky's lights showed in gross foreshortening a naked girl enthusing over Pippet, whatever that was, something comforting and desirable, stimulating, something. 'Aboard,' yelled Willett to Val. 'Imposs,' shook Val. 'Aboard,' buffeted Willett, buffeting him aboard.

The raft bore them some little way uptown, soaked, shivering, lurid in lightning. It made manically, already dissolving to plank and lath, for a building high enough to have still twenty or so storeys showing above the flood level. The name of the building flashed in Egyptian italic an instant – THOTHMES. A hotel? Damned silly name for a. The raft hit the façade clumsily but kindly just beneath a windowsill and then disintegrated further. Willett grabbed a metal support of the hoarding before it leapt into the tiger-jawed waters and hit with it at the window. He was pulled away by wind and water and then shoved back. He hit and hit inaudibly, but the window was responding. Willett stepped onto the sill with rare grace for one of his bulk, then fell in, glass yielding. Val was borne away and screamed. He was borne back and was grabbed, grabbed and was grabbed. Willett pulled him in there, to lovely dryness. It was a hotel, a bedroom, abandoned, lightning showing brutally a bed unmade. Val wanted to lie on it, made or not. 'Up,' Willett insisted, over the thunder.

To their surprise there was a dim light on the corridor, evidently a domestic generator snug above the waterline. But the elevator bank seemed to have fed on some profounder power, for it would not work. The two walked to the emergency stairs and clattered up, taking their time this time. Val, ridiculously, looked at his watch, ticking healthily away, time and the hour running through the roughest night. Four twelve of a wet morning. He'd missed that plane. To be on the safe side they climbed five storeys. Safe side? The building was shaking; probably it would hold, though, till the tide went out, if it went out. Explosions popped from all over the city. Through a landing window they saw the greater towers of Manhattan lightning-drenched but still standing. 'This,' Willett panted, 'will. Do.'

They came out on to dim-lighted deep purplish corridor carpet. Many doors were locked, but one, RAMESES SUITE in cursive metal on the wall by it, was open and welcoming. Hasty evacuation here – bed a Laocoon of sheets, an open wardrobe even displaying neat suits. In the bathroom fine primrose towels unused; toilet articles, male, on the marble wash-deck. A sitting room with bar. Another bedroom, bed made or perhaps never used. The lights were dim, emergency obviously, but to their joy there was hot water in the faucets. Val, drinking raw gin naked at the bar, let Willett soak his mountainous body first. In heavy jocularity he dialled 4 for room service. A mechanical voice said that room service was temporarily suspended. The telescreen gave out nothing. The radio delivered urgent official words, unintelligible under static. There was nothing in the still-humming refrigerator except for soft drinks and fruit-flavoured yoghurt – papaya, boysenberry, butterscotch and bitter orange. Healthy fare, but it would not do for Willett.

* * *

Walked, then. Freud was aware of his mere five feet seven when walking with the immensely tall Jung. Jung had more energy, too; Freud, the great walker, was growing tired. Jung talked away:

'It's possible, of course, that my reservations about your far-reaching views are due to lack of experience. But don't you think a number of borderline phenomena might be considered more appropriately in terms of the other basic drive – hunger? Not sex, but hunger. Sucking is hunger. Kissing is sex. The child confuses the two. They coalesce psychologically – one of them contains constellated aspects of the other.'

'Perhaps,' Freud panted with caution. And then: 'Speaking of hunger – have you had supper?'

'Supper? *Supper?*' Jung laughed and made the empty night Vienna street echo with it. A cat scampered. Freud wondered if the word had perhaps a special, obscene, meaning in the German of Zürich. He did not like the tonalities of this brand of German. There was a disdainful neighing quality about. 'Supper, aha. Let us not talk of supper. Listen, my dear revered professor, let me tell you about one of my difficult recent cases – one I cured, needless to say, with your method. A twenty-year-old Russian girl, ill for six years. When she was three she saw her father hit her older brother on the bare arse – I beg your pardon, fundament. It left a very powerful impression. She had the conviction that she'd defecated on her father's hand. From the fourth till the seventh year she tried to defecate on her own feet – or rather she pressed her heel against her anus – sitting on the floor, of course – and tried both to defecate and to prevent defecation at the same time. She often held her stool back for two whole weeks. It gave her a blissful shuddersome sensation, she said. Later, of course, she turned to masturbation. What do you think of that, revered professor?'

'A nice story. The sight of her brother's spanking took her back to her second year. Her own anus – possible genuine defecation on her father's hand – why not? It's not uncommon. Her father's caresses in infancy. Anal erotism. Transference to you, of course.'

'Oh yes, very powerful. A pretty girl. A student.'

They sat in a near-empty café. Chairs were upside down on tables for next morning's sweeping. Jung did not touch his coffee, now cold.

'Not just a matter of free verbal association. I limit the freedom.

I use a stopwatch. I time the space between the word given and the response. I always carry a stopwatch. Here it is.'

'Swiss-made?'

'Oh, certainly Swiss-made. Shall we try?'

'You haven't even tasted your coffee. Would you like a glass of something stronger?'

'Alcohol? Never touch it.'

'Your Calvinistic upbringing? The clean predestinatory faith which teaches sober living? That ties up with watches, doesn't it?'

'You joke. But I detect a note of disparagement. Never disparage the prohibitions of religion or the mystique of religion. We're surrounded by oceanic mysteries. As for drink – alcohol obfuscates the mind. This you know. The ear and eye alert, the finger sensitive to the trigger of the stopwatch. Of course, you have been trying to put me off my demonstration. Asking me about alcohol and Calvinism. You don't wish to put your brain in my hands.'

'I've already,' and he lighted a cigar, 'completed my self-analysis.'

'Give up that weed. It too is obfuscatory. Let's just take this as a mere informal friendly parlour game. Ready?'

'If you wish.' He coldly watched Jung click the thing on.

'Pork.'

'I beg your pardon?'

'Pork.'

'Prohibition.'

'Grass.'

'Keep off it.'

'Mother.'

'Inhibition.'

'Sister.'

'Exhibition.'

Jung sighed, clicked off, put away the stopwatch. 'So, honoured professor. I see resistance.'

'Oh, my dear colleague,' Freud said kindly, 'I have to resist, don't I? I must savour the delights of authority.' And then, with a kind of parodic Mosaic ferocity to mildly looking Joshua, 'I discovered the unconscious mind while you were still dabbling in your urine.' Then the loving Moses. 'Still, you're remarkable. Brilliance, I think. I think now our cause is safe. I know it. The great wind will blow out of Zürich. Vienna – ach.' He spat a brown gob on the dirty floor.

Jung looked inscrutable and not at all in its direction. A police matter in Zürich.

Bells bells bells and a gorgeous Sunday morning. They walked about the great baroque Ring, and Jung was loud above the ringing.

'I entreat you, my dear esteemed revered professor, to look beyond your consulting room. And I do not mean look out to our clinic in Zürich, or to Budapest where Ferenczi is at work, or to Berlin where Abraham has started. No – look beyond medicine to the whole of civilization. You bid us understand the dark mysterious forces of the unconscious, but only to exorcise them as devils. We understand, or will soon, the urges which lead to the creation of music, poetry, this glorious architecture that surrounds us and seems to me, at this moment, a miraculous solidification of the sweet jangled yet ordered syncacophony of the bells. We understand that art is a kind of neurosis, but does that make us reject beauty? Decidedly not. As for religion – we understand. Religion can be therapy. I cured one old lady of her hysteria by reading the Bible with her. The Bible does not lose its authority because we now know it is founded on dark Oedipal urges. The religions of the world – they point to the truth of a collective unconscious, the world-form, God in many shapes and with many voices – ' He paused for breath. Freud said bluntly:

'Religion is the oppressor. True, it has given us art, music, architecture of unsurpassable beauty, but that does not prevent it from being a roof over the heads of shivering people scared of engaging the huge windy blackness without. Man invented God because he knew no better – the great unpredictable father, indulgent or angry, loving or vengeful. But God had no real independent existence. Outside man there is nothing, *nothing*.'

But the bells clanged, hurled, howled, raised their throats to heaven and drowned Freud. And Jung smiled towards the sky, nodding as if acknowledging the greeting of an acquaintance.

Dinner with the family, and the children drank it all in. It was a pity Minna was no longer with them, off travelling in deepest Europe, about her own affairs. She would have shown a dark sardonic eye when the tall soldierly Switzer, his spectacles drinking the light, his stuffed veal neglected, spoke of the long dark road that led to the Freudian glimmer.

'A recurrent dream, Frau Doktorin, and a great wind blowing. I toiled against this wind, and in my hand was – this – ' He took Freud's matchbox, ready for the digestive cigar, struck a light and cupped the spunk in his paws. 'Behind me was the shadow of a great black giant following following – but I had to go on, guarding from the extinction of the wind the little bright light sheltered in my hands. I awoke after the hundredth repetition of this dream, and behold – the meaning was revealed to me. The figure, the great black giant, was my own shadow on the swirling mists, brought into being by the light I carried in my hands. The little light was my consciousness. I had begun to understand the nature of man. And how – ? Because I had read the works of my beloved teacher and leader here. My dream had been striving to tell me the truth – but it could not, not until His Excellency here had provided the key to my dreams.' He blew out the match and handed the spent stick to His Excellency, who deposited it solemnly on a breadplate.

A good story, but he should not have told it again, word for word, at the house of Freud's mother, whom he insisted on seeing. Great men and their mothers or something. Freud's mother said:

'His Excellency?'

'That,' Freud said, 'goes along with the title of Professor, mamma, but you needn't use it.'

'Ach, to me,' she said to Jung, 'he'll always be the little boy playing in the dirt.'

Jung beamed at the reduced, though temporarily only, father figure, beaming: 'And what can be cleaner than dirt? I am not like you people of the great city. I was brought up in the country, among cows and bulls and cocks and hens and the muddy fields. Dirt, they used to say when I watched the bull with the cow, the stallion with the mare, the cock with the hen, hens rather – but even then I had the feeling that dirt is only a dirty word for the earth that the rain has fertilized, the life-giving mud that begot the whole civilization of Egypt. You must, all of you, come to Switzerland, to my house on the lake, sail with me in my boat, cook fish in the open air, chop down trees, carve wood – '

'Do you good, Siggy,' Freud's mother said, 'get that hump off your back and the smoke out of your chest. He smokes far too much, Dr Jung, I'm always telling him it's a filthy habit.'

'Ah,' Jung beamed, kindly looking at Freud taking a deep suck at a cigar that would not draw, 'sheer devotion – that's all it means. To you, to you, to you, *gnädige Frau.*'

They went to the railway station not quite two hours early. As the train steamed in, Jung said: 'So you will think about it?'

'I will do more,' Freud said with enthusiasm. 'I will say yes and again yes and consider that the matter is already in your hands.'

'A giant,' Jung nodded, assessing the five-foot-seven figure tailor fashion. 'You are altogether remarkable. And yet – there are depths I cannot reach, waters where strange fish lurk – I cannot quite as yet altogether make you out – '

'You will.' Jung mounted, boarded, and was soon beaming from a window. 'Close and closer, my dear Carl. We're together in this great adventure.' It seemed easier somehow to say that a second or so before Jung was pulled away from him towards Zürich. They waved at each other and, when the train had vanished, Freud took out a cigar, cut the end, lighted it, then sucked and sucked. To hell with what the sucking meant. That sort of thing could go too far. Then he strutted off to re-engage dirty Vienna.

There they were again, assembled for the Wednesday meeting, Otto, dear little faithful Otto, with pencils ready sharpened. 'Gentlemen,' Freud said, 'at last we are emerging from obscurity. I think we are entitled, at last, to ennoble our group by giving it a more dignified name. I suggest: the Psychoanalytic Society of Vienna.'

Adler at once said: 'The Freudian Society of Vienna.'

'I am touched,' Freud said, 'and gratified by Dr Adler's concern with the honouring of my humble name. But the movement must not be associated with a mere personality. It is not the creation of Sigmund Freud, merely his discovery. Shall we put it to the vote – unless, of course, there are other suggestions?'

'Is it not possible,' Adler said, 'that other schools of psychoanalysis will develop? Meaning – other societies?'

'Other schools?' Freud said in faint puzzlement. 'I fail to understand. There is only one possible school –'

'At the moment,' Adler said, 'the Freudian school. Hence my suggested name for our organization. But we must consider the future. You say that already in Switzerland this man Jung is talking of future developments – '

'But there I am, somewhat embarrassingly, honoured in the name they have chosen for their group. Let us have none of that here in Vienna.'

'There is,' Adler asked, 'no talk of a Jungian school, a Jungian society?'

Freud was sharp, somewhat. 'Of course not. He's a young man. He's made a beginning. But he still has much to learn. It is we who must teach him. Vienna is still the mother of psychoanalysis, though a bad mother, a vicious mother – '

'I thought,' Stekel said, 'you said Vienna was a father.'

'I may change my metaphors occasionally.'

'I see.'

'What do you see, Dr Stekel?'

'The Freudian Society of Vienna,' Adler said. 'I suggest we put it to the vote.'

'Very well,' Freud said somewhat testily. Adler, Stekel and Otto Rank stuck their hands up. Freud looked astonished at good faithful Otto. Otto guiltily dropped his hand and recorded the votes. 'The Psychoanalytic Society of Vienna?' All except Adler and Stekel stuck them up. 'Good. Next item. The first international psychoanalytic congress.' He beamed warily. There was a bit of a buzz of talk. He rose above it. 'The venue – Salzburg. The dates – to be fixed. The arrangements to be in the hands of Dr Carl Jung.' One or two frowns, long faces, murmurs. 'You will understand, gentlemen, that it was not possible to discuss this matter with you. Jung paid me a brief visit only. I could not convene the group. The notion of an international congress was, moreover, Jung's own idea.'

'Ah,' Adler said.

'What do you mean – ah?'

'What I said. Ah.'

'Was I,' Freud said with some heat, 'to reject his offer of help – more than help? He is in a strong position there. The Freudian – the method is used in his clinic. The clinic itself is perhaps the most distinguished psychiatric institute in the whole of Europe. He has authority. He also has energy. More, he expressed willingness. You who have grumbled so much, some of you, you know who I mean, at the failure of our movement to expand beyond the walls of our ghetto – you now seem aggrieved that at last we are becoming a name in the world.'

'*You*,' Adler said, 'are becoming a name.'

Freud was irate now. 'Is it my fault that I hit on it first? Did anything prevent any of you from discovering psychoanalysis?'

'Only,' Stekel said soothingly, 'a lack of talent, dear Sigmund.'

'What did you call me then?'

'Sigmund. It is your first name. Sigmund Freud. Sigmund.'

Sigmund, or Freud, grunted, not knowing how to take this. Rank was writing, and Freud glanced over to see what he was writing.

'Strike that out,' he said. 'Dr Stekel's uninvited familiarity is no part of our official proceedings.' He then beamed, much in the manner of Dr Jung, on the group. 'Salzburg, gentlemen. A pleasant town. Associated with a particular musician, I forget for the moment whom.'

'Wolfgang,' Stekel said. 'Wolfgang Amadeus Mozart.'

Eine Kleine Nachtmusik played, along with a fountain, in the rococo square. The hotel was on a side of the square. Freud and two other men walked, limped rather, into it. Walking round the town, sight-seeing, the cobbles hard. In the hotel vestibule Dr Carl Jung came forward beaming and crushed Freud's hand in his great Swiss paw. With him was.

'Dr Jones of London,' Freud said, 'Dr Brill of New York. Dr Jung. Dr – '

'This,' Jung said, 'is Professor Bleuler, revered head of our clinic.' A grey man, demeanour grey, not much blood in him.

'I,' Freud said, 'am overwhelmed, Herr Professor. Dare I hope to believe that at last – '

'Converted?' Bleuler was quick with it. 'Me converted? You dare not hope to believe, Herr Professor. I am here purely as an observer.'

Jones said: 'You'll be converted, sir.'

'If I am, it will be totally against my will.'

'As with all the best conversions,' Brill said in twanging German. 'St Paul, for instance.'

'An inept analogy,' Bleuler said.

'Speaking,' Jones said, 'as a member of one of the lost tribes of Israel, may I say that – '

'I thought,' Bleuler cut in, 'you were English, Dr er er – '

'Jones. Welsh. Jones is a common Welsh name. We sometimes call ourselves one of the lost tribes – '

'I thought,' Bleuler said, 'the Welsh were Christian.'

'Do my sense antennae deceive me?' Brill with American forthrightness said. 'Is it possible that I'm hearing the buzz of religious division? Psychoanalysis, surely, is international, transcultural, supra-religious – '

'We Swiss,' Bleuler said, 'are what we are, sir. John Calvin hammered our faith into us a long time ago.'

'This, Herr Professor,' Freud said, 'is embarrassing.'

'You are mistaken, gentlemen,' Bleuler said, 'if you think I reject psychoanalysis on theological grounds. Cultural grounds, possibly, yes. The Jewish attitude to the family is, you will admit, very different from the Gentile.'

'The whole concept,' Freud said, in a voice that not yet clarified feeling had rendered hollower than he could wish, 'stands or falls on the assumption that all human beings are much the same. I hope to convince you, Herr Professor. Dr Jung, my profoundest thanks for the efficiency with which you have organized – '

'Yes yes yes, it was nothing.' He frowned at a round ebullient mannikin who, bowing round Professor Bleuler, had nearly tripped departing bowing Bleuler up. This mannikin approached Freud with wide gestures of reverence, saying:

'Sandor Ferenczi of Budapest. The apostle to the Hungarians. At last I meet the saviour of the world's sanity. Let me kiss your writing hand.' Freud put it in his pocket. 'This is such joy. Dr Jung, your servant. I have used your word-association technique with marked success. In Budapest I am known as the mad doctor with the stop-watch. Gentlemen – ' and he bowed and bowed at Jones and Brill ' – at last we join together to affirm the new philosophy of love to the whole unloving world –'

'Love?' Freud wavered.

'Of course, love. We kill the irrationalities of hate We destroy sexual neurosis. We cancel the errors and terrors of the bed. We restore to the patient the love of himself and the love of others. Ergo, it is a mystique of love and a technique of love. What, dear dear professor, are you going to lecture to us on, about, concerning?'

Freud said heavily: 'A recent clinical case. The case of the rat man.'

'The – ?'

'Rat man. A man obsessed with rats.'

'Rats,' and Ferenczi grew wide-eyed and trembling. 'I can't stand rats. It is an irrational, I know, it is a wholly unreasonable, an instinctual, I cannot control, the repugnance, rats I – ' He began to see rats emerging from nonexistent holes in the immaculate cream walls of the vestibule. A rat climbing up that red velvet swag there? Jones said:

'A drink, I think. A schnapps, say.'

'Yes,' Freud said, 'a drink.'

Jung said: 'I don't drink. Nor does my chief Professor Bleuler. The surest way to his heart is not to drink.'

'A drink,' Brill said, 'nevertheless.'

They went off for a drink, Jung looking inscrutable, Ferenczi dithering at imaginary rats.

'You see you ain't wanted, brother,' says the first thug to Trotsky, 'not here.'

'I see how much I *am* wanted,' says Trotsky. 'Here.'

'We don't want no foreigners,' says the second thug.

'Telling us how to run the country,' says the third thug.

'You gonna leave nice and quiet, without causing no trouble?' says the first.

'Comrades,' Trotsky says gently, 'do not threaten. All my life it has been threats. Some of the threats were carried out. Some were not. But I've never before had to face threats from my fellow socialists.'

'Our socialism ain't the same as yours,' says the second. 'Comrade.'

'You gonna go quiet?' says the third.

'Call him Lertzing, not his real name. Thirty, an advocate, excellent cultural background, highly intelligent. But not sufficiently intelligent to overcome suicidal impulses – perpetual desire, when shaving, to cut throat with razor. Suicidal impulses connected with fear of great harm happening to the two people most important in his life. His father, the young woman he had been in love with for ten years. Sexual life? Masturbation between ages of sixteen and seventeen, intercourse at twenty-six, frustration at lack of sexual opportunity, physical repugnance at very thought of prostitutes. I took him back to the age of four, when sexual experiences began with governess, Fräulein Peter, man's name, note, as I noted. Allowed to creep under her skirts and play with her genitals. Fräulein Peter, most accommodating governess, permitted him to undress, caress her. Not unnaturally began to have erections which he took crying to his mother, frightened, complaining of pain. Convinced that his parents knew everything going on in his mind. Began to believe was speaking his thoughts out loud, that he was the only one who could not hear them. During consultations persisted in the fear his father was going to die. Then I discovered his father had already died many years before.'

'I was born on a farm,' says Trotsky. 'I broke stallions on the Russian steppes. I worked, I suffered, I starved. For people like you. There's not a spare ounce of fat on me, comrades, but look at yourselves – swollen with beer, ice cream, popcorn. Now what do you say?'

'This,' and the first thug prepares to hit Trotsky in the kishkas. Trotsky dodges. He grasps a chair by its two hind legs. He floors one of his assailants and sends another one off howling. But the one remaining is game. He comes for Trotsky with a bigger and heavier chair. Stag fight, with geometrical antlers. Olga comes in, a cheap fur coat on for the cold. On the table on the dais she sees the copy of Marx's *Capital*. She hits the thug with this on the back of the head. He turns, bewildered. Trotsky takes his chance and cracks him on the occiput with the front edge of the chair seat. The thug drops his own chair and sobs. Trotsky says fervently:

'Dear sweet pretty adorable little comrade. What's the book? Ah. Karl Marx fits every situation.'

'I think, comrade,' Olga says, 'what you could do with is a drink.' Trotsky nods gravely and then smiles. He offers her his arm.

'The pathological condition was brought to a crisis when Lertzing was participating – as so many of us here have done – in military manoeuvres during his compulsory service. He lost his spectacles. He knew he could find them if he held up the route march he was on, but he decided against it. Resting during a halt with his company commander, a captain of a sadistic disposition, Lertzing became distressed when the captain spoke of a brutal punishment meted out to men who had transgressed army regulations. The patient became most distraught when recounting this punishment to me. He was somewhat incoherent. I understood, through his hesitant description, that the delinquent was tied up, a pot was turned upside down on his buttocks, there were rats in the pot, and these rats were permitted to bore into the wretched man's anus.'

Ferenczi fainted.

A little bar in Manhattan, West 55th Street; its name the Kokolka. Olga and Trotsky are at a table. A man in Russian peasant dress plucks softly at a balalaika. The waiter brings vodka. Olga says *spasibo*. Trotsky says:

'A put-up job. A put-up job. I must remember the expression.'

'In America,' Olga says gently, as to a child, 'socialism is the road to capitalism. Nobody wants the classless society. I told you – we had our revolution in 1776.'

'You said *we*. You said *our*. But you're a Russian.'

'I'm an American. You talk of internationalism. This is the only true international society in the world.'

'It's here it must come. It has to. Marx said that. The revolution, he said, will come first to those countries that have the highest industrial development. England. America.'

'Well, Marx was wrong, wasn't he? Socialism is for the poor peasant countries. Russia. China.'

'China? Nonsense.'

'Yes, comrade. You always know best, comrade.'

'It now began to occur to Lertzing that this boring of rats into the anus was actually happening to both his father – dead, remember – and his very much alive fiancée. The image of the boring gnawing rats was obsessive, but he could only fight it by shaking his head vigorously and saying to himself: 'Whatever are you thinking, whatever are you thinking?' Now, while still on manoeuvres, Lertzing obtained new spectacles, which were delivered to the regimental post office. The captain brought the package containing the new spectacles and said: "You must pay the sum of three crowns eighty to Lieutenant Nahl, who has already paid the cash due on delivery of this package." Now in the mind of Lertzing this order to pay became an order from his father – his dead father, remember. He wished to pay the debt, but at the same time he did *not* wish to pay it, else the fantasy about the rats would come true with regard to both his father and his betrothed. His guilt became intense. He believed that his father had called out his name before dying, telling him to come and say farewell, but he had disobeyed the paternal summons. His guilt prevented his continuing his legal practice and further studies.'

Ferenczi had come to. Bleuler kept shaking his head.

'Comrade. Sweet pretty little adorable – I'm sorry. It's a habit.'

'I know it's a habit. A formula. It's not the words I object to. It's the meaninglessness of the words.'

'I never use words without meaning. Oh yes, I do. Bloodsucking capitalistic parasites. Fawning lackeys. Jacks in office. I'm too glib.'

'Call it eloquent.'

'You think,' says Trotsky, 'I'm stupid.'

'Not stupid. Innocent.'

'Well – there are worse vices than innocence. There's innocence for you.'

'What?'

'The song he's singing. Pushkin, isn't it?'

'I probed deeper and learned more. Lertzing began to tell me frankly how many times he had wished for his father's death. In this latter part of his life he had a good, if coldblooded, reason for wanting it. He would inherit a sizeable sum. He would be able to marry the girl he loved – a poor girl without a dowry. He told me how, when he was a child, he had bitten somebody, and his father had punished him for this with a very severe beating – yes, you will have guessed, on the fundament. The themes, gentlemen, are beginning to coalesce. Lertzing began to see connections. "Bite," he said. "Bite him. That's what rats do – bite." '

Ferenczi fainted again.

The singer sings to his balalaika:

'Ya vas lyubil; lyubov' yeshcho, bit'-mozhet,
V dushe moyey ugasla nye sovsyem;
No pust' ona vas bol'she nye tryevozhit;
Ya nye khochu pyechalit' vas nichem.
Ya vas lyubil byezmolvno, byeznadyozhno,
To radost'yu, to revonst'yu tomim;
Ya vas lyubil tak iskryenno, tak nyezhno,
Kak day vam Bog lyubimoy bit' drugim.'

And Trotsky, who discovers he knows his Pushkin better than he had thought possible after all these years, speaks the words softly:

'I loved you. And love for you has not yet burned out of my soul. But don't let my love cause you distress any more. I don't wish to bring you grief. I loved you silently, hopelessly, sometimes in joy, sometimes in jealousy. I loved you so sincerely, so tenderly. Ah, may God grant that you be so loved by another – '

Olga starts quietly to cry.

'It took me months to discover the precipitating cause of his mental sickness. It had occurred six years before. His mother informed him that he must forget his love for this poor girl without a dowry. He must marry the daughter of a wealthy cousin and thus become rich, successful. But he didn't love the girl. He loved the other one whom he couldn't marry for lack of money, his father inconsiderately refusing to die and enable him to inherit. Still, he was tempted by his mother's proposal. He evaded a decision by falling ill – not uncommon, gentlemen, as we know. His illness was characterized by the fantasies and obsessions I have already recounted.'

Ferenczi had come to again.

Trotsky gently puts his arm about her, but she is not having that. She says, disengaging roughly, 'I must look for another job.'

'Sweet pretty darling Olga. No, no glibness now. I thought we were to work together. I thought perhaps you would go back with me to Russia, so that we could continue to work together.'

'I shan't be coming in tomorrow. I must look for another job. We can't work together.'

'We can. We will.'

'Now the long-expected transference began. He converted myself, his analyst, into the wealthy cousin with the marriageable daughter. He imagined that a certain young girl he had seen by chance outside my apartment was my own daughter, and that I was forcing him to marry this girl. He raved at me, struck me – when I was unable to dodge quickly enough – for asking him to abandon his one true love and marry for money and position. Then I became his father, smacking him on the buttocks. Then I was the sadistic captain. Then I was Fräulein Peter, the governess. I became an object of love, scorn, rage. Things began to clarify in the patient's own mind. I do think that at this point Dr Ferenczi, to save himself further distress, ought to leave.'

So with expressions of regret and shame Ferenczi kissed his hand and put his hand to his heart and, with further gestures, left. Bleuler seemed to consider leaving too, but Jung's strong hand held him back.

'No. We quarrel. I get angry.'

'I don't mind you getting angry.'

'I know you don't. And I don't mind if you get angry with me. That's the trouble. I don't want to get *involved*.'

'With the socialist movement?'

'No, you idiot.'

He sighs. He sings, *parlando*, variations on words he has sung, *parlando*, before, though then alone. She looks at him, wondering.

All through history
Mind limps after reality.
And what's reality? I don't think I know.

There's no mystery
In physical causality.
Matter. Is that as far as mind can go?
The shape of – a face.
The dream of – an embrace –
Impertinent irrelevancy, totally
And categorically supererogatory –
Quacks, brays, bleats, noises.
The truth may well be that the root of all human miseries and joys is
Something any good Marxist is shocked even to find himself minimally even vestigially thinking of.
The reality may be may be may be

'Rats, gentlemen. Rats and the patient's anal erotism. He had, I discovered, suffered almost continual irritation of the anal tract as a child. Worms. His parents had called his penis a worm. Instead of making the more usual identification of faeces with money, he associated money with rats. One day, paying me, he said: "So many schillings – so many rats." His father, in the army, had spent so much money on gambling that he was known as *der Spielratte*, the playrat. His own revulsion towards the sadistic captain proved to be mingled with a strong homosexual attraction. He had been trying to punish himself for this. After eleven months of daily sessions he was able to look squarely at the elements of the fantasizing that had been long locked in his unconscious. He saw that he had no occasion to feel guilt towards his father. Once the rat obsession was dissolved, I was able to pronounce him cured. He is now practising the law with vigour and success. He is also happily married. I think we may now take a *Kaffeepause* and, in twenty minutes, reassemble to hear Dr Jung on some aspects of dementia praecox.'

The assembly applauded and then broke up. Jung and Bleuler looked at each other. Bleuler nodded, not unimpressed. Ferenczi, hearing applause, looked in, sidled in. Freud said:

'We've killed the rats, Dr Ferenczi.'

'No no no no – don't mention them – *please* – '

* * *

'You've had a tough day,' Olga says. 'Three blocks to the subway and then you're home.'

'And you?'

'Eleven blocks. Downtown.'

'To your lonely bed. To my lonely bed.'

'Yes, I guess so. Our lonely beds, comrade.'

But they leave hands clasped. *Kaffeepause.*

The band played Strauss. Jung's and Bleuler's glasses of water were improper for a beer garden, but Freud and Jones and Brill and Ferenczi grasped foaming steiner. They talked with animation, loud because of the band. The Vienna delegates were at another table, those of them not already retired to bed. Late hours. After midnight. Dr Freud there fresh as a daisy with these foreigners. Adler and Stekel nodded their distaste, drank up and left. Something not quite proper going on. Next morning –

'No,' Otto Rank said in incredulity. 'No no no.' Freud shushed him. Jones was telling his audience about *Hamlet*. He said:

'Did Shakespeare himself understand why Hamlet had to delay and delay and delay before killing his uncle the murderous usurping king? We do not know. But what we may suspect is that Shakespeare was unconsciously driven by an Oedipal situation in his own life to dramatize an Oedipal situation in the life of the gloomy prince of Denmark. Hamlet's uncle had murdered Hamlet's father. Could Hamlet himself really seek revenge when he himself had wished to kill his father? Here psychoanalysis proffers an answer to a problem that has exercised literary critics for at least two centuries.' Jones stepped down from the little dais to applause from the assembled delegates. Otto Rank turned angrily to Freud and said:

'That was my idea. I told you that idea. Did you talk to Dr Jones about it?'

'I may have mentioned it in a letter. Does it matter much? The idea was anybody's for the taking.'

'It was my idea,' very hotly, 'mine.' He got up petulantly and stalked off.

'Come back, Otto. Ach, stupid young idiot.'

Things not going too well for some reason. The human element;

more, the national, racial. As Freud passed them purposefully on his way to Jung's room after the day's meetings, his fellow townsmen looked at him coldly. He smiled, bowing. They bowed, unsmiling. Stupid idiots. At the foot of the main staircase he found Jones and Brill and Ferenczi waiting. They would go together. They climbed.

Freud knocked and heard *Herein*. Opened, entered. Jung and Bleuler were seated, Bleuler on Jung's bed, Jung on Jung's chair. They rose. Jung said:

'It seems a little conspiratorial, does it not? Sit where you can, gentlemen. A bed seems an appropriate place.' They sat gingerly, Freud and Brill on the bed, Jones on the window ledge. Bleuler remained standing. Bleuler said, though grimly:

'You have your convert.'

Up from that bed, hand-shaking, the relief, the satisfaction. Bleuler did not seem to wish to be touched. Grimly he said:

'I have heard some remarkable things. It has been a remarkable conference. I trust this will be an annual event.'

'To your colleague Carl Jung,' Freud said, 'most of the credit must go. And, Herr Professor, talking of annual events – '

'You mean the *Jahrbuch*,' Bleuler said.

'The – ?' Jones queried.

'*Jahrbuch*,' Jung said with clarity. 'Yearbook you would term it. Professor Freud and I have already discussed the need for an annual international publication devoted to psychoanalysis.'

'With Zürich as its sponsor,' Freud said. 'Specifically the Burghölzli Clinic in Zürich, whose reputation extends even to New York – am I not right, Dr Brill?'

'Let me say how delighted I am, we are, that Professor Bleuler should,' Brill said. 'Ha – I think I may be jumping the gun – '

'I should be honoured,' and now Bleuler smiled, 'to accept the post of co-director – along with Dr Sigmund Freud.'

'The honour,' Freud said, 'is all ours, mine. How can I possibly express my gratitude, satisfaction – I think we must all agree, gentlemen, that there can be only one possible editor – '

Jung looked modest.

'The problem here, dear dear professor,' Ferenczi said, 'is that, though I handle German well enough in speech, and I naturally assume that a *Jahrbuch* is to be, though international, published in German, my written German leaves much to be – '

'I did not mean you,' Freud bluntly said.

'Honoured honoured honoured,' Jung murmured. Ferenczi's crest was down.

'So,' Freud said, 'what more can I – can we – except perhaps order a bottle of er – something?'

Bleuler sternly said: 'You have converted me to the doctrine of the sexual aetiology of the neuroses, Dr Freud, but you will never convert me to alcohol. *Never*.'

'Mineral water I was about to say,' Freud lied.

'The *Jahrbuch*,' Ferenczi cried, 'must be a work of beauty, a labour of love. Love, it must *exude* love.'

Some coughed. Jung broke in: 'I believe the photographer is waiting for us. It looks like rain. Shall we go?'

They went, elaborately courteous about who should go first. Freud bowed out Bleuler. Below, on the gravel path behind the hotel, the photographer waited indeed, a broken-toothed eager young man in a dirty tall collar, one shoulder slightly higher than the other. He beamed. You stand here and you there and you, sir – Freud and Jung in the middle. Jung very tall, Freud terribly diminished. Freud frowned, Jung caught the frown. Some empty beer crates stood by the drainpipes and the water butt and some discouraged creepers. Jung finger-clicked at a hovering hotel servant in striped waistcoat. The servant saw what he meant. Soon he saw, standing out of the shot, this little bearded one with the cigar on a beer crate, higher than anyone. The photographer called for a smile. Jung smiled inscrutably, Freud genially. The other Viennese did not smile at all. A magnesium flare flared and the shutter clicked, and the picture entered the future.

Two hours early at the station, naturally. Stekel and the rest were not quite so early. A passing porter saw a group of mature professional-looking gentlemen giving voice at each other. Soon Stekel said:

'The consensus, in conclusion, is that you behaved high-handedly, discourteously, ungratefully, exhibiting neither local patriotism nor natural amicality.'

'Amicality?' Freud said. 'You mean friendship. Hard accusations, Dr Stekel. You mean I cultivated new friendships and neglected old ones.'

Adler said: 'You treated the entire Viennese delegation like a lot of poor relatives. You took us for granted. We, who are the blood and bones of the movement – '

'You make it sound like an abattoir.'

'Don't make silly little jokes,' Stekel said. 'We've had enough of you as the comic Jewish raconteur with the American and the Hungarian and the Englishman and the Switzers.'

'The – ?'

'Zürichers Zürichers Zürichers.'

'Oh,' Kahane said, 'let's come to the serious charge.'

'I'm on trial?' Freud said.

'You may say that,' said Kahane. 'You hold a secret meeting about starting a yearbook of psychoanalysis, and who was at the meeting? I will tell you. One Englishman, one Hungarian, one American and two men from Zürich. No Viennese.'

'I was there,' Freud said.

'Stop it, do you hear?' Kahane cried. 'You're selling our movement to a pack of foreigners.'

'Oh, let's go further,' Freud said. 'I'm selling the movement not just to foreigners but to Gentiles. Isn't that the crux of the matter? We have to remain Jewish and *gemütlich* and incestuous. Idiots. I have to spread the light. I have to hug and kiss and flatter the unconverted. The best tribute I could pay to you was to ignore you, take you for granted. You know about the rabbi who railed at the man who slept during his sermon. The man said: "Well, would I sleep if I didn't trust you?" '

'There we go again,' Stekel said. 'All right, I'll come out with it since you brought up the Jewishness. That man Jung – he's an antisemite.'

'Did he tell you so?'

'All the Swiss are antisemitic,' Adler said. 'It's in the blood.'

'There are Swiss Jews. I had a patient who was a.'

'There's wet fire and hot ice,' Adler said. 'Listen. This man Jung. You think he's the great loyal disciple, the man who'll carry the torch all over Europe. Nothing of the kind. I've watched him, watched his eyes. He'll betray you, he'll betray us all. You make him editor and you put into his hands the instrument that will pervert our science into a Swiss Gentile travesty. You trust too much and you trust in the wrong places. You see Jung as Joshua to your Moses, but you're wrong. You scorn the loyal and you butter up the potential traitors. It makes me sick.'

Freud fixed him with his eyes. 'Look into your own soul sometime, Dr Adler. It's only Jung I have to fear, is it? Only Jung can be the traitor. The Viennese Jews are too holy and loyal and good to dream of defection. Bear my words in mind, Dr Adler. We'll see.' Adler snorted and turned his back. 'We'll see, won't we, Dr Adler?'

The train came in. Freud let them scramble aboard. He scornfully waited till the whistle blew and then found a compartment of his own.

The advance party had done good swift work on CAT. An electrified wire perimeter enclosed a square mile of flat earth on which little grew. An electromagnetic roof hovered invisibly above to keep out air intruders. In the middle of the field, brought in at the end of March, lay the great hulk of the moonliner *Tallis*, its name already deleted but its new name *America* only so far stencilled in. Surrounding it, but at a respectful distance, were prefabricated huts of great solidity, for work, for sleep, for minimal recreation. The huts on the periphery housed army troops. The fifty elite were lodged, in greater comfort and privacy, nearer the squat ship, each hut divided into four large apartments, each apartment accommodating two men or two women, but never a woman and a man. There was a small assembly hall or lecture theatre equipped with cinematic apparatus. It was here, the morning of their arrival – the true bright morning, not the black parody – that Professor Frame had proposed, in a near-final moment of glory, to outline the project to the CAT team. Paul Maxwell Bartlett, brutally but reasonably, had pointed out that for a dying man to speak, in the inspiratory way that was needed (he stressed the *inspiratory* cruelly), about a project concerned with salvation, with, yes, life, was out of order. Head of Project, he had insisted that he himself give the inaugural address. There was a brief altercation, in which Vanessa joined, but there was no question as to who must win.

Bartlett wore black surrogate leather and very well-cut black boots. He stood on the little dais and surveyed his buzzing audience without fear, with a measure of histrionic contempt rather. Vanessa's heart was heavy, heavier still when Bartlett began with: 'There should be fifty-one of us here, but there are only fifty. Dr Valentine Brodie, cybernetically appointed our official chronicler or archivist, met an unfortunate, indeed fatal, accident last night in New York City. We shall, I think, contrive to find without difficulty a substitute for him among ourselves. The recording of events is hardly to be termed scientific. It calls for no specialist skill.' Vanessa sobbed drily and those near her – Felicia DeWitt and Mackenzie Eidlitz – looked at her with brief curiosity. Then they gave all their attention to Bartlett. He had more cruelty to deal out before he got down to business. He said: 'The founder of the project we call CAT, Professor Hubert Frame, is, as you will know, with us here, though in a very marginal capacity. He is a sick man and is confined to his quarters. He is not a member of our team, though without his brilliant work, and that of his daughter, fortunately very much with us, this team could hardly have been brought into existence.'

He paused, did an upstage turn, then swivelled abruptly to frown at them all. 'Professor Frame,' he announced, 'is going to die, but we are going to live. The whole of the population of the Commonwealth of Democratic Americas is going to die, but we are going to live. It is our duty to salvage human knowledge in the face of human cataclysm. The day of the cataclysm is coming, Cat Day as we may whimsically call it, and the identity of the world-destroyer is known to you all. Lynx, most vicious of cats, is already showing his claws in earthquake, seaquake, moonquake, flood. Soon he will leave, but only to circle the sun in a year much briefer than ours. Then he will return and make straight for our hapless planet. Before that day, Cat Day, our preparatory work will have been done, and our ship, laden with the fruits of men's scientific inquiries, self-sufficient microcosm of our own creation, will be making for Jupiter, our first posting inn on the long journey to another world. That world may never be reached, but our search will never give up. We shall breed new generations of spacemen and spacewomen, and they in turn will breed. We are not ourselves, we are humankind. Humankind must survive, and we humble insufficient creatures are the chosen instruments of its survival.'

He relaxed as far as his temperament allowed, smiling grimly as if to deprecate the rhetorical tone he had, in justice to the imaginative nature of the enterprise, been compelled to employ. He said: 'You are all specialists in various fields relevant to the scope of the project. As philosophy was once regarded as the clearing house, or interpretative unifier, of the various sciences, so we may regard ouranology as the discipline that binds together the various specializations necessary to the creation of a space microcosm. Dr Vanessa Frame, our coordinating ouranologist, is, as it were, the possessor of the blueprint of the ultimate body – ' There were smiles and sly glances at Vanessa, sex rearing its blessed head even now, but Bartlett seemed unaware of the *double entendre*. 'You, the engineers, clinicians, physicians, even librarians, are, as it were, the several organs of the body. My function? It is quite simply to control, maintain project discipline, be ultimately responsible – to whom, you may ask? I say to the spirit of future man – for the success, if one may use so utilitarian a word, of the whole glorious and terrifying venture.'

Professor K. O. Eastman, a lithe savannah-blonde diastemoploionologist, was tentatively raising a finger to raise a point. Bartlett made a dismissive gesture, like a karate chop. 'Wait, please. Questions later. Or rather I hope to anticipate all possible questions before I have done. You all know where you are – in the state of Kansas, between Hays and Hill City, an area chosen for its centrality and hence immunity from tidal damage, also its negative seismic record, also its comparative isolation. You know where you are, but, I must say it now, you will never be in a position to divulge our whereabouts to the outside world. Security must be, security will be, absolute. Doomed mankind, if they knew of us, would be envious and, in the final phases of apocalyptic panic, be very willing to destroy us and the hope of the race. You, and I with you, are prisoners of the project. You were chosen not solely for your supreme skills, not even solely for the combination of those with superlative records of personal and ancestral health. You were chosen also because you have no family commitments. You leave friends behind, true, even perhaps mothers and fathers, but you are unburdened by responsibility for wife, husband, child. The time will come for mating and the duty of breeding the first space generation, but that must wait. Our primary dedication is to work.'

Nat Goya was raising his hand in a dithering manner and stuttering a vocable that sounded like *but*, but Bartlett waved the proposed interruption away sternly. 'To help us in our work, we have a military body of engineers, technicians, pioneers, both male and female. The restriction that applies to ourselves applies also to them. They too have no family commitments, are granted no furlough, but they have a sufficiency of amenities and have been instructed in the great advantages of belonging to the project. The true nature of the project, of course, they do not know precisely, nor must they. But, even if they knew, they would be content to remain here till the end, having been made to realize – through televisual and other forms of indoctrination – the horrors proceeding, or due to proceed, in the world outside. They are well disciplined and are under superb officers. They are unarmed.' A chill went through the assembly as he said: 'Arms there are in this camp, but under my personal control, securely locked away in an armoury whose location I alone know. They will never be for the use of the military.'

'But,' dithered Nat Goya, 'there must have been a – '

'Silence,' cried Bartlett. 'Have the goodness to wait. You will,' he told his listeners, 'wish to know about supplies. In terms of commissariat we are already remarkably equipped. In terms of the materials necessary for your work, the basic requirements stipulated in the Frame prospectus are already in process of fulfilment. You will indent for further supplies, from hydraulic cranes to microfiches, through Dr Hazard.' He nodded towards a squat black man of superb musculature, who rose slightly, bowed slightly, frowned much. 'I can assure you that security will not be jeopardized even minimally in such necessary contacts with the outside world as are involved in the securing of your supplies.' He glowered at his audience an instant as if he knew how strong was its collective desire to jeopardize security and how purely self-indulgent would be its requests for supplies. 'Three centres – Kazan, Barnum and Wollcott – are at the disposal of the project. Loading will be effected by automation after telecomputering of needs. Pilotless vehicles will pick up supplies. One final, perhaps minor, point. To emphasize the essential unity of your various tasks, to promote a sense of quasi-military discipline, you will all wear uniform. It will be the uniform that I am already wearing. It is smart and serviceable, as you can see. The quartermaster, Lieutenant Wetmore, will be at your disposal all day in his store. Consult the map outside this auditorium for its location and the location of other departments. If there are questions you wish to raise, perhaps you would be good enough to arrange an appointment with me through my secretary Miss La Farge. And now Dr Frame will discuss matters of allocation with you.'

He strode out; Vanessa came forward. She began by organizing the lowering of a cinescreen and the projection of images of the interior of the spacecraft, and prepared to talk about the allocation of specialist zones of activity. But young Nat Goya dashed after Bartlett and caught him as he left the building, prepared to march purposefully to Project HQ and his office. 'Dr Bartlett,' he panted, 'there must be some mistake.'

'Mistake?' Bartlett frowned as the Kansas sky frowned.

'I'm a married man.'

'You're a – '

'Married man. With a child expected.'

Bartlett thought five seconds and then said: 'Impossible.'

'But it's true. I can show you the – '

'Nonsense. Computers don't lie.'

'They do if they're wrongly programmed. The information on me couldn't have been up to date.'

Bartlett doubly drilled him with fierce Napoleonic eyes. 'You can take it that your marriage is dissolved. I see no alternative to that. Like all of us, you're married to this project.'

'That's absurd. I'm married to a girl I love. I want her here.'

'*That's* absurd.'

'Or I want to opt out of this. If it means having to die, I'd rather have it that way. With her. With our child.'

'No.' Bartlett shook his head very sternly. 'Oh, no. There's no fat on this project – except for that Brodie man who isn't here anyway. You're the only microagronomist we have.'

'There's Belluschi. There's Audelan.'

'No,' Bartlett said. 'You need to have your priorities regularized. In a way you're a godsend. We can test the technique right at the outset. Report to Dr Adams after Dr Frame's briefing session. A session, incidentally, which you should be at.'

'Dr Adams? Dr Maude Adams?'

'Immediately after the briefing session. That's an order.'

'You mean I'm going to be brainwashed? Into forgetting my wife and loving CAT? No, Bartlett, I'm not having it.'

'I should hate to have to use disciplinary measures so early in the in the – ' Bartlett twitched minimally. 'Go on, now. Do as I say.'

'I'll go all right. I'll go straight out of that front fucking gate and I'll – '

Bartlett had taken a stick microphone from his breast pocket and intoned a frequency. 'Provost captain? Be good enough to send a sergeant and two men to Zone A. At once. Thank you.'

'Christ,' Nat Goya said. 'Police state tactics.' He shrugged. 'All right, I'll go. But you've not heard the last of – '

'With an escort. Until you're made to see sense and behave in a civilized manner.'

'Civilized manner. Oh Jesus.'

That expletive, children, was being used as a vocal gesture of shock but also as a genuinely pious ejaculation, by another man at that moment. Dr Calvin Gropius, with his wife Maria and his eldest son James, was proceeding by car towards Dallas, Texas. They had flown to Oklahoma City from Sacramento, California, after the disastrous rally which had been cut off from the eyes of Val Brodie and Willett and the other televiewing drinkers of that New York bar now drowned in dirty flood water. In Oklahoma City James Gropius had resided until the earthquake destroyed his home but not, he, they, thanked God sincerely, his wife Jennifer and their daughter Jessica. These two, having been forewarned in a dream, had gone to the home of John Gropius (second son) in Dallas, where they still, as a blepophone call had confirmed, rested in safety. Calvin Gropius, learning of terrible events on the California coast while still in Sacramento, had also learned of seismic disturbances inland. He had blepophoned James's number in Oklahoma City, but a recorded message at the central exchange had twanged that all private lines were temporarily out of order and that the caller should contact 405 5534–2349. This turned out to be a highly operative number, that of a temporary rescue centre on the outskirts of the city, and Calvin Gropius had made eventual contact with his son. The times seemed to call for a family reunion. The Will Rogers Airport was still functioning, though the Thaw, Whitehead and Toscanini car-hire services were all equally disorganized. It had eventually been a matter of stealing a Durango 99, idling outside the terminal building while the driver went in to get news of flights, or so James presumed. James stole the car, but he told his father that he had been merely lucky enough to hire it. He now drove it towards Dallas, just having crossed, by a very solid and imperturbable bridge, the raging Red River.

'Jesus, Jesus, help us all, forgive us all.'

The news trickled in faintly over the car radio. The citizens of New York caught unprepared, the disastrous flooding of the Potomac and the evacuation, to a location not yet announced, of the Commonwealth Government, the end of London and the whole northern French coast, a fissure all the way down the great continent of Africa, Russia's blaming of the destruction of Leningrad on the filthy monopolist capitalistic decadent world. How much was true, how much mere improvisatory rhapsodizing it was hard to tell: the announcer stuttered and kept breaking into his endless bulletin (as if to find time to invent new enormities) with a tape of a Utah choir singing Sir Arthur Sullivan's 'The Lost Chord'.

Seated one day at the organ I was weary and ill at ease –

'What's going to happen, Calvin? What's going to happen?' Maria Calvin kept up the hopeless litany. She was a mature beauty, under fifty, metallically smart, well-read in the Bible, not overintelligent.

'I don't know, I just don't know.'

'You should know, you ought to know.'

'Quiet, dear, quiet. Or else pray, yes, pray.'

'What's going to happen now, mom,' James said, 'is that we're all going to be together. Dallas is a safe place, nothing much happens in Dallas. John will be there, and Rufa and the kids, and Dashiel's coming over from Fort Worth. And Jay and Jay will be waiting for us, safe, sound and lovely.' He meant Jennifer and Jessica, his wife and daughter.

'But what's going to happen to all of us?'

'A guy told me,' James said, driving into a filling station, 'that this will last only a couple of weeks. Lynx will come closer and then go. Then there'll be a great calm, a lovely great peace, and we'll all get to thinking it never really happened.'

'But there's our apartment and Rachel and Judith.' Rachel was the cat, Judith the Teutprot servant.

'It's high, mom, real high. Safe as houses.' He pondered the simile and its ineptitude and growled: 'My stamp collection, all my fucking – Sorry, dad, mom.'

'All right, son, you're overwrought, God will forgive you.'

'I guess I just forgot myself.' He growled merely growls now.

The filling station was attended by a tough thin old man who knew his Bible better than either Dr or Mrs Gropius. At least, he knew it better in its Italian version. '*E vidi,*' he recited, filling them with Sharpas Super. '*Ed ecco una nube bianca, e sopra la nube uno seduto simile a un figlio d'uomo, avente sopra la sua testa una corona d'oro*. All a there,' he said, 'in a Bibbia. Enda world comin.' He was an Italian Protestant, one of the Mid-West Florio congregation. He gave them accurate change and wiped their window, exhorting them, in Italian, to repent. They nodded tiredly. He went to his seat, picking up a pornograph in bright colours. He was reading it with relish as the Gropius family resumed their Dallas journey.

'Jesus help us, Jesus forgive them.'

It was beginning to grow dark, and Lynx was rising, red and veined like a bloodshot eye. The moon seemed smaller. Mrs Gropius shivered and resumed her litany:

'What's going to happen, what's going to become of us, Calvin?'

'Oh, for Christ's sake shut up, dear. Put your trust in the Lord.' He was very weary.

'Yeah, I guess we ought to do that,' James said cheerfully. 'Put our trust in the Lord, like you said.' He had earned his living as a salesman of sanitary installations in presbyteries, manses, and other sacred residences. As for a less peripheral concern with religion, well, he left that to his father. One holy guy in the family enough.

'Family enough?' Dr Adams said, a very lissom dark-haired woman of thirty, to Nat Goya. 'That's what he said? The project is family enough?' She leaned against the surgery wall, legs crossed, arms folded, looking at Nat Goya, who sat in a kind of dentist's chair. 'All right,' she said to Sergeant Tiziano and his two men. 'You can go.'

'We got orders, lady.'

'The term,' she said coolly, 'is *doctor*. I have a right to see my patient alone. *Sergeant*.'

'He told us to stay, lady doctor.'

'Who?'

'Boss Cat, we call him.'

'Boss Cat,' she grinned. 'Very good. I myself will see *Boss Cat*, sergeant, and explain about responsibility and that sort of thing. All right, go.'

'If you say so, lady doctor or maybe it's doctor lady.'

'I do.' And they left. Then, door shut, she searched the beautifully appointed surgery for microphones, even telecams. She found a minute microphone, no bigger than a coin that was called a *dime*, very small, in the wall-plug of the examination light, and she pulled it out. 'There,' she said. She wrote rapidly on a prescription block: *Not happy about these dict. methods. You're free man. Giving water inject. Maybe other mics*. She showed this to Nat, then stuffed it in her white jacket pocket. She filled a syringe with water and watered Nat under his epidermis. Then she stuck plaster over the puncture. 'Come back at the same time tomorrow,' she said, 'and I'll see how you're getting on.'

'Thanks, Doc Adams.'

'You're welcome, *Doc* er Goya.'

'I'm beginning to see that he's right. The project is family enough.'

'You'll see it even better when you wake up tomorrow morning.'

He grinned and left. Having left, he did not grin. Sergeant Tiziano and his two dogfaces were in the corridor. 'Has our orders,' the sergeant said. 'Did it, did she?' They saw that she did. Nat Goya went away. The escort did not follow. Medical science had its own inbuilt escorts.

Nat got his briefing indirectly from Drs Belluschi and Audelan. 'Tomorrow at 0800,' Dr Audelan said. 'The foodfields are here, you see, in Bays 3A, 3B, 3C.' He had a plan of the ship. Nat Goya hardly listened. His mind was full of Fort Worth.

Two men, children, had actually settled into Fort Worth, having come all the way from New York straight with hardly a stop. There were wicked men in those days, and these were two of them. It was not their primary aim to be wicked but to make money fast and easy, and wickedness was unfortunately involved in the process. They had a fine old Sicilian name, Tagliaferro, and they were the sons of the famous Don Tagliaferro, who had christened them Gianni and Salvatore. Their father, and the rest of the great family of Tagliaferro (which, as you will know, means Ironcutter), had regarded the coming of Lynx as an impertinence hardly to be combated and so best ignored. They were in Princeton, New Jersey, a fine old university town full of fine old Sicilian names. Gianni and Salvatore had argued loud and long with their father, a thing not known before, and had said that this heavenly visitant was going to be the death of New York and possibly of New Jersey too. Gianna had read a book, a pamphlet really, full of the prophecies of an ancient guy called Jack the Seer, and this book gave a nasty prospectus of life for the current year, beginning on Lady Day. Floods and earthquakes and other disasters. Bad for business. They had talked with a guy in a bar who had advised them to go west, young men. So they had come west to superintend some aspects of the family business in Fort Worth, Texas.

The Florentine Hotel had long been fronted by a third cousin called Paolo, or Paulie, Praz, a suspiciously northern-sounding surname. Paulie had been responsible for certain irregularities, involving heavy feathernesting, and had been taken, on instructions from New Jersey, for a little trip to Lake Arlington, where leaden boots had helped to effect a rapid quietus. The boys who did the job were trusted death mechanics of the Tagliaferro family and they had been given, as a reward, a brief holiday at the Hotel da Rimini in Miami, Florida.

The installation of a non-Sicilian, even a non-Italian, as a replacement for Paulie, was not, in those days, considered all that irregular. Protestants, it was known, could be trusted more than Catholics, especially by Catholics. Customers liked to see a fine upstanding American college-boy type in charge of a gambling palace. It made them feel more at ease. Sicilians, for some reason, had rather a bad name. This guy Dashiel Gropius was a good guy; he was the son of a big Protestant preacher you saw on TV, hence a walking guarantee of cleanliness and fair dealing. There was no shadiness in his aspect nor in his accounts. He was no womanizer, no drinker. He read big fat books in his spare time. He liked running things. The hotel cuisine was good, though a bit Frenchified. The brothers were happy to set themselves up for a time in a couple of nice suites in their family hotel and consider the extension of their business in the Fort Worth area. Their families they had sent to live in another family hotel in Peoria, Illinois. They did not want them here for the moment. They wanted to taste of the local talent. Besides, the inevitable trouble with the Maranzana family which would be occasioned by the extension of their business in this area might be dangerous for their wives and children. They might send for them later.

Gianni, however, was troubled. He spoke, troubled, in the Trapani dialect of West Sicily, to his untroubled brother. He said: 'Suppose it happens. We were told at school by the nuns. The end of the world. What do we do?'

'Nothing we can do, *ragazz*. A short life and a happy one.'

'You think it can happen?'

'Anything can happen.'

Gianni was silent for a space, still troubled. Then he said: 'Hell. You think there's really a hell?'

'The priests say there's a hell.'

'If the end of the world came, there's where we'd go? We've done bad things. We'd go to hell for them?'

'*Babbo* has done worse, worse than killing.' He was referring to their father, Don Tagliaferro, who had, among other things, once personally cut off the penis of an enemy and made him eat it, or as much of it as he could. 'Hell, sure we were taught it's there. The big thing is to put off dying. Of course, *Babbo* may not go, not with all the masses. Better get those *puttane* in Illinois buying a few masses. They've nothing else to do.'

'But we may not like what you say be able to put it off. It's coming, *fratello*. I can feel it in my balls. What do we do?'

'Now? Have a drink. Always best to have a drink when the cold fist hits you on the back of the neck. *Un whisky liscio.*'

A neat whisky was what was in the hand of Val Brodie as he sat down, in white silk shirt, Taxis woollen suit of baby blue, and soft grey Gucci shoes, to a foredawn meal with Willett, whose bulk had rendered it difficult for him to find anything fresh to wear. He had, however, unexpectedly, bizarrely, come across male Scottish evening dress in the Ptolemy suite, and he now wore kilt, sporran, stockings complete with dirk, an oversize pyjama jacket all spots, and a bulky hunting coat of leather with pockets for hares and rabbits, possibly even stoats. In one of these pockets he had stowed a couple of precious *trouvailles* – mini videocassettes he had come across in a kind of library in the manager's office on this top floor. The tartan, Val knew, was of the Mackenzie clan.

They ate alone in the top-floor restaurant (named the Cleopatra), though they were not sure whether they were alone in the entire hotel. They heard odd movements, as of a great upset stomach, doors banging, feet hurrying, but these might have been engineerings of the tidal gale which, however, was now dying down. The restaurant had its own emergency power supply, like so many in those days of strike-bound public utilities and comparatively cheap nuclear installations. They sat to litres of fruit juice from the refrigerator, steaks, fried eggs, sausages, pork chops, cold Balmoral pie with mustard pickle, ice cream with strawberry purée, champagne (Ballart, 1984), brandy (Zacatecas, b.o.f.i.), much very strong coffee.

'The skywalk,' Val suggested.

'Hole up here for a bit,' Willett said. 'Nothing wrong with up here.'

'My view is,' Val said, 'that the tide will rise even higher tonight. Higher still tomorrow night. We want the highest hotel in Manhattan.'

'The Neogothic?'

'The New Gotham, yes. There ought to be a skywalk from the roof here. We'll see after breakfast. No immediate hurry. More brandy?'

Skywalks, boys and girls, ladies and gentlemen, were a feature of the Manhattan skyline in those days. There was much helicopter traffic, many heliport roofs, some of them in the service of hotels. You could disembark from the chopper, walk by skywalk to the reception area on one of the upper floors of your chosen midtown hotel, then be taken *down* to your room. The upper area of the city was called Alto, as the lower was called Basso. Having finished their bottle of Zacatecas, cooled it with more champagne and refired it with more coffee, and lighted up long Solzhenitsyn panatellas taken from the restaurant's smokecase, Val and Willett went up, following a notice that said TO THE GARDEN OF THOTH, to a ruined mess of greenery on the roof. They saw that there was indeed a covered skywalk, battered somewhat by the gales but still intact. The skyscrapers, they were relieved to notice, still stood in proud defiance and had also sheltered the skywalks from the fury of sea and sky. They looked down to see the water level falling as the sun rose. When it fell totally, they knew, they would see a street littered with thousands drowned.

'New Yorkers,' Willett puffed sadly. 'They will not be told. Everything left to the last moment. Public orders ignored. Public orders badly given and hardly at all enforced. Too much individuality. Too much incredulity. New Yorkers have seen everything and live in a perpetual state of apprehension. There is nothing new to make them feel new fear. Millions dead, I have no doubt. The subways choked with dead. How many, I wonder, will have gotten through the tunnels to New Jersey?' He shook his head, puffing. 'This walkway or airwalk or whatever it is leads to the roof, by a series of gentle stairs and corridors, of the Witherspoon Hotel. Then we mount, gently again, to the Valentino. Then the Neogothic.'

'New Gotham.'

They walked, peering through the tough durovit at the skyline. The Brooklyn Bridge was shaking in the wind. They could, they thought, glimpse the plinth whereon the Statue of Liberty had once stood. Soon, on its heliroof, they stood beneath the gigantic steel sign of the New Gotham. But the A and the M had gone, dislodged by fierce winds or struck by lightning, and the hotel spoke of what would now never happen, though it had often been prophesied – the coming of a new savage disruptor of western civilization from the fierce heartland of barbaric warriors. A morning wind suddenly blew with Gothic ferocity, straight out of the dawn. 'For God's sake – ' Willett cried tardily. The huge steel G, evidently only hanging on by a single rivet, flew down at Val and a serif clonked him on the temple. Then it clattered and clattered on the roof and at length lay still. Val too lay still. He had fallen heavily. 'G,' Willett said to himself, 'coming from the wrong direction. Val, Val.' Val was out and bleeding badly. His teeth madly clutched a panatella still smoking. 'Val.' Then: 'Jesus

Christ all damnable mighty.' Willett threw both panatellas away and dragged Val by his armpits. It was difficult. 'G,' bitterly. Panting, near-expiring, he got Val wound round him like a sousaphone in a fireman's lift.

Val came to at twilight, wondering where in the name of. 'Thank Christ,' Willett said. 'Quick, drink this, these I would say.' He gave him a potent analgesic ready watered, then hot strong tea, sweetened and rum-laced, from a thermos jug of large size. 'A foul headache, I should think,' said Willett, 'but the cut isn't deep. I checked, I medicated, I bound. But I was getting worried. You've been out too long.'

'How long?' Val felt the bandage, felt pain rattle in his skull like a stone in a gourd.

'G hit you yesterday morning.'

'Yesterday mor – '

'You were right about the tide getting higher. It seems to have engulfed that mock-Egyptian place we stayed in. Here seems safe enough. This is the penthouse suite, called, for some reason, the Ezra Winter.' Val took in blurred and agonizing luxury – beechleaf-green walls, olive curtains, chunky fawn furniture, a cocktail bar shaped like a stylized golden galleon. He was lying not in a bed but on a great couch as big as a bed. 'We are not alone,' Willett continued. 'There are others here with the same notion as ourselves – to ride out the storm, wait for a total tidal recession, and then – Then what?' he asked. 'Or will talking exacerbate the pain?'

'I think I'd better sleep.'

'But you've done nothing but sleep. No, unfair. It wasn't sleep. Will you eat something? No. Look, I'll leave you in peace for an hour or so. I have dancing lessons to give.'

'*Dancing less* – ' But Willett had gone. Val, shaken fully conscious and almost painless by this revelation of the frippery of dancing going on (seriously too: *lessons*, for God's sake) while New York drowned, meanwhile being terrier-shaken ratlike, suddenly felt a deeper and more awed affection for Willett than he had previously known. Willett had, then, dragged him here painfully, knocked out by G, whatever that meant, and tended him. If he had been alone last night's sea–sky bacchanal would have done for him. (Out as long as that, for God's sake.) He slept smiling, hearing the wind rise, feeling protected. He woke to dark with a monstrous light on him and he screamed like a child. Then he knew: Lynx. The destructive planet intruder. But surely Lynx had been different – a red sore eye, all veined? Now Lynx had a silver disc attached, its circumference edged in red, glued to the planet below the planet's centre. The moon and Lynx, lord and vassal, conjoined this night in a one-way tug. Then his senses, shocked to deadness by the vision, came alive to fear of the consummation of all things coming. His room rocked like a ship's crow's nest, the whole slender strong hotel beneath him creaked and groaned like a main mast, hail and rain whipped the window, fire tore at the sky and thunder rumbled open-mouthed a punctual second after. The pain in his skull temporarily knocked away, he went tottering to the window to look down and was aghast at what he saw: cream-topped waves dragoning and hurling three storeys down. This must surely be the tidal limit. In panic he went to what he took to be a bedroom but saw only glacial bathroom fittings, white hued silver and blood by the fireballs in the heavens. 'Willett,' he called, back in the living room, going to first one door and then the other. There was no sleeping Willett, only two neatly made beds. He shook his way to the corridor and found dim blue light, as in that other hotel so long ago, an emergency supply gamely holding up. He heard faint music. He followed its source and came to a well-carpeted broad stairway leading up to what was called the Jacob Riis Ballroom. He climbed the stairway and swung open a massy door, blued gilt in the dim light. What he saw astonished him more than the tidal madness without, the red and silver flameglobes.

Candles, candles, candles. A stereo player thundered out civilized defiance at the elemental rage clawing and bouncing the building: the *Blue Danube* waltz belting from wall and wall and wall, men and women, youths and girls, swirling to it, with Willett a ferocious master of ceremonies, beating out the time on the parquet with a broom handle as bandmaster's mace, crying: 'Dignity, grace, rhythm, for God's sake.' Faces sweated in candleshine, bodies swung, turned, swayed. This, Val thought sadly, this: you'd never get this in a spaceship. He sat down on a chair by the door, comforted by light, people, harmony, civilization. Never get this in a fucking spaceship. He decided to go down with *this* ship, so long as Willett was captain. Earthship, that had weathered so much, that held the dust of great men and women in its bowels. To hell with that cold contrived future in the heavens, the spaceship horror. And then he saw in his mind's viewing room Vanessa, cool, unperturbed, watching calibrations, taking readings. A woman he knew, a woman who had been his wife.

The heavens were hers: he would crumble to nothing with the dirty earth. His body relaxed to heroic resignation. Only the dead were great. He left the dancers, returned to the Ezra Winter suite, fell into one of the beds, raised his fist feebly like a wool-stuffed mock-Beethoven at the tempest in the heavens, then passed out like a child.

In pain from his cancer and his prosthesis, Freud could not sleep. French champaign in summer moonlight brought no ease. Anna put down her cheap English novel again. She had remembered something – her briefcase. 'Mail,' she said. 'I'd forgotten.'

'Last post,' Freud said in English. 'Retreat.'

'There'll be mail awaiting us in London. Forwarded. Unless the Nazis confiscate it.'

'Anything interesting there?'

'There's a strange letter from America,' Anna said. 'From a certain Samuel Goldwyn.'

'A doctor? Professor?'

'He makes cinema films. In Hollywood. *Himmel* – he wants to pay you one hundred thousand dollars – '

'To psychoanalyse him?'

'No. To be in charge of a series of films. About the great lovers of the past.'

Martha smiled broadly, unseen of her husband and daughter.

'He comes too late with his offer,' Freud said. 'Anyway, poor Ferenczi was the right man for that job. Always bubbling about love. He loved the films too. I couldn't keep him out of the New York movie houses. What year was that, Martha?'

'America? Oh, before the war sometime. I don't remember. You sailed from – I don't even remember that.'

'Bremen,' Freud said, as though announcing a great truth. Bremen harbour in sunlight, full of shipping and ship's sirens. Gulls wheeling. Ferenczi at the window of the quayside restaurant, bubbling.

'I can see her – that's her – there are people already going aboard – oughtn't *we*?'

This was not a train. Freud and Jung sat together calmly at a table, like seasoned sea voyagers. The waiter was taking their order. Freud said calmly: 'When you've had your hamburger steak, Ferenczi. It is that you want?'

'Wienerschnitzel,' Ferenczi said, coming back from the window.

'In Bremen?'

'Wherever you are, beloved Professor, to me it is Vienna. Wienerschnitzel. With noodles.'

'And,' Freud said, 'I think, a bottle of Sylvaner, well chilled.' The waiter went off. To Jung Freud said: 'How much is Fordham University paying you?'

'Not quite so much as Clark University is paying *you*. I forgot to order a bottle of mineral water. Never mind. The pay differential is as it should be. Talking of mineral water, I have a letter from Bleuler. Foolishly I left it in my suitcase. But you can read it on board.'

Freud chewed bread. 'The same old theme, I suppose?'

'Indeed. He read it to me before sealing it. He thought it mignt be – well, impertinent. He still can't stomach the word *sex*. It's not right for Switzerland, he says. The term *sexual* is going to get him burned at the stake. You too, of course.'

'In effigy only,' Freud growled. 'What does he want – infibulation? Pantheality? Corporeality?'

'Love?' Ferenczi suggested.

'Sexuality is sexuality,' Freud growled. 'Evade the term and you're exhibiting a neurosis. Sex sex sex. What's wrong with the word?'

'You have to accept, Herr Professor,' said bland Jung, 'that not everybody sees with your eyes. Perhaps in you there's a certain predisposition – '

'Nonsense.'

'If I may put it more delicately, perhaps the study of sexuality may be – well, a surrogate? I say no more. I have no wish to inquire into your personal life. Though, on board, I suggest we might exchange dreams.'

'Put my brain in your hands again?'

'And mine in yours.'

'Yours is there already. Ah.' The wine had arrived. The waiter poured it. He started to pour it for Jung, but Jung put his big masculine hand over his glass. Ferenczi said:

'Come, celebrate. We're going to take the great message to the New World.'

'Mineral water, please,' Jung said to the waiter. The waiter was an old man, a kind of museum piece with grey muttonchop whiskers and a tailcoat constellated with tokens of long-served dishes. He nodded, pouring, with deference. Freud said:

'It won't hurt you, you know. Didn't your St Paul say *in vino veritas*? Or is it the *veritas* that worries you?'

'I'll take just a mouthful then.'

'Bravo,' went Ferenczi.

'Fill the gentleman's glass,' Freud said.

And so they solemnly clinked glasses. Food came. They ate, Freud and Ferenczi with sea-air appetite. Jung picked at his fish. He said:

'I was reading on the train from Zürich about these bog corpses that have been found in Northern Europe. A newspaper article, though of some length, scholarly. You know about it – the presence of humic acid in the bog water tans the skin and preserves it, along with the hair. Natural mummification. You can see what men and women looked like thousands of years ago. Of course – this is the city where they are – the peat-bog corpses of Bremen. Pity there isn't time to see them.'

'Not,' Freud said, 'the most discreet topic for mealtime talk. You know poor Ferenczi has a queasy stomach. You'll be talking of rats next – '

'No no no no no. *Please*.'

'Besides,' Freud said, 'you're wrong about the location. You won't find those corpses in Bremen. They're further north – in Denmark, Sweden – '

'*Of course*.' Jung smiled. The marine sunlight filled his lenses. 'I knew all the time. Now what on earth induced me to import them to Bremen? What would your *Psychopathology of Everyday Life* say about it? Nobody makes an error without a reason – '

The other two saw with surprise Freud tremble and look glazed. His fork fell, then his knife. He silently began to tumble from his chair. A dead faint. 'Quick,' Jung ordered. 'Take his feet ' The strong Switzer had his torso firmly clasped. Thank God the restaurant was near empty. 'Where?' Jung asked the astonished waiter. The waiter led them to

Freud surfaced in the manager's office, on a couch. 'Thank God,' cried Ferenczi. 'Dear professor – drink this.' He held a glass of Jung's mineral water.

'I'm all right,' Freud said, sitting up. 'More overworked than I thought, perhaps. Or something I ate in Munich. Very strange. I don't faint. I don't collapse. This was the first time.'

The ship's siren urgently hooted.

Glorious August sea weather. Freud and Ferenczi strolled on deck. 'Where's he gone?' Freud asked.

'He's indefatigable,' Ferenczi said. 'He's working on the Anglo-Saxon mind. A rather intelligent cabin steward who claims to have read something by Dr Jones.'

Still, as Freud now spoke he looked cautiously at companionway entrances, as if fearful that Jung might spring athletically up and hear what he was now about to. 'Drawing on your psychoanalytical experience, Ferenczi, give me a diagnosis. Of why I collapsed. In Bremen.'

'Oh, that. If I were you I'd put it out of my mind.'

'Very loyal, Ferenczi. Come on.'

'A somatic thing, dear professor. Tiredness, indigestion, excitement.'

'No,' Freud cried, so emphatically that a strolling old couple stared. 'It was shock, Ferenczi. It was evasion of a terrible truth. Jung wanted to kill me.'

'*What?*'

'Oh, not consciously. Not with a knife or gun. He's anxious to lead our movement, and how can he do that if I'm still alive? He wants me dead. He transferred those corpses from Scandinavia to Bremen. Mine was among them.'

'I think,' Ferenczi gently said, 'sometimes – please please don't misunderstand me – you're too anxious, beloved professor, to see the world in the colours of Greek tragedy. The prince killing the king –'

'Crown Prince, that's how he sees himself – '

'But life is also quite a dull drab ordinary pleasant affair – a little neurosis here, a little neurosis there, not harmful. Carl Jung has a great affection for you.'

'And great ambition for himself, wouldn't you say?'

'For our cause, dear professor. He bursts with desire to spread the word. He has youth, energy, self-confidence, a certain glamour.'

'And I grow old. Not too old, however. Not old at all, by God. I'll show them – '

He looked to the horizon, where there was as yet only sea. The wind ruffled his beard. He took off his hat to feel the cool fingers of the wind play like a mother with his hair. The sun caught a tuft of his hair. Ferenczi saw it, a gilded horn.

Jung in his cabin had his stopwatch out. The steward was changing the sheets of his bunk in a leisurely manner, not averse to playing this big soldierly doctor's game for a while. Jung said:

'God.'

'Father.'

'Mother.'

'Cake. She baked good cake.'

'Green.'

'Blood. I fell on the grass when I was a kid. Cut my head open. On a stone it was.'

'Look,' Jung said in his Swiss singsong but otherwise excellent English. 'You needn't give me all this information. Just respond – a word for a word.'

'But,' said the steward, a pared man with a strong blue jaw, 'if you didn't know *why* I thought of blood when you mentioned green you'd go off and tell Dr Freud I was mad, wouldn't you? Let me give you a bit of advice, doctor. Don't meddle with people's brains too much. Very delicate piece of machinery the brain is. Like a clock. You should know all about clocks, coming from the place you come from.'

'Let's try again. Knife.'

'Father.'

'Sister.'

'Bed. I was in bed with my sister when my father came in. He went for me with his fists so I went for him with my pocket knife. Then I ran off to sea. Got all you want now?'

He had finished his deft making of the bed. Jung sighed and stowed his stopwatch.

'And,' the steward said, 'I've got no neuroses at all.'

They stood, the three of them, at the taffrail, and they saw for the first time the skyscrapers of Manhattan. 'The confidence of the son who's prevailed against the father,' Ferenczi said. 'Look at those phalluses. No neurosis there.'

'Virgin soil,' Freud said. 'To be planted with a million analysts' couches.'

'I must confess,' Jung confessed, 'to a sensation of being already overwhelmed. I fear being lost, absorbed – '

'Ah,' Freud said somewhat phlegmily, cigar stuck between strong teeth gleaming as though ready to chew the whole continent. 'Wait till they hear what we have to tell them.'

'You sound,' Jung seemed to admire, 'as if you own the place already. Ambition. It is, I suppose, a fine quality.'

'There's only one ambition worth having, Carl. And that is *to be first*. Having fulfilled that ambition, I have everything. Including this city.'

Which sidled coyly nearer, its harbour frantic with shipping, its pinnacles superb in the sunlight.

Superb at night too, punching the stars. The air had a vinous property. It promoted various kinds of appetite, including basic animal physical. Freud chomped his steak with relish at a restaurant table where ate also Ferenczi, Jung and the welcoming Brill. They had not waited for Jones. Democratic manners. Eat when you are hungry. They were already at the strawberry shortcake and coffee stage when they saw Jones cockily striding in towards them between animated tables. He greeted and was greeted. Freud said:

'How are the neuroses of Toronto?' The little orchestra struck up, as in Freud's honour, the *Blue Danube*. Jones said:

'Very active. Fighting the good religious fight against the Freudian devils. But we'll win.' A waiter came. 'A steak,' Jones ordered. 'Rather bloody.' And to Freud: 'We have to remember that North America is a return to the Garden of Eden.'

'Before the serpent got into the undergrowth?'

'I gave a lecture the other night – in Winnipeg. A lady afterwards said that Europeans might dream of sleeping with their mothers but Canadians were different. Canadians, she said, respected their mothers even when they were asleep.'

'You'll meet resistance,' Brill said, pouring more coffee for Freud. It was not as good as Viennese coffee.

'I've always met resistance.'

'You have to woo,' Brill said, 'not attack. Seduce, not shock.'

'Keep sex out of it,' said Jung.

'In the Swiss manner,' Freud unkindly said. 'In other words, lie.'

'No, Herr Professor. Come slowly to the truth. Dance the dance of the seven veils.'

'Titillate. That's obscene. There's nothing obscene about nakedness. Have no fear, gentlemen. I'll be academic, dull. I'll make incest sound like algebra.'

After dinner Brill said he had to get home: his wife had been murmuring lately about his late nights, which she did not altogether believe were spent in academic service, spreading the light about the sexual aetiology of the neuroses. Freud and Jung and Jones and Ferenczi went to a cinema. Freud sent ample cigar smoke curlicues into the projector beam, watching a man on horseback racing a train amid Californian scenery of great aridity, gently amused. Ferenczi was so volubly excited that members of the audience shushed him.

'Amazing! Astonishing! The art form of the future! The only medium that can convey the quality of dreams!'

Freud looked behind him at the back row, seeing young people making furtive love. He said, less loud than Ferenczi:

'*That's* what the cinema's for. A dime's worth of amorous dark.' He too was shushed. Coming out, they stood a while in the vestibule, Freud puffing benevolently at the emerging amorous young. Jones improvised a limerick:

'The young things who frequent movie palaces
Know nothing of psychoanalysis.
  But Herr Doktor Freud
  Is not really annoyed.
Let them cling to their long-standing fallacies.'

Jung was prudishly embarrassed. They went out, and their eyes were drawn to the pinnacles, long-standing phalluses. They saw a hot-dog stand.

'We'll have one of those,' Freud said. Sausages laden with dripping sauce were thrust into slit buns. They munched with relish and with relish, all except Jung, who genteelly sipped a Coca-Cola. 'Fellation,' Freud said.

'Sex,' Jung rebuked. 'Sex sex. You think of nothing but sex.'

'Nothing,' munched Freud happily.

Not so happy at that lecture, where was that lecture? A Freudian block. A large audience. Ferenczi, Brill and Jones on the platform. Freud said:

'The discovery of the sexual origin – more, the infantile sexual origin – of neurosis was not a discovery I was eager to make. I anticipated profound opposition from the Viennese medical confraternity, but the reality far outdid the expectation. I was drenched in odium, bespattered with ordure. I remembered the words of the great Oliver Cromwell, the British hero after whom one of my sons is named: "I beseech you, in the bowels of the Lord God, consider that you may be wrong." But the sea of vilification continued to wash over me. The the – ' He was in some distress. He looked awkwardly at

Brill and Jones. Jones had read his symbolism. He got up, ready to lead the way. Freud said unhappily to his audience: 'Forgive me. A call of nature. I will be back.' The audience buzzed. *Call of nature*, an obscene phrase. The learned professor clearly did not altogether appreciate certain *nuances* of the language he otherwise spoke so well. Freud and Jones hurried off.

They hurried down an underground corridor, trying all doors. Freud was desperate. At last they heard running water. '*Gott sei dank.*' Jones waited patiently outside a closed closet. The voice of Freud came from within, plaintive over noises less articulate.

'Those damned hot dogs. It was the relish, as they call it.'

'Don't tell Jung. He'll say *I told you so.*'

'Why are these damned places so hard to find in America?'

'Puritanism. You have to pretend that calls of nature don't exist. Everything hidden away.'

The sound of flushing came through.

No trouble in that other place, in Boston, Massachusetts. A triumph, you could call it.

'I am aware that in this city of Boston in the Commonwealth of Massachusetts puritanism was decreed for the early American colonies. I am drawn to puritanism. I see in it an immense intellectual rigour, an ascetic devotion to the virtues of hard work, a dignity and a disdain for empty pleasure, qualities which define the personality of John Calvin, creator of the Swiss character. But I am not drawn to its reticence about sex, its cultivation of sexual repression as a virtue, its traditional insistence on regarding sex as the snake in the Garden of Eden. In Boston I see the fusion of the better part of puritanism and the better part of American liberalism. I am proud that it is Boston that has given so powerful and gratifying a welcome to the science of psychoanalysis. This city of English Calvinism and Irish Catholicism is large enough of soul to welcome a heretic Jew from Vienna. But we are all together, regardless of the contrary tugs of contrary theologies, prepared to seek a new America, a new Promised Land, in which the soul of man shall be free and the life of man suffused with dignity and happiness.'

An immense clamour of clapping. Some stood to render homage. But two Irish policemen at the rear door, chewing gum, looked at each other wrily. And was it then that, gowned in the hood of a doctor of laws, he simpered at Brill's reading of the citation?

'Sigmund Freud, of the University of Vienna, founder of a school of pedagogy and therapy already rich in new methods and achievements, leader today among the students of the psychology of sex, and the new science of psychoanalysis, is hereby'

Overwhelming applause. And afterwards a reception. He clinked a glass with Jones. 'You're conquering Canada. I've made a start in New England. And Jung's spreading the word in New York. The infancy of psychoanalysis is at an end.'

A phrase he had used before, perhaps prematurely, and appropriated by Dr Carl Jung, clinking a glass of water against a glass of gin held by an academic of Fordham University.

'The infancy of psychoanalysis is at an end. A fine speech, Dr Jung.'

'I might have added that the psychoanalysis of infancy is also at an end. Thank you.'

'It was a relief to know that these – excavations into the human soul are not an essential part of the doctrine. A relief to know that, well, sex – '

'Please,' Jung cut in, 'don't regard my discourse as a rejection of the Freudian position. It's just a question of – well, of moving on. We honour our pioneers but we do them no honour when we refuse to build on their foundations. We may say that the Freudian generation already belongs to the past.'

A fidgety professor, emaciated and blinking all the time, whom Jung adjudged ripe for the couch, said: 'The pioneers overstate, I guess. Throw exaggerated emphases on to things in order to gain attention. So – we don't have to worry about incest any more.'

'Incest?' Jung sang. 'A fantasy symbol for something else. A failure of adjustment. The whole stress on sexual components in neurosis must now be modified. It was startling and perhaps salutary at first, it claimed all the attention of our great pioneer, my master and friend, but it was only one aspect of many – '

'Will you,' a priest fluted, 'be writing something on psychoanalysis and religion, Dr Jung? Some of your er adumbrations in the lecture were of fascinating import.'

'I fear that my esteemed master, rejecting the faith of his fathers, assumed that other faiths were as rejectable. Religion is increasingly confirmed as satisfying a numinous passion in all of us; it is no mere large-scale projection – as, if one may say so, on a cinema screen – of the mother, queen of the sexual heaven, and the father, grim king of punitive hell.'

'I think,' the fidgety academic said, 'a lot of us are going to sleep more easily in our beds after your lecture, Dr Jung. We had thought the psychoanalyst to be – well – '

'A long-nailed monster,' Jung said promptly, 'digging in the detritus of buried memories? Ah, no. Come to Zürich and you'll see that we're no more frightening than dentists, and we hurt much less. After all, we have to see our patients socially. We don't want anal erotism crawling over the dining-room floor.' A little inept, he thought as he sipped his water. But they laughed the laughter of relief.

It was a cold wet day in Vienna. Freud had, for some reason, packed away his waterproof. He must some time think what the reason might have been. For the moment one might consider it in terms of a new fearlessness, the spitting of his Viennese enemies reduced to a benign summer shower, his habituation to the sunlight of American esteem. But the rain of Berggasse was heavy, and he protected himself from it with his red doctoral gown, which for some reason he had placed near the surface of his toilet bag. He heard thunderous applause, but it was only real thunder. A cold dog looked at him, raising its snout from a sausage skin in the gutter. Freud looked back. The dog yawned. Freud schlepped his baggage wearily to Number 19.

The sunset is getting later. Trotsky, his hair in need of cutting, his cravat in disarray, his shirt dirty, his hands in his skimpy overcoat pockets, walks away from the strong wind that is blowing out of the gates of the sun. He is in Central Park. He is haggard. He sings:

Driven driven driven by the wind,
Riven like a lightning-struck tree –
Frightening to see
In one like me
Who has striven striven striven day and night,
Given all the might in his mind,
Fighting to find
The right, the right.
Then out of the west

The wind blew,
Shattering my rest:
The wind is you.
All that I thought worth treasuring
Is no such thing now, snow in spring now.
Driven driven driven like a leaf,
Given up to grief and to joy,
A toy boat on a raging sea
Is storm-tossed me,
Who have striven striven striven so hard to be free.

That girl there, striding north; is that she? No, it is not. She has gone, she has lost herself in this vast city. 'Love love love,' he cries to the still-bare trees. The wind ruffles his hair in unfeeling jocularity.

Val woke to daylight and near tranquillity, to find Willett, half Scot, half American hunter, looking down on him.

'How do you feel?'

'Better. That was one hell of a night.'

'Yes, I'm aching all over. So are the others, I should imagine. Oh, you mean the tide. I think we've had the worst of it now. Time and the hour run through the roughest – Perhaps I've given you that citation before. Shakespeare. I played Macbeth in Minneapolis, at the old Guthrie. Shall I bring you breakfast, or do you think you could manage to walk to the Pickwick Coffee Shop? A Mrs Williams and her daughter are running it, enjoying it too. There's nothing like occupation. It's on the floor below this.'

'If you could just bring me some orange juice and coffee – '

'But you must be *starved*.'

'Yes, I think I must be.'

'Ham and eggs. Sirloin steaks. Pancakes. Corned beef hash with poached eggs.'

'I'd better wash first.'

And so they ate breakfast, in cheerful enough company. There seemed to be a general feeling that New York, the world for that matter, had seen the worst. A man called Mr Weill was bitter about lost trade, the ruination of stock, the difficulty of restarting a men's garment store. A Mrs Wolheim tried to cheer him up by recounting something she said she had heard, thinly, distantly, on a radio broadcast from what was now called Commonwealth HQ, meaning presumably the new Washington: no shortage of government money to tide (ha) over, a mere matter of going to specially set-up CBF offices (Commonwealth Bureau of Finance) and drawing one hundred dollars a day. In inland towns and cities, of course. New York, no. Mr Terhune said there had to be a boom coming when all this was over, especially in the construction trades. The mortician's trade too, said a Mr Steinweg gloomily: all those bodies to be collected, identified, interred or incinerated. He was revealed later himself to be a mortician: the gloom was a professional mask. Val held his peace. After breakfast he would talk to Willett.

He talked to Willett up in the living room over a bottle of Presidio cognac (b.o.f.i.). There were certain things that Willett had certainly guessed; now he was to have as near professional confirmation as he could hope to obtain. 'You know,' Val said, 'or I think you know – '

'Yes?'

'That it's all going to be over.'

Willett nodded vigorously with even a sort of satisfaction. The satisfaction of not having to leave the party before it finished? Everybody saying good night together? 'I couldn't understand,' he said, 'why there was so much humming and hahing. Why couldn't the big men be out with it? I always thought scientists believed in the dissemination of truth.'

'The truth is very hard liquor. Panic. Murder. Wait till the people learn the truth. Not from others' lips, from their own agony.'

'What precisely is going to happen?'

'There's going to be a brief period of peace and calm. Optimistic clearing-up, I suppose, and a lot of free money around. A lot of goods to be used up. The sensible will know the worst from the fact of the general prosperity. No more future to save for, no virtue in thrift. No money spent on war, defence, feeding the starving half of the world.'

'How about the moon?' Willett asked.

'The moon?' It seemed, on the face of it, a frivolous question. 'The moon,' Val said, 'is, I think, already being drawn into the gravitational field of Lynx. Lynx's mass is very much greater than the earth's. We'll miss the moon during our period of tranquillity. No more destructive tides. No poetry, either. No popular songs. A lot of our literature will become meaningless.'

'Not meaningless,' Willett said. 'Just sad. My son,' he said, 'is on the moon. I used to get letters from him. I don't suppose there'll be any more letters.'

'I didn't know you had any family,' Val said, surprised.

'Oh, yes. My third wife left me six months ago. I have a daughter in Beckley, West Virginia, another in Philadelphia, two sons, twins, inseparable, in Springfield, Illinois. I never hear from any of them, but I used to hear regularly from George. George on the moon. He's been around the moon a bit, has George. Maupertius, Clausius, Cassini, even Hell. Has there been trouble on the moon?'

'Moonquakes? Without doubt. And now the moon is dragged away from us. But it will be back.'

'With Lynx?'

'With Lynx.' Val traced ellipses and circles on the coffee table with a brandy-wet finger. 'Lynx is entering into its first year as a member of this planetary system. It will be a brief year – not much more than two hundred days. There seems to be some ancient inexplicable law about distances having to be maintained between planets. I've had it explained to me, but I was little the wiser. Remember, I'm only a writer of fantasies, not a scientist at all. *Am*,' he then said bitterly. 'Why do I keep saying *am*?'

'Go on about Lynx.'

'Remember that earth itself goes round the sun. At present our position, ironically enough, is favourable to us. We could have been much closer to Lynx. But in the fall the two solar orbits will be very close indeed. The gravitational pull of Lynx, which we're feeling already, will then be irresistible.'

'So it's earth that will do the colliding?'

'We shan't think of ourselves as the assailants,' Val said. 'Even the specialists are using Ptolemaic terms, not Copernican. We suddenly think geocentrically. We always have, really. We will till the end. Lynx will rise, with our moon sidling around it. Lynx will approach. Lynx will be incredibly large in the sky. Lynx will hit. But every bit of our soft and shifting geology will yearn towards the tough male mass of Lynx. We offer ourselves, as children of earth, to the jaws of the beast. Sorry,' he grinned. 'That's the writer coming out. The bad writer,' he said with disgust.

'I take it,' Willett said, 'that this place where you were going was not what you said.'

'No. A spaceship taking civilization in microcosm into the great darkness, looking for a new light, a fresh habitable planet. Strictly speaking, I should be out there in the middle of the American land mass looking for it. A soldier who's lost his outfit looking for his outfit. I'm AWOL.'

'But you don't know where it is?'

'No, and I don't care where it is. You and I stay together.'

Willett took in several litres of dusty air and then let them out again. Noisily. 'Your place,' he said, 'is not only with the duty you were chosen to perform but also with the wife of your bosom.'

'I'm freed from the duty by not knowing where it is. That frees me also from my wife. Though the law says now that she's not my wife. I don't think I love her, anyway. Perhaps I'm not capable of loving a woman. Going to bed, yes, feeling a transitory tenderness. But engaging the mind, the psyche, of a woman – no. Perhaps that's why I failed as a writer.'

'You didn't fail as a writer,' Willett pronounced. 'I read one of your books – it was a serial on radio – '

'So,' Val said, smiling, 'it was you. There was always something about your voice that sort of pricked me somewhere – '

'Yes, it was me, I. *The Desirable Sight*. Would that be it?'

'Very much it.'

'There was a passage in it that stuck in my head. Let me see if I can – ' He sat back, shut tight his eyes, then hawked as if to bring up the passage from the back of his throat. 'Somebody says something like this: "The future hasn't come into being yet, and the present is a hairline thinner than the thinnest imaginable hair. There is only the past, and the glory of the past is not order, for order is an abstraction imposed by that non-existent thing called the present. The glory of the past is riot, profusion, a chaos of flowers. But there is another glory too. The past has beaten the forces of destruction: possibility became fact, and fact cannot be willed away ever, not even by God. Let us not dream of the future which does not exist and can exist only by becoming the present. Let us not dream of living in the present, since the present has no existence. Let us glory in having added more and more to the past, increased the roar of its music and the chaotic profusion of its flowers." ' Willett coughed modestly and took a swig of brandy. 'Something like that,' he said.

'It sounds good the way you say it. You almost make me believe in myself.'

'I was always good at that sort of thing,' Willett said with some complacency. 'Fine words, sound. They don't have to mean much, of course. Still, don't let me hear you talking of your failure as a writer.' He looked at the sunburst clock on the wall. 'I have another lesson to give,' he said. 'This time the mazurka.' He left. Val watched his big back on its way to his duty, along with the rest of his huge frame. He smiled with sad affection.

That night was the most terrible of all the terrible tidal phase. Both Val and Willett woke, heavy with brandy, to the smashing of windows, the unwished bounty of red and silver light, lightning like giant probing tendrils, sea and thunder vying for intensity of terror of sheer ragged noise, and the silver-red medallion of the sky partners in destruction flashing in and out of the torment of clouds. Val felt his hair turning to a nest of porpentine bristles as he tried with a dry mouth to say: 'Christ, look, the water – It's up to, up to – ' It was crashing, dirty grey-green-white sloggering knouts, at the window sill. Willett said nothing. Instead he grasped Val's arm in rough fatherliness and dragged him out of bed and to rapid dressing and then out of the room. The corridor was already filling with panic. Willett shouted:

'The whole damned creation is doing a mazurka. We must make for the highest building in Manhattan. The Partington Complex. If that isn't enough – well, we've had good times together. Come on,' he barked. And he led the way to the sky reception area, already filling with thirsty water. On the heliroof, fearful of being dragged down by the hurricane to the sea that brimmed the streets, they made, thirty or so of them, tight embracing groups of eight or ten, turning themselves into a single tottering beast with many legs and arms, wheeling drunkenly to the nearest covered skywalk. It swayed with furious irritability as they tottered across it in pairs and trios. Somebody, Mrs Stoke or somebody, screamed that it was going to go down, but Willett's voice thundered, 'Damned nonsense.' They came into the terrible open again on the roof of the Newman Tower, whipped and pushed and dragged savagely, drenched breathless, jeered at by the intermittent monstrous light up there. A single beast of sixty legs, they sidled towards the next skywalk. Val, clutching tight a frail girl called May Roth, felt her slipping, was conscious of the vibration, if not the noise, of desperate screaming. She was pulled from the joint grasp of weakening arms by a violent windstream and was to be seen, sickeningly, backing as in a dance, to the roof's edge.

She went over, arms out, as if begging for applause. Thunder gave it. 'On on,' Willett's great silent mouth must be yelling.

They fought the final pitch to the vast roof of the Partington Complex, which spread out on all sides of the central strong slender tower like a playing card poised on a pen tip. Val and Willett were among those who had reached that desperate near-haven when the violent voices of air yelled derision at the swaying tunnel poised over an infinity of black Atlantic, and they saw the desperate pleading arms of the others, their useless crying mouths, as the skywalk buckled at an Olympian wind buffet into an inverted V, sending some sliding straight into the maelstrom, others fighting to hold onto the apex of the inverted deck of the skywalk, bleeding hands slipping on blood, and then, gracefully, taking its time, the skywalk was an arrow pointing to Lynx as in protest, then it fired at the ocean below and plunged.

The way into the Partington Complex via the roof consisted of an ornate deckhouse, now much punished, with a fancy ironwork gate tormented by the elements to a nest of serpents. That gate, broken free at the catch and massively though soundlessly clashing, offered but weak opposition to their crawling panting entrance. They – Val, Willett, ten or so others, all men – found themselves broken, bloody, torn, breathless in a great empty upper hall, whose chairs and tables and magazine stands danced drunkenly from one wall to another with the sway and shudder of the whole structure. There were no beds to seek in this tower dedicated to commerce. Under the perilous clicking of emergency lights in the comfortless space it was enough for now to lie agonizingly filling dry lungs, hoping dawn would come soon, feeling a faint grim satisfaction that, if moon and Lynx were to get them now, they had done their utmost, scaled their highest mountain.

The group was assembled in Freud's consulting room, smoking hard. Anna came in to remove the coffee tray. She smiled shyly at her father and left. Stekel said:

'Growing up.' Freud said:

'I beg your pardon?'

'Your daughter. Growing up.'

'And so?'

'I merely remarked that your daughter was growing up.'

'I see.'

'Nubile.'

'I beg your pardon?'

'She is nubile. Of marriageable age. Your daughter.'

'I am well aware that my daughter is nubile, which means, as you are kind enough to inform me, of marriageable age.'

'That's all right, then.'

'Oh, let's get on with it, shall we?' Kahane said irritably. He meant the close examination of the contents, format and editorial voice of the *Psychoanalytische Jahrbuch*, of which they all had copies before them. 'This man Dr Hans W. Maier,' Kahane said, 'he ought to be whipped. He's a damned traitor. I told you this would happen. I always said that once you let the damned Zürich quacks get hold of this publication you'd have trouble.'

Freud tried to hide his uneasiness. 'He's a member of the Swiss Psychoanalytic Society. He ranks high in the Burghölzli Clinic. Tread carefully, Kahane.'

'But damn it,' Kahane cried, 'you're always going on about the pure Freud doctrine. How much of it have you got in this damned hundred-page article? It's nearly all that bloody man Bleuler, the man you said was a convert. It practically says the unconscious mind doesn't exist. That sex is for dogs and bitches, not pure Swiss citizens. Look at it this way – this *Jahrbuch* goes round the world. What are they going to say when they read this stuff? Freud's publication, right? Well, Freud doesn't believe in his own theories. He lets this man say that it's no more than a lot of hocus pocus and jiggery pokery and copulating on the analyst's couch.' And he pointed at Freud's own chaste couch, crammed with cretonne-covered cushions. There was a strong mutter of agreement. Rank said:

'Expel him from the Society is my suggestion. Make sure he doesn't pay his next year's subscription – letter going astray, that sort of thing.'

'Wait,' said Freud, 'I beg you. Think. We have to be politic.'

'We're not politicians,' Adler growled. 'We're psychoanalysts. Some of us.'

'What's that supposed to mean?' said Stekel.

'Yes, yes,' Freud cried, 'psychoanalysts whose concern at the moment is keeping the science alive. Consider our situation. In Vienna we remain unsupported by a university or a clinic. In Zürich the

Burghölzli Clinic uses our methods. Zürich publishes our yearbook – '

'It's not our yearbook,' Stekel said, 'it's theirs. They use it as they like. They publish long articles denying the validity of the very thing they're supposed to uphold and propagate. And your friend Jung is no longer at the Clinic. He's quarrelled with his boss. Bleuler and Jung spit at each other in the street.'

'That's not allowed,' Kahane drolly said. 'Not in Switzerland.'

'Nonsense,' Freud cried at Stekel. 'Bleuler's still a member of the Swiss Psych – '

'That means nothing,' said Adler. 'As this article here shows. It's become a general term, not a trade mark of Freudianism. A term that can be stretched to mean anything they damned well like. Including anti-psychoanalysis. I vote that this Maier be kicked out – '

'You can't vote,' Freud said. 'We have no jurisdiction over the Swiss branch of the movement. All I can do is write to Jung.'

'That,' Kahane said, 'will take us a long way.'

Fiercely Freud said: 'I tell you this, you idiots – the only hope of our prevailing in Europe lies with Jung and with no one else. We have no hope at all here in Vienna without university support. The future has to be ordained in Zürich.'

Kahane said sadly: 'I never thought it would be like this. Having to rely on a gang of antisemitic Switzers. They don't even drink. They're unnatural. And,' with somewhat factitious resentment, 'I object to being called an idiot, Herr Professor.'

'Oh, all right, not an idiot then. I'm the only idiot here. I was too innocent. I thought men of science could behave like rational beings – debating, accepting criticism and opposition like gentlemen, arguing things out amicably – '

'You'll never get that from the Swiss,' said Adler. 'There's something in the climate. Their blood's thin. They have cuckoo clocks.'

'I fail to see,' Freud said, 'what cuckoo clocks have to do with it.'

'Oh, I could write a whole essay about that,' Stekel said. 'Not that the Swiss would allow me to publish it. The sexual symbolism of the cuckoo clock. The penis tamed and kept in a little house. The acceptance of cuckoldry as a fact of the household.'

'Wait till the Nuremberg Congress,' Freud sighed. 'We can sort everything out at Nuremberg. Perhaps Nuremberg beer may help to promote a, well, kind of torpid reasonableness.'

'They don't drink, Herr Professor,' Otto Rank said.

'It's the home of unity,' Freud said helplessly. 'The city of the guilds, Hans Sachs, tolerance, that sort of thing. Well, we'll see.'

A strong evening wind blows the skirts up and hats off of young women and men going home from work, getting off subway trains, buses, street cars, stylizing their movements into dance steps, singing:

1917 –
The scene won't alter.
Two months have gone
Since Trotsky first called to
His comrades.
Europe's still at war,
And gory headlines
Show what's going on –
All corpses and breadlines
And bomb raids.
And still they haven't told us what we'll get yet.
America's not in it,
But the President may talk
Any minute.
Get ready, New York.
1917 –
Some green is glowing.
Spring's ripe to burst,
The Hudson is flowing,
And the snow is going away.
We'll know the worst
Or else still be okay
Before 1917
Has seen
The first
Of May!

They dance off home.

In the offices of the *Noviy Mir*, Bokharin, Voldarsky and Chudnorsky look glumly at Sasha sweeping. Nearly everything has been cleared out of this main room except a few chairs, and a rickety upright piano has been imported.

'It's a nonsense,' says Bol. 'Triviality and frippery.'

'It's in the great Russian tradition,' Chud says.

'Imperialist tradition.'

'What other tradition do we have,' says Chud, 'yet?'

'The revolutionary process,' says Vol, 'can make use even of bourgeois techniques if need be. That's laid down. Somewhere.'

'But ballet,' says Bok. 'A leg show. And what does Natalia Trotsky know about it?'

'It was her ambition,' says Vol. 'In the old days. Besides – '

'She's right,' says Chud. 'If revolution's an international process it needs an international language.'

'We have an international language already,' says Bok. 'Russian.'

'You'd be surprised,' says Chud, 'at the number of Americans who refuse to learn it. Including Russians. Him there, for instance.' He means Sasha, who is still more or less sweeping.

'We'll see,' says Bok. 'One thing is true, and that's for sure. *He's* not getting the message across. Lev Davidovich. Not now.'

'You heard him last night?' asks Vol.

'I heard him,' says Bok.

'We both heard him,' says Chud.

'A big crowd?' asks Vol.

'Packed. It was Philadelphia.'

'What did he say?' asks Vol.

They sing.

BOK: Instead of the strife
Of capital and labour,
He spoke of a life
Spent helping out your neighbour.

CHUD: His sabre
Has stopped flashing.
He's shoved it in its sheath.
No more gnashing
His teeth.

VOL: That is no way to start a revolution.
It throws a cold douche on
The very idea.

CHUD: He didn't once clash
The hammer and the sickle.
BOK: He'd willingly cash them
For a wooden nickel.
CHUD: He's fickle as a virgin,
All ifs and ands and buts.
BOK: Got no urge in
His guts.
VOL: That is no way to start a revolution.
BOK: It throws a cold douche on
The very idea.
VOL: He seems hand in glove
With the swine who ring the bell
In the Sunday morning steeple.
BOK: With the parasites who sell
The opium of the people.
CHUD: Brotherly love yet. Brotherly love.
VOL: His red is red paint.
He talks like Dostoevsky.
CHUD: He'll turn into a saint
BOK: Like Alexander Nevsky.
VOL: He's deaf.
CHUD: Schi-
Zoid.
BOK: A poet.
Like Pushkin –
VOL: Only bad.
CHUD: He doesn't know it
Makes us mad.
ALL: That is no way to start a revolution,
It throws a cold douche on
The very idea.
And we want a revolution
This year!

'He doesn't know where she is?' says Vol. 'You're sure?'

'Sure,' says Bok. 'Last place in the world he'd suspect.'

'He sees the messages,' says Vol.

'She doesn't,' says Chud, 'put her name on them. Comrades, she's doing well. A nice harmless American Russian secretary in the Imperial Russian Consulate. And she's a – '

Bok shoves his fist on Chud's lips and indicates the back of sweeping Sasha.

'He doesn't know Russian,' says Vol.

'He mustn't see her,' says Chud. 'If he doesn't see her he'll get over it.'

'Two months,' says Chud, 'is nothing in geological terms.'

'Does Natalia suspect?' asks Vol.

'Natalia has her ballet. Shhhhhhhh.'

For now there enters

Men were at work painting AMERICA on the hull, using a uricon-based mix guaranteed to resist indefinitely the encroachments of the abrasive dirt of space. Silver on black – simple, elegant. It had not yet been decided whether to add the numeral I to the name. There were, it was known now, other spaceships in preparation, all, by presidential fiat, to be christened after the land of their creation – II, III, IV: the line would stretch literally to the crack of doom. To call this protoploion anything other than plain *America* was somehow to diminish the achievement, to make it appear primitive and experimental and, in a sense, already a dead thing.

The great ship rested on an artificial sea of synthetic foam and, in high winds or even earth tremors, would rock gently on it: its gravitational system was its own and built into it. It was endowed with a quality of spatial excess or marginality essential to what was no mere vehicle but a whole self-contained world. The ploiarchal, or navigational, area was small in comparison with the living and working quarters; the nuclear propulsion device was negligible in size, as were the power generators or heliergs. The whole structure was three decks high. One would go upstairs to bed – fifty double cabins, ten bathroom-toilets, a commodious automated laundry. The middle deck housed the galley, under the control of Dr Rosalba Opisso, assisted by peripatetic robots, the dining hall, the recreation area (cinema, games room, library, microviewing booths). The main or first deck was dedicated to work. It was a university in miniature, with micro-archives, lecture rooms, laboratories, computers. A sterile area of some size, at the stern of the craft, was given over to the vital task of providing nutriment – protein surrogates, vegetable matter, complex vitamin constructs. There was, near it, an engine for converting the waste products of the body into aliments. Below this deck lay the intricate electronic economy of the whole organism, including the gravitational magnetotechnasma of brilliantly original design. Dr Guinevere Irving was in charge of the atmosphere, the flow of the carefully controlled mixture that converted the perpetually expired into the perpetually inspired. Hospital facilities were tucked away in a side pocket rich with elevators which rose to the whole height of the ship. There was much much more. Children would be born, brought up, educated, and would grow to maturity and death at a rate of population growth which would never exceed the maximal hundred for which *America*'s economy had been designed. The eventual dead would be disposed of unwastefully – converted to fuel and nutriments.

Running all round the ship at mid-deck level was a walk of more than a kilometre and a half in perimeter, but there were no ports or lights looking out onto the dispiriting show of space. Instead there would be, according to Owings Merrill Skidmore, regularly changed stereoscopic vistas of country, sea and townscape, or works of art, or kaleidoscopic fantasy, the illusion of infinite clothed space, not the true nakedness outside.

Young Nat Goya, microagronomist, had promised himself that he would, before any work was started in his department, be out of the concentration camp in whose midst *America* was set. He had simulated to Boss Cat Bartlett, whom he cordially detested (nor was he alone in this), the lineaments of a man brought, by cunning medicine, to single-minded devotion to the enterprise. He was no longer, his faint smile said, a devoted husband and potential father. But he was going to get the hell out of here.

He had wandered round the camp, just inside the electrified periphery, looking for an unattended gate, but guards were omnipresent, efficiently changed every six hours on the second, and, though they were not equipped with firearms, they had coshes and nightsticks and walkitalks and loudhailers. There was no need of perimeter floodlights, since the whole Kansas sky was a nightly day, what with bright red Lynx and the silver moon. To burrow under the wire was a dream derived from old scratched movies about POW camps in World War whatever-it-was, I, II, III. To diminish Nat's chances, a disaffected corporal named Stanford Everard Whiteboy had himself attempted escape when on guard duty, making a run for it. Brought back, he had been brutally punished, publicly too, on the orders of the military commandant, Colonel Fernando Jefferson. This was to stress the urgency of the CAT project.

His best way out, so it seemed to Nat, was by means of one of the driverless vehicles, remote-controlled by Captain Truslove's transport section. He had wandered round this area, on the pretext of looking for Dr Ebenezer Hazard, supplies coordinator, who was supposed to be there consulting about a particular bulk order on the depot at Kazan and the number of vehicles required to bring it in. Nat had a brief opportunity to examine the structure of a Speight van. He was even able to look underneath it and observe the simplicity of design – the axles, a kind of hook perhaps connected with traction, and a long laterally placed metal bar probably used for the yanking open of a kind of booby hatch which afforded a view of the engine not provided by the lifting of the hood. Nat, being an adoptive New Yorker, knew little about automobiles, either gas-powered or nuclear-driven. About this kind of autoautomobile he knew nothing at all. But it seemed to him that he might conceivably fit himself for a brief space under a vehicle like this, hands gripping that hook, or perhaps a bit of rope affixed to it, feet resting painfully on the lateral bar. The vehicle would leave the camp and, at a decent distance down the road, he would let go and drop, relaxed, flat as a corpse, and be free.

As an earnest of his forthcoming desertion of the project, he worked very hard on his aspect of it, supervising the installation of the auzesis trays and even manhandling some of them himself. He scrupulously requested permission for a further injection of the magical substance from Dr Adams, telling Boss Cat that he had had a disturbing dream of his wife weeping and did not wish any more such incubi. Dr Adams, who was now close to open expression of her dislike of Bartlett, gladly injected him with distilled water.

It was when the moon had become a frank satellite of Lynx and Lynx already seemed to be retreating that Nat went to Dr Hazard with an urgent indent for heliodiscs and even asked when he could expect them.

'There's this order going out to Kazan tomorrow,' Dr Hazard said, unsuspicious. 'I could telly this addition to it now. There'll be two Speight vans leaving at 0800.'

'I'd be grateful if you would. Twenty, HD/369 gamma size, as I've specified here.'

'In quint? Right. No trouble.'

The following morning nobody could but be pleased at the sight of Nat Goya, in tracksuit, jogging round the camp, young, athletic, shaking out harmful juices, sweating away useless impertinencies like sexual desire. At one point, near the transit lines, he got a stitch, also a crick in the calf, and limped panting, looking for a spot to rest. He did not think anyone saw him when, lying low, he inched under a Speight van. He took from his tracksuit pocket a little thick hemp, fixed it to the traction hook, and knotted himself a handhold. With difficulty, as in a bed too short, he managed to fit his soft-shoed feet onto the pullbar. His watch had recently given him the time: 0751. He would not have long to wait. If, that was, he had chosen the right truck. The position was fucking agonizing. But not long to wait at all now.

At 0800 the first of the long day's camp sirens sounded dismally, as though an air raid were expected. Promptly vehicles began to move, one at a time, down a shallow ramp. To his relief and joy, Nat found that his was one of them. There was one immediately behind, as he could tell from the noise and the occlusion of light, and this might present a problem when the time came for his drop; he did not wish to be mangled by unstoppable wheels. He was aware of a gate sliding automatically open. He heard the yawn of a guard and another guard answer his fatigue or boredom with 'Yah, you're right at that.' Then he was on the road. The position was desperately painful, and he would, he thought, have to endure it for several kilometres. What electronic eyes were peering beyond the confines of the camp he did not know. He must take no chances.

After, he judged, twenty minutes of agony at high speed, his hands on fire and his feet numb, a thing happened he should have expected but had not. The vehicle came to a sudden halt, as also the one behind. There was a traffic light to be obeyed, and the automatic drivers were automatically obeying it. This meant that they had come to a town or village or the outskirts of one.

He dropped, boys and girls, ladies and gentlemen, sore, half-dead, but unharmed. He dropped, swiftly crawled out from under, painfully stood, saw a sidewalk and limped to it, then looked warily about him. The light changed and the vehicles went on their way. He had arrived in a town of one street only, and he had arrived, apparently, unnoticed. There were few people about, and those who were saw with little curiosity a young man in a track suit panting, stiff, having perhaps run too much before breakfast and now probably wanting breakfast. There was, he saw, a place in which to take breakfast – Jack, Joe and Curly – as also an Untermeyer General Store, a Stokes dress shop, a Bellow–Mailer hardware shop, and a grim building called the Chapel of the Flowers of Beulah. He went to see Jack, Joe and Curly, but not for breakfast. He wanted to use the telephone. He had coins, he had made sure of that. He had the number. He nodded at an old man slurping coffee and at an unshaven young man in dirty white behind the counter, Jack, Joe, not Curly, because he was bald. Or perhaps because he was bald they called him Curly. He went to the wall telephone, heart desperately thumping. He knew the number by heart. He dialled with a tremulous finger. He nearly fainted when he heard her voice.

'Darling, angel, sweetheart, it's me.'

'Who?'

'Me, Nat, your husband, remember?'

'Oh, thank God, oh Nat, I love you, I love you, I. Where are you, Nat? Here?'

'No, honey, not yet, I'm – ' The name of the little town was up there on a police notice about a certain escaped and dangerous Geoff Grigson. 'I'm in a place called Sloansville. I escaped.'

'Escaped?'

'Oh, it's a long story, they only have unmarried people here and they didn't know I was married and I told them but it made no difference and now I'm on my – '

'Oh my love, oh my dearest – '

A hand on his shoulder and another hand gently detaching the handset from his own hand and. It was a man with a stormy plump Irish face, known to Nat from a distance only previously. The name Lee Harvey O'Grady, his trade that of astunomicologist. Nat had not inquired into the meaning of the term, but now he thought he was going to begin to know it. O'Grady said:

'You enjoy your little run?'

Primed by the word, Nat tried to make a run for it. But there were two military policemen waiting outside, smiling, as pleasant as you could wish. There was also a car with a police driver, chewing something, looking with interest at Nat.

'We're going back,' O'Grady said, 'nice and quiet and no trouble. Can't have jeopardizing of security, can we? You might have breached security very nastily if I hadn't grabbed you in time.'

It was a silent drive back, except that O'Grady hummed a little tune, the while examining his nails. 'Thanks, men,' he said as the vehicle stopped in the transport park. 'You and me,' he said to Nat, 'are going to see Boss Cat.'

Bartlett sat in his austere but sizeable office. He said to Nat, who stood before him, O'Grady behind him, his stormy Irish face smiling faintly and plumply: 'It was, of course, very foolish. What worries me is that you didn't realize the foolishness. That argues a lack of intelligence. I wonder sometimes at the viability of cybernetic selection. You see, you were nowhere to be found in the camp at 0800. Therefore, you had to be out of the camp. There was only one way for you to leave. It was all very foolish. The question is: what are we going to do with you?'

'Throw me out,' Nat mumbled. 'I'm no good to the enterprise.'

'You're no good to the enterprise,' Bartlett agreed. 'As for throwing out – throwing, I would say, comes into it, wouldn't you agree, O'Grady?'

'He didn't jeopardize security,' O'Grady said.

'Throwing *to*, not *out*.' Bartlett turned right around to look at O'Grady, who grunted and smiled dourly at the same time. Bartlett turned back to Nat and confided: 'A certain Dr Damon Scribner is being summoned. You know him?'

'My field. Mid-Western University. Author of *Space Trophimonistics*.'

'Correct, correct. *Throwing to*. You know your Bible? Daniel and the lions. Nathaniel and the lions.'

'My name's Nathan.'

'A matter of small importance. A name will hardly be worth attaching to what you're going to become.'

'What are you going to do?' Nat could hardly believe that, for so minor and moreover abortive an infraction of rules, he was to be, well, punished. This was not the Mafia. He had been brought up in a liberal tradition. 'What exactly – '

'Dr O'Grady here will have you safely escorted to the Provost Captain. We delegate punishment to the military. They have experience of that sort of thing.'

The disciplinary action chosen for Dr Adams was less drastic and was promulgated by Bartlett himself in public. She was arraigned before a court of which both judge and jury were the same man. The entire CAT team was ordered to attend. The time was 0600 the following day, a recessive Lynx, along with its moon, lazily setting. The place was the assembly hall. Bartlett sat at the little table on the dais: Dr Adams, dark, lissom, smart in her black uniform, stood below him. Bartlett said:

'This is a court of law. Our laws are emergency laws and our procedure must be emergency procedure. Dr Maude Quincy Adams, you stand accused of violation of an order. You were instructed to administer to Dr Nathan Goya a particular medicinal injection, designed for his own physical and mental good and for the good of the project. You failed to obey the instruction. Do you admit this?'

'Oh, I admit it.'

'Have you anything further to say?'

'Yes. A question first. What has happened to my – patient?'

'You will not ask questions. You may make, if you wish, a statement.'

'Very well, I state this. That the purpose of this mission, as I see it, is to salvage human civilization – '

'A tautology. Civilization is necessarily human.'

'No. Your view of civilization is an *in*human one. If the civilization we are met in this camp to salvage is merely a matter of intellectual and technological knowledge, then it is not worth salvaging. Justice, compassion, fairness, humour – even a modicum of decent human inefficiency: where are these? It is not only my opinion that the dictatorial methods you are using will wreck the project. You were in the navy. You probably know the phrase *a happy ship*. You are at this moment commanding a very unhappy one.'

Bartlett sighed and shook his head. 'The time will come for what you call compassion. Also fairness, humour, though never never never, under my command, inefficiency. But the time is not yet. This project is the most audacious the world has ever seen. It must not fail. We must transform ourselves into unfeeling mechanisms until we are assured of its success. Then the virtues you speak of will have time to flower. Not before.'

'What,' asked Dr Adams again, 'has happened to Dr Goya?'

'Dr Goya,' Bartlett said, 'is unfortunately no longer with us. *Unfortunately* – a conventional term I ought to apologize for using. Dr Goya should never have been chosen in the first place. His substitute will be arriving tomorrow.'

'What,' Dr Adams repeated with heat, 'has happened to Dr Goya?'

'Dr Goya,' said Bartlett patiently, 'has been struck off our strength.'

'He's dead, isn't he?'

'Dr Adams,' Bartlett said sternly, 'we are concerned at the moment with your er misdemeanour. You say you admit to its ah perpetration. We must think of an appropriate disciplinary response to that.'

'*We*,' the accused mocked. '*We* are not allowed to think of anything.'

'I, then,' said Bartlett. 'I do not propose to dismiss you from the project – '

'Meaning *liquidate*,' said Dr Adams.

'But I hereby direct that you receive habilitatory treatment from Drs Fried and O'Grady. I hereby direct those two officers to initiate this treatment as from today. And I shall arrange for a military escort to accompany you, Dr Adams, as you proceed on your regular duties, until such time as I am satisfied that rehabilitation has been effected. This court stands adjourned.'

The incineration of the battered body of Dr Nathan Goya took place in the camp crematorium at 0300 hours. There were no obsequies.

Old Nuremberg and its sights. Wagner's *Meistersinger* overture. Freud and Ferenczi were walking in earnest talk. An astonishing thing happened. A man came round a corner, smoking a cigar, his beard greying, his eyes steely, his face the face of Dr Sigmund Freud. He walked on, steely eyes surveying some empyrean of higher thought; or else the problem of paying a bill or ridding himself of a mistress no longer wanted. Freud nearly fell. Ferenczi, concerned, held him upright.

'Oh my God,' breathed Freud. 'My double. You know what that means, Ferenczi – death, approaching death. That's the second time I've seen him. The other time was in Naples – '

'How long ago?'

'About ten years.'

'And you're still alive.'

'That was the premonition of the premonition. This is the real warning – '

'Nonsense, Herr Professor. Come and drink some beer. You're beginning to sound like Jung – all this superstition and mysticism – '

So they sat at a quiet indoor table and ordered the local brew. 'Call it a warning,' Freud said, 'that things had better be set in order. That's why I asked you to come a day early. We know not the day nor the hour.'

'What do you want me to do?'

'When the papers have been read and the discussions held – I want you to take charge of what amounts to a general policy meeting – more, a meeting that will define the nature of ourselves as a permanent organization.'

'Me in charge? I'm honoured.' There was a fleck of beer foam on his smile.

'You're the obvious choice. You're not Viennese and you're not a Zürich man. You've done wonders in Budapest, and how? By being likeable, by going about things cheerfully and discreetly. You'll be ideal as chairman.'

'Honoured again, overwhelmed. But I fear your Viennese colleagues. They won't like it.'

'I'm sick of my Viennese colleagues. Wrangles, dissensions, small-mindedness. Adler and Stekel sarcastic, mumbling in corners about socialism, treating me as an old fogey. No, it has to be you, Ferenczi.'

'You said something about a permanent organization – '

'We have to set up an International Psychoanalytic Association with constituent societies in Austria, Germany, America, Hungary, England – all the countries that are ready. I want Carl Jung to be elected President of the International Association – *for life*.'

'Are you sure? Really sure?'

'Yes, I'm sure. Vienna can never be our centre, nor can London. Zürich has been receptive to our science from the start – despite dissensions which may be regarded as evidence of vitality. Another thing – the yearbook which is our organ, our voice. We have to guard against the intrusion into its pages of stupidities.'

'Like Maier's article?'

'Exactly. Carl Jung must have the right to examine all articles submitted and decide what should or should not be published.'

'I see no harm,' Ferenczi said doubtfully, 'so long as you are on the governing board.'

'You mean I may be removed from the movement? By revolution?

By death? Close your mind to that, Ferenczi. It's the only way to live – to close one's mind to unpleasant possibilities.'

'Or certainties.'

'What do you mean?'

'It was you who mentioned death, not I, dear Professor.'

'And when I'm dead, who can run the organization? Can you, from Budapest? Can Jones, from London? Brill, from New York? We have to accept the truth that only Carl Jung is qualified to be my successor. Qualified in terms of originality of mind, in strength of character – '

'The very qualities that will draw him further and further away from your own doctrines, the pure Freudian milk – '

'No, no. He's my natural successor. My friend, my son.'

'And, of course, he's in Zürich. That's the real point that has to be made.'

'Yes, yes, dear Ferenczi,' seeing eyes moist and lips, still foam-flecked, turned down, 'you too are original, you too are strong. But you don't happen to be in Zürich. You too are my son, never forget that. Order more beer.'

And so Ferenczi, all charm, took the chair in the hotel salon and addressed the assembled delegates, saying:

'Gentlemen, I think I express the general feeling of the congress when I say that we have had altogether admirable papers and discussions of immense vitality. I may instance Dr Adler's paper on pyschic hermaphroditism and Professor Abraham's on fetishism, as well, of course, as our leader and founder's contribution on the future of psychoanalytical techniques.'

There was a smattering of applause for the leader and founder, which he acknowledged with a flick of cigar ash onto the carpet.

'We come now,' Ferenczi said, 'to what may be termed the business aspect of our congress. It is proposed that we form an International Psychoanalytic Association, with branches in all countries where they are ready to be formed. I take it that there will be no dissentient voices raised to this proposal.'

None, loud applause rather. Freud sucked his cigar to a bright glow as his own contribution to the positive clamour.

'The headquarters of the International Psychoanalytic Association,' Ferenczi said, 'will be Zürich. Dr Riklin here has expressed himself willing to act as executive secretary. He will collect dues, supervise publications, officially recognize new chapters as they open in Berlin, Budapest, London, New York – '

An immense chill settled on the Viennese contingent.

'It is proposed,' Ferenczi said, 'that the life president of the Association shall be Dr Carl Jung.' First chill, now murmurs. 'As life president,' Ferenczi went on, 'he will be responsible for the organ or voice of the Association, the *Psychoanalytische Jahrbuch*. All materials to be published therein will henceforth be subject to the approval of the president. Only by such centralized control can our science remain a science, unsullied by contributions which strike at its dignity and truth – '

Stekel stood and cried: 'Dictatorship. Tyranny.'

Adler stood and cried: 'We're sick of the dictatorial hand of Zürich. We Viennese are the founders of psychoanalysis. We will not permit it to fall into the hands of foreigners.'

Irate, Freud stood and cried: 'I, sir, am the founder of psychoanalysis.' Ferenczi quietened the tumult with his gavel. A single voice, that of Kahane, cried:

'Why is Vienna always put down in favour of Zürich?'

'I will tell you why,' Ferenczi said, with uncharacteristic hardness and crispness. 'Because they are all university-trained psychiatrists, and you are not. Because you Viennese are unrecognized in your own city. You are unsupported by a university, a clinic or even a provincial hospital. Because your approach is unscientific. You, Dr Stekel, are known to invent psychoanalytic cases. You, Dr Adler, have drawn psychoanalysis into the doubtful realm of politics. The conduct of the Viennese, who by rights should be the most loyal supporters of the great Viennese who founded our movement, is unscientific and unacceptable. That is why Zürich must be the headquarters of the International Psychoanalytic Association.'

The response to this statement was shameful. Viennese and Zürichers tore unhandily at each other. Stekel and Adler tried to manhandle Ferenczi, who screamed protest in Magyar. Dr Jung strode to the chairman's table and grasped the gavel. He hammered and hammered with it on wood not bone and cried:

'This meeting is adjourned. This meeting is – '

By then a heartsick Freud was on his way out. He climbed the stairs wearily to his first-floor room, where his first act was to take a small bottle of cognac from the chamber-pot cupboard and glug some into a toothglass. He lay on the bed with it, sipping and hopeless. When a knock came he called *Herein* with little voice. Otto Rank came in. He said:

'Herr Professor, I think you'd better come to Stekel's room. All the Viennese are there. They're very angry. They're threatening to walk out of the congress.'

'Oh my God,' Freud groaned. 'All my fault. I thought I could trust Ferenczi. I told him too much. I was indiscreet – '

'You've been human, Herr Professor, no more. Try and persuade these others to be human.'

Freud could hear the angry babble before, erect and ready, Rank behind him, he knocked. Betrayal of the worst kind the betrayal of innocence I don't call it innocence I call it sheer damn overbearing pseudopaternalism well he always said we should not trust our father figures. He walked in and they shut up then. They just looked at him sullenly. He said:

'I've let you down, haven't I?'

'Why,' Adler said, 'did Ferenczi attack us?'

'He was playing a role,' Freud said tiredly. 'He thought it was my wish that you should be attacked, he misinterpreted my – expressions of dissatisfaction – '

'And now,' Stekel said, 'the whole world is made to believe that I invent all my cases. I've a good mind to sue him for slander.'

'I chose Ferenczi to speak for me,' Freud said, 'because I thought I knew Ferenczi. I apologize for my stupidity and for the indiscretions that Ferenczi uttered. I beg you, in my distress, with all humility, to forget what happened just now.' No one had risen on his entering. He had been standing, but now Kahane offered him his chair. Freud thought of taking it but then shook his head. Adler said:

'There's no forgetting. That's the whole basis of Freudian analysis.' Stekel said:

'We've been loyal for eight years. We've toiled through the wilderness bearing the ark of the covenant. We've endured the attacks of our enemies, *your* enemies. The men of Zürich go their own way, taking from your doctrines, ours, what they wish, then, if they wish, abandoning them.'

'Jung,' said Kahane, 'the man you want as permanent president, he only pretends to believe. He cast doubt – here at this congress – on the sexual origin of the neuroses. He talks about ghosts and poltergeists – '

'He believes,' Freud said doggedly.

'He believes,' said Adler, 'in Jung, the Züricher almighty, creator of heaven and earth. A real heaven, with a God in it modelled on

Jung himself, a clean Swiss earth untainted by sex. This is your president. This,' he said, 'is your successor.'

'We need the Swiss,' Freud violently said. 'A new medical science cannot be established without the support of a university medical school. Jung's clinic – there lies our only hope. Let me say another thing. It's only through Jung that we've been saved from being regarded as a purely Jewish movement. Our enemies are mostly antisemitic. We needed the broad base of neutrality. We may be Jews, most of us, but our science is universal.'

'Are you,' asked Adler, 'ashamed of being a Jew?'

'At least,' Freud cried, 'I didn't turn my back on the religion of my fathers to become a Protestant, as you did, Adler. A Jew when it suits you to be, a Christian when the wind changes. I'm sorry. Forgive me. God knows we have enough dissension without, without wanting to foment it here. Enemies – I'm sick of the sneers of enemies, the accusations of immorality – Freud the Viennese libertine who seduces patients on his couch, Freud who should be investigated by the police – that's what the Germans say. And Jones in England actually persecuted by the authorities, thrown out of two clinics, the Boston police raiding Brill's home, looking for dirty books. Enemies, enemies – the work I've done, the structure of truth I've tried to build up over twenty years – I don't want to see it destroyed. I want the temple to stand in a green place among mountains. I want a sick world purged and made well. And it's nothing but sneerers and smiters – attack after attack – enemies, enemies – they want to see me starve – they'd tear the very coat off my back – ' And now he sat on the chair and began to sob into his hands. There was silence except for the sobs. At length Kahane, though quietly, broke it, saying:

'I think I speak for all of us when I say that – Zürich is acceptable as the centre of the Association. We also agree to Jung's presidency. But not for life. For two years only. After that – a free election.'

Freud wiped his eyes on a crumpled handkerchief with a design of blue spots. 'I accept,' he said.

'We reject,' Kahane said, 'Jung's jurisdiction over our published writings. We reject censorship. We express our fear that Jung, given total control, might drag Freudian psychoanalysis onto paths of his own devising.'

'I sought,' Freud said in a low voice, 'only protection from bad work, heretical work – like that wretched essay of Maier's. I will suggest that we have an editorial board, drawn equally from Vienna and Zürich.' The tension was lessening. 'I go further. I wish to resign from the presidency of the Vienna Psychoanalytic Society. I recognize that my natural successor is Dr Alfred Adler. I go further still. I propose a journal of our own, published in Vienna. I nominate Dr Adler and Dr Stekel as its joint editors.'

'Accepted,' Stekel said, 'with thanks.'

'Accepted,' Adler said. 'If it is the wish of our group that I undertake the office of president, then I propose here and now that we cease our cosily domestic meetings –'

'My house,' Freud said, 'or, rather, my consulting room – is always open to you. But I recognize that it – implies a kind of paternalism which is no longer applicable.'

'Public meetings,' Adler said. 'Weekly, as before, but with doors thrown open so that all may enter. Lectures.'

'Meaning,' Freud said, 'less free discussion. Less informality.'

'Can we afford informality?' Adler said. 'We may not relax, not yet. Perhaps not ever. We must confront the world with weapons, with tactics and strategy. We're an army, not a clutch of coffee drinkers.'

'It was never obligatory,' sighed Freud, 'to drink my wife's coffee. Well, then – Do we shake hands? And then go down to dinner?'

Adler wiped his right hand on the seat of his trousers and then offered it to Freud. So did the others, but without wiping.

Trotsky. Quieter, less ebullient, though with an American city-slicker suit and a bow tie with a pattern of blue spots. He says, in English: 'Hi, fellers.' His three colleagues look sadly at each other. Vol says:

'You put in for US citizenship yet?' Chud says:

'For the Episcopalian Church?' Bok says:

'How is Comrade John D.?'

'Comrades, don't mock,' says Trotsky. 'You see in me a walking breathing living model of the dialectical process. The thesis called Trotsky meets the antithesis called New York. They clash, they fight, they attempt reconciliation. The synthesis, whatever it is, will be something never known before. It certainly will not be the old Lev Davidovich.'

'But what the movement requires,' says Bok, 'is the old Lev

Davidovich. Do you forget what Lev or Leon or Leo means?' He roars theatrically, advancing on Trotsky. Trotsky backs away, granting evidence to his colleagues of an unwonted debility. But he says, firmly enough:

'Comrades, I am no king of beasts. I do not want power. Understand absolutely clearly that I do not wish power. A humble servant of mankind, a lover of my fellow creatures, a mere nameless worker for the cause – I aspire to be no more. A lover, comrades. In none of the textbooks of socialism is human affection expressly forbidden. Who knows? – if the workers actually *like* each other it may even contribute to their political solidarity.'

'Is,' asks Vol, 'human affection part of the substructure or of the superstructure?'

'That will have to be worked out,' Trotsky says. 'Comrade Stalin is good at that sort of thing.'

Chud says: 'I fear, Lev Davidovich, I fear –'

'Fear Comrade Stalin? What nonsense.'

'I fear that you will be absorbed by this city and its decadent culture. What shall we tell them in Russia? That Trotsky, comrades, has become a New Yorker?'

'No no no,' Trotsky says. 'There's a dynamic contradiction in me, altogether healthy. It's like digesting a heavy meal. I'm divided, but only temporarily. Let me put it this way.' He sings:

I don't like it.
BOK: What?
TROTSKY: I like it.
I don't like it.
VOL: What?
CHUD: What?
TROTSKY: Liking it.
I like these folks
Who like being slaves,
I like their jokes
And Gillette shaves,
Their talk about limeys and wops and kikes.
I like their likes and dislikes.
BOK: I don't like it.
TROTSKY: What?
BOK: Your liking it.

TROTSKY: I don't like it.
VOL: What?
CHUD: What?
TROTSKY: Your not
Liking me liking it.
BOK: New Yorkers don't talk:
They rattle the larynx –
CHUD: Snort and squawk
Through the nasopharynx.
VOL: How do they cook
This stuff that they scoff?
Even its look
Puts me off.
TROTSKY: But eating's not a feast
Here in Manhattan –
It's an existential function instead.
The waiter's not a priest
Burbling Latin,
Pouring extreme unction on your head.
CHUD: But what do they think a drink is?
A device to wet the dry,
For shovelling sugar into the pancreas,
For getting high.
VOL: Highballs. Uncivilized.
BOK: Manhattans. Dry
Martinis.
CHUD: I
Am getting thirsty.
TROTSKY: What I mean is
I don't like it.
CHUD: Everybody gets thirsty.
TROTSKY: Liking it.
I'll end up liking liking it,
Liking the lack
Of political spleen
In the white and black
And shades in between,
The subway beneath,
And the El above.

What I really don't like is that possibly –
THE OTHERS: Yes?
TROTSKY: The liking may turn into love.
BOK: I don't like it.
TROTSKY: How can you not like it?
The pretzels are as salty
As in Petrograd,
The elevators faulty,
The drains as bad.
The women are striking
But the workers not.
I am liking the women a lot.

(*he speaks*)

Generalizing, comrades. I am turning New York women into a kind of general thesis. I know you think I am thinking of one particular woman. She was just the forerunner of them all. I am safe, I can assure you. She has gone. I will never see her again. Never. I'm getting over her. I think. I'm sure.

(*the song is resumed*)

VOL: I don't like it.
TROTSKY: What?
CHUD: He doesn't like
Your even tentatively liking it.
TROTSKY: What's wrong with Times Square
And the Great White Way?
The champagne air?
The boats in the bay?
Staten Island ferry?
The towers in the sky?
Ice cream and blueberry
Pie?
BOK: But you can't like the slaves
Of this roaring colossus
Who don't have Karl Marx on their shelves.
No one rants and raves
About killing the bosses –
They want to be bosses themselves.

TROTSKY: I'm not ignorant of their ignorance,
I loathe their excess of phlegm,
I loathe their lack of bile,
But I don't loathe *them*.
VOL: Heresy. Dangerous.
BOK: You can't separate
Thinker and thought.
CHUD: Like and hate
At one and the same time.
TROTSKY: Precisely. So I'm
Not liking it, liking it.
I was tempted to climb
Up the Statue of Liberty
And spit on the flibberty-gibberty
Civilization beneath.
I said: I don't like it. The wind blew it back in my teeth.
You'd better like it, it said with a shout,
For this is what liking and loving and living's about.
BOK: I don't like it.
TROTSKY: Ah, shut up.

The song ends, the clock strikes seven. 'She's late,' Trotsky says.

'The clock's fast,' says Chud. 'But *we're* late.'

'Where are you going, comrades?' asks Trotsky.

'Dinner,' says Vol, 'with the Boilermakers' Union.'

'I thought,' says Chud, 'it was with the Federation of Railroad Wheeltappers.'

'Meaning,' says Trotsky, 'you don't want to see Natalia's ballet?'

'We'll all be there,' says Bok doubtfully, 'for the first night. Or perhaps the second. Much depends on the *real* work. For now, comrade, we'd only be in the way.'

And now there enters

Freud had a chow named T'ang. It was cavorting in the weakening sun of October in the park, lifting its hind leg, sniffing, panting, looking back occasionally at its master, who was walking with Otto Rank. Rank said:

'Why not?'

'Because you're not medically qualified.'

'I have an arts degree. At last, thanks to you. And let me say now, now that I've come so far – I shall never forget. All my life I shall, oh, glow with gratitude when I think what you've done for me – time, love, money – '

'No more gratitude,' Freud said. 'Especially about money. Money is as necessary as defecation but just as negative. Listen to me. Psychoanalysis is still a branch of medicine, even though you seem to regard it as an art.'

'You yourself have said it's an art, Herr Professor. Another thing, Hanns Sachs isn't a doctor, yet he practises psychoanalysis. He practises it with your blessing.'

'Not my blessing. I tolerate him. He's a lawyer, and law is a grave discipline, like medicine. Besides, he's old. But you – well, you know the prejudices. A young man with no medical degree, asking a woman to lie down on a couch. Talking to her about orgasms and masturbation. No. We have to be made respectable. A medical degree excuses everything.'

Rank watched T'ang ease a long turd on to the grass. 'You can't actually *forbid* me,' he said.

'No, Otto. I'm not your father and, anyway, you're not a child. I'm only your very much older brother. I can only solemnly advise. Or warn.'

'What a waste. I've learned so much these last eight years. And you say that I mustn't use what I've learned.'

'Write. Write articles, books.'

'When I come up with an idea – like the reason for Hamlet's delay in killing his uncle – it's stolen by somebody else. Like Dr Jones. And because Jones is a doctor he's listened to. His theory about Hamlet must be important, because he's a medical man. But I'm just a dabbler –' Freud said guiltily:

'I shouldn't have discussed that with Jones. But it *was* a remarkable idea. The Oedipal Hamlet. I couldn't resist talking about it.'

'So I go back to my garret and shiver. Try to write articles that nobody will want to read.'

Freud showed surprise. 'Garret? What do you mean? You're the paid secretary of the Vienna Psychoanalytic – '

'I was when you were in charge.'

Freud showed shock. 'You mean – Adler got somebody else?'

'Adler has made bigger changes than a mere change of secretary. I've heard about the new Adlerian psychology. I've had time, you see, to listen around. I'm one of the unemployed now.'

Freud looked at him sickly. Then he called T'ang. T'ang was reluctant to come.

There was no doubt about the Adlerian pedagogical skill. He had a most musical, Willettian voice, and he was very persuasive. 'I ask you,' he told his audience, 'to consider these two terms of post-Freudian psychology that are fundamental items in its armoury. The first is: inferiority complex. The second is: masculine protest. Let us now see how these two concepts fit into an observed neurosis. The aetiology of a neurosis cannot be considered primarily in sexual terms – here the Freudian doctrine shows itself to be naive. The neurotic is forced into using sex as a device of protest – masculine protest to overcome an inferiority complex. Masturbation, for instance, does not indicate a sexual neurosis, a sexual maladjustment. The neurotic masturbates in defiance of the feminine principle, the demon that threatens his masculinity. He wishes to avoid love, which may be thought of as a giving of himself to the demon. The basis of the Freudian doctrine is, as you know all too well, the Oedipus complex, in which there is an infantile fixation on the mother as the source of a gratification which the Freudians regard as wholly sexual – leaving out of account other pleasure elements, such as warmth, food, comfort, and deeper elements, such as the need to be secure against the buffeting frightening world outside. The infantile mother fixation, according to Freud, finds in the father an object of hostility, as the powerful and vindictive god who will punish the child for daring to love the mother, punish him with castration. Dramatic, tragic, true, but a doctrine with a purely aesthetic appeal far removed from the observed reality. What Freud calls the Oedipus complex is a masculine protest – a wish to possess the mother out of a desire for power. We accept as fundamental the principle of psychic hermaphroditism, positing that in all of us there is a masculine element and a female element. But I say that a neurosis arises when the masculine element is threatened by its opposite. The resultant inferiority complex is the enemy which the analyst must seek to destroy. The Oedipus complex, so called, is a minor part of the whole dynamic, a phase of the masculine protest – no more.'

Freud was on his feet at once, coldly controlling an anger that had no wish to be controlled. He said:

'I have listened with close attention and growing disquiet to Dr Adler's discourse. I am appalled by the reactionary tone of his alleged innovations. He has abolished the unconscious, he denies infantile sexuality – '

Adler was truculent. 'I do *not* deny it. I merely deny its primacy, which is the fragile cornerstone of your whole theory. A neurosis arises when the subject is not sure whether he is male or female –'

'This is not new. I myself have propounded the principle of bisexuality, which you now make pretentious with your – your psychic hermaphroditism – '

'Let me make one point clear, Herr Professor,' Adler said in a kind of mockery of ingratiation. 'My whole discourse, my whole doctrine, would have been impossible without your teaching. What I am trying to do is to create a harmony between the old and the new – '

'The new?' Freud cried. 'You mean the reactionary and the retrograde. Let me make one point clear to *you*, Dr Adler. You are not a psychoanalyst. You're a biologist, basing your heresy about psychical inferiority on organic inferiority. You're a sociologist, concerning yourself with man's fulfilment in society. I don't doubt the value of your theories. What I do doubt is that they can form a basis for a valid psychoanalytical doctrine.'

Stekel stood up. Stekel said loudly:

'Now let *me* say something, Dr Freud. You used the word *heresy*. It is the word I have long expected to hear from your lips. It represents at last the candid declaration of yourself as not only the creator of a doctrine but as its monopolist, its arbiter, its judge, its supreme pontiff. We are sick of your dictatorship. We hereby declare a reformation.'

The auditorium was dark, the light concentrated on Adler, upright on the podium. Freud could not see where the murmurs and more articulate noises of agreement were coming from. He listened for support for himself. He heard some. He said with heavy sarcasm:

'Your purple rhetoric proclaims your essentially journalistic soul, Dr Stekel. I gave you and your *heretical* colleague leave to edit jointly a new Viennese journal of psychoanalysis. Not one publisher will accept it so long as you are co-editor. That surely speaks for itself.'

'You compound your pontifications with irrelevancies.'

'I merely warn Dr Adler, whom I respect, though I deplore his deviations from the truth, that he had best look to his real friends, not his opportunist hangers-on.'

'That is a slander. I will take action.'

'Do so. I say to Dr Adler that, as a sociological corollary, addendum or appendix, his observations about the inferiority complex and all the rest of it might well find welcoming arms here, *here* – but he preferred to be led to the gestures of disaffection and revolt by a glib and opportunistic dabbler and scribbler.'

'I will not have this,' Stekel cried, and, at the same moment, Adler thundered, blazing:

'I will not be diminished in this manner. I am not led. I lead. The truth leads. It's clear that there's no longer room for me in this organization. I accordingly resign as its president. I resign also from the co-editorship of the *Vienna Journal of Psychoanalysis*. I hereby proclaim the inauguration of a new association, to be called the Society for Free Psychoanalysis.'

Freud groaned in pain as Adler's supporters applauded. He said: 'This is an intolerable moment, a desperate one. This is the first time in nearly ten years that I've lost a disciple.'

'I was never a disciple,' Adler said loftily. 'A colleague, rather. And it is not I who am lost to the movement, Dr Freud. It is you yourself who are lost. You started a revolution. You refused to allow it to develop. You *froze* your revolution. You wished for stasis, for turning flesh into stone. That is not the way of science. You have betrayed the spirit of science, the open-mindedness of science, the dynamism of science. And you, sir, have the gall to speak of *heresy*.'

He got down from the rostrum to applause and a few boos. Freud began to leave, feeling broken. He was avoided. Even Otto Rank kept out of his way. Outside on the steps of the building there were two murmuring groups, but Freud's group seemed to be murmuring against its own leader. Freud went wearily over to Adler and said:

'I admitted mistakes when I made them. I incorporated other men's discoveries in the growing corpus of truth about the human soul. I have not stood still. I am not as you presented me. There must be – you must have – there has to be some other – What, Adler, is your real reason for this desertion?'

'Why should I,' Adler hissed, 'have to live under your shadow?' And he stalked off into the dark. Stekel followed him, having shown snarling canines to his former master.

* * *

Summer came, and the licking of wounds. There had been too much tide; now there were no tides at all. The moon had left the sky, but it was still, though very dimly, in contact with the selenostations of earth. Thin messages came through from Vitruvius, Zagut and Schneckenberg. A farewell message came from Sheepshanks. The moon had been very badly knocked about, and now it was nearer the sun and very hot, except at night, when it was very cold. It was very near to its new host, whose barren features had been closely annotated. Much hydrogen steaming away, scars of ancient space battles, an interesting axial irregularity. From the space stations in terrestrial orbit there was no news: something had gone wrong, but none on earth knew what.

The government of the Commonwealth of Democratic Americas was revealed as having moved, with the disastrous flooding of the Potomac and an earthquake that had destroyed the White House, to Dallas in Texas. The Trinity river there had overflowed its banks and made a lake of Rochester Park, but Highland Park had been virtually untouched and the Dallas Country Club, with its imposing gateway on Mockingbird Lane, its fine drive leading to a splendid building overlooking Turtle Creek, was now the presidential residence. There had been no word about the recall of Congress. An emergency situation still obtained; power lay undistributed among the three arms of federal rule; the President was a kind of Boss Cat Bartlett, but a milder and more intelligent one.

In early July, just after the uncelebrated Day of Independence, he talked with his aides, Bidu Saarinen and Florenz Zenger, both New Yorkers. They walked in the grounds of the New White House, as the Dallas Country Club was now called. The white paint was, on this fine day full of butterflies and birdsong, being renewed. You required two things only for a White House: a president and a can of paint. Jack Skilling, visibly older since his Christmas meeting with Hubert Frame, stooped, his right leg painful and making him limp, his hair greyer and sparser.

'Well, Flo,' he said, 'what are you going to do in outer space?'

'Read Toynbee. Perfect my chess game.'

'Yes,' the President said. 'I shall read all of Henry James. James and games. The games, mark my words, will survive, but James and Toynbee will not. There'll be nothing to refer them to. What humanity will salvage from its long history is a few structures, a few rules in the void. Is it worth launching fifty billion dollars' worth of ironmongery just to keep a handful of gamesplayers in austere leisure? What do you think, Bid?'

Saarinen shrugged, wiping his sweating blue-black forehead with a snowy handkerchief. 'Life is curiously sweet,' he said. 'If we can't have real butterflies we can at least read about them and see them flashing on a cinescreen. I'm grateful for the chance to live out my life – even in dead outer space.'

'No guilt?'

'No guilt, sir.'

'No sense of our taking advantage of our position?'

'Why should we be overmodest, sir?' Zenger said. 'We have skills, we have knowledge. If we reach a new earth, or if our children do, we shall know how to set up a community.'

'No,' Skilling said. 'That's not it at all. We're just glad at the prospect of saving our skins. But I'll be frank with you, gentlemen. I hope to be cut off before then – in my boat, in a hunting accident. I've no right to outlive one of the best presidents this country ever had, the womanizing handsome clever bastard.' The others knew whom he meant – a man who had been assassinated in his forties in this very town.

'Do you propose to prepare a statement?' asked Saarinen.

'About the end of things and the salvation of the presidential staff? No, I don't think so. I think we have to pretend that the horror's all over. The return of life to the littoral, the reconstruction of shattered cities – why not? We don't, thank God, have to worry about money.'

'It all seems a terrible waste,' said Zenger. 'Do you propose the rebuilding of Washington?'

'Why not? The White House, the real one, must go up again. Meanwhile the President stays in Dallas.'

'And Congress?' asked Saarinen.

'I don't think we need to be in too much of a hurry to recall Congress. God knows how much of Congress is left. God knows how much of the Americas is left. As for the outside world – I refuse to think of it. I want to eat lunch today.'

Already eating lunch in a fine house on Fitzhugh Avenue, southeast, children, of State Fair Park in this same city of Dallas, was pretty nearly the whole of the Gropius family. This was John Gropius's house, John being the second son of Calvin and the vice-president of the Newbold Construction Company. His wife, a pretty woman named Rufa (after her father Rufus – a silly name, it was generally thought, doggish, wuffing, inappropriate to a woman so soft, gentle, undoggish, even unbitchy) was feeding their youngest, Sam, with a spoon and gently chiding their middle child, Joe, who was splashing Jell-O onto their eldest, Wilhelmina. James, Calvin's eldest, was rejoicing still in his reunion with Jay and Jay, Jennifer and Jessica. There were so many stories coming in still of bereavement, some grotesque, some heartrending. The dream: Jennifer never tired of recounting her dream. It was a very simple dream, highly biblical with its angel warning of fire coming to the city, its resounding injunction in high Jacobean diction: 'Go ye then to Dallas, safe in the Lord.' And, by Christ, James thought, here they were, safe in the Lord. Though he could have done with less talk of the Lord now that the troubles were over and the government money was coming in and everybody should be having a darned good time. It was the old man who kept grimly going on about the Lord.

There was only one member of the Gropius family absent from the table. This was Dashiel Gropius, youngest son, whose work kept him in Fort Worth. He managed a great hotel, the Florentine, on Arlington Heights. This hotel was at the moment booming, what with the influx of coastal refugees into the town, the lavish cash handouts from the government, the leisure which was so easily filled with cabaret entertainment and gambling. For the Florentine, modelled on many a great hotel in Las Vegas, a noted gambling city, children, offered not solely bed and board but also song and dance and a variety of games of chance – roulette, blackjack, craps, as well as what were called fruit machines or one-armed bandits. Calvin Gropius was not happy that his son should be engaged in such profane work, but he accepted philosophically that at least one of his brood must react against the father of it, and that one great religious believer was probably enough for any family. Still, he would have been happier if. Never mind. He was addressing his family, less Dashiel, gravely over the dessert and coffee.

'You delude yourselves, as does most of the country, and perhaps most of the world that is left, that we have had our disaster and we may now resume life as it was before.'

'Don't preach so, Calv,' said his wife Maria. 'Not to us, dear.'

'Life as it was before,' repeated Gropius, 'except that we don't any longer have a moon.'

'Such a shame,' said Rufa, tears in her eyes. 'Little Sam will never know what it was, the moon, I mean.'

'Oh, it will be back,' said Gropius grimly. 'And nobody will be happy to see it.'

'The moon.' James Gropius waved the moon away, like an appendix or other unnecessary organ. 'We can do without the moon.' There was no money in it, he seemed to say.

'That planet will be back,' said his father, 'lugging our moon along. I have been talking with men at the state university in Arlington. They say that the population at large has been kept in ignorance to avoid panic. They approve of this, as I do myself. The presidential policy, in so far as such a thing may be said to exist, is to allow the people to resume life as it was before, to meet an unavoidable end without special preparation for it.'

'Spiritual, you mean?' asked Jennifer.

'No,' said her father-in-law. 'Spirituality is not the affair of government. Though there was a time when it was, in Geneva, Switzerland, under the man whose name was given to me at the font. And in New England, many centuries ago. No. I mean, alas, that the final disaster will hit a land disorganized. For to what can organization lead? To anyone's salvation? Not this time, ah no. Chaos, and government impotent.'

'It's a long time off, dad,' said James, chewing a brazil nut.

'We shall never celebrate Christmas again,' said his father. 'Think of that. We shall never see another Easter. Unless unless unless –' He sighed, closed his eyes, then opened them. 'Why should the righteous be destroyed with the sinner, O Lord?' He was looking up at a spot of dried damp on the ceiling. He now looked intently round at his family, including little dribbling Sam, and said: 'You remember Genesis 6?' Oh Jesus, thought James, nodding brightly. 'Listen to the word of the Lord,' Calvin Gropius said, giving out the word, which he knew by heart: ' "And God saw that the wickedness of man was great in the earth, and that every imagination of the thoughts of his heart was only evil continually. And it repented the Lord that he had made man on the earth, and it grieved him at his heart. And the Lord said, I will destroy man whom I have created from the face of the earth; both man and beast and the creeping things and the fowls of the air; for it repenteth me that I have made them." '

'That always seemed kind of unfair to me,' James said. 'I mean, the beasts hadn't done any harm.'

Calvin Gropius ignored him and turned his fierce eyes on his daughter-in-law Jennifer. 'What comes next, Jennifer?' he asked. Jennifer said:

' "But Noah found grace in the eyes of the Lord. These were the generation of Noah: Noah was a just man and perfect in his generation, and Noah walked with God. And Noah begat three sons –" '

'Yes yes yes,' her father-in-law said impatiently. 'Where is the ark for the family of the righteous?' They all looked at him. Then John said:

'You mean it ought to be us?' His father said:

'If only God would speak. An angel spoke to Jennifer here and saved her from the fire and ashes of Oklahoma City. The Lord spoke to Noah.'

'It was a dream,' said Jennifer brightly. 'If you like, I'll dream a dream and He can speak to you through me.' She smiled. 'I'm good at dreams,' she said simply. Calvin Gropius resumed reading from the holy book printed in his brain:

' "And God said unto Noah, The end of all flesh is come before me; for the earth is filled with violence through them; and, behold, I will destroy them with the earth. Make thee an ark of gopher wood – '

John, whose trade was ordering the construction of things, like God himself, said: 'It was simpler in those days. Nowadays Noah would have to build a spaceship. If by the destruction of the world you mean, you know, what the professors are talking about. It won't happen, you know, dad. But it shows where the Bible goes wrong. I mean, it's not a good guide for today. If God destroyed the earth, Noah and his sons would have to get off in a spaceship. And they couldn't do it, could they? They'd have to get somebody to build it for them, and have a government grant of fifty billions or so.' John had an instinct for estimates.

'Look,' said Calvin Gropius with such concentrated ferocity that his wife wondered about this Lynx disease she'd heard of, men going wrong in the head because of the gravity or something. 'Listen. If anyone is going to be saved, we are. We are the righteous. I've preached the Word to this whole nation, and to other nations too – well, Great Britain, South Africa anyway, that French trip was a flop because of the language problem – and if anybody has the right to call himself the patriarch of the nation, it's myself. And if I'm Noah, you are Noah's family.'

'Would there be animals?' asked twelve-year-old Jessica. 'Clean and unclean beasts, like it says?'

'It's a nice idea, dad,' John said, getting up from the table, his table, this was his house. 'If it was just a matter of an ark of, you know, gopher wood and that other stuff with shit in it, sorry, mom, it's in the Bible, I could put that in hand tomorrow. Cost you about a million, done properly. Well, perhaps not tomorrow. Next month, say. There's talk about a lot of contract bids coming up. The Coast, naturally. I'm on my way. See you all at dinner.' He kissed his wife and kids and went out humming 'The animals went in two by two, hurrah, hurrah.'

'If anybody's to be saved,' said Calvin Gropius, 'it's us. And now – grace after meals.' He joined his hands and closed his eyes. 'James,' he said, opening them, 'stop chewing. John,' he said, 'should not have gone out like that. Never mind.' He closed his eyes again and started to give thanks for the lamb chops and the Jell-O.

Meanwhile, life having begun to return to New York City, Val Brodie and Willett (at last dressed as a non-Scot) were holed up in the penthouse suite of the Peter Minuit Hotel, which overlooked Park Avenue. They had undergone bad times together, but there was now a sense of deflation, of the rebirth of normality and law and order and cops and having to pay bills, which made them almost nostalgic for great waves and winds tugging at them. Periodically, in this fine tideless summer weather, they would go out onto the balcony and look down at the rapid restoration of the old civic pattern. The bone-dry streets had been cleared of dead and other debris by a kind of pressed militia under brutish men with guns and mouths ever ready with insult and obscenity. Val and Willett naturally wished to keep out of the way of any improvised conscription that was going on, but they recognized that forced massive manpower was needed to dry out, clean up, polish what had once, children, been known as the Big Apple. An apple was a kind of fruit; some of you may have seen a picture of an apple.

They were subsisting, not too tastily, on canned goods they had lugged from various storerooms of hotels at various skywalk levels, not that many skywalks had survived the ultimate high tide. In the clothes closets of their two bedrooms they had the entire spectrum of Hiss Soups, Seth Low Tasty Stews, Mensch Spongemeats, Piccirilli Pasta Yums, Moshowitz Kosher Puddings. They had cases, agony to manhandle, of hard liquors and Marquis de Lafayette Good

American Wines (b.o.f.i.), as well as some genuine vinous relics of dead France, Spain and Italy. They had instant coffee and a water heater. The water in the roof storage tanks was pretty foul and had to be thoroughly boiled, so they drank mostly from the heady wholesome bottles. The question, much debated over these same, was: what were they going to do?

Val had been studying the whole business of the impending collision of earth and Lynx, mainly with the aid of a couple of paperback books he had picked up from a bookspinstand in the skyrecep level smokestore of the Rutherford Hotel. The books, like everything else, had been soaked but had dried out in humps and bumps and waves and bleary lines of blurred type. The books were called *Astronomy, Folks* and *Ah, The Stars* – silly catchpenny titles. In the early evening, after a meal of Hiss and Seth Low and Moshowitz and good Baton Rouge brandy (b.o.f.i.), Val tried to explain what he saw as the situation to Willett, who was in a kind of white moygashel tent suit. They both smoked long Joe Papps, of which they had a fine store, as well as of disposable gas lighters.

'Here it is, you see,' Val said, showing Willett a humpy diagram. 'There's the sun, a hell of a size, and then the planets kind of keep their distances, as in a kind of ritual dance. Mercury's nearest, then Venus comes next, then Earth, then Mars, then you get the mansize stuff – Jupiter, Saturn, the big boys – then Uranus and Neptune, fairly bulky, and last tiny Pluto, right on the edge, sometimes called the asshole of the solar system. Now what I don't understand is why Lynx doesn't smash up Mercury or Venus or, for that matter, following the rule of the dance, just get in, say, between Venus and us and go spinning merrily around, minding its own business. I mean, why *us*?'

'And why, for that same matter, does it have to have our moon, with poor young George on it?'

'What I don't want to start thinking about,' Val said, 'is some kind of predestined pattern, with God knowing all about it, creating man, knowing before he created him that he was going to be a wicked bastard, and so setting up this nice little cataclysm to get rid of him.' He looked gloomily at the diagram before him, the page a terrain of little hills, the crude colours run together with the (punitive?) waters.

'It may not happen,' Willett said. 'The general view is that it's not going to happen.'

'Scientists have been wrong before,' Val said. 'I mean, the forecasters let everybody down very badly over the first of the tidal attacks. Still, I wish to Christ I'd listened more carefully when Vanessa and her bastard of a dad were talking about it.' He glumly traced on the diagram with a chewed pencil the sun routes of both earth and Lynx and couldn't for the life of him see how a collision was inevitable. 'If,' he said, 'it's *not* going to happen, we ought to start deciding what to do with our lives.'

'There'll be no television for a long time yet. Nothing for me. No theatres. I have money, of course.' And he patted his right breast, where a wad of hundreds lay snug. They had robbed, both of them. They had met a remarkable phenomenon in the Chemical Bank Skywalk 30 – a safe opened by lightning. They had also found cashboxes and cashdrawers here and there, full of crisp or soggy green. 'But, God, God, life's more than having money. You, I take it, will start teaching again.'

'I had my orders,' Val said. 'I ought to do something about reporting someplace. But whichplace? And,' he said fiercely, 'we ought to stick together. You and I, we're a sort of gestalt.'

'What's a gheshtalt?'

'A combination of persons to create a fuller sort of organism.'

Willett grunted, not unkindly, and said: 'I think we might risk a stroll through the city. I wonder if there's anybody running this hotel yet? Anybody interested in the paying of bills and so on?'

'There's no maid service. The elevator doesn't work.' Their rooms were dry enough now, though tatty, everything lumpy or wrinkled. They had had sheets and mattresses out on the terrace in the hot sun. The armchairs had steamed out their load of damp in the same blessed fire. Still, a sense of grubbiness pervaded the place: there was a strong smell of ditches and marshes and rotting apples.

'The worst of being up here,' Willett said, 'is not the going down but the coming back up again. I wonder if there's anything *really* happening down there? Bars, grills, Madame Aphrodite, that sort of thing.' He went to the balcony to peer down at the street scene. People, no cars. 'Christ,' he said, 'there are lights coming on.' Val came to see. There were, too. Lights, one or two flickering skysigns – OLMSTEAD, VOORHEES, ISIDOR STRAUS.

'We'll go,' Val said.

'How do we get back?'

'We climb the stairs.'

'Are you mad?'

'It's only fifty floors.'

'You *are* mad.'

When, somewhat furtively, they reached the corridor, locking the door with the lockcard that had been kindly awaiting them on the hallway table when they first entered (the door being then flung wide, clothes scattered, evacuation of the former tenants evidently hasty), it was perhaps no surprise to find the elevator working. This did not, however, elate Willett; he did not altogether relish the end of the days of anarchy. But in the reception area below they found nobody. Some quirk of a timeswitch somewhere had brought light and power back to the hotel. They cautiously went out onto the sidewalk. They walked south of a very green though treeless Central Park and found people, not many, walking dogs. 'Mad, mad,' muttered Willett uneasily. 'It's almost as though it never happened.' They saw signs of reconstruction work – men working lights, floodlamps already flooding. On West 57th Street they entered Jerry Towle's Bar and Grill, a hostelry they could not recall having seen before. It smelt of a very damp grave, but there were drinkers and a cheerful barman.

'Scotch,' Val said. 'Very large.'

'Very expensive,' the barman said. 'There won't be no more Scotch when existing stocks is finished, friend, friends. There ain't no more bonny Scotland.'

'Jesus,' said Willett with awe. 'Television.'

The other drinkers had been watching a blank crackling screen, waiting. In very crude and blotchy colour the Stars and Stripes fluttered to the blurred brass of the old song that honoured them. Then there came the cheerful face of the President.

'Christ, he looks old,' Val breathed. The President said:

'My friends, I speak to you from the White House, Dallas, Texas, the present centre of government until such time as a certain other White House, in a certain city in the District of Columbia, has been rebuilt and restored to its former glory. We have had, to say the least of it, difficult times. Now we count our dead in resignation to the will of heaven and, in obedience to the law of life, start to reconstruct our shattered country. You will hear rumours, put about by the forces of subversion for its own sake, to the effect that the worst is not yet over, that the destructive planet Lynx will plunge back into our, alas, now moonless sky, and resume, on a greater scale than before, its wanton work of destruction. This rumour is wicked and false.'

Willett and Val looked at each other over their whisky. One never believed a politician. Or did one? Some of the drinking watchers were believing.

'The world has known many disasters. But man has always come through, by his skin and teeth. I would ask all of you to remember that the disaster that has struck the whole world has been blessedly merciful to these United States that make up the American Commonwealth. Our littoral has been devastated, and the devastation of the rampant oceans has pushed far inland, and where it has not pushed the earth itself has not been slow to erupt in its own mode of devastation. But our basic resources remain intact – skill, materials, and equipment, of which, on a nationwide scale, but a fraction has been lost to us. Work, rebuild. Be, during this difficult time, obedient to the civic and federal authorities. Let life start again. God bless you all and good night.'

That was the end of the evening's transmissions, except for five minutes of commercials – CRUNCHTHUMP GRAVELATORS, WARREN AND WETMORE WETMIX, IF IT'S GOODY'S IT'S A GOODY, and so on – followed by an ancient movie of a rich girl falling off a horse and developing brain damage. This film broke down after the doctor had delivered his prognosis, and the service sputtered out. An old man without teeth sat next to Willett and said:

'Sure is good to be back. With my wife's folks in Oshkosh, Wisconsin, till the lakes flooded. Then in Indiana. Sure is flat, Indiana. My daughter's there with this guy. I tell 'em why don't you get married like regular folks, but there's no telling these kids.'

Warmth, warmth, human warmth flooded in. Scotch at fifteen dollars the shot warmed. Soon Willett was going on about flutch calf-lollies, turdy-guts and shitten shepherds, referring chiefly to a group of droop-mouthed youths in, God bless their innocence, Lynx shirts.

'Sure has what they call a voke abble airy, your friend there.'

Girls came in, and Willett had his arm round one gat-toothed giggler with famished speed. 'Honeybunch,' he called her, 'piggesnie, heartsease, bedworthy bundlesnuggle,' and so on. She giggled. Then two men in uniform came in, one with a clipboard, the other with a pistol in a verdigrised holster. The uniform was a sort of overwashed blue, denoting some store that the floods had got at. In default of collar dogs or breast badge, they wore cloth brassards which said NYC CLEANUP. They picked up the droop-mouthed youths first.

'Work card?'

'What sordour shitsa work card?'

'I think,' Willett said, 'it would be wise to get out of here.' He unhanded his heartsease honeybunch. 'Some other time,' he told her. 'A matter of an urgent appointment.'

Outside the barroom door another NYC CLEANUP man was waiting, armed. 'You wait,' he said, 'till you been seen about in there, buster.'

'Ah, Jesus,' Willett said.

'Work card?' said the man with the clipboard, inkpencil at the ready. He was the overbearing sort who never learns humility, not even from cosmic disaster.

'Never heard of work cards,' Willett said. 'Sounds like an unwholesome innovation. I am an actor, freelance naturally. I work when I'm able to work. My friend here is a university professor.'

'Work card?'

'What *is* all this?' Val asked.

'If you've no work card you get temporary drafted into the city clean-up force. Thirty dollars a day and all found.'

'But I can prove,' Val said, 'that I'm on the staff of – ' But, of course, he couldn't prove anything. 'What do we have to do?' he asked in resignation.

'You wait outside there with Officer Grogan till we collects ten. Then you march.'

'Where to do we march?' asked a little chewing man they had pressed.

'You'll see, brother.'

Outside Val looked up at the sky and said to Willett: 'Do you see what I see?'

'What do you see? Oh. Oh yes. You'll see brother, indeed.'

'Not much point in cleaning up,' Val said.

Martha Freud and Emma Jung were taking together a *Jause* of coffee and cake. Sun streamed into the living room of 19 Berggasse, enriching Martha's Mediterranean darkness, etiolating the Swiss prettiness of Jung's wife. 'Upset him terribly,' Martha was saying. 'He gets headaches. I tell him to take a powder for it, but he won't. He says it's a psychological headache or something. But I say it's a physical pain, and he can't deny it. But he won't take anything. He's against drugs, as he calls them. That's because of that old cocaine business.'

'He thinks cocaine addiction is all his fault?' Emma Jung spoke a pinched birdlike kind of German.

'Well, he was the first to tell everybody about cocaine. How marvellous it was and so on. He often dreams about injecting people. He says a syringe is a guilt symbol. Men always take these things so seriously. More coffee, dear?'

'No, but I'll have one of those delicious-looking cream cakes. We can't get them like that in Zürich.'

'You must take some back with you.'

'Oh, Carl's all against Viennese self-indulgence, as he calls it. But I *like* Vienna. Cities were made for women, I always think. Men like to be in the great outdoors, chopping things.'

'But you have a lovely home on the lake there.'

'You'd get tired of it. I do. Not much company, you know. Except ghosts and poltergeists and things.'

'You don't mean it.'

'Oh, Carl's always seeing things. The occult, he calls it.'

'Oh dear.'

'Yes, I know what you mean. Your husband's very sceptical, isn't he?'

'He has to be, dear. There's so much nonsense going about now. This man Adler with his inferiority complexes and so on. Adler's giving him a lot of headaches. Take something, I say, but he won't. Men can be very stubborn.'

Emma nodded sympathetically and chewed her cake. She was so wholesome a young woman that the cream round her mouth looked like toothpaste. 'Mmmmmmm. Scrumptious.'

And in this glorious summer weather Freud and Jung walked up the hill to the apartment, talking about her.

'She's charming, Carl. You're a lucky man.'

'Yes, I am. Charming and accommodating.'

'In what way?'

'The test of a good marriage is the length of the leash. Or the fact that there's no leash at all.'

Freud could not help being shocked and showing it. 'You mean,' he said, 'infidelity?'

'Now you sound like my father. A man needs a certain – width of sexual experience, don't you agree?'

'I've been faithful. I've never been with another woman. Martha and I – we've been faithful. I must confess that – once in Rome – I found myself walking towards the brothel district. Quite unconsciously.'

'Then you walked away again? Hm. I've mentioned it to you before – this matter of the surrogate. Don't you think – if you'd had more sexual experience, you'd be less inclined to be preoccupied with sex?'

'I've never been preoccupied, as you put it. I leave that to my patients.'

'It's a point worth thinking about, don't you agree?'

'Is this,' said Freud, watching the sun go into temporary occlusion behind a cloud like a silhouette of Franz Josef, 'a prelude to your renunciation of infantile sexuality? We don't want another Adler prancing about in Switzerland, do we?'

'We have to survive. There's a lot of anti-sex feeling about. We have to tread very carefully. Renunciation? That's a terrible word. Never never never. Jung is a good Freudian.' They went in.

They went into Freud's study. Jung's eyes withheld comment as they coolly ranged the accumulated litter of jujus and totems and statuettes. He cleared his throat and said: 'The factuality of occult events.'

Freud looked up startled from lighting a cigar. 'Eh?' he said. And, then puffing, 'I hope to God that isn't the title of a paper you're going to write.'

'No. The factuality of. I like the sound of the phrase. When you put something into words, even if the idea seemed impossible before – well, the words give it a kind of validity.'

'The spirituality of grilled sausages.'

'Now you're mocking me. Or perhaps not. That goes too far, I think, though. But occult events – they happen. There has to be a place for that sort of thing in any theory of the mind.'

'They don't happen to me,' Freud said surlily.

'You mean things happen to you that can't be explained. Because they can't be explained you reject them, you pretend they never happened. Now what do you think of this extension of your view of the unconscious? Two divisions, one personal, individual, the one we can probe on the analyst's couch, the other – well collective, parallel to the inherited brain structure, this being the general form, common to all humanity. This collective unconscious deals with things that the individual mind can't explain – psychic phenomena, God, myth. The collective unconscious – it explains much that you leave out.'

'You're turning to mysticism, Carl,' Freud growled. 'I don't like it. It gives me a headache.'

'The more we can explain – art, religion, psychic phenomena, telepathy, psychokinesis, prediction of the future – the more our science moves towards completeness.'

'It's a lot of mumbo jumbo, Carl, and I'm not having it.'

Jung then ouched in sudden pain. He pressed his hands in pain to his belly. 'Ouch. Red hot. Like fire.' And then from the bookshelves there cracked violently out a report like a pistol shot. They rose, both of them, expecting to see the shelves fall or else a door open made of book spines and armed anarchists emerge. But nothing looked different. In triumph, still holding his belly, Jung cried:

'You see – the factuality of the occult. A catalytic exteriorization phenomenon.'

'Nonsense.'

'Nonsense? It happened. And it's going to happen again.'

It did. A loud cracking gunshot. Freud tried not to look uneasy. Jung stood wide-eyed. 'You see,' he cried.

'Poltergeists, eh? Demons.' Freud sat down, nodding grimly. 'You arranged this. It's a trick. You're trying to force me into a belief in séances and trances and the rest of the nonsense.'

'And the sudden red hot pain I had down here – how do you explain that?'

'You've got bowel trouble.'

'Never. Don't mock me.'

'All right, then. Did that cause the cracking noise, or was it caused by it?'

'Now you're laughing at me – or trying to. You know it's no laughing matter. And you know that this thing happened. I can explain it, but you can't. Poltergeists – elemental spirits.'

'No,' Freud said. 'Green wood. New green planks for bookshelves, put in a few days ago. They're drying out.' Another cracking report confirmed or denied it. 'There you are. Drying out, you idiot. All this damned nonsense about poltergeists. Watch it, Carl. We're already regarded as sexual criminals. It's a good deal worse to be classed with the table-tappers and fortune-tellers. Let's keep our sanity.'

It happened again. 'Poltergeists,' cried triumphant Jung.

'All right,' cried fierce Freud, 'poltergeists. Another word for green wood drying out. Idiot.' Jung clasped his belly again in a sudden shaft of red hot, of. Freud responded by clasping his brow. 'Damned idiot. God, this headache.'

'It may be,' Jones said, as they walked about Munich, 'that Jung is your headache.'

'No. It's Adler and Stekel and the rest of the heretics. I cast them out,' grimly, passing an ornate baroque front from behind which organ music pulsed, Brahms or somebody, 'of the bosom of Mother Church.'

'And they've crept back in in the form of a headache? No. It's Jung.'

'No. No. No.'

'Watch that horse dung there.' For they were crossing the street. 'Listen,' Jones said on the other side. 'Here's a strange thing. I nearly didn't come to Munich. Jung sent the invitation to the congress to another Ernest Jones – my father in Wales. He also put tomorrow's date instead of today's. An unconscious slip, but we all know what it means.'

'A gentleman wouldn't have that kind of unconscious. But still – '

'A gentleman wouldn't give you these headaches.'

'No. No.' A shoeblack looked up from blacking a gentleman's shoes outside a tavern. 'Yes yes,' with shoeblack's drollness. Freud said: 'Carl is all right. Carl is fine. Carl is your future leader – '

Jones soothed. 'Yes, Herr Professor. Everything will be all right.'

Freud tried to sleep off the headache without success. He was late going in to luncheon. Jung was plying knife and fork and talking. Freud hid behind a pillar to hear. 'Incest?' Jung was saying. 'I think we must not make too literal an interpretation of it. A symbol, no more. A spiritual symbol. It has a profound religious significance – we find it in all the mythologies.' Without turning, he said: 'Do sit down with us, Herr Professor. The roast beef is excellent.' Supernatural awareness of Freud hiding behind a pillar. Freud, abashed, came from behind it and sat down. A waiter came to him at once. 'A forking of the roads, dear professor,' Jung said cheerfully, a fine underdone gobbet on raised tines, 'inevitable, nay desirable, but it doesn't mean a forking of the road of friendship and affection, does it?' He forked it in.

'Forking? Knifing?' Freud was confused. 'Forgive me, that was silly. No, my dear Carl. I'm learning something of the value of deviation.' Roast beef was brought to him. He ate with a reflection of Jung's own cheerfulness. Then he began to feel unwell.

'How,' Jung asked, 'is the headache?'

'Tell me,' Freud said, 'why is it, my dear Carl, that in your lectures, in your published writings, why is it that – ' The bit of beef would not go down. ' – you no longer mention the name of – of Sigmund Freud?'

'Why should I?' Jung blandly said. 'Those days are gone. Everyone knows that Sigmund Freud is the father of psychoanalysis. There's no need any more to mention your name. You should rejoice. I certainly do.'

The bit of beef went down. Then Freud fainted. It was Bremen all over again. Jung, as then, picked him up like a baby and carried him off.

Freud came to with his collar and tie and shoes and jacket off, on his own bed in his hotel bedroom. Jones looked down on him, concerned. Freud, weak, said:

'Where is everybody?'

'The session's begun. Abraham is lecturing. How are you now?'

'He gave himself away,' Freud said languidly. 'He wants to be loyal. But he wants to wear the crown. Now. He can't wait. He wants me dead. He wants me never to have existed.' He closed his eyes tiredly. Jones could hardly hear his next words. 'How sweet,' Freud said, 'to die.'

Very much alive, tied, collared, shoed, jacketed, cigar alight, he went in with Jones to the chandeliered salon. There was noise. Jung was saying:

'On Dr Abraham's paper I have this comment to make. There is the same old hoary stress on the literal incest situation. The Oedipus doctrine has not advanced one centimetre since it was first enunciated. Abraham insists on the strict observation of the letter of what are now commandments long superseded – thou shalt believe in the sexual aetiology of the neuroses, thou shalt believe that thou didst desire thy mother in infancy, thou shalt have no other God but thy avenging father who has come hither to shear off thy testicles. Surely we have advanced some miles on the great road of psychoanalysis, but, from the address you have just heard, one would hardly think so. Dr Abraham, though he holds a lonely fort in Berlin, is still addicted to the stale whipped cream of Vienna.' Protests, protests, Ferenczi on his feet and gesturing, the Viennese snarling, Jung banging his chairman's gavel. 'No further discussion. We will now move on to the next paper. Dr Ferenczi will speak about three recent homosexuality cases. In view of our lack of time, Dr Ferenczi, I fear we must cut that down to *two* cases. Come on, start, please. Time is precious – '

Freud was appalled. He had let his cigar go out.

Fury and humiliation in his bedroom. Ferenczi, seated on the master's bed, bounced as he cried:

'His presidency must not be renewed. We must all leave our ballot papers blank – '

'He has a majority,' Freud said in weariness. 'He's bound to be re-elected. Blank papers – a futile exercise in in in – '

'Why do you continue to support him, Herr Professor?' Rank said. 'Why, when he seems intent on destroying everything you stand for?'

'He is not his own master,' Freud said in slow tiredness. 'He's divided. Between loyalty and ambition – and what is so wrong with ambition? The Swiss medical authorities are fighting him – the Church, the press. Can you blame him if he wants to believe that sex hardly exists in adult life, let alone in infancy? Remember this – he fought for us when we were beleaguered. It's in his hands that the match flame burns. A threatened flame. Only he can carry that flame to the future.'

'It's not your flame,' Rank cried. 'It's his.'

It was Rank who chalked up the votes. He announced: 'Fifty-two votes for the renewal of Dr Jung's presidency of the International Psychoanalytic Association. Twenty-two ballot papers are blank. Dr Carl Jung is herewith re-elected to the office of president.'

The Swiss applauded loudly. So did some others. Jung ignored the applause and strode up to Jones, who stood, not applauding, at the back of the salon. Jung was in an unwonted though quiet fury. He said to Jones:

'You – you left your paper blank, didn't you?'

'I'm sorry, Jung.'

Jung seemed to spit. 'I thought,' he said, 'you were a *Christian*.' He strode off. Jones strode after him. Jones cried:

'What do you mean by that? Do I smell the stink of antisemitism? Are you deserting Freud because he's a Jew? Answer – ' But Jung had left the room. As Vol and Bok and Chud have.

* * *

Into the room Natalia. She is not at all like the historical wife of Leon Trotsky, being tall, slim, supple and given to dancing. She enters in black ballet tights covered with a fur coat. Where did she get that coat? Trotsky has not seen it, he thinks, before. What is it? Sable? Muskrat? Rabbit dyed? With her comes a troupe of young New Yorkers from a ballet school in South Manhattan. Natalia says to Trotsky:

'Well, little darling, now we'll convince you. The historical process presented simply, movingly, entertainingly, and not a word spoken. We don't need words, do we, sweet darling little comrades?' Hearing that conventional endearment, Trotsky shudders somewhat. 'And where,' cries Natalia, 'is our little Petrushka?'

'Pete, ma'am,' answers a young bony boy with very long fingers. He struggles out of his overcoat and goes over to sit at the piano.

'Not ma'am,' says Natalia. 'That is bourgeois and stands for madame, which means my lady.'

'Yes, Comrade Natalia.' And he puts in order the manuscript music he has brought with him. The ballet students take off their outer coats and are seen to be in black ballet dress. They change into their ballet shoes and start to sing, while Pete accompanies them:

A word is just a pen mark,
A babble of sound.
It means one thing in Denmark,
Another in France,
But all the world round
People speak dance.
A word is just a bubble
Of air from the lungs.
It's hardly worth the trouble
To try to enhance
Your knowledge of tongues:
People speak dance.
With all due deference,
A bourgeois reference
Neatly makes the point.
The Bible tells of Babel,
But only dance is able
To put that joint out of joint.
You don't need French or Spanish

Or Russian or Greek.
Linguistic problems vanish
Away at a glance.
There's no need to speak
When you speak dance.

(*They punctuate the song with dance postures*)

You don't need to call
On blah blah blah.
You can say it all
With an entrechat.
And if you have some-
Thing else to say,
Let it come
In a fouetté.
Stop grunting over grammar
Like old-fashioned fools,
And make each tootsie hammer
Due south of your pants.
In all the best schools
Teachers teach dance.
The past indicative,
Labial fricative –
Don't those sound obscene?
Just throw away your syntax
And strew the floor with tin tacks
And be a Mexican bean.
So let's have no more anguish
With adverbs and verbs.
Let language go and languish,
Teutonic, Romance,
And the speech of the Finns and the
  Magyars and Croats and Serbs.
People speak dance!

They are now ready for the ballet. A big chair, like a throne, is upstage. Trotsky slumps in a plain office chair and watches. The telephone on its little table rings.

'We'd better answer it,' Trotsky says, slumped.

'Take if off the hook, somebody,' cries Natalia. 'We don't want disturbances. All right, *tovarishchi*, we begin.'

So Pete, content to use the telephone's ringing as a sonic adjunct until someone takes the instrument off the hook, storms into his music, which is gloomy but has learnt dynamic tricks from *Le Sacre du Printemps*, already four years old. The ballet is simple. The corps de ballet, as workers, go through weary and resentful mechanical motions. A monster with an Uncle Sam costume encourages them, leering, by lashing them with a rod surmounted with a big vulgar dollar sign. He has a bodyguard of two gangsterlike men with guns. Tired of hitting out at the workers, he slumps into the throne chair, takes a whisky flask from his hip pocket, and drinks deep. Then he sleeps. His snores are incorporated in the rhythm of the music. The leader of the dancers, a vigorous well-balled male, appeals to the gunmen to join their side, to shoot the boss, to help inaugurate the Revolution, but they refuse. The ballerine bring to the fore an aged greyhaired woman, worn out with work, whom the thugs recognize as their mother. They throw down their arms. They take off their flash suits, disclosing workers' uniforms beneath. The workers use the boss's staff of office and oppression to poke him awake and then trample him underfoot. Limping, snarling, he limpsnarls off. The leader twists the dollar sign at the top of the staff into a hammer and sickle. General triumphant dance, in which the staff, symbol of power, is passed from hand to hand and is finally held by all. C major crashes on the piano.

Natalia claps her hands and cries: 'Good. Fine. Very eloquent. There are one or two little things we have to put right. Now, watch me – ' She snakes gracefully into a dance position. But the dancer who has played the workers' leader says:

'We haven't finished yet.'

'Not finished? Of course you've finished. What more is there to say?'

'This.'

The workers work, their leader with them. Then he detaches himself from the group to supervise them. Some dancers are out of rhythm, going their own way. The leader good-humouredly tries to put them right. They refuse to be put right. Soon everybody is going his or her own way. He grows angry. He summons the two former thugs and reinstates them as gunmen. He twists the hammer and sickle back into a dollar sign, puts on the Uncle Sam hat let fall by its previous wearer, and lashes the workers into their former imposed conformity. But during this final action the door opens and Olga appears, breathless, urgent, very agitated, gesturing that she has something important to say to Trotsky. Trotsky gets up with equal urgency and attempts to cross over to her, but he becomes entangled with the dancers. He falls and is trodden on, though unhurt. Natalia, certain suspicions confirmed, shouts to her dancers:

'Out, everybody. Take a break, a breath of fresh air. We discuss later what you have done wrong.' So the dancers grab their coats and their outdoor footwear and leave, though reluctantly. There is going to be Russian trouble, and they would like to see it.

'So,' says Natalia, when the door has closed, 'this is the *Amerikanskaya* they tell me about – '

'Who tell you about?' cries Trotsky. 'Tell you what about?'

'Please, please,' pleads Olga, 'this is urgent – you're in grave danger – '

'You can say again he's in grave danger,' says Natalia. 'I heard all about it, you shameless decadent New York hussy – '

'Who do you hear what from?' cries Trotsky.

'It's the Tsar, it's the government,' pants Olga. 'They got a message in the consulate – '

'All right, Natalia Ivanovna,' says Trotsky, 'you're going to get the real truth now, not what the gossipmongers have been saying. I've never been a liar and I'm not going to start now being a liar. And if you're going to start talking about blame and sin and the rest of the bourgeois nonsense, remember that no man is free, every man is driven by history, destiny, call it what you will – '

'You have to leave,' cries Olga, 'get out of New York, go south, cross the border into Mexico. They want to arrest you – '

'So it's the truth we're going to have at last, is it?' blazes Natalia. 'The thing right out and no more not eating your meals and crying out in your sleep – '

'A man is driven – ' repeats Trotsky. He sings. They all sing.

NATALIA:
Plenty of words,
He always had
Plenty of words.
Like notes
With birds
His throat's
Full of words.

TROTSKY:
Driven driven driven
By the wind,
Riven like a
  lightning-struck
  tree.
Frightening to see
In one like me,

OLGA:
You have to leave,
You have to go.
I know
All the cables they
  receive.

And first they had

Falser than false,
Like other men,
Falser than false.
How well
He tries
To tell
Filthy lies.
All his talk
Of saving New
York
From the tyranny
of money
Could be funny
If it weren't sad,
Disclosing the bad
In all his words.
He always had
Plenty of words.
Most el-
Oquent
But hell,
He's so bent
On lies.
How he tries
To throw dust
In our eyes –
Trotsky the
saviour!
I'm just disgust-
Ed with his
behaviour.
Falser than false,
Friend of the
worker,
His life's a waltz
Or a mazurka
Of lying words.
Let him preach to
the birds!

Who have
Striven striven
striven
Day and night,
Given all the might
in his mind,
Fighting to find
The right, the right!
Then out of the west
A wind blew,
Shattering my rest:
The wind was you.
All that I thought
worth treasuring
Is no such thing
now –
Snow in spring now.
Driven driven driven
Like a leaf,
Given up to grief
And to joy.
A toy boat on a
raging sea
Is storm-tossed me,
Who have striven
striven
Striven striven
So hard to be free.
A snowflake in a
July sun
Is all I've done
Who have striven
striven
Striven striven
That everyone
Might be free –
But there's little
freedom I see
In me!

One most disquieting
Telling of rioting
In Petrograd.

Others came
About you and your
friends,
Putting the blame
On your socialist ends.
The one that smothers
Your hope of revolution
Talks of your execution
To encourage the others.

You're going to hang
high, you
They're going to
shanghai you.
It's illegal, we know,
But they plan your
arrest.
Go, go –
Don't stay to test
The legality.
The reality
Is that they'll get you
somehow.
Go now, now.

I know you're no
stranger
To this kind of danger,
So listen to what I say –
Don't stay
To pack your bags. I'm
Telling you there's no
time
Go, go right away!

* * *

You will have been wondering, boys and girls, ladies and gentlemen, how Professor Hubert Frame was getting on during this eventful spring and summer. Lying quiet in a little white room in the CAT hospital, his respirator plugged into the mains (the camp, of course, had its own generator), often under sedation, his heart action kept steady if faint through Dr Sophie Haas Fried's administration of the drug Diegerticon 5, he was informed regularly as to the progress of the great work by his daughter Vanessa, who also told him frankly – not caring much whether there was a hidden microphone around or not – about the unhappiness of the ship, the fervent and growing dislike and fear of Boss Cat Bartlett.

'Distrust as well?'

'Oh, he's the soul of efficiency, if soul's the right word. That's the trouble. Efficiency through tyranny. Just a life of hard work and sterile devotion to the cause. To him, really. More and more he talks of loyalty to him.'

'I heard some story of exemplary harshness. I'd like to know the truth about poor young Goya.'

'Bartlett says it was the military going too far. But now there's O'Grady ready to try the latest astunomological techniques on dissidents. Maude Adams has been turned into a most efficient automaton. I never saw the necessity of an astunomologist on the team.'

'Hm,' Frame went, in the faint voice which was nearly all exhausted breath and very little glottis. 'It comes from the Greek for policeman. The Natsci committee, as you'll remember, was worried about space hysteria, hysterical dissidence, the need for an expert in pacification. One can never be sure. Policeman sounds horrible, of course. O'Grady is highly skilled in techniques of pacification.'

'That sounds horrible too.'

'Yes. You think O'Grady ought to go?'

'I think Bartlett ought to go.'

Frame could see clearly (sorry) framed in the window the great bulk of Lynx, bloody red, with a tiny moon beside it, newly arisen and ready to terrorize coastal evenings again. 'We're not in charge of the project, Vanessa. We invented it – '

'You did.'

' – But we're not in charge. We don't tell anybody to go. Bartlett could deliver you to the murderous rapists, presumably, and on me he could literally pull the plug. I think, however, I ought to have Bartlett in here.'

'You won't *have him in*, father. He's not a schoolboy, you're not a school principal. He might one of these days *deign* to come in.'

'I think I have certain rights. Perhaps if you told him I'm going to die. I am, of course.'

'I'll ask. Request. Bow humbly and beseech.'

'I ought to have a talk with him. The Bartlett file – it just doesn't give any real idea. Does any file? I've been thinking of someone else – someone with a useless file. Val, I mean. Before I – go – '

'Don't talk about going. Don't talk about poor Val.' She held back a sniff.

'How do we know it's – *poor* Val?'

'What do you mean?'

'Oh, never mind. He wouldn't have lasted five minutes with Bartlett, from all you tell me of Bartlett. Or – mad, isn't it? – Bartlett might not have lasted five minutes with *him*.'

'What a strange thing to say. You never liked Val. You despised him.'

'I suppose I despised in him what I despised in myself – self-indulgence chiefly. My self-indulgence – tobacco, this project. His? Drink, fornication, science fiction. Perhaps I should have fornicated more and smoked less. Val at least had the grace to keep his science fiction between hard or soft covers. I've been reading some of his verse. You gave me this little volume in error.' He indicated with his chin the worn book on top of others on the bedside table. 'It was sandwiched between Toynbee's and Coneybeare's studies of history. Mad to read history when history's at an end. Val has a poem about the end. I know it by heart –

> Here on the final pyre
> See that page with its curled ends
> Rolling into the fire.
> Here's what the poet sang:
> This is the way the world ends:
> Not with a whimper, BANG.'

The little explosion was too much for him. It took him some time to find breath enough to say: 'Do ask Bartlett to come and see me. I shall have to sleep soon.'

Bartlett was chiding Dr Louise Boudinot and Dr Georges Auguste Ewing in his office, while O'Grady sat silently behind him. Ewing interrupted the chiding to say:

'Christ, wouldn't you say you'd reached the limit, Bartlett? If a man and a woman can't – Christ, we'd done *nothing*, and even if we had – '

'The time,' Bartlett said patiently, 'will come for sexual congress, but the time is not now.'

'You call that sexu – ' gasped Louise. 'A kiss, you call that – '

'There's no time for fleshly indulgences,' Bartlett pronounced. 'There was a point 05 error, a significant error, in the calibration that Drs Irving and Herodotus were engaged on. And they were merely pawing each other.'

'Holding hands,' said Ewing.

'What do you suggest, O'Grady?' asked Bartlett.

'Nothing now. Put out a general warning. Next time a dose of eireneutis 6a.'

'Christ,' said Ewing.

'Gamma phase report in tomorrow,' Bartlett ordered.

'I need at least another two days,' Ewing said, sweating slightly. 'I'll have to stay up all night two nights running. Be sensible.'

'Dr Adams will be glad to be of help,' Bartlett said. 'Overjoyed.'

'Jesus Christ.'

When Vanessa was admitted, Bartlett this time alone, she found him affable. 'A drink?' he said, going to his fruit and vegetable juice cabinet. She shook her head and told him her father's request. 'Yes,' he said thoughtfully. 'He has a certain claim on my time. Though he must have read the progress reports.'

'He finds reading increasingly difficult.'

'I'll go now. No need for you to come. Perhaps you'd be good enough to check on whether Dr Ewing's gamma phase report has actually been *started*. I don't trust Ewing. Ewing needs treatment.' He gave Vanessa no time to confirm or contest that but marched out. When he got to Frame's room in the hospital, next hut to Project HQ, he entered without knocking.

'Good of you to come, Bartlett. Do sit down.' Bartlett remained standing. He said:

'Was there anything particular you wanted of me?'

'When will you be ready?'

'Six weeks to the day by my calculation. Everything is going as planned, except for some extra work still to be done on the gravity apotha. It seems to be a matter of accepting natural pull in the initial stages and then effecting a tangential glance-off, using Jumel's megaproagon.'

'I've no doubt of your having,' sighed Frame, 'every technical aspect of the venture under iron control. Have you, however, ever considered what the venture is really for?'

Bartlett smiled meagrely. 'The salvaging of Western civilization in microcosm. Your phrase, I think.'

'Ridiculous, isn't it, Bartlett?' Bartlett smiled still, though less easily. 'How much do you believe about that civilization nonsense? When I spoke to the President, months ago, eons ago, I spoke of man's achievements in science, art, architecture, music, philosophy. False political rhetoric. What do I care about such things? What do you care?' Bartlett held his smile but let the uneasiness out, like a slowly expelled breath. 'This project was designed for the glory of Hubert Frame, scientist and smoker. But who will give him the glory?'

'When our *America* reaches America Nova, the name Frame will be given to the first community established there. That is already laid down in the conspectus.'

'Again I ask – what do you care? What's in it for you, Bartlett?'

'I was chosen. I do my duty.'

'You do your duty,' Frame echoed with what sarcasm his dyspnoeal voice could emit. 'But what reality do you serve? Beauty? Love? Truth?'

'Power,' Bartlett said without hesitation. 'Power is the reality. Manifested at so many levels – the power of one heavenly body over another, of one man over many – '

'Fifty men and women,' Frame said, showing no surprise at Bartlett's avowal. 'Not many to have power over.'

'You're wrong. A race of my making will colonize America Nova, wherever it is. I have no doubt that man will survive, the kind of man I shall mould. I shall fix the parameters for ever once the voyage is begun. I have already thought much about the – desirable image. I shall make the new race.'

'So your fellow astronauts are in for an unhappy time. At least you don't give me the hogwash you give to them, or so my daughter informs me – a time of totalitarian discipline to be followed by an endless era of happy freedom. That argument never worked, did it? The end justifies the means, and the means determines the nature of the end.'

'Unhappy,' said Bartlett, having picked out that one word and disregarded the rest of Frame's breathy flow. 'Human emotions are a great nuisance. I have fine brains and fine bodies working for me, for the project I should say, but their emotions are a great nuisance, a damnable source of ultimate sabotage. Soon there'll be leisure to eliminate emotions – love, hate, that sort of hindrance, that sort of nonsense. What we take with us into space is not the whole of human experience – just a part of it, the useful part. No literature, music, art. Those are disruptive, the stuff of dissidence. Man will have a new chance. A chance to understand the nature of power.'

'God help them, God help me. I wasn't big enough to *frame* such a venture.' He stressed the verb bitterly. 'I should have listened to my son-in-law more than I did. I can't give you my blessing, Bartlett. Perhaps in hell or purgatory I shall have a wry laugh at *homo Bartlettianus*, learning the reality of power in Bartlettland on Bartlett, habitable planet of the Bartlett galaxy. But there are other ships going into space, Bartlett, other *America*s. Remember that.'

'Space is very big,' said Bartlett. 'Big enough for more than *homo Bartlettianus*. Well then, I go without your blessing. Have you anything more to say?'

'No more commerce between us, Bartlett.'

'You're probably ready to die, I should think,' Bartlett said coolly. 'Shall I – pull the plug on you? A corporal work of mercy, as the Christians put it. Pull out the plug, wait five minutes, push it back in again. Professor Frame is dead. A grand burial with the buglers blowing taps. If you want a really big funeral you'll have to have it tomorrow. The day after tomorrow the troops are leaving. They've done their work.'

'I should like,' Frame said with equal coolness, 'to see the great ship before I go. See what might better have been left as a dream – a hunk of science fiction. Will you grant me that?'

'Gladly. Some day next month?'

'If I'm still alive.'

'Oh, that can be arranged. No problem there. Keeping people alive is one aspect of power.' And, with no more words, he left.

The day after the next day the troops went off in their trucks to their bases in Kansas, Indiana, Illinois, as far south as Kentucky and Tennessee, leaving a cadre of a platoon, corporal, sergeant and lieutenant for residual work. Bartlett insisted on a kind of passing-out parade. He wore naval uniform for the occasion. It was noticed by the observant that he had promoted himself to full admiral. He was terrifyingly smart, every inch an officer. When the troops had gone he presided, still in admiral's uniform, over a special dinner in the mess at which, exceptionally, alcoholic beverages were available. He gave a little speech:

'Now, ladies and gentlemen, we enter into the final phase of the operation. The er donkey work has been completed. Now it is all a matter of fine eye, keen brain, total utter and ultimate dedication to the preparation of *Bartlett*.'

There were murmurs, even vinous laughs.

'My apologies. *America*, as we rather too grandiloquently call it. A slip of the tongue.' It was not. Everybody was damned sure it was not a slip of the tongue. And then Bartlett quoted: 'We few, we happy few, we band of brothers.' A chill of a new kind whooshed through the assembly. Nobody had heard Bartlett quote poetry before. Dr Abramovitz and Dr Da Verranzano smiled zombyishly over their orange crush, since they were among those not permitted alcohol. They did not seem to have heard the line before. After several sessions with Dr O'Grady their professional bibliothecological knowledge had become severely limited. *Henry V*? *Tom Sawyer*? *Portrait of a Lady*? Never heard of them.

At this time Edwina Goya was still with her Aunt Melanie in Fort Worth, Texas. Aunt Melanie was a widow of pre-Lynx vintage, not badly off, living for the day, a player of bridge, a great sceptic who called that big light in the sky, *our* moon circling about it, a lot of wicked nonsense. 'Thief,' she said sometimes, '*arrant* thief. Stealing like that and then coming back to mock at everybody. Sneering at us from the sky.' She was not above shaking her fist at it and shouting at it to go away. It did not go away.

Her house was in Haltom City, southwest of Richland Hills, a decent well-built stone house on Conkling Avenue, just by the People's Burial Park. There was enough room in it for two women not to get under each other's feet, but Aunt Melanie saw little of Edwina. Edwina kept to her bed, nursing her belly (everything going just fine, little lady, Dr McBean said) and reading devotional poetry, thinking in a confused way about Nat and what might have happened to him, doubting totally that she would ever see him again. She repeated to herself the name of the town Nat had uttered on the telephone, Sloansville. It meant little, as there were some fifty Sloansvilles in the United States. And if she ever found this place, near the fiftieth

Sloansville, they would of course, would they not, welcome her in, saying: Come and join your beloved and distract him from his work. The trouble was that, with the growth of the child in her womb, the memory of Nat became dimmer in inverse proportion. To resume love, Nat and herself, for the brief time left? Less important than to ensure the survival of the child she carried. Otherwise, what colossal wicked waste. A child crushed in the ultimate ruins. What was God's view of that? Her volumes of devotional poetry returned no answer.

Sometimes she read the Holy Bible – it made little sense for her, or for the world on which Lynx was to pounce – chiefly because its diction and rhythms were inextricably woven into her memory of the patterns of one particular voice. The voice was that of Calvin Gropius, a man who proclaimed for her the vital energy that transcended, or lay immanent in, all the quotidian details of life. In a sense, Gropius was the father of this child kicking in her womb. She had had but to invoke his image, and the image of his voice, when lying with Nat, for her to be flooded with a force of intolerable vital joy. And if she loved Nat it was, she had to be honest with herself, solely as the catalyst of the rending ecstatic process. Her child, Gropius – the two concepts danced in a rhythm which she could now read. It spelt *survival.* Gropius, where was he now? Perhaps dead, shattered in earthquake or engulfed in tigrine waters. But in a sense he could never die. He transcended the accidents of both disaster and decay. If anyone on the doomed earth ought to survive – The two, she saw the two together. Her child and the avatar of divine energy.

'Edwina,' said Aunt Melanie one morning, bringing her ungrudgingly her breakfast tray – coffee, toast, papaya juice – 'Edwina, Jonathan's coming home.'

'Jonathan?'

'Oh, come, child, *my* Jonathan, your cousin Jonathan. He's coming on furlough. Private first class Jonathan Putnam, *my son.* Now you'll have somebody to talk to. Somebody your own age. My Jonathan. Do you mind changing bedrooms, dear? This was always Jonathan's room.'

'Jonathan. I've not seen Jonathan since – he came to see us in Hawaii, didn't he? Hawaii – ' Her mouth squared for tears. Her aunt would stand no nonsense, saying:

'Stop that, girl. No news is good news.'

'Dad and mom, oh my God. Hawaii sank like a stone. All of it. Like so many stones.'

'Be cheerful now. Take what comes, girl. Your mother was my sister, remember. But I'd like to kill that great fat thief of a thing in the sky.'

Jonathan was not of Edwina's age; he was somewhat younger, demonstrating youth in pimples and gawkiness. Edwina came down from her room to the fine homecoming dinner Aunt Melanie had prepared. Jonathan ate heartily of the roast turkey, stuffing, cranberry sauce, roast and mashed potatoes, braised celery, with strawberry shortcake to follow. Edwina picked at a bit of cheese and a breadstick.

'Come, dear, eat,' said Aunt Melanie. 'Remember you've two to feed.'

Jonathan was slow at taking in the meaning of this: he was still only a private first class in the Engineers. But then his face beamed. 'Gee, that's good news,' he said. 'And when do we get a look at your husband, Eddie?'

'Never, as far as I can tell,' Edwina sniffed. 'Never. Excuse me, I think I'll go to bed.' She got up from the table, her half-chewed breadstick clattering down to her plate.

'Oh, come, girl,' said her aunt. But Edwina could be heard running upstairs.

'What happened to him?' Jonathan asked, wiping turkey gravy from his uniform shirt with a napkin corner. 'Was he in the coast floods?'

'No, he was in a thing called Cat or something and they wouldn't let him out. She's not heard from him. Of course, as I keep telling her, Jonathan, he may be alive and well and get furlough as you've gotten it.' Jonathan's mouth was open wide. 'Don't show what you're eating, dear. It's not nice.'

'Cat, you said? C.A.T.? The moonship project? Gosh, mom, that's where I was.'

'But you said you were working on electrical generators in Kansas, dear.'

'Yeah, I know, mom. I didn't say more 'cause it's still supposed to be, you know, Top Secret, TS as they call it. We were told no talking about it on furlough. But that's what it was, the moon job. Finished our work, so off we march. So, then. So that's where he is, was. Small world, kinda. What's his name?'

'A Spanish kind of name. Not Jewish, I know that, just the opposite. There was some great artist with it, Edwina tells me. Goya. I said before, Jonathan dear, don't open your mouth like that.'

'But I know about the guy. Doc Goya. He got out.'

'So Edwina said. He got out and telephoned to this very house. Then it seems like they took him back in again.'

'Yeah, they did that all right. And then I was on the incinerator party. He's dead, mom. Gee, that's terrible. Eddy's husband. There was a lot of, you know, talk about it. This guy they had in charge, Boss Cat they called him, gosh, he was terrible.'

Jonathan's mother was thoughtful. She brought a bubbling percolator of coffee in with the strawberry shortcake, set both down, was thoughtful. 'The question is, Jonathan, whether we let the poor girl live in hopes. Or out with it. Our family was all brought up on the truth.'

'It's a terrible truth to have to tell her.'

'I think she ought to know, Jonathan. You're the one who knows the truth. You're the one to tell it, dear.'

'It's the kind of thing,' said Jonathan, a veteran in army *mores*, 'you tell a guy only when he's drunk. I mean, there was this guy in our outfit, when we were still at Camp Pollock, Dayton. His pal, his closest friend, you know, got chewed up by one of these excavators they call crushers. They got him very drunk and then they told him. It cushioned the shock, the medical officer said. Instinctively correct, he called it. He was okay when he'd gotten over his hangover.'

'You're not getting Edwina drunk,' said his mother.

'But suppose I take her out, mom? You know, on the town? A couple drinks only, you know. Tell her quietly.'

'Well,' said his mother, sipping coffee thoughtfully. 'She has to be told somehow, Jonathan. Poor girl. Poor boy, for that matter.'

It was not until two evenings later that Edwina consented to go out with Jonathan in his Poe Speedbird, Edgar Allan as he called it and as other Poe-owners called theirs. Though only a private first class, he was not unwise in the techniques of holding off bad news. He took her to the Malinda on Sagamore Hill, to the Comanche off Lancaster Avenue, Meadowbrook. Lynx and his stolen moon were big in the sky, and there was much drunken excitement about. She had two martinis and he talked about buddies, officers, the time when he had had two days' shore leave in Hawaii when on his way to Fiji and they had, he thought he remembered, swum together. Treacly water with Diamond Head looking down. At the mention of Hawaii she wished to cry. He quickly got on to a movie he had recently seen in camp, *Baa Lamb's Ass*, meant to turn you on but it didn't. He had had a girlfriend there in the other ranks' dining hall, a waitress, sort of. A sweet potato of a girl, Cindy Wadsworth by name. She said:

'Let's go to the Florentine. Arlington Heights.'

'But that's a great big gambling hotel, Eddie. You wouldn't want to go there.'

'Gambling. It's a picture of life. Take me.' He didn't understand, but he paid for their drinks (plain Coke for him, driving) and they went off. The Florentine was massive, gaudy, not at all Florentine. Its Italian connections were not at all northern. It was, after all, owned by the Tagliaferro brothers, who were very southern. 'I like it,' Edwina said, brightening as she sat at the huge leather-bound bar in the main gambling hall. People were gambling away C-notes like quarters. A handsome, broad, sleek man in his thirties, in space-depth blue tuxedo, white-teethed, abundant black hair, armed with a controlling vitality she found disturbingly familiar, came up to the bar and said to the head barman:

'Put the new price plan into operation at nine thirty, Jack. All brands.'

'Check, Mr Gropius.'

'Everything okay, Jack?'

'Everybody thirsty, Mr Gropius.'

The man laughed and turned away from the bar. Edwina put a hand out and touched. He turned, politely smiling.

'Your name,' she said, 'is Gropius?'

'That's right, miss or madam. Dashiel Gropius at your service. Is everything all right?'

'Are you,' she could hardly get the words out, 'any relation of.'

'I'm always getting that question,' said Dashiel Gropius. 'The answer is yes. My father is, for his sins or mine or somebody's, the great Calvin Gropius. Does that answer your question and quieten your heart, miss or madam?'

'I need to see him,' Edwina blurted. 'I *must* see him. A very important message. Is he around?'

'Around? Here? That's good. No, he never comes to the haunts of sin, not even to preach. He's in Dallas. He wouldn't thank me for divulging his er present hermitage, but that's where he is. At Number 57 Fitzhugh Avenue. Southeast of State Fair Park. Go and see him. Go and pray with him.' And, smiling sardonically but pleasantly, he re-entered the smoky brilliant electric gambling area.

'Thank God,' said Edwina. To Jonathan's surprise, she kissed him, swiftly, sweetly on the lips. 'You're a blessing, Jonathan. If it hadn't been for you – let's have another.'

Jonathan was glad to buy another. He said:

'Eddie, there's something I have to tell you. But not here. Over at that table there. See, that guy's leaving.'

'Very mysterious. Why can't you tell me here?'

'You may want to be some place, you know, dark and quiet. It's bad news, Eddie. Does Cat mean anything to you? You know, C.A.T., Center of Advanced – I mean, I was there. My outfit was there, doing the dirty work. We weren't supposed to know where it was, but it was Hays Hill, Kansas. It's about, well, I guess you know who it's about, Eddie.'

'He's dead, is he?'

'Doc Goya he was known as. A good guy, clever and, you know, young. Well, of course, you know all that. I'm sorry, Eddie.'

She betrayed no expression, sad or otherwise, but drank off her martini thirstily. 'Another, please,' she said. And then: 'I thought he might be. God rest his soul, as my devotional poets would say. Thank you, Jonathan.'

'Don't thank me, Eddie. I just thought, well, mom thought – '

'No, thank you for bringing me here. Everything's going to be all right now, I think. Everything.'

The train moved on towards Paris. They could hear aircraft flying overhead. They flew low, their noise was temporarily deafening. 'War in the air,' Freud said. 'But not a new war. The same war. What's wrong with Germany?'

'Adler was the man to ask,' Anna said. 'Not us. Not Jung.'

Freud pondered that. 'Inferiority complex, he'd say. The protest of the masculine element. But Hitler – he's really a woman. And Adler was a damned traitor.'

'Try and sleep, Sigmund,' Martha said.

'Anna will see the end of it. Not you, Martha, nor I. Well, I'm on a different side now. Fool that I was – ' Made the mistake of being patriotic, he was thinking, as he looked down tunnel after tunnel of time. Of regarding Germany as the great protective father. He, the original Jewish Oedipus. He could not remember where it had been, this watching of grainy war-actuality film in the company of Ferenczi. Ferenczi, Hungarian son of the doomed Austro-Hungarian Empire, to whom the cinema had promised nothing but delightful dreams. Men marching too fast through a silent hailstorm. The Kaiser with his withered arm and a spike on his helmet to impale falling sparrows, his moustaches too spiked. And Freud himself, parodying the Emperor's Hymn: *Alles alles über Deutschland, gegen uns die ganze Welt* . . . Picture postcards from neutral Zürich, depicting neutral Alps. Jung too busy to write long letters, only brief progress reports like wish-you-were-here messages from holiday sun. Jung doing well in Zürich.

In Zürich, in the restaurant named Zum Roten Kreuz, there was an upright piano. On this played Wolf-Ferrari, diminutive and shock-headed, trying out the Intermezzo for his opera *The Jewels of the Madonna*. In a furtive corner over gentian liqueur sat Lenin and a shifty-eyed informant. The train? Seven seventeen. To the Finland Station, comrade. It's coming, it's coming. Is Trotsky still in New York? We hear nothing from Trotsky, comrade. At a bigger table sat James Joyce, an Irish expatriate who was trying to write a large book about the prewar time. With him was the woman he was living with, a deep-voiced woman with a peasant's accent. There were also two children, a boy and a girl, the girl somewhat charmingly louche. The son, like the father, wore glasses. Jung sat with them. He had come in at the end of their luncheon. He took coffee to Joyce's absinthe. He said:

'I don't understand your objection, Herr Joyce. It will be a matter of a few word-association sessions, reminiscences, a gentle examination of your childhood.'

'I don't like *conditions*, Herr Doktor.'

'Mrs McCormack is making you a very generous offer. Look at Wolf-Ferrari over there, listen rather. He's composing again.'

'He's not composing very well.'

'He will be. He's suffered a long silence. But I unfroze his mind for him.'

'My mind doesn't need unfreezing. The river flows very nicely, thank you very much. If only I had more time.'

'You waste too much time in here, Jim,' said the mother of his children.

'Well,' Jung said, 'you have your chance. Mrs McCormack is very rich.'

'I have no objection to wealthy patronesses. But I object when they make having my head examined by you a condition of their patronage. Psychoanalysis indeed. Literary artists know more about the human mind than you fellers have a hope in hell of knowing. Ha. My craft is ebbing. I am yung and easily freudened. One of these days I'll show the lot of you what the unconscious mind is really like. I don't need any of you. In a sense I *am* Freud.'

Jung looked gloomily guilty at the name. 'Yes?'

'What's Freud in English?'

'Joy.'

'Joy and Joyce. There's little enough difference. Except that I add C and E for Creative Endeavour. I spit in all your eyes.'

'Stop that now, Jim.'

'I *contain* the lot of you.'

Lenin and his confederate quietly left, the confederate carrying Lenin's battered suitcase.

'There's another that thinks he knows it all. Comrade Lenin. He's off to start a bloody revolution.'

'Stop that swearing, Jim.'

Bloody enough. Freud and Ferenczi watched more snowy film of the end of the old Russian régime. 'People's republics,' Freud said. 'We're going to have one here. No more father figures.'

'No more neuroses?'

'Oh yes. Get this war over and we'll be in business again.'

This was business not easy to accomplish. Freud sat with sceptical army officers in a plain office full of plain chairs. Major Waldheim said:

'I don't understand your objection, Herr Doktor. Electric shock therapy *works*. The military hospitals are discharging patients with incredible rapidity. The men are *cured*.'

'They're glad to say they're cured. They're running away from electric shocks. But they're still shell-shocked.'

'It's like this,' Colonel Rosenstrauss said. 'I look at electric shock treatment as the kind of kick in the teeth these scrimshankers need. Sheer damned hysteria. Another word for malingering.' Freud said:

'You take me back forty years, colonel. Hysteria is another name for neurosis. Neurosis is a genuine disease. You can't cure it with a few volts of electricity.'

'I think,' said Captain Heller, 'all this is a lot of civilian nonsense. Some men are cowards and some men are not.'

'Why?' Freud asked.

'Some people are red-haired, some black, some bald. Some are Jews, some Gentiles. A matter of what's bred in the bone. What you scientific chaps call heredity.'

'This you know?' Freud said. 'You have scientific evidence?'

'The obvious is the obvious. Why drag science into it?'

'So,' Freud asked, 'what do you do with your so-called cowards?'

'Shoot them,' Major Waldheim said.

'I thought,' said Freud, 'that was the enemy's job.'

An officer who had not so far spoken, Major Schilling, now spoke, and reasonably. 'I think the Herr Professor is trying to tell us that, in effect, there are no real cowards in the Imperial Army. Is that it?'

'There's no Imperial Army any more,' the colonel said angrily. 'There's no Austro-Hungarian Empire. We're a republic now, God help us. All this business about looking to the army of the future and the shell shock of the future is a matter of – what's the word, damn it?'

'Hypothetication?' suggested Captain Heller.

'That'll do, I suppose. Hypo whatever it is.'

'You're wrong,' Freud said. 'There'll always be armies. And there'll always be men stupidly shot by their stupid officers for so-called cowardice. Such men are *sick*. And their sickness goes a long way back. The stress of battle is only the excitatory pretext. The true cause goes back to childhood – '

'You will not, Dr Freud,' the Colonel said, 'attribute stupidity to officers of the army. As you have brought up the word, it is a word I have heard applied to your own theories, along with more op op op opprobrious terms – '

'I think,' Major Waldheim said, 'that no further advantage is likely to be served by this discussion – '

'I think,' Major Schilling said, 'this board of inquiry ought to know that Dr Freud has cured innumerable cases of neurosis. That his reputation is worldwide – though the world does not seem to include the city of Vienna. That he was the only Viennese medical man to be chosen by the United States commission for the administration of the presidential fund to relieve the distress of our Austrian children.'

'So,' said the colonel, 'you think shell shock's a disease? A neurosis? Something you and your chaps could cure?'

'I say this,' Freud said. 'When a man displays hysteria under fire it's because there's something underlying, repressed, an aetiology probably sexual – '

'Oh God help us,' the colonel groaned. 'Oh Lord God Almighty.'

'Look, colonel,' Freud frowned. 'I've been in this psychoanalytical trade for a long time. Rather longer, I should think, than you've been in the killing trade.'

'No need to get offensive, is there?'

'Institute a department of army psychiatry. Get your shell-shock cases on to the psychiatrist's couch. Dig out the real cause of your so-called cowardice.'

'Bit late, isn't it?' said the colonel. 'The war's over.'

'War's never over,' Freud said. 'There's always war. But human lives are still precious. Even the lives of private soldiers. Do you want a written report – a considered recommendation?'

'I hardly think so,' the colonel said. 'We carry on with the electric shock treatment. To be honest, Dr Freud – your name – well – '

'Stinks all over Vienna?'

'I wouldn't be quite so blunt.'

'It smells very sweet in the rest of the world,' Major Schilling said. 'Or so they tell me.'

'Not in Switzerland,' Freud said.

'If you call in at the cashier's office on the way out,' the captain said, 'he'll give you the agreed fee. I hope you brought – ah, I see you did. Thanks for your ah help. Good day to you.'

Freud bowed curtly and carried his small suitcase out. The officers looked at each other.

'He's a great man,' Major Schilling said.

'He's a damned civilian,' Major Waldheim said. 'Shall we break for luncheon?'

'What luncheon?' growled the colonel.

In the cashier's office Freud's suitcase was being stuffed with inflated banknotes. 'Ten million,' the cashier said.

'What can I buy with this? A cabbage?'

'If you can find a cabbage. Sign here.'

In her cold kitchen Martha Freud, older, thinner, was trying to make a dish out of a handful of dried beans. Freud said: 'See – a great treasure. A cigarette. It cost five million. I'd give my soul for a cigar.'

'There's a sick soul in the waiting room,' Martha said. 'It's really peacetime now. People have started having neuroses again.'

'A patient?' Freud dithered in excitement. 'Oh, my God – ' And he dashed out to see.

'Anton von Freund,' he said, writing it down. The man on the other side of the desk was, matching his name, smiling and agreeable. He said:

'I'm called Toni. Sandor Ferenczi calls me Toni.'

'Ferenczi?'

'We've been friends for a long time. I've also been under treatment with him. He said – well, if the master can't come to Budapest, you go to Vienna, Toni, he said.'

'Ferenczi showed you something of my method, then? You know the basic elements?'

'Yes, but I'm still not cured.'

'Tell me your story.'

'I've had cancer of the testicles. Naturally, I've been operated on. Pretty drastic, I'm afraid – the removal of one of them. My doctors tell me that the possibility of a recurrence is – well, fairly remote. They also say that there's no reason why I shouldn't resume a normal sex life. I – well, my wife is young, attractive – There's no physiological obstacle – nothing psychological that I can discover, or my friend Ferenczi either, but – well, I can't. I can't, Herr Professor. My sexual life seems to be at an end. Why?'

'So short a word – *why*. I'm delighted to make your acquaintance, Herr von Freund. Two names in an auspicious conjunction. Freud, Freund. Joy, friend – '

'My friends call me Toni.'

'Toni. Shall we start?'

Freud ached for a cigar as he sat, hidden from his confessee, at the head of the couch. 'The masturbation continued,' Toni was saying, 'despite my father's warning. But the guilt grew worse. The penis grew dead – it became a dead thing – '

'As if your father had already cut it off.'

'Exactly.'

'I think then – with luck – this could be one of the shortest cures on record. The removal of one of your testicles has become tied up with your infantile fears of castration. There's nothing wrong with your genitals now – we have your doctor's word for that. You've confused one fear with another. The castration fantasy – we've all had it. You must start freeing your libido. It will take a little time. But I don't foresee any difficulty.'

'When do I come again?'

'Tomorrow. Any time you wish. Alas, I have too much time.'

Toni got up from the couch. He stood, looking down on Freud, and said: 'You've revealed certain things to me. Now I must reveal something to you. Ever since I heard about you from Ferenczi, ever since I read your books, learned of your cures – I've had a vague notion of doing something for you – advancing your fame, making your books more easily available, making possible the publication of new books – without the opposition and inefficiency of commercial publishers – '

'My own dream. We all have our dreams.'

'This is one that's going to be fulfilled. You know my trade?'

'I never ask. Perhaps I should. Sometimes it's relevant.'

'I'm a baker. A seller of bread. But on rather a large scale. The world doesn't know that it needs psychoanalysis, but it does know that it needs bread. I'm rich, Herr Professor. I propose putting one million crowns into your account.'

'But this is – ' Freud spluttered. 'I can't – '

'I mean one million old crowns, pre-inflationary crowns. Let me translate that sum into a stable currency. A quarter of a million United States dollars.'

Freud, shaken, sat at his deak. He automatically opened his cigar box. There was, of course, nothing there. 'Our own publishing house, is that what you mean? The Psychoanalytischer Verlag – '

'Exactly. Publish your works – in all languages – a definitive edition. The world's been shocked by a terrible war. It's no longer shockable by a mere – well, guide to mental salvation.'

'What can I say?'

'You need a cigar, I think. Ferenczi told me about that amiable vice. I have something for you.' He lifted his briefcase from the floor by the desk. He took out a box of Romeo y Julietas. Freud trembled as he tore at it with his nails, lifted the lid, inhaled, took out a deep brown cylinder of bliss, cut the end with a pocket knife, found matches, lighted up, breathed in smoke and exhaled in a kind of ecstasy more appropriate for the hearing of Beethoven. The cigarette that had cost five million he dropped into his wastepaper basket. He smiled at Toni and said:

'I still don't know what to say.'

Toni smiled back.

It took some time for the physical conditions of life to revert to normality. Freud and Martha sat in a restaurant one evening and felt normality in the restored heating, heard it in the string orchestra, smelt it in the goulash and the castellated desserts. Their steaks came.

'Meat,' mumbled Freud, knife and fork busy, mouth full. 'It's like eating ancient history.'

'I'm worried, Sigmund.'

'Don't worry while you're eating. It's bad for the digestion.'

'It's a terrible lot of money.'

'The bank loan, you mean? It's only a matter of waiting for von Freund's money. I had a letter from him today, remember. It takes a little time, he says, to free money for export. Martha, for heaven's sake put out of your head any notion that he's a man who makes promises he won't fulfil.' And he scooped fried potatoes onto his plate.

'It's not that. It's a question of *can't* fulfil. Governments are very funny about money these days. Sigmund, you've borrowed so much – '

'We had to secure the premises. Wait till you see them. We'll take a stroll after dinner.'

'I'm worried, Sigmund.'

She was right to be worried. A few days later Freud sat in their living room, shaken, a copy of the *Wiener Tageblatt* in his hands.

'Admiral Horthy. Did you ever hear of him before?'

'Not before now.'

'This is the age of revolutions and counter-revolutions. They call this a counter-revolution. Meaning a dictator, inevitably antisemitic. That's Horthy. And all bank accounts frozen, again inevitably. That's the end of our publishing house. Unless there's a counter-counter-revolution.'

'But all the money you borrowed – ' She was near tears.

'The bank will have to wait. We'll appeal for funds at the Berlin Congress. It's poor Ferenczi I'm thinking of now. Counter-revolutionaries don't like psychoanalysts. They're scared of the truth. Don't worry, Martha. Everything will be all right. But – poor Ferenczi. I'd dreamed of Budapest as a great psychoanalytical centre. These damned politicians. They're the real enemy.'

A military band blared, thumped and jingled down the Kurfürstdammstrasse. That jangling belltree was a Hungarian import. Ferenczi looked old and broken as he moaned over his coffee in the little café. He groaned:

'Where? *Where?*'

'It can't last,' Freud said.

'Not *asked* – *forced* to resign. And they've even closed down the clinic for the treatment of war neuroses. Where can I go?'

'Back to Budapest. Fight.'

'I'm no fighter. Besides, I've no status – my patients are leaving me – because I'm no longer a member of the Hungarian Medical Society, no longer at the university – '

'*Fight.*'

'You have friends,' Jones said, 'fellow fighters. How about Anton von Freund?'

'He's dying. Cancer. It's spread upwards – to his liver, his lungs. Say what you will, you can't contain cancer. It grows. It kills.'

Freud suddenly and surprisingly felt a sourness in his cigar. He removed it from his mouth, frowned at it, shrugged, restored it.

'There's work for you in the publishing house,' Jones said.

'He was a good man,' Freud pronounced. 'But I thought I caught – well, the smell of death on him. He's not dying of a diseased mind, that's one thing. Yes, the publishing house, Ferenczi. His memorial. Though not, alas, his money.'

'Everybody's money,' Jones said. 'We should have thought of it a long time ago. It's *ours*.'

'Will it never stop?' Ferenczi moaned. 'This damned persecution.'

'No,' Freud said, 'never. But you still have to fight it. *Fight.*'

There were two hundred and thirty-nine delegates in the hotel ballroom. Freud addressed them from the creaking rostrum.

'We have arrived, ladies and gentlemen. Psychoanalysis is at last an accepted fact of the modern world. It will be persecuted still, mocked, reviled, but it cannot be dislodged. Perhaps that term, implying as it does a rock or stone or monolith, is not an apt one. Psychoanalysis is rather a river with many tributaries. It flows into the sea of truth. It cannot be deflected. As an earnest of its everchanging never changing properties, I propose to you today a new view of the mind, or should I say a new terminology of the mind. I think we must be done with vague terms like conscious and unconscious. We must think instead of the human soul as containing an uncharted entity which I call the id – a seething cauldron, a stormy lake of instinct, suffused with primal energy, open to somatic influences. Then there is the ego, which seeks to substitute reality for the mere shapeless gratification which is the concern of the id. Then finally there is the superego – the representative of society within the psyche, the watcher, concerned with morality, the guardian of the ego, as the ego is the watchdog of the id – '

Looking at his notes on the lectern, preparing to turn a page, he was mildly surprised to see a fleck of blood on the hand ready to turn. He ignored it and continued:

'Psychoanalysis is the discipline, the tool, the instrument which enables the ego to control the id – '

A sizeable fleck. A sizeable fleck too back in Vienna when he spat into the wash basin. He examined his mouth in the mirror. Martha came in in her dressing gown.

'What is it, Sigmund?'

He came away from the wash basin, shrugging. 'A little blood. A swollen gum, I think.' He tested with his tongue. 'A bit rough. Nothing.' He went in to breakfast.

Martha brought in fresh coffee. Freud bit a piece of bread and then looked at the slice. A bloodstain on the white. Martha saw it.

'Nothing,' Freud said, hiding his disquiet.

Val and Willett were employed on the ghoulish work of unblocking the Ghersom Tunnel which ran under the Hudson and connected, along with other tunnels and battered bridges now under repair, Manhattan with the New Jersey mainland. Ghoulish because the blocking had been done by cars with bodies in them, as also bodies without cars. Val and Willett operated a Marquet truck on which cadavers were piled; they drove it to Dump 4; they tipped their freight into the great hole to which, at the end of the day's work, Lynx and moon in their crescent phase rising, fire was lavishly set. There was an unofficial team which stripped the bodies of whatever was unspoiled and still useful – rings, watches, dental bridges, money, credit cards and the like. This was the ultimately ghoulish. No, not quite the ultimately. There was a dribbling mad necrophile who had to be kept away from fleshly mauling. He was eventually shot by Murphy, the man in charge of Dump 4.

It was Murphy who, during the lunch break one day, came up to Val and Willett and their bread and cheese and beer (rations were issued at the Dorothy Draper Museum, at present a workforce hostel, when the parties left in the early morning). He had a little book in his hand and he said to Val:

'This you?' He thrust the book, a lumpy, wavy, water-spoiled paperback, at Val's nose. Val saw his own picture on the back cover.

'Good God,' he said, taking it. 'I'd almost forgotten this existed.' The title was *Not to Call Night*. The blurb said: 'This brilliant first novel by one who bids fair to become a great name in world SF . . . '

'I had a look in it,' Murphy said. 'Ain't nuttin doidy in it.' This seemed to be a reproach. A man said, chewing cheese:

'Doidy? A doidy book?'

'*Not* doidy, Milligan,' Murphy growled. 'If you want sumpn doidy I'll take ya to see *Baa Lamb's Ass* at the Truman Capote.' The workers looked at Val, who flicked through his book with tenderness, surprise, distaste; looked at him with the mixture of awe and contempt that working men always accorded chance-met writers. Dis guy's a rider. What's he ride? Not rider, stoopid, he writes books. Doidy books?

'Read us some out,' Milligan said. 'A sex bit.'

Willett jocosely grabbed the book from Val, opened it at random and began to improvise: ' "Panting with desire she seized him and said: 'Now, now, I can't wait.' He held her off contemptuously, disdaining the proffered opulence of her half-naked flesh. Then she . . . " ' His voice faded out. He looked at Val, frowning. 'When did you write this?'

'The date's opposite the title page. 1990. 1986. A hell of a time ago.'

'You remember what it's about?'

'The blurb says, surely. About a heavenly body preparing to hit the earth, isn't it? False alarm. A lot of earthquakes, though. Is that right?'

'Listen,' Willett said. 'Listen carefully. There's a character here called Dr Bodley. Does that ring any bells in the corridors of your creative skull? This Dr Bodley says: "If I had to choose a site comparatively immune from seismic shocks, however hard they hit the rest of the American terrain, I'd opt for a little place called Fordtown in the state of Kansas, midway between Hays and Hill City." Where did you get that information? Guess work? Pure fiction?'

'Ain't nuddin doidy in dat,' Milligan said.

'I used to work pretty hard on background,' Val said, brows knitting, trying to remember. 'The critics were always quick to leap on writers who hadn't done their homework. I should think that's a chunk of exact information. Why?'

'Idiot,' Willett bawled. 'Shitabed lobnoddy, foolish loggerhead. Your turdstrewn catcamp is in such a place. Didn't they ever talk about the kind of site they were after? Your wife, your wife's old man?'

'A spot,' Val pondered, 'comparatively immune from seismic activity.'

'That's where we're going,' Willett said, chucking the rest of his bread and cheese to a spotted loll-tongued pooch that had joined their party some days before.

'You guys are going,' said Murphy, who had been listening intently but without comprehension, 'back to woik.'

'There are other places,' Val said. 'These United States, as they were formerly called, are full of good quakeless land.'

'We have to go somewhere,' Willett said, 'and soon.'

'I told you the position,' Val said. 'I'm off the team now, no doubt about that. Discharged dead, probably. And you've never been on it.'

'We'll cross that bridge,' Willett said, 'when we come to it. We'll negotiate that tunnel,' he varied.

'Back to woik,' Murphy announced, and he blew a whistle.

'Till when?' asked a polite educated dark man who alleged he had taught Arabology at Columbia. 'When do the floods start again? We have our preparations to make.'

'Don't know nuttin about that, buster,' Murphy said. 'We goes on till the mayor says to stop.'

'Fuck the mayor,' the dark man said evenly and without rancour.

'You don't wanna say that, buddy. That's kinda like what they has in the old movies. High treason, it's called. You wanna watch that mouth, little buddiuddy.'

Dump 4 was on the New Jersey side of the tunnel. At three in the afternoon, Val jerked the lever for the last time and sent his last freight of corpses thudding into the great smoky hole. The scavengers frisked about like rats, opening dead mouths, tugging at dead fingers. 'Okay,' cried Val. Willett let in the clutch. They were off. Voices shouted after them. They fancied they heard gunshots. In three-quarters of an hour, after a passage of sickening bumpiness on broken roads, they were on the outskirts of Newark. Their truck was gasoline-driven. They filled up from a self-serve pump, stuffing dollars into the mouth of the machine. Fat gas glugged in. Val noticed a shop opposite with a temporary nameboard tacked up: WHITEHEAD GUNS.

'Guns?' Willett said. 'You can actually buy guns?'

'The inalienable right of all Americans. Guaranteed by the Constitution. The pursuit of happiness, also of enemies and harmless uneatable animals. Come on, we need protection.'

An old man, chewing an afternoon bever, was glad to serve them. 'It's lead,' he said, 'does the protecting. Had 'em in lead, all of 'em, down there in the cellar. When I came back from my sister Ethel's in Macon, Georgia, I fould all gone but the cellar,' He cackled. 'But it's cellars that count, wine, guns, money. You can't beat cellars.' He sold them a Hamster hipfirer and two .45 Schultz pistols, together with some yellow boxes of ammunition. They paid out hundreds of dollars.

Near Reading in Pennsylvania, they ate ham and eggs and cheesecake in a diner and stocked up at a hypermart on canned goods, at a liquor store on liquor. Lynx's crescent was a grotesque lewd mockery of its attendant moon's. Reading had had little trouble last time and expected no more this. But outside Harrisburg they found an end-of-the-world-is-coming group shouting hysterical slogans about the need for repentance, to the laughter of passing motorists. At a motel outside Pittsburgh they stayed the night. It had been a long drive but the truck was speedy. Tomorrow they would need something speedier, as well as more comfortable. They had their thieves' eyes on a Tallahassee '00, evidently abandoned, parked outside Chalet 9A, which was empty and open. They lay on the twin double beds of the room they shared, smoking long turd-coloured Columbus panatellas.

'Hopeless,' Val repeated.

'A matter of degrees,' Willett said. 'One thing's less hopeless than another. To stay in New York would have been ten-point hopelessness on a ten-point scale. A day added to life – it's something. Even to be in Kansas will be something like three-point hopelessness. Besides,' he puffed azure, 'I have rather a fancy to be saved.'

'Why?'

'A bonus. A gift. I don't insist on it, of course. A man's a fool to insist on anything. I'd rather like,' he said innocently, 'to be in a spaceship. It fulfils a childhood dream.' Rain suddenly burst from a million simultaneously pricked bags in the Pennsylvania sky. When, like a brilliantly organized hissing high-violin effect, it had played a few measures in moderato tempo, lightning performed jaggedly on the skyline visible through the wide uncurtained window, and hundreds of drummers thumped thunder. Then there were, as from extra orchestras hidden in the wings, deeper thumps and grumbles afar. The Coke bottles on the middle bedside table clanked together, and their contents danced, even splashed. 'An earthquake,' Willett guessed. 'North of Pittsburgh. We got out of New York just in time. The tides will be starting again.'

They were determined to get some sleep on this trip. Val had a bottle of five hundred Aupnia tablets. They took three each, sluicing them down with shaky Coke, and settled to slumber. It came tardily, but it came. Their portable alarm digiklok, picked up from the travelling bag of another westbound fugitive in the hypermart when he (she with him) was paying his snakelong check, woke them at six. Crescent Lynx and moon setting, the rain ceased, the distant seismic rumbles audible still, flashes on the horizon, they got up wearily and stiffly. Chalet 9A was still tenantless, and its door swung. The Tallahassee '00 would not yield to Willett's omniclef. 'Bugger,' he said in stage Britishry. 'Let's try that one over there.' He meant an Abaco station wagon in high-gloss aubergine. It started like a dream. They were on their way, bags and guns rattling at the rear.

They breakfasted at a diner just over the Ohio border, five miles or so from Wheeling, and made Columbus easily by midday. Again, as they sped on with full bellies, the sky yawned open and vomited haily rain, lightning did its act with thunder trundling grumbling after. Just beyond Dayton the car broke down. 'Christ pedicate the bastard,' swore Willett. The tank was half full of gas; there was something subtly amiss with the engine. Val got delicate fingers to work on the guts under the hood, but to no avail. 'Christ blast its soul to fucking Tophet. Christ deliver it a fiery message of abomination.'

The name of the Redeemer was being used less blasphemously in the headquarters of Calvin Gropius, 57 Fitzhugh Avenue, Dallas. It was also being used less frequently. Gropius found the New Testament hardly relevant to the situation he knew was coming. The Book of Revelations was good for pertinent rhetoric but hardly for a programme of action. The holy name was heard less in his mouth than in that of his visitor, Mrs Edwina Goya, widow and prospective mother. Outside the rain whished down, and more damp began to appear on the living-room ceiling. 'Do you not consider yourself,' Edwina asked, 'to be the living vicar of Christ?'

'That's what they call the Pope,' Gropius said. 'If there still is a Pope.' He and his family – Maria his wife, his son James, his two daughters-in-law, his grandchildren, the other two sons being at work, a brindled cat that had come in from yesterday's rain and had adopted the household and had been christened Joachim – looked at this strange girl with the swelling belly, not too curiously, certainly not fearfully: the human beings there were all used to cranks, it was one of dad's occupational hazards.

'Listen,' said Edwina, on the edge of her dining chair, 'I have the facts, I have the knowledge. I'm not talking now like one of the chiliastic fanatics of California. The world is going to end. Not with the Lord coming in glory, flanked by archangelic brass. Just a very unfortunate cosmic accident, something to be explicated in terms of physics and not at all by theology. Do you understand me? Going to end, and going to end soon. And there's a spaceship being made ready in the state of Kansas to salvage a load of scientists. Is this right? Is not this flying in the face of the Lord's will? Doesn't the Lord Jesus Christ want the righteous to be saved, not the knowledgeable?'

Gropius looked warily at her. He knew the eyes, wide, fired, capable of adoration. He said:

'I must confess I have waited for a sign – a message – a dream, perhaps – ' Jennifer said brightly:

'I'm the one who gets the dreams. There was this one before Oklahoma City got hit by the quake, and this angel – '

'Yes, yes,' Gropius said wearily, 'we've heard all about that. What you say,' he told Edwina, 'makes all too much very sad sense. In the days of Noah, righteousness and the woodworker's skill were enough. Christ's own career shows how those two attributes were, in a sense, cognate. Today, alas, we have the age of many and diverse and exceedingly complex specializations. Righteousness is one full-time job, technology is another.' That last neat phrase had actually been spoken by his son John at dinner the previous evening.

'Well, the ark is in preparation,' Edwina said, 'and I know where. It's your duty in Christ to confront them, confront the murderous head of the team, and make your demand in the Lord's name.'

'Murderous?' said Gropius.

'The bastard murdered my husband.'

'Don't you swear in this house,' Maria said, 'and don't you tell my husband what his duty is.' But her husband cut in with:

'They will laugh. They will tell me to go away. The Lord's word means nothing to the breed of atheist scientists.'

'So,' said Edwina, 'you have so little faith in the power of the word of a messenger of the Lord. You did not show this lack of faith when you preached to your great rallies.'

'It was different then,' Gropius mumbled.

'Different, yes. No danger threatened. Religion is a toy for the good times, is it, not a weapon for the bad?'

'Don't speak to my,' Maria began, but her husband said:

'What am I to do?'

'Demand. And if demanding is not enough, threaten.' James Gropius gave a little laugh, very short. 'The Lord's men were never afraid of fighting giants. David felled Goliath with a kid's catapult. Joshua ordered the moon to stand still. Moses fought. Fight. But threaten first. That's the Lord's way.'

Gropius looked at his loved ones, and even at the cat who washed a furred drumstick. 'If it were true,' he said, 'that there was this chance of the salvation of the righteous, a bare chance only, would you come with him who has followed the path of righteousness and preached the word of righteousness to the many?'

James shuffled in his chair. His connections with religion had always been marginal – filial, hygienic. He heard the big words and thought: Jesus, that crap again. Jennifer said:

'I'd rather wait for a dream, I think. I mean, it was the Lord's angel in Oklahoma City, and that was only an earthquake. For the end of the world I think I ought to have like an archangel telling me. Though,' she added, 'this is Dallas. Perhaps the heavenly host don't like the idea of coming to Dallas.'

'They came to Sodom,' Edwina said. 'Look, there are other ways than dreams. The way of an unknown woman coming out of the blue in a hire car and a yellow raincoat. A messenger of the Lord, if you like.' Maria Gropius pursed her rouged lips. James said to Edwina:

'What's in it for you?' It was said without insolence. He had said it often before, in his gleaming trade, to men who brought visions of big orders – the toilets of the new Sacrecinema in Ponca City, for example, which was to be devoted to holy movies – *Quo Vadis*, *Ben Hur*, Zeffirelli's *Jesus*, that sort of thing. He waited for Edwina to answer. Edwina said:

'I don't care whether I live or die. But I have this child within me. And the father of this child, the earthly father, has been done to death by the atheist scientists who run this atheist project which must be redeemed by the touch of the Lord. I want this child to live. Because I believe this child is the Lord's child.' She looked firmly at Gropius, and Gropius separated his neck from his shirt collar. 'Without my message you would have no hope of salvation. There is hope now, good hope. Not certainty, but hope. That's what's in it for me,' she told James.

James nodded. It seemed fair. 'You want in on Noah's Ark,' he said. Edwina said:

'The certainty can only come about through the strength of the Lord. Through the Lord's threat, and if the threat fails, the Lord's thunderbolt.' Thunder afar heard that and grumbled assent.

'Guns,' Gropius said, 'you mean guns? I never handled a gun in my life, except for duck-shooting.' He turned to his wife and said: 'Maria, sweetheart. Would you come, dressed only in the hope?' James grinned at that, mom bare naked except for hope. They might let her in at that.

'It's not going to happen,' Maria said.

'*It fucking well is*,' hissed Edwina, neck stretched forward, lips spread. 'And don't say anything about language language, because the time has come to stop dithering and act. The time is very short,' she said to Gropius. 'If we leave, we should be leaving tomorrow.'

'But,' Rufa said, breaking her wide-eyed silence, 'it's Sam's birthday the day after tomorrow. We have this little party.'

Edwina said nothing. Nobody said anything. Then Edwina tightened her raincoat belt about her lost waist and said to Gropius: 'I'll be back this evening. No need to invite me to dinner,' she added, as Maria looked doubtfully at the table in the dining alcove, not enough places, not enough roasting beef. 'It's your duty in Christ. God send you the fucking dream, if that's what you want. Good afternoon, all.'

'A queer girl,' Jennifer said, as they heard her car start. 'Sometimes she sounds religious and sometimes she doesn't.' Calvin Gropius ached nostalgically for *true* religion: a great lighted rally in a vast stadium, Bible-thumping, the crowds coming down to the front to pledge themselves to Jesus, a light supper after, eyes of adoration. He then felt sick.

'I don't know,' he said. 'I just don't know. Let us get down on our knees and pray for guidance.'

'I have to go to the john,' James said.

Edwina drove grimly to the Florentine Hotel. There was the faint gut-rumble of an earth tremor and the rain emptied passionately. She parked outside the hotel's main entrance, where there were already many cars. Inside, gambling and drinking proceeded, passionate as the rain. She asked a sort of undermanager for Mr Gropius.

'He's busy right now.'

'This is important,' said fierce Edwina. 'It's about his father.'

'His dad? Wait here, lady. See what I can do.'

Edwina waited while he blepophoned. The image of Dashiel Gropius was disclosed on the miniscreen in high colour, shirtsleeved, working at a desk. 'Send her up,' said his voice.

She went up with the sort of undermanager in an elevator upholstered in mauve plush. He knocked at a heavy-looking door of brass-embossed teak. A light flashed above it. Edwina went in. Dashiel Gropius politely rose. 'Good afternoon, miss, madam. We met before, I think.'

'Listen,' Edwina said. 'Listen carefully.'

'Do please sit down. A drink?'

'Martini. Listen, there isn't much time. Whatever they tell you, we're in for big trouble. The trouble's so big that there's no point in government doing anything about it. We have to face it on our own.'

'Lynx?'

'Lynx. There's going to be a collision. Now, please don't look at me as if I'm mad. I'm not a scientist, but my husband was. He's dead now, but he told me everything before he died. The government ordered the building of a spaceship – maybe more than one, I don't know. But there's certainly one standing ready in the state of Kansas. I know where, I know precisely where.'

'Where?' He gave her her martini, which she drank thirstily.

'Never mind where for now. I've been trying to persuade your father that his duty is to get his family together and get on that spaceship. With me, too. I have a child to save. To hell with me, but this child has to live. Do I make myself clear?'

'Go on.' But he drew nonchalantly on a long gold-tipped Penhaligon, faintly smiling.

'Christ,' she said, 'we've all seen too many movies, read too many trashy books. About the end of the world, I mean. It's just a chunk of old-fashioned folklore. But now it's really going to happen. How can I make you believe me?'

'Why did you come to me anyway?'

She smiled a smile faint as his own. 'You're a man of action, I suppose. A man of the world. I don't think it's going to be a matter of the great Calvin Gropius crying "You know who I am, God's voice. Let my family into the ark." I think it's going to be a matter of a fight.'

'Do I look like a fighter?' He smiled more broadly.

'Ah, shit,' she frowned. 'I know all about gambling. It's dirty work and dirty people are behind it. People get knifed and shot. I should imagine your bosses have names like Leopardi and Tortarella and Bonicelli.'

'A bit like,' he agreed, 'but those names are too northern. The Tagliaferro brothers, to be exact. Nice people, but excitable. If you talked to them about the end of the world they'd probably believe you, making the sign of the cross all the time. Tell them about a spaceship and they'll say, or Gianni will, "Bought one a dem for my eldest kid." As for fighting, they'll fight. They're used to it. Submachine guns in guitar cases, Frobishers, Magnolia sevens with thirty-centimetre silencers. Whether they'll fight for a Protestant Voice of God is another matter. Besides, I don't think father would like to have them in his ark. Not even as animals.'

'You don't believe,' she said sadly. 'I'd go myself, alone, yes, but that's not what the thing's about. Your father's a great force, bigger than he knows, and I don't think it's anything to do with what he believes.'

'I think I agree with you there. I always felt that. That's why I got away from him at the age of fourteen. I wanted to be a force of my own, not just a satellite. I think I see something else you mean. He's anti-science. Instinct, superstition, myth. You think he's a force that ought to be saved.' He grinned. 'In order to save others. Martians or something.'

'Not Martians. Look,' she said, 'you're bright. Why do you do this kind of thing?'

'Because I'm bright.' He went to the private bar and brought two more martinis. She was parched and took her glass gratefully. He said: 'I got a message this afternoon. From Ottawa, Illinois. Southern Chicago's in ruins. An earthquake.'

'You're not kidding?'

'I'm not kidding. It happened last time – earthquakes, tidal waves.

It's happening again. It can't go on happening, can it? It's got to end somewhere.'

'Call the first time a warning. Get on that spaceship before that too is in ruins. That spaceship's bigger than Chicago. It's the hope of mankind.' Rhetoric, rhetoric – how the hell did one keep rhetoric out? 'I wanted to believe, like everyone else, that the damned intruder was just looking in then moving off. Or getting into a rhythm of coming and going. I see now how plain the whole thing is, and I wonder why nobody believes. Last time the earth was in one position in its solar ellipse, now it's in another. *It's going to happen*. What are you going to do?'

'Are you seeing my father again?'

'Tonight, after dinner.'

He grinned. 'I can see you're not the sort of messenger mom would want to invite *to* dinner. I think I'll be there.'

'One very small thing, pure curiosity. How did you escape a holy name? I mean, Dashiel is a bit profane, isn't it?'

'George Dashiel. Mom insisted on the Dashiel in the middle because it sounded refined. Name of a French general, approximately. There was a writer called Hammett who had it. You may have seen an old movie called *The Maltese Falcon* – '

'The dragon fighter is the bit I trust.'

That night the two crescents were blood-red and, it seemed, much closer. There were earth tremors in Fort Worth. There was some panic in the gambling halls of the Florentine, quickly calmed by drinks on the house. George Dashiel Gropius, getting into his car, *believed*.

'Driven,' cries Trotsky, 'by secretions in my glands, driven by destiny – whatever it is, I have no shame. I want you, Olga. I've trodden the streets of this city, searching for you. Now that I have you I won't let you go. Natalia, listen. You know that marriage is a bourgeois institution. You know that impulses of this nature can't be withstood, Natalia – '

'Yes,' cries Natalia. 'Just what Dr Goldstein was saying to me in New Jersey. He talked of love, but he didn't talk about marriage being a bourgeois institution. He wants to get me where I can be safe.

me and the children, and not tied up with bloody revolutions. He wants to give me a real home –'

'What have you been doing with Goldstein? What's been going on there?' Olga yells louder than either:

'Listen, for God's sake, listen. You're in danger, Trotsky. They're going to try to get you on board the *Isaac Brodsky* – it's tied up there now, Pier 16. They want to take you back to Russia. They're going to make you stand trial. On a charge of disaffection, treason, anything they can damned well dig up. Listen to me – get home, pack a bag, take a train south. Get to Mexico – you'll be safe in Mexico – '

Natalia does not listen, nor does Trotsky. Natalia cries: 'He says what a woman like me wants out of life is more than being in exile all the time, hounded, always in danger – '

'Offered marriage, did he? All right, get a divorce. On the grounds of an adultery that never happened. I won't stand in your way. Go on, marry the bourgeois swine – '

'And I take the boys too.'

'Take them – they're yours. As the proverb says, it's a wise child that knows his own father – '

'What's that you said then? What are you accusing me of?'

'Oh my God,' Olga cries, tugging at Trotsky and being tugged away by Natalia. 'Don't you hear? Haven't you heard what I said? They're coming for you, you've got to –' But Natalia slaps her viciously and says:

'American slut.'

'Don't you do that,' cries Trotsky, getting weak punches in. 'You leave that girl alone.' And to Olga: 'Get out of here, wait for me at you know where – '

'Oh my God,' sobs Olga. 'It's a madhouse. They're coming for you, do you hear me? You've got to get – ' Natalia is on to hair-pulling now. 'I'll tell my stepfather. But it may be too late for the police. Go on, get out, go.' And she herself goes.

'Wait for me,' cries Trotsky. 'At the place where they sang that thing of Pushkin's.' But she is quite gone.

'Pushkin, eh?' cries Natalia. 'Love songs for you and the filthy American slut –'

'All right,' blazes Trotsky. 'You're always saying that fidelity was a bourgeois notion. Motherhood a biological reality and fatherhood a legal fiction. Now we know what's been going on in the dark evenings, don't we, with me away at committee meetings – '

'Legal fiction! Fiction all round in your case. What kind of father have you been, putting your sons in peril – '

'If they *are* my sons!'

'Making them a bad second to your political nonsense, me too, a very bad second – '

'Ah, go to Goldstein, fat on workers' blood, with his automobiles and his chauffeurs and his false socialism. Go and join the American ladies – you, who used to call yourself a daughter of the Revolution – '

'I'll go all right. You won't ever see me again, you dirty hypocrite.'

'Hypocrite, is it? Dirty, is it? Go if you're going, but I'm going first – ' He looks round for his overcoat and finds it bundled up on the seat of the piano.

'That's right, go to your Pushkin and your Newyorkskaya whore – Take her off to Mexico as she suggested, hypocrite and lecher.'

'What's that about Mexico? Did she say something about Mexico? I didn't hear what she said with your screaming and yelling and vulgar abuse – '

'Ach,' spits Natalia. 'You bourgeois sentimentalist, you lackey of the discredited romantics, you – *Trotskyite*.' And she goes out, slamming the door in the face of the cleaning man Sasha, who is trying to come in. He comes in, sucking his teeth, looking coldly at Trotsky. He notices that the telephone is off its hook, so he recradles it. Then he says to Trotsky:

'*Nye dobriy malchik, pravdo?*'

Trotsky looks at him open-mouthed. 'You speak Russian!'

And Sasha goes on speaking Russian, with a patrician accent. 'Ah, yes. It was quite an effort putting on that er *phony* New York accent.' *Phony* seems to go well into Russian. Sasha takes his worker's bunch of keys from his overall pocket and firmly locks the door.

Trotsky gapes still. 'What did you do that for?' he says. 'Who are you?' And he goes to the door, hardly able to believe that a snotnosed menial has locked him in. 'Why did you do that? Give me that key.'

Sasha seats himself. 'No,' he says. 'You're staying with me. You've nowhere else to go, have you?'

'Ah, I see. One of the enemy. One of the grand discreditors. You told those stories to my wife.'

'*You're* the enemy, *gospodin*,' Sasha says. 'You're guilty of treason against the State. You've advocated the assassination of His Majesty Nicholas II, Emperor of all the Russias, God bless him and protect him from rogues, liars, killers like you and your associates. You've preached the throwing-over of the established order. You're going back to Russia to stand trial.'

Trotsky approaches him tottering, with his claws out. 'You're mad,' he says. But Sasha pulls a revolver, nicely oiled, from his overall pocket. He says:

'Sit down, Lev Davidovich. Your mistress, your *American* mistress, knew all about it. I think she tried to telephone earlier, but the instrument was off the hook. She's been working in our consulate here in Manhattan, sending sly news items to this newspaper of yours – items about the deplorable state of our motherland. We let her. We have nothing to fear from the truth. The truth is that it's you and your insurrectionist colleagues who are responsible for the bloodshed and unrest. They're going to make an example of you, Lev Davidovich.'

There is a knock at the door. His gun pointing, Sasha gets up to open it. Two pompous men come in, impeccably overcoated and bowler-hatted. The hats they doff in apparent deference to Sasha. They look coldly on Trotsky. 'Welcome,' Sasha says. 'May I introduce Alexandr Gregorovich Kamarin and Ivan Pavlovich Doktorov, consul and vice-consul respectively at the Imperial Russian Consulate here in New York? You gentlemen know who this ah *comrade* is.'

Kamarin speaks. He taps his left breast. 'I have here a warrant. It came in the consular bag by the *Isaac Brodsky*. The *Isaac Brodsky* sails back to St Petersburg in two days' time. You will be on it, under lock and key. You will be on it tonight. Prince Komisarjevsky will make all the necessary arrangements.'

'Prince Komis – ' Trotsky realizes that this personage is none other than the cleaning menial Sasha. He takes a deep breath and says: 'The Tsar and his jackals have played many illegal tricks in this wretched time of our oppression, but this is a piece of illegality impossible of fulfilment. This is a foreign country, a free country – '

'Ah, interesting,' Sasha says. 'The land of the bloody dollar is free, is it? Fascinating.'

'I'll call the police,' cries stoutly Trotsky.

'You'll call nobody,' Sasha says. 'We have a motorcar waiting in the street below. In a few moments you are going to have vodka splashed on your face, Lev Davidovich. See, Ivan Pavlovich has the bottle ready. You will leave as a drunken man. With a gun pressed to your ribs. New York, incidentally, will be rather glad to see the last of you –'

And now the telephone rings. They all look at it, and then at each other. But it is Sasha who lifts the receiver. He says in English:

'This is the office of the *Noviy Mir.*' And then: '*Chto? Kto? Da. Da. Khorosho.*' He puts the receiver down and looks gravely at Trotsky. 'This,' he says, 'is not a matter of politics. I am therefore able to express my regret. Your son has disappeared from home. One of your sons – Seryozha seems to be the name. It was the other son telephoning.'

Trotsky turns frantically on the three. 'This is another piece of Tsarist brutality, is it? What have you done with him, where have you taken him? Kidnapping, eh? For the ransom of a signed note of repudiation – a confession of guilt. You won't get it, you swine. Let me get at that telephone – let me get to the police – '

'This,' says Doktorov, 'is not us, *gospodin*. I join his highness in an official expression of regret. I've no doubt your son will be found. That must be your wife's affair, I'm afraid. Our mission must be accomplished. Will you come quietly or in the role of a struggling screaming drunken man?'

'Brutality and madness,' Trotsky cries, tearing at his hair. 'You show what you are. I'll come if you let me call the police. I'll come only when I know he's somewhere safe. Seryozha, Seryozha – what have they done to you?' He struggles to grab the telephone. Sasha wonders whether to hit him on the head with the gunbutt. The telephone rings again. Sasha lifts the receiver. Trotsky cries: 'They've found him! Have they found him? Tell me, you swine!'

But Sasha, speaking in English, is listening to astonishing news. 'Yes. Yes. I see. Amazing. One moment, please.'

'Have they found him?' Trotsky screams. 'Let me get to that – Give me that – ' But it is to Kamarin that Sasha hands the instrument. Sasha says: 'I'm going. My mission is temporarily frustrated. I hope you find your son.' And with great speed he leaves, gun pocketed. At the door he sketches a bow. And then he can be heard clattering down the stairs.

* * *

Freud sat in the surgery of Dr Hajek, a man with greying raying hair and thick spectacles. He said: 'Something came back to me from my old days at the medical school – "beware of painless bleeding". It's a kind of growth, apparently. Small but rough.'

'Let me see.' And Hajek examined the open mouth and throat of Freud with a metal spatula and a portable lamp. 'Nothing much,' he said at last. 'Leucoplakia. On the mucous part of the hard palate.'

'It will go away?'

'Hard to know whether it will or not. Best to cut it off.'

'That's drastic.'

'Do you want a second opinion?'

Dr Deutsch, a young man getting untimely fat, examined Freud in Freud's own study. 'Hajek's diagnosis was right,' he said. 'Leucoplakia. It will grow. Best to excise it now. Meaning tomorrow.'

'Dr Deutsch,' Freud said. He hesitated. Then he said: 'I think you know what I want you to tell me.'

'No,' Dr Deutsch said promptly. 'You're not going to die. It's a simple job. I'll telephone Hajek now and set it up for tomorrow morning. A cut and a scrape and you'll be right as rain.'

But Freud did not like this jauntiness.

Next morning he sat in a kind of dentist's chair, his coat and collar off, a bib around his throat and chest. Hajek sprayed the inside of his patient's mouth with a local anaesthetic. Freud recognized the taste and smell. He said, licking:

'My old friend cocaine.'

'Your dubious discovery.' Hajek's hair rayed in the sunlight from the one window.

'Tell me one that isn't. America, for instance?'

'I'm putting a wooden wedge in to keep the mouth open. Nurse,' he said. The nurse was a gaunt straight dark Swabian. She handed the little door-stopper over. 'Now. I have to cut – quite a way back.' The nurse took the knife from its boiling bath. Hajek cut. Blood spurted. Freud coughed, retched, spat out the wooden wedge.

'Keep that open,' cried Hajek. 'Nurse, hold it open.' She held it open, blood-slippery, so that Hajek could work fast. Hajek probed deep. Hajek hit an artery. Blood gushed into Hajek's mouth and eyes. Blood flowed unstaunched. Hajek made a desperate final cut and Freud spat out a tumour like a raspberry. Freud spat blood as well, but the flow of blood saved him the trouble. The nurse brought a gauze packing. Hajek applied it. He said:

'I thought it was a superficial lesion. But it went deep. So deep that I seem to have hit a major blood vessel. But I got it all out. We'll have to keep you in this chair till the bleeding stops. Nurse, hold this wad in place. Did you tell your wife you were coming here – for this?'

Freud agonizedly shook his head.

'I'll telephone.'

He went off quickly. The nurse clucked Swabian commiseration as she held the gauze pack tight. There was rich blood everywhere.

Freud sat alone in the waiting room of the clinic, holding a new gauze wad in his mouth. Martha and Anna came in, worried, Anna carrying a night bag. 'Why didn't you say?' complained Martha. 'Didn't we have a right to know?'

Freud shrugged: didn't think it worthwhile, thought it would be nothing. Hajek came in, annoyed about something. '*Gnädige* Frau Professor, *gnädiges* Fräulein – a damnable thing – not a single free bed in the whole clinic.'

'What is it, Dr Hajek?' asked Anna.

'What *was* it, you mean. A small benign tumour. It's out now, nothing more to worry about. But we hit a blood vessel. He can't go home till we have the bleeding under control. Pardon me – I must try again – for a bed I mean – '

He found a small dark room for Freud with two beds in it. One was already occupied by a cretinous dwarf who was in and out of that bed constantly in his restlessness, his striped nightshirt stained with the juice of his last meal. He tried to communicate with Freud. Freud was equally inarticulate. He held a new gauze pack, the sixth or seventh, to the ruptured vessel.

'*Dann die wurfen in Gegenbuchlichkeit so holen lassen wurden guggurggugrafholzenharfen duftenangekommen urgh.*'

'Argh.'

'*In menschlichen Warfengegenslichtigsauersdensogegengekommen.*'

'Argh. Orgh.'

He started to bleed again. He sat up in the bed, gagging, loosening the pack. The bleeding became intense. The dwarf gurgled, wide-eyed.

'*Blutblutblut und Eisen. Ein Reich ein Volk ein Oesterreich.*'

Freud rang the bell but nobody came. Blood galloped. Rang and rang and rang. Only blood came. The dwarf leaped out of his bed with circus agility and ran off in his stained nightshirt gargling.

Hajek and Deutsch stood over Freud, looking gravely at him. The bleeding had stopped. The dwarf too stood, looking with a greater gravity. Freud said, weak:

'Biopsy report?'

'Negative,' said Hajek.

'Sure?'

'A benign growth. No carcinoma.'

But the dwarf shook his huge empty head and said: '*Nein nein nein. Es gibt ein verfluchtegegengekommenen kark kark kark inomos. Dort. Dort dort und dort.*'

Freud looked at him as though he were the only one there qualified to deliver a prognosis.

He sat in his study, bright summer sun pouring in on the idols and totems and Dr Deutsch. Dr Deutsch said:

'Have you heard of Professor Hans Pichler?'

'No. Has he heard of me?'

'No. He ought by rights to hear of you when he develops a neurosis. You're hearing of him because he's the finest oral surgeon in the country.'

'I see. So it's not all over.'

'No. There's a new growth. I've taken the liberty of making an appointment for you.'

'Soon?'

'Tomorrow.'

'Whatever he does – whatever happens – this is the last time I speak as a free man.'

'I don't understand. You'll always be a free man.'

'A diseased body is as tyrannical as any upstart dictator. Let me foresee – an indefinite period of dumbness. Dr Freud, the man with the words. Dr Freud, the slow of speech.'

'Like Moses.'

Freud nodded enigmatically, took a cigar from its box, sniffed it, crackled it, lighted it.

'How many a day?'

'About twenty.'

'Your mouth has been a silent sufferer.'

'Hardly silent. Silence, I see, belongs to the future. So let me utter to the sky and the winds and the smoke-blackened ceiling of my study my last loud curse on the generation of traitors – Alfred Adler, Carl Jung, and all their wretched epigones.'

Deutsch prepared to leave. 'It won't be so bad, I promise.'

Freud puffed hungrily and grimly shook his head.

Dr Hans Pichler was a youngish dapper man, sure of himself. His consulting room was bigger than that of Dr Hajek. It shone with steel. On the walls were tastefully framed diagrams of the human vocal organs. Hajek, who had come to assist in the consultation, saw, in a flash of sunlight, that this Pichler belonged to a new world – he looked like an American – while he himself represented a dying Vienna. Pichler washed his hands and accepted a towel from a blonde nurse who looked like an import from Manhattan, saying:

'Professor Freud – you're a psychoanalyst but also a man of science.'

'I never,' Freud said grumpily from the shining polished chair with its rods and springs and pedals, 'considered that one excluded the other.'

'Forgive me. I should say: also a physician. I mean this: you can accept the truth.'

'More. I insist on the truth.'

'Well, then – you have a cancer of the mouth. A serious condition, I fear. I shall, of course, have to operate. This will leave you with a hole in the hard palate –'

'I knew it. The end of speech.'

'No, no. We can plug the hole with a prosthesis.' He pointed to a chart on the wall with his newly clean left hand. 'Keep the nasopharynx artificially separated from the oral pharynx. Your speech will not be noticeably over-nasalized. You will have to perform exercises to keep the soft palate mobile. But – to the operation. I'll have to perform it in two parts. First, the teeth on the right of the mouth will have to be removed. Then I cut the neck – there, see. That enables me to reach the external carotid artery and apply a ligature. Then I remove the upper cervical lymph nodes to stop the carcinoma spreading to other organs – '

'A general anaesthetic?'

'Unfortunately, no. We can't have you choking on your own blood. This growth – it was originally confined to the hard palate, but it's spread to the jaw and the tongue and the cheek. There's a lot of cutting to do.'

'So the body at last has its revenge.'

'I don't understand.'

'Never mind.' Freud sighed profoundly. 'It's a long story, Dr Pichler.'

Dr Pichler was ready, in the operating theatre with its hard sharp light and its locally anaesthetized patient, to start work with his scalpel and hammers. Freud heard a voice he had been waiting to hear, that of his cancer. It was a high-pitched voice which combined the singsong of idiocy with the droning parsonical. It spoke through the bones of his head:

'I'm attached to your hard palate, Professor Freud, but, as this doctor will soon discover, to your velum or soft palate as well. You are going to feel a hammer pounding away. The bone will be cut. You'll hear the rasp of a little saw. And then they'll throw part of me into the waste bin. My dead body. But I can soon develop another living body. You're a physician, Professor Freud – or were. You can't kill me, you know that.'

'The revenge of the soma on the psyche. I was always asking for trouble.'

'A dangerous thing to do, Professor Freud – to assert that certain diseases have a purely mental cause. But you seem to have proved it. The soul has a separate existence. It can ignore the body. And how can the body express its resentment of this enforced divorce? Only by being sick. By dragging the psyche down. That's my job, Professor Freud. You're going to suffer.'

'I can stand suffering.'

'Don't be too sure. The golden-voiced Professor Sigmund Freud, Freudios Chrysostomos, full of wisdom, muttering like an idiot. The prosthesis they'll put in your mouth – it won't fit very well, you know. It will press on the tissues and inflame them. An unending condition of agonizing ulceration. Prosthesis after prosthesis. The latest models from America, but none of them any good. Every word you utter a station of the cross, if you'll forgive the Christian image. And all the time I'm growing, silently, invisibly. They cut a portion of me off, but I'm still there. And at the end there's only me. Ah – here comes the hammer.'

Freud heard his hard palate pounded sickeningly like an obdurate rock. Then it ceased its obduracy and shattered.

In his study he looked at himself in the small blue mirror, souvenir of Florence. Sixty-five years old, beard and moustache fuller but greyer. Thinner, worn. Eyes in pain. He put down the mirror and took a cigar from the box. He tried to put the cigar in his mouth but he could not open his lips. He tried to pry open the lips with a clothes peg he took from a glass jar that contained trombones for clipping papers, gilt two-pronged paper fasteners, nibs. He opened his mouth by force and reached into the inner fiery cavern. He released the prosthesis and pulled it out, grunting and moaning. It lay, the offending plaque of bakelite and metal, on the desk top in a little bath of foam and saliva. He sobbed and put his head in his hands. The door opened quietly. Anna walked in.

'You've taken it out.'

He nodded, nodded, nodded.

'You must not do that. The tissues will shrink. You must get used to the prosthesis.'

'Gne mnostern.'

'All right, the Monster. I'm going to put it back in. And every day I'm going to take it out and clean it and then put it back in again. Is that understood?'

He nodded, nodded.

'Try and open your mouth.' She picked up the prosthesis, dried it on tissue paper, then started the labour of fitting it in. 'No sympathy from me. No self-pity from you. That's our covenant.'

He was sleeping alone now. Not that he slept much. He was sitting up in his lonely bed, trying to read Montaigne in the original, a hot-water bottle against his agonized jaw. No, the bed was not lonely. He had his cancer for company:

'Professor Freud, what do I say by way of greeting at three o'clock in the morning? *Gott grüss*, I suppose, as this is Vienna. Well, we're both awake. You because I keep you awake. I because sleep is not in my nature. All these prostheses, monsters as you call them, plugging the hole. None of them any good, as I forewarned you. What a waste of hard-earned money – six thousand good American dollars for that new model from Chicago, and worse than all the others. Inflamed tissues. Ulcers. A boiled egg for dinner and you dribble most of it through your nose. Undignified. No, don't think of suicide. Montaigne, a great sceptical, tolerant Frenchman – he ought to help you to develop a condition of stoical suffering spiced with good humour. I want you alive, sir. I need your living body. Just go on accepting me. You can still do a lot. Write books about the human soul. The soul. Oh, I believe in it. I wish sometimes I could get at it. Conquer the whole human kingdom.' Freud groaned and tried to settle to sleep. He thought he heard the soft laugh of his cancer.

* * *

The maimed, indeed dead, Abaco station wagon provided at least shelter for Val and Willett while hail rattled from the black sky and the cracking and frank opening of the earth could be heard in desperate rumbles from all over the horizon. They sat glumly in the assailed and rocking Abaco, pushed into a layby, watching healthy vehicles push west. Lightning attempted crude forky images – the number 58729, a caricature of a long-dead maiden aunt of Willett's, a firework setpiece of the battle of Marengo, a collapsing city skyline, a word that looked like BANANAS. The crass thunder imitated nothing but itself, or the drums of a Berlioz orchestra imitating itself. Then: 'Good Christ,' cried Willett. He saw lightning swoop down and knife with many blades something on the road far ahead. An explosion, then a great pile-up. Squealing of tardy brakes, torturing of metal, audible under the hail. Car after car after car after car concertinaed into car after car after car after car to make a long sorry polychrome shattered metal monster python. Thunder roared silly triumph; the Abaco rocked beneath Val and Willett like a boat. They had to sit there open-mouthed, looking at the endless metallic chaos sprinkled, dredged, full-floured in hail. Till the hail left off. Then they got out, each with pistol stuck in belt, Willett with the bigger gun slung by its sling over his shoulder, Val wearing a bandolier of bullets, their pockets stuffed with bullets. They squelched down haily grass off the main road, Willett looking back to deplore waste a moment – all those cans, liquor – and they proceeded, squelching in their heavy work boots, by a deserted and long-neglected side road, towards the border of Ohio and Indiana.

Eventually they came to a farm. A scrawled poster-sized message in the window of the farmhouse said, supererogatorily, GONE AWAY. A few forlorn chickens clucked, in a paddock a horse grazed with a companionate donkey beside him. The neighbouring field was riven by a great smoking ditch. Dirty greasy cloud rolled richly over the sad farmscape. Val and Willett had no difficulty in forcing the warped front door of the homestead. Inside they found the comforting musty cabbagy smell of a house long lived in but never well enough aired (enough air outside without having to have it inside too) and a gross black cat that cried its neglect. They found unrefrigerated milk not yet sour and gave the cat a basin of it. It ran grrrrrring thirstily. They found a hanging flitch of smoked bacon and a basket of brown eggs. There was neither electricity nor gas working, so they made a fire in the old-fashioned kitchen fireplace, using chairs for fuel, and fried a fine early supper, sluicing it down with canned beer and applejack.

The sky had cleared and was brilliant with firepoints, but Lynx and moon, steadily continuing lunation and lyngation, were vast and growing nearer, the half moon visibly, if one watched long enough, rounding to hide behind her master. The two watched from the great bed of the master bedroom. 'It's going to be the moon,' Willett said after a time. 'The moon will hit us first.'

'The moon will regret it,' Val said. 'It will shatter to bits and pieces.' And then: 'Us? What do you mean – us?'

'We are earth,' Willett said simply. 'We're not *mind* careering in outer space. We're tree and grass and root and dung and water. Earth, earth is us. What a shame, what a fucking shame. There has to be a God, there has to be an eternal sensorium just to hold the memory of the smell of tobacco and frying bacon and the look of gentians and dawns. Otherwise, what a waste creation was.'

'The universe can afford waste.'

'Well, I say balls to a universe that can afford to waste a Keats or a Shakespeare or a Charles Ives or a Vaughan Williams. Balls, balls, balls.' And then Willett, having taken four knockout tablets, bawled himself into heavy sleep.

They left the nameless farm the following morning, after a night curiously peaceful, Willett the heavy on horseback, Val, lighter, on the placid donkey. When they came to swifter and less uncomfortable transport, they would kiss and fondle the beasts goodbye and leave them to Indiana grass. Now they took a maze of small bad roads towards Indianapolis, a hell of a long journey. They ate bacon sandwiches in a noon full of cloud swirling in and choking the bloody sun. Behind them was a din of violent earth tremors. Ahead, so far, nothing. They had yet to discover that much of the state of Illinois was jaggedly rent, from Chicago to Decatur, and that the city of wind lay in ruins, the wind singing fiercely over it.

Hooves were still plodding inferior road when they came, at nightfall, to a scene of riot. It was a town called, so a signpost had signalled, Carson, a one-street nothing. Lynx and moon illuminated ghastlily liquor-maddened dancers. Stores had evidently been broken into, and strong waters were glugged down, sicked up, used in jocular baptism. The whole small population was circling in a claw-buttock dance to an old man's drunken accordion – major triad followed by dominant major ninth: one two one two – and the bashing of a big battered drum by a boy. Val and Willett sought to ride through unnoticed, but Val was pulled from his donkey and, with greater difficulty and much post-Rabelaisian language from him, Willett from his nag. They were offered bottles of Roma Rocket, whatever that was, and a fluid that reeked like coarse calvados. Naked girls, all ill-favoured, offered sweat-wet bodies. Some men were piling chairs, tables, anything inflammable, in the middle of the single street. Val and Willett fought off their hosts, who then became truculent, so yielded at last to the offers of drink, though not to the proffered steaming mots. The speech was mostly unintelligible – thick deformation of some local version of English – but it seemed to be about certain fundamentals: drink, copulation, riot, end is upon us.

A man with only a torn shirt on, lustily aswing below, whooshed canned gasoline onto the mess of wood. A naked middle-aged woman, aswing above, threw a flaring butane lighter. The fire broke at once into a vermilion paean to fire, leapt high. Its worshippers leapt about in a leaping dance. 'Out of here,' said Val, looking for a way out.

'The burro!' someone yelled. They were not yet ready for a human burnt offering; a donkey, parody of human servitude and long patience, a long-eared Jesus, would serve for the moment. They wanted to seize the living beast and drag it to the flames. Val's heart sank; he knew that now, for the first time in his life, he had to use real violence. Man should ennoble himself for his end, awaiting it in dignity. It could not be avoided, this drawing of the pistol ready loaded, the thumb trembling on the safety catch. Then: thank Christ, he did not have to fire. Willett was in first, cracking a loud shot Lynxwards, then another. The gesture was enough. They mounted, kicking bare sweaty bodies, guns butting hairy arms. They slapped their steeds' necks and got out at a half gallop, singed.

Ten miles or so on they came to a burnt-out farm, with corpses of cows, chickens half burnt, their scorched legs pathetically pointing up at the causative horror in the sky. They took shelter in the barn, their beasts with them comfortably chewing hay. There was plenty of light, God knew. They feared being jumped on by Lynx-crazed wanderers in the dark. They still had a long way to go. Hungry, they gnawed at a half-raw rooster. Sweet water dripped from a yard tap. They slept badly. They woke to the heaving of the earth, though gently, as of a great body still in sleep. Huge hail balls hurled down for half an hour. Dawn was sick-coloured, clouds scudding thinly, swiftly. 'This is no life,' Val groaned, 'no life at all.' His skull ached, his limbs creaked, his arse was on fire with the ass ride. Their beasts lay on their sides, their flanks heaving in sleep still, unresponsive to the dawn. It seemed a shame to wake them. They set themselves to walk to find an abandoned vehicle.

Having trudged a bumpy road in silence, they came to a main road empty of life, with a grounded signpost pointing to Columbus. Ohio? No, they were out of Ohio. America was full of Columbuses. To their surprise and cautious joy they saw a Howard Johnson motel intact, mock steeple and all on the contingent restaurant. Cars were parked or abandoned in the car park, which was humped up grotesquely by a past mild tremor. They went into the restaurant, empty but clean, chairs set neatly on a floor that sloped, but not yet enough to topple the flimsy functional furniture. They found sour milk and horrible dry buns. They munched, then filled their pockets with candy bars. At one end of the restaurant was a display of videodiscs. Willett, chewing, went curiously to examine them. 'Good God,' he said, twice. 'They're here. The ones the flood took.'

'What? Why?'

'Never mind. Ah, a mailman's sack.' There was, too, full of mail never now to be delivered. 'We must collect what we can where we can,' spilling the letters on the floor, putting his filched discs in, adding his chocbars and a couple of wrapped dry loaves. They went, munching, to look at cars and found a Trussel 95, a veteran Newsmobile, a shining new Duffy. The Duffy did not need the ministrations of the omniclef. The ignition key was set firmly waiting to be turned. Thanked be Almighty God.

When they came close to Vincennes, along the highway crammed with cars and bodies crushed, the highway itself bristling with huge sharp chunks of broken road, they sighted the Wabash in terrible frothing flood. They ran along its flouncy horrible skirt till they saw a nameless steel and concrete bridge swaying frighteningly. 'We can do it,' said Willett, who was not driving. They could and did, but the bridge responded to their speed like a dead tooth in a live mouth, wagging perilously to the puff of speech. Then they were in Illinois. Twenty-five miles along a near ruined highway they saw the hair-raising deep slash, north–south, that stretched down the state. To right and left it spread without visible end. They got out of the car, stood on its muddy edge and surveyed it.

'It's possible,' Willett said. A mile-deep slope to a trough of turbulent water that did not, for all its fury, look deep, a mile-high slope beyond up to flat country. Tree trunks lay everywhere, the disturbed earth gave off a smell of spring ploughing. The horizon all around challenged them with interested grumbles. A flock of black-white birds soared up from nowhere, twittering, chattering, were lost in a sudden swoop of bitumen-coloured cloud. 'All right?' said Willett. With no further word spoken, they coasted down, zigzag, avoiding stones, trunks, sculpted boulders. The car sploshed in the furious broth of the trough. The wheels turned impotently, the engine strained. Then, as if destruction were on their side, a subterranean belch followed by a head-high spume, grey like bad meat, lifted them. They sailed up the slope, the car game but in agony. They stuck in a tangle of oak roots. A tremor bore them clear, sailing an instant in air. They were in a flat placid field. The thunder roared derision, but where was the lightning? It was not thunder, it was the earth straining, boiling, breaking.

'I could lie down,' quoted Willett unconvincingly, 'like a tired child and weep away this life of care.' Then he banged vigorously his companion on the shoulder and cried: 'Enjoying it? It's life, God help us. It's something to tell your grandchildren.'

'If,' Val said, 'I have to slaughter the whole fucking crew, you and I are getting on that ship.'

Howls premonitory of slaughter meanwhile were heavily audible to Dashiel Gropius in Fort Worth. They came from one of the Tagliaferro brothers, probably Gianni, crying useless revenge. Dashiel's suite faced theirs on the top floor of the Florentine, a floor which had no corridor but instead a carpeted central area onto which the four suites opened. Dashiel could divine what the howls were about – failure to get through to the albergo in Peoria, Illinois; earthquake news from Springfield, Illinois, before radio communication with the outside world ceased. Dashiel was packing a bag and wondering what to pack. Shirts, socks, shoes, a suit. It seemed petty, inadequate. This was not a weekend trip to Florida. This was a voyage to the ends of space. So they hoped, so they hoped. He packed a box of Havana Hermositos and a litre flask of white rum. He would travel in leather boots, suede one-piece catskin, heavy hunting jacket. The tremors that had been picking delicately at Fort Worth suddenly bit, hard. He was pitched nearly over. He sat down, sensibly waiting for the spasm to pass, and smoked one of his gold-tipped Penhaligons. Well, whatever lay at the end of the journey, it was all over here. The power had failed at the city plant and here there was no emergency supply – typical Tagliaferro false economy. Last night a minimal tremor and lights out had started screaming, swearing; a man had broken his leg. That was while he had been out, in Dallas, with that girl Edwina and his family. The Florentine was finished. The brothers must know it was finished, but one thing at a time. A passion of grief behind locked doors had first to spend itself.

When the earth quietened, Dashiel took from a drawer the .45 Beaufort he had never yet had occasion to use, together with the still-sealed yellow box of ammunition. He loaded the gun carefully and stuck it in his belt, the soft leather belt that gave a waist to the catskin. The light from the window, though it was full morning, was dim, all stewing ferrous cloud shot with tarnished brass. He packed the rest of the ammunition.

Quite a girl, this Edwina. John had been the prime scoffer. She had railed against him, but he had prevailed on behalf of himself, his family, James and Jay and Jay. He had, he said, the finest possible shelter under the house, proof against doomsday the builders had said. It had its own power supply, refrigeration, heating, the lot. It was stocked with enough canned food to last a year, even with ten incumbents, and had an independent water supply and a waste products converter. Damn it, was he not in the construction trade? Had they not all lived under long threats of nuclear war? Well, the shelter was now to prove itself under the actuality of something rather less terrible. The horrors would pass, and they, not he, their father, would emerge on to an earth ready once more for reconstruction, while he, their father, went into outer space and to certain death shouting impotent biblical texts.

The girl, delightfully pregnant, Edwina, had told him not to be a fucking idiot. She had drawn on the living-room wall, plain, cream, and apt for drawing with a fat felt pen, the irrefutable simple diagram that spelt doom. John was not impressed. It was really all to do with having known the biblical language of doom from babyhood. It was a dad thing, a Bible thing, nothing to do with real-life possibilities. Dad's thunderings had not helped; rather they had made the diagrammatic reality suddenly become remote and mythical. 'All of us, Noah's family, seek the ark of salvation, armed with the Lord's righteousness' and all that palookeroney. Poor mom had not known which way to turn. She had said:

'John's right, Calv, John's practical. I'll stay with them till things blow over. I mean, it's only like you going off to preach, dear, isn't it, and it always gives me a headache, that Sacramento rally last time was terrible, and I said to you never again.'

'But this is different, this is the end, this is the last day, this is the Day of Judgement.'

'Yes, dear, the Day of Judgement.' Indulging him, the Day of Judgement being as much part of the furniture of their family calendar as the Fourth of July.

'Your duty as a wife, as the helpmeet of the last living servant of the Lord.' Oh Jesus, all that crap again, James's grin kept saying.

'I'm a mother too, Calv, don't forget that.'

And then dad, in his divine foolishness, had said: 'This girl here, this brave Edwina, she knows her duty.' Mom's eyes had gone hard at that. A long agony of contrary gravitational pulls – my boys, my boys, my dear grandchildren; my husband in the potential clutches of a designing female (more, more: whose is that child she's carrying? Is it possible, is it just possible, men are all the same, even the holiest, holy, what in God's name does *holy* mean?). Then many tears and holding on to her strong sons and snatching her grandchildren in desperate arms, but finally the brave tearful decision. Very well, her duty. Dad put strong arms about her. 'Praise to God, who has shown his servant the light. Praise him, praise him.' He had very nearly called for a fucking hymn, with Jennifer at the piano.

Dashiel did not care greatly, in the primary bodily sense, whether he was saved or not. The soul was a doubtful entity. Religion was proving itself mere crap in the face of true doomsday. The thing to do was to act, go through the motions of action. The girl Edwina was no fool. She could cite scripture when she wanted to, but her arguments were hard and practical. If anyone could lead them on to that salvation ship it was the charismatic Calvin Gropius. Must the Lord's word perish with the perishing earth? She had a child to save, and she was right. Why let the miraculous process of gestation end in destruction, a child brought forth only to die directly? But for him, Dashiel, action, just that.

Was that child really his father's? Could it be possible? Was that why she burbled, becoming briefly mystical and foolish, about the divinely appointed mission of the child? An illegitimate Gropius messiah, a divine by-blow? The world was full of surprises. He grinned at the banality of that, hearing a sickeningly long rumble on the horizon.

Well, now came the walking out. Quietly, leaving the brothers to their grief. There was not much point in staying to explain, say goodbye. He took a deep breath, squinted about the dark room as if to remember its comforting details in exile, then prepared to leave. He was not in the least surprised when Salvatore Tagliaferro came in, leaned on the little bar and looked at Dashiel, white, strained, but ready for more than a wallow in a tub of grief. Salvatore had instincts.

'I thought,' he said, 'you might be leaving us, Dash. I thought you might be telling us you'd be leaving us.'

'I didn't,' said Dashiel with care, 'want to intrude on your grief. Everything's over. We all have to go our own ways.'

'Grief,' said Salvatore. 'That's a short sharp word for what Gianni's going through. A bad language for grief, the English language. Gianni wants to kill the whole world. Me – I get over it. Nobody lives for ever. I gave them a good life – Lucrezia and little Annamaria. But Gianni wants to kill the whole world.'

'A good reason perhaps,' Dashiel said, 'for my not wanting to say goodbye to him. He might see me as the only killable bit of the world available.'

'Naw,' said Salvatore, 'he loves you like a brother, like he loves me. But now he's on to hell and he's going to hell and his wife Susanna and those kids he adored are angels looking down on him burning in the fires of hell. I tell him he's been a good man and only killed three guys that were bitter enemies anyway, and leave out the violence that didn't kill, and he'll go to purgatory. But then he screams that the pains of purgatory isn't what he wants either. In a terrible way is Gianni. Where you going, Dash?'

'I'm going with my father and mother.'

'Lucky you still got them, Dash. Me and Gianni, we ain't so lucky. And where are you going with your father and mother, Dash?'

'I don't really know, Salv. Nor do they. We're going with somebody who knows where to go.'

Salvatore thought about that. Then he said: 'Your dad's a big name in the Protestant religion, right? He's got connections? He's gonna get you and the rest of his family out of what they call – what is it, Dash? – Boomsday, zoomsday?'

'Nobody gets out of it, Salv.'

'So why move? Why not stay till the roof falls and puts you outa your misery?' He grinned affectionately. 'Or makes Gianni's miseries begin.'

'You have to do something at a time like this. You've got to move. You could be moving from something bad to something worse, but you've still got to move.'

A renewal of howls of grief came from Gianni's room. Salvatore shook his head indulgently but also in mild sadness. 'We gotta give Gianni time to make a good act of contrition, pay for a few masses, see a priest maybe. Your dad's a kind of priest?'

'Protestant. Not what Gianni wants.'

'Still, we're coming with you, Dash boy. Sit down. Have a drink, a good stiff one, *liscio*, wait till we're ready. Where you go we go. Gianni might even turn Protestant. I've heard a lot about your dad. Always wanted to meet him.'

There was a large explosion in the centre of Fort Worth. Lake Arlington could be heard roaring like an angry sea.

'Hello,' says Kamarin to the telephone. 'Yes, the *Noviy Mir*. Who? What news agency? From where? London. I see. I take it there is no doubt of – No. I see. I see. Authentic. Thank you.'

'What the hell is going on?' rages Trotsky like an angry sea. 'Have they found him? Is he dead? My Seryozha – I want my son, you swine.'

Kamarin speaks gravely to Trotsky. 'Lev Davidovich Trotsky, the telephone is all yours. Before you use it, however, you must witness something.' He takes out the warrant from his inside pocket and solemnly tears it. 'The Tsar's authority has been liquidated. The Revolution has begun. Comrade.' He shudders somewhat at the term. He goes bravely on. 'My colleague and I, until we are replaced or liquidated or, which is much more likely, resign and become ragged teachers of Russian here in New York, now represent a People's Republic. Call at the consulate at your leisure and you will be given a visa. For your return to Russia as a free man and, I should imagine, one of the leaders of the new State.'

But Trotsky cannot take this in, not yet. He is at the telephone even while Kamarin is addressing him, trying to get through to the police. What he says on the telephone is inaudible owing to the following song which Kamarin and Doktorov now start to sing:

KAMARIN: The first thing we do
Back at the office
Is turn the Tsar's face
To the wall.

DOKTOROV: But first order two
Brandy-laced coffees.
My mind can't embrace
This at all.

BOTH: Change, change,
They have to have change,
No matter how strange and bizarre.
But why can't God and his angels
Let things stay as they are?

DOKTOROV: It's something that I
Shrink from admitting.
The whole thing may prove
A bad dream.

KAMARIN: We'll go out and buy
Clothes so ill-fitting
They'll fit in the *nouv-*
Eau régime.

BOTH: Change, change,
They have to have change,
No matter how strange and bizarre.
But why can't God and his angels
Let things stay as they are?

KAMARIN: From his burg they'll pull St Peter –

DOKTOROV: Drag poor Petro from his grad.

KAMARIN: What will it be to-
Morrow to our sorrow?

DOKTOROV: Marxgrad?

KAMARIN: Engelsgrad?

DOKTOROV: Britishmuseumgrad?

KAMARIN: Trotskygrad?

BOTH: Whatever it will be, it will be bad.

KAMARIN: We'll get two cloth caps
At a sale on Second Aven-
Ue. Then we'll rub doit
On our shoits.

DOKTOROV: Swill beer from the taps
In a Fulton Street tavern
And learn how to floit
With the skoits.
BOTH: Change, change,
They have to have change,
No matter how strange or bizarre.
But why can't God or his dark angel
From Novgorod up to Archangel
Let things stay as they are?

Trotsky puts down the telephone receiver in gloom. 'They tell me not to move,' he says. 'To stay here and wait. They're doing all they can, they say. So I *can't* leave.'

'Our sympathy, comrade,' says Kamarin. 'No hurry about leaving.'

'What?' frowns puzzled distraught Trotsky. He has ceased to live in a public world.

'Call at the consulate at your convenience.'

'For my deportation? My enforced repatriation?'

Kamarin shudders. 'You can call it that.' He and his colleague try to give the clenched-fist salute, but their arms seem to revolt. So they add a last verse to their song.

KAMARIN: It's not very nice –
With fingers close-packed you
Must pull your fist in-
To your arm.
DOKTOROV: It's just a device
For hiding the fact you
Do not have hard skin
On your palm.
BOTH: Change, change,
We all have to change,
So screw the Tsarina and Tsar.
But why couldn't God and his angels
Let things stay as they are?
DOKTOROV: Were.
KAMARIN: Were if you prefer.
BOTH: Why couldn't you, comrade or sir,
Let things stay as they were?

Are they addressing God or Trotsky? No matter. They leave. Trotsky has not at all taken in the news of the start of the Revolution. He has his only son on his mind.

Otto Rank rushed into the hotel lobby with his luggage. The delegates were already moving into the hotel ballroom to hear a lecture. Jones saw Rank and said:

'Where have you been? I wrote to you and got no reply.'

'Not in Vienna,' Rank panted. 'In the United States. Lecturing. How are things?'

'You've heard no news? Had no letters from Vienna?'

'I was lecturing. Moving around. Why – what's happened?'

'We'd better go in.'

There was an audience of about three hundred. On the rostrum Anna Freud, looking absurdly young but firm with her father's authority, clear-voiced and crisp, told them:

'The situation of "real anxiety" differs from that of "morbid anxiety" in that the nature of the danger is evident in the former, whereas in the latter it is unknown. In morbid anxiety the danger may emanate from dread of impulses in the id, from threats from the superego, or from fear of punishment from without. But with males it is always a fear of castration – with females more characteristically the fear of not being loved. We must learn to distinguish between the vague sense of danger and the ultimate catastrophe itself, which we may term the trauma . . . '

Rank was slow in taking in the situation. The daughter introducing the father. But the father did not appear. He grew white and felt sick. He said tremulously to Jones:

'He's dead?'

'No, not dead. He merely has cancer of the mouth.'

Rank's hysterical laughter was startling. He could not control it. The lecture temporarily stopped. All looked with horror. Jones got him out, still screaming with laughter, and pushed him into the elevator. On the third floor he dragged him, the laughter abating now, to his own bedroom. There he quietened. Jones took a bottle of cognac out of the wardrobe, tooth and drinking glass from the washstand.

Calmer, lips cognac-wet, Rank was able to say:

'It's irregular.'

'She's only his voice. She merely read the paper he wrote.'

'There's a loss of authority. She's only a girl. She has no qualifications. She didn't even finish high school.'

'She's his daughter. Isn't that authority enough?'

'I see. All in the family.'

'You're in the family too.'

'I know. He called me his younger brother. But I never felt like that. I've always been a son.' He spoke with an exaggerated rising intonation. Jones said:

'I think I begin to understand that hysteria. Do I detect a certain – guilt?'

Rank mumbled now, eyes down on his cognac glass. 'I was forbidden the right to practise. But I was told to write. I've been writing. I've never done anything I shouldn't have done. I've nothing to feel guilty about.'

'Nevertheless you're guilty. *What* have you been writing?'

'A book. I published it. In Germany.'

'Without showing it to him? Without discussing its content?'

'He'd have laughed at it. Rejected it. I had to go my own way.' He looked up at Jones with a certain hostility. 'And I had to keep it to myself. If I'd told him he would have discussed it with you. And then you'd have given a lecture on it. The great man Dr Jones, a *real* doctor. Rank's not a doctor, don't listen to him.'

'I don't understand.'

'Oh yes you do. The Oedipus complex and Hamlet. You published your lecture. Everybody thought it was marvellous. But it was my idea.'

'I didn't know,' said Jones. 'It was just a notion – something that came up in discussion. But, well, ideas are common property. It's what you make of the ideas that matters.'

'Mine,' said Rank with some truculence. 'This new idea is all mine. And what I've made of it is mine. And I've nothing to feel guilty about.'

'Meaning that you've broken away. Like Adler. Like Jung.'

'Yes.' Rank gave himself more cognac. 'Like those two great *doctors*. Why shouldn't I break away? Sons have to leave their fathers sooner or later.'

'You were supposed to be a younger brother, not a son.'

'I wasn't good enough to be a brother. Now I *am* good enough. Brothers in achievement, each going his own way. My book is – epoch-making.'

'I've heard that before,' Jones said drily.

Rank had left his luggage with the porter, but he had kept his dispatch case firmly under his arm. He now began to open it. 'Ferenczi,' he said, 'said so. Ferenczi said it will supersede the Oedipus complex.'

Jones was uneasy. 'And Ferenczi never said anything to him either?'

'Scared, like me. Scared of the Mosaic thunder and the breaking of the tablets of the law on our heads. But we've nothing to be scared about now.' He took out a book, a very thick one. 'Here it is. I know your German's good enough. It's good simple German, with none of his flowers and figures of speech.'

Jones handled the book gingerly but he did not examine it. He looked at Rank instead, right in the eye.

'What have you against me?' he said. 'There's something, I can see it. Do you resent my – continuing fidelity?'

'Stop talking about him all the time. Look at the book.'

'*The Birth Trauma* . . . Are you sending him a copy?'

'No. No. No.' Rank began to laugh again. His hysteria was subdued but still alive.

'*The Birth Trauma*,' said Anna, handling it gingerly. 'Do you want me to read it to you?'

Freud smoked vigorously, ill and old, slumped in his desk chair. Anna faced him. He said, with painful nasality:

'Sum it up.'

'Well, he says this. He says that neuroses don't spring from infantile sexual causes. Neuroses spring from being born. Some are affected more than others. It seems to be a matter of physical constitution. The child comes from a warm comfortable place, his mother's womb. He's dragged out, slapped, forced to breathe air. He faces the hostile world outside his mother. He never gets over it.'

'Nonsense.'

'Listen to this. "Birth is both the first of all dangers to life and the prototype of all the later ones that cause us to feel anxiety, and the experience of birth has probably left behind in all of us the expression of affect which we call anxiety. Macduff, in Shakespeare's *Macbeth*, was not born of his mother but ripped from her womb. For that reason he was unacquainted with anxiety." '

'What damnable nonsense. I told him that. It was a joke.'

'No joke now. What this seems to mean is this – that the mother becomes important as a place, an environment, a source of life. You make her a love object. Something to fight over with the father. He seems to have created something new – a pre-Oedipal situation.'

'No. No.'

'There's something in it.'

'Are you too turning against me, Anna? Is there nobody left who's loyal? Curse Otto Rank. I gave him everything. This is how he repays.'

'You'd better lie down, father.'

Freud crushed out his half-unsmoked cigar in the brass ashtray. He got up unsteadily and tottered into his consulting room. Then he lay down in great pain on the analytical couch. He tried to escape into sleep but the cancer was not having that:

'Infidelity? Disloyalty? And how is Dr Jung getting along these days, Herr Professor? He doesn't take kindly to such as me. A very fit man, big and strong, his body unsullied and unweakened by drink or tobacco. Of course, it all depends what you mean by cancer, doesn't it? Never mind. *I'll* never leave you.'

'The Jew,' Jung said, 'who is a nomad, a wanderer, has never yet created a civilization of his own. He has never made his own culture, and he never will. All his instincts, all his talents require a more or less civilized nation as a host for their development. The Aryan unconscious has a higher potential than the Jewish. In my opinion it has been a grave error in medical psychology up to now to apply Jewish categories indiscriminately to German and Slavic Christians. This most precious secret of the Germanic peoples – their creative and intuitive depth of soul – has been explicated as a morass of banal infantilism, despite the warnings of such as myself. My warnings earned the suspicion of Sigmund Freud. Freud did not understand the soul. Has the formidable phenomenon of National Socialism – on which the whole world gazes with astonished eyes – taught him and his followers any better?'

The applause was considerable. Swastika brassards danced on applauding official arms. The Berlin sun came briefly out to smile on Jung. Jung smiled and inclined.

Jung borrowed a certain jauntiness from the men in jackboots who accompanied him down the swastika-decked corridor to the office of M. H. Goering. M. H. Goering rose fatly from his desk as Jung entered.

'Delighted to see you, Dr Jung. I was present at your lecture. I was impressed. Ah no, that's inadequate. Overwhelmed.'

'*Danke sehr*. Are you by any chance related to – '

'Our esteemed head of the Luftwaffe? There's a family resemblance, they say. My cousin. We call him fat Hermann, and he doesn't like that. A drink?'

'Thank you, no.'

'To business, then. I know your time is precious. We take it as a great compliment that you should come to Berlin to lecture and visit our clinics. I have a proposal that will, if you accept it, give us the greater compliment of your even closer liaison with our city. And with the Third Reich itself. Last year – June 1933 – we reorganized the German Society for Psychotherapy.'

'I knew.'

'Of course. The International Medical Society for Psychotherapy we call it now.'

'Not the National Socialist etcetera etcetera?'

'Well, no. We look outward to the whole world, not inward to the party. Though, of course –'

'In time you hope that the terms will coincide?'

'It is the Führer's hope, Dr Jung.' The Führer looked down from a picture above the drinks cabinet. 'For myself, I'm a doctor and I try to keep out of politics. Though, naturally, I accept intellectually and emotionally and with intense patriotic devotion the principles for which the National Socialist Party stands. That is why I was so delighted to hear your words of this morning. We have lost our president, Dr Jung. He resigned when we changed our name and our policy.'

'Resigned?' smiled Jung.

'Let us say *resigned*. There were certain pressures, of course – party pressures. He belonged to the wrong race. You and I do not, Dr Jung. We stand for an Aryan psychotherapy and not the Jewish heresies of Sigmund Freud. I'm offering you the presidency of our organization.'

'But – well, I'm honoured, of course – But I'm Swiss.'

'These petty national boundaries, Dr Jung. You're a German. You subscribe to the mystique of the German race. Dr Jung – President of the International General Medical Society for Psychotherapy. It has a good ring, has it not? We shall have a journal for you to edit. I shall be more than happy to assist.'

'Honoured, honoured, highly honoured. Aryan psychoanalysis.'

'International psychoanalysis. With the Jews left out. Will you drink something now?'

'Nothing alcoholic.'

'Like the Führer himself.' He opened the shining drinks cabinet and took out a small bottle of Apollinaris.

'And Dr Ferenczi –' (deep in Freud's left ear) ' – that delightful Hungarian follower of yours. One of your sons. You called him son to his face, didn't you? The apostle of love, Professor Freud. How is *he* getting on?'

In Ferenczi's consulting room a girl named Ilse lay on the couch and sobbed. Ferenczi sat listening, holding her hand.

'And I feel rejected. Cast out. By everybody.'

'Unloved, Ilse?'

'Unloved.' She burst into tears. Ferenczi kissed her hand and then her bare arm. He said:

'We must feel close, Ilse. You must transfer your feelings to me – hate, resentment, love – You must hold nothing back. Only that way can you be cured.'

He took her in his arms, kneeling to do so, and smothered her wet face with kisses. She responded ardently. He broke away.

'A moment.'

He went to the door to be sure that it was securely locked. It was. Then he returned to his patient. The couch was a wide one.

'You feel better now?'

'Much better.'

'But' (deep in his right ear) 'you and I don't worry about betrayal, do we? I live. You live. I grow. You grow. Visits from great men. Einstein. H. G. Wells. Your photograph in the magazines. Medals. Awards. No Nobel Prize, of course. You're still not respectable enough for that. But other things. Many. Ironical, isn't it? You'd give them all to be rid of me. But I'm staying, Professor Freud. I'm staying till the very end. You're sleepy now? Good. Sleep. I'll watch over you.'

* * *

Lynx and moon were gibbous and menacing over the state of Missouri. Between St Louis and Jefferson City, Val and Willett became fully aware for the first time of what the term *lyncstatic* might mean. 'Lyncstasy,' Val muttered, 'lyncstatic asylums.' The whole of the small town of Wilcock was a lyncstatic asylum. Its buildings were down and its drainage ruined, and it stank of incontinence like any ward given over to cortical decay. The people were bedding down in the ruins, eating raw flesh and poisoning themselves with foul water. As Val and Willett tried to drive down the single street, there were men decorated in rooster feathers, armed with cudgels, brisk to stop them and ask their business. A much befeathered fat young man who stank of raw alcohol asked: 'Are you on the way to the putting out of the big light?'

'If,' said Willett carefully, 'that is what you require.'

The fat young man turned to his henchmen with a gap-toothed sneer. 'To talk of requiring,' he said, and they laughed. To Val and Willett he said with truculence: 'Don't let the big light hear you. You must abide the rising of the bigger light. Come out for the eating.'

'We've already eaten,' Val said. 'Thank you very much.'

'Eaten, yes, as the wontcocks will. You must eat of Smith to put off the doom.'

'Smith?' Willett asked. The befeathered group pointed. The toothless bald head of an old man leered from a battered and bent lamp standard. He had been bound to the lamp standard by the neck, and his belly had been roughly slashed open. Finger joints and toes had gone, and there was evidence that thin slices of flesh and skin had been shaven off his limbs and torso. Days dead, perhaps weeks: there was a rich scintillancy of maggots in the belly hole. Val retched. Willett of the stronger stomach was unmoved. He said: 'We have eaten of the grandfather of Smith. In a far place of many waters.' And he kicked and punched Val. 'On our way,' he growled. The car growled, pushing forward, and the feathered belaboured it with sticks. Thunder spoke from the western horizon. They turned to it, as though to interpret its loud DAAAAAAA. The car got away, Val still retching. There were loud shouts of 'Eh! Eh!' behind them, men waving cudgels, feebly running.

'Drawlatch hoydens,' growled anew Willett at the ghastly skylights. 'Gaping changelings. Lubbardly louts. Jeering companions. Oh, Jesus. Well, better to go in madness, perhaps.' The car coughed. The car jittered and jolted.

'A matter of gas,' Val said. The fuel needle signalled nearly nothing.

'Jesus Jobbernol Goosecap Christ All Grouthead Gnatsnapper Mighty.'

They had to abandon the car and trudge towards Jefferson City. Afar, down a side road, they saw what looked like the ragged remnant of a battalion marching. The soldiers coughed and coughed, as from Somme mustard. 'Keep in step there,' yelled a sergeant. What was their mission, whither were they marching? Would they march in mindless automatism till the world ended? Willett quoted, growling:

> 'These, in the day that heaven was falling,
>   The hour when earth's foundations fled,
> Followed their military calling
>   And took their wages, and are dead.'

There was a great abandoned factory, half in ruins, though with a chimney smoking blackly in the red and silver light, near to a town called Houseman. There was a great car park, and there was a brace of orange and violet trucks with the name ILLIONS on them. Simple omniclef stuff. This time Willett drove. The next variety of lyncstasy they saw was at, and Val Brodie shuddered, Brodie. But it was of a kind long known in America – a group of white-robed end-of-the-worlders, crying wolf no longer. An emaciated elder spoke to a congregation bearing torches that stank of animal fat:

'. . . And I saw a new heaven and a new earth: for the first heaven and the first earth were passed away; and there was no more sea. And I saw the holy city, new Jerusalem, coming down from God out of heaven, prepared as a bride adorned for her husband . . .'

Since the time when, a bride adorned for her husband, Maria Gropius had vowed obedience, a deep-down potion of truculence must have been preparing itself. Now she was tasting the strong brew and spitting samples of it at Gropius. Gropius was driving silently. To the right the Ozark mountains were leaping, like the mountains in the Song that is Solomon's. The Bible was true, after all. And in ways you'd never expect. Behind their car, whose back was stuffed with Maria's useless clothes, jewels, frivolous gewgaws, was, he knew, the car of their son Dashiel, and his companion was Edwina Goya. Behind again, though this they did not at first know, was the flashy Concordia '00 of the Tagliaferro brothers, Salvatore driving, Gianni in the back surrounded by a whole arsenal – Kopple submachine guns, Lefferts hipfirers, a Munsey Angel, pistols galore. Gianni knew no Shakespeare, but he was paraphrasing a speech of King Lear's with more punch and economy than the self-indulgent master had ever used: 'Why should a fucking mouse have life and they be fucking dead?' In the leading car, which had just skirted Tishomingo, Maria was showing equal fight:

'You've no right to do it, Calv, you've no right to drag me, and I wouldn't be going with you if it wasn't for the little foul-mouthed bitch back there with Dashiel, it's a wife's duty to save her husband from sin, I'll say that, I've always said it, but you've no right to talk about any other kind of duty, duty to the messenger of Christ's word and all that shit . . .'

'What did you say then? What was that word you used then?' This was absurd. The sky was red and silver fire with heavy oily cloud scuds, noise barely excluded from the noise-excluding windows, and here she was nagging away as if the world were going to go on for ever, which, of course, was what she believed. A knowledge of the Bible, he admitted to himself sadly, distractedly, rarely had much to do with an understanding of it. He said: 'You're distraught, dear, and no wonder. But get this once for all into your thick skull, dear, that the girl has one thing in mind and one thing only, and that is to save her child, and she thinks that I'm the only man in the world who can do it. A lot of people, Christ help them, have believed in my supernatural powers, God help me. But she's right about the other thing she says, that the Word of the Lord has to be taken into the high places, and I'm the only man, God help me again, to do it.'

'High places. Word of the Lord. All that shit when the roads are crammed with the wrecks of cars and the rivers flooded and those mountains there shaking with the earth tremors. Why are we going to Kansas? Why couldn't we stay in Dallas till it's all over?'

'It's not going to be all over, dear, for the hundredth time. This is the End of the World. Remember the phrase? *The End of the World*. It's in the Bible. The Last Day. The Day of Judgement. *Remember?*'

'Oh yes, the Day of Judgement.' And then, less sarcastically, 'Oh Jesus, oh Jesus lover of my soul.' For the road in front of them was cracking and throwing up slivers of itself. They lurched as on a switchback. 'Stop the car, stop it. Oh Lord Jesus save me.'

'I'm going on. It's our only hope.'

She screamed as an elongated trapezoid of crumbling metalled road flew at the windshield. 'Go back, Calv. Turn round and go back.'

'No, we're going on. Pray, dear, pray hard.'

'I *was* shitting-well praying. Oh Lord Jesus forgive my sins.' They sped into sudden calm. 'Tell me,' she said, 'tell me the truth, Calv. We're near to God now, so you have to tell me the truth.'

'What truth, for God's sake? I've always told you the truth, haven't I? I've always told everybody the truth. God's truth.'

'I don't want God's truth, I want the real truth. I mean that girl. Tell me the truth as you hope to die. Is she carrying your child?'

'Oh God preserve my sanity. No. Or rather yes.'

'I knew, I knew, I knew.'

'Her child and fifty thousand other children are my children. Will that satisfy you? I've spent my life fornicating. I'm a ravening sex monster.'

'There's no need to be sarcastic, Calvin. You're not a sex monster. At least you've never been a sex monster with me. If we're on to the truth, you've never been all that good in bed. You've got to admit it. Have you?'

'I've always had other things on my mind.'

'I'm going back, Calvin, while there's still time. I'm young still. I have my life to live.'

'Sex, is that it? You're thinking of getting somebody who's good in bed? Not like me, your husband, faithful, always faithful, always too damned faithful. Christ, even the patriarchs had handmaidens.'

'Was she your handmaiden, Calv? Tell me the truth. I promise to forgive you.'

Ahead the road was blocked by a fallen sequoia. He had to stop the car. Behind he was aware of the following car coming to a halt. And a car behind that. Who was in that third car? Had it been with them all the way from Dallas? Well, let who would seek salvation. He said: 'Go back, and let me do my duty. A man's duty comes first.'

'You've always let your duty come first. Never your wife.'

'I've given you children. Your children have given you grandchildren. Go back to them. Let me concentrate on my duty with a clear mind.'

'That's what you've always wanted, isn't it? To be alone. With a *clear mind*. Thank you, Calv. Thank you very much.'

'Let's not part like this. Let's part in love. Confident in the Lord's love and his salvation. We shall meet in heaven, Maria.'

'The sweet by-and-by,' Maria said. 'All right, get out. You can go with that foul-mouthed little bitch behind. Dashiel will keep you from any funny business.'

'For the five hundredth time – '

'And when you come back from Kansas with your tail between your legs, don't expect me to be waiting with the pot roast ready. I may be in Miami. I may be at Palm Springs. I'm entitled to a bit of life without the shitting Word of the Lord in my ear all the time.'

He sighed deeply, getting out, yielding the wheel to her. 'So,' he said, 'it's come to this.' The earth and sky were strangely quiet, as though interested.

'Yes, Calv, it's come to this. See you in the sweet by-and-by.' She turned the car deftly and took the road back. Things remained quiet. The perturbed elements were awed to silence by this demonstration of woman's perfidy. Wearily, Calvin Gropius went over to the car of his son. There was a side road somewhere back there. That might get them to Guthrie, where they aimed to spend the night. Maria Gropius had already sped past it, not, unlike Lot's wife Sara, looking back.

And so, by diverse routes, our parties worked jerkily towards their unforeseen conjunction in salvatory Kansas.

In Kansas, Professor Hubert Frame had his respirator batteries charged and was ready to examine what was the final concrete expression of his theoretical studies. He could not, of course, walk. O'Grady's strong arms lifted him without effort from his bed into the solitary wheelchair that the camp clinic possessed. His daughter stood by, sniffing.

'Stop blubbing, girl,' he said. 'Nothing to cry about.' Bartlett, in smart black with a CAT brassard on his left arm (a stylized puss, back view, sitting up straight), was ready to escort him to *Bartlett, America* rather. Frame, as he was trundled through the twilight, gibbous Lynx and moon newly arisen, admired the wide sky, which he had not seen in its fullness for many months. 'The increase in size,' he breathed, almost inaudibly. 'Astonishing. Double acceleration, of course. One is reminded ironically of one of those old comic films. In which two lovers. Moving from opposite directions. To. Embrace each other. Cannot slow down. So go past each other. Miss. Won't happen here. No missing here.' He was taken to *America*, great, hugely elegant, where the whole team waited. He, Bartlett, Vanessa, O'Grady got into the elevator and were lifted gently onto what was known as Level A. When the dying professor appeared on the ring concourse, as it was called, most of the team subduedly clapped. Frame waved feeble acknowledgement.

He was taken round, elevated to Level B, and then to Level C. There was no doubt of Bartlett's efficiency, alas alas alas. The concentration on living space, the human need for sheer spatial freedom, had not entailed any skimping on technical essentials. The ploiarchal area, for instance, where Drs McGregor and McEntegart flicked their switches in demonstration, made their screens glow, set talking their radiocommunication devices, was positively palatial. Frame heard reports from *Americas II* and *III*, from the Australasian ship *Southern Cross*, from the European Community's *Defrit*, stupid unrousing name. Moon stations came in faintly. Frame admired the three-layered hospital, the incredible foodfields, the ample dortal area which, when the population began to grow, would still be ample. He saw the library, functional and wholly technological, and the audiovisual facilities, dedicated to knowledge not diversion. He admired the automated foremater, which would fabricate you a garment in a microsecond after digesting the designational input. He frowned at the appearance of Dr Maude Adams, the two bibliothecologists, others. They looked dead, themselves automated dead matter, going through certain programmed motions. He said, with a sharpness that was clearly though painfully audible, to Bartlett:

'Have you been pacifying?'

'It was necessary.'

Frame asked for a microphone. He said into it: 'Ladies and gentlemen, we ought to toast our enterprise. Is there any champagne aboard?' There wasn't. Bartlett frowned. O'Grady shook his head, frowning. Frame grinned bitterly and produced from a roomy side-pocket a leather-bound brass flask. 'Whisky,' he said. 'A token sip, doctor?' he said to Dr Adams. O'Grady tried to intervene. Bartlett put out an arm, saying:

'Alcohol is expressly forbidden to certain of our crew members. A matter of –'

'A matter of depacifying,' said Frame. 'Its effects, of course, can be dramatic. Drink, doctor. Drink, I insist.' She drank, dead-eyed. An automatic drinker. To Vanessa he said: 'A word in your ear, my love.' He gave her the word. 'This is it. I may as well go here.'

'No!'

'Yes. One thing still on my conscience. I lied to you. I said that Val was dead. He may be, of course, by now. But I knew nothing of his er biotic status at the time we flew here. I'm sorry. I didn't want him on the project. I think I was wrong. I'm sorry. He may be alive, he may be trying to reach you. I have a dying man's hunch.' He nodded grimly at Bartlett, who had taken the flask, with some difficulty, away from Dr Adams. 'Hope, my dear. Hope that he'll come to you.' Vanessa, very white, put her hands to her face. She couldn't even sob. To the assembly at large Frame now said: 'Ladies and gentlemen, I have lived a full life and now I am going to end it. A full life, but not a successful one. I know nothing, despite the fullness. I know much of science but nothing of life. Now it is too late to learn. But it is, remember, now time for you to begin. If you want a motto to blazon over that screen there, the one that will show you the pulsing universe you are to travel through, that is now showing you earth and Lynx moving inexorably to collision, the motto might be this: *Scientia non satis est.* Knowledge is not enough. Let us now see how well your cadaver-recycler works. Eat me, drink me. Rather sacramental, isn't it? God be with you, which is the meaning of.' He smiled, switched off his respirator, breathed desperately out 'goodbye', wide-eyed, blue-skinned. His eyes looked poisonously on Bartlett an instant, and then they looked on nothing. His head collapsed on to his right shoulder. There was a silence. Dr Adams, of all people, led the few who shed a tear or so. Bartlett was efficient as always. He ordered Dr Durante:

'You heard what the professor said. Trundle him into the recycler. Not the wheelchair – that may still be needed.' Pale, Dr Durante obeyed. The recycler was to the left of the foodfields. It was a simple matter of disengaging, with the help of Dr Sara Bogardus, the spent body from its chair and pathetic apparatus, and then introducing the mere chunk of morphology to the atomizing chamber. They did this, shut the heavy doors, then set the apparatus working. There was no sound, no flashing of lights. Silently, the task of salvaging protein, carbohydrate, phosphorus, fluids cleansed and potable, and converting waste to fuel for the ancillary heating engines was consummated. Frame would live in them and for them.

Bartlett said, with the brutality which they now knew was stitched into his nature: 'So much for the past. Our work is nearly at its end, our work of the present. We take a deep breath and prepare for our work of the future. There will be a general meeting this evening after dinner. 2130, the usual place. Very well, dismiss.' They dismissed. Dr Maude Adams said to Vanessa:

'I don't feel at all well,' and leaned on her.

'Come to my quarters,' Vanessa said. She gunned the frowning

O'Grady with her eyes, the eyes of a woman just bereaved. 'I'll look after you.'

And so, boys and girls, ladies and gentlemen, after a meal more frugal than usual, not in honour of the dead but as an earnest of the eternal space diet to come, an evening began that shall live for ever in our annals.

During dinner, the diners were aware of unaccustomed earth tremors. They all looked at each other, fearing for their ship, though it was mounted on a mound of elasticom which, theoretically at least, enabled it to ride terrestrial tempests as a seaship rides the sea. Still, they were unaccustomed. Louise Boudinot nearly ran out to check that all was well. Bartlett, the imperturbable, banged his knife handle on high table and said: 'Calm calm calm.' They were calm.

They were, naturally, less calm at the general meeting, watching Boss Cat take his place on the dais. They feared, with justice if past experience were to be trusted, new curtailments of amenity and longer working hours. They did not at all expect what he gave them. He said:

'The time has come, as I have already intimated, to think of the future. To think, indeed, of more than our own future: of the future of the race. We have to breed a race, ladies and gentlemen,' frowning as if breeding were a hard necessity imposed upon them by the stern daughter of the voice of God. 'Before we breed, we must mate. As soon as we are under way into shallow space, the mating process will begin.' Some of them began to stare at him, open-mouthed. He said: 'I have spent time and close study on the question of mating. I have not consulted any of you on this matter; indeed, there is no one properly to consult, since we do not possess a professional zeugaromatologist on our team. But I have completed a final list in which I am confident that every relevant factor has been taken into consideration. I would ask you all to pay close attention as I read out the list and to note carefully the mate chosen for each of you. I do not imply any derogation in putting male names first. After all, the mating process is traditionally initiated by the male.' The open mouths opened even more. Not a breath was heard. The thumping earth, muffled by the sound-proofing, was forgotten. 'So then,' said Bartlett. 'In alphabetical order.

'Dr David T. Abramovitz will mate with Dr Jessica Laura Thackeray. Dr Vincent Audelan will mate with Dr Gianna da Verranzano. Dr Paul Maxwell Bartlett, Head of Project, will mate with Dr Vanessa

Mary Frame. Dr Robert F. Belluschi will mate with Dr Belle Harrison. Dr Miguel S. Cézanne will mate with –' The first one to snigger was, strangely, Dr Adams. Bartlett looked down at her in total surprise. 'Please. Dr Cézanne, as I say, will mate with Dr Guinevere Irving. Dr Douglas C. Cornwallis will mate with Dr Minnie Farragut –' But now the single snigger had opened the door to laughter. Some laughed, then others. It was a hell of a time since any of them had had a good laugh. They laughed, some, more, more still. O'Grady frowned. Bartlett was frankly puzzled and looked for a cause of laughter – an open fly, a cat micturating against his table leg. He tried to continue: 'Dr John R. Durante with Dr Kathleen Orlinda Eastman. Dr Mackenzie Eidlitz –' But he could not be heard. The laughter was very nearly total. Even the clinically pacified were laughing. Laughing, it seemed, was a solvent of even the most potent chemical conditioner. Bartlett, white, horrified, yelled: 'Silence. Silence. Silence.' That only made it worse.

Dr Eidlitz was bellowing like a sealion. Bartlett picked on him and said: 'Dr Eidlitz, control yourself. Mating is a serious business.' For some reason that began to touch off a risory nerve in Dr O'Grady. Bartlett did not at first notice: O'Grady sat somewhat to his rear. He said: 'If, of course, there are any compatibility problems, Dr O'Grady will be only too happy to supervise the clinical staff in effecting adjustments.' He looked at O'Grady and found, shocked, horrified, that O'Grady was showing big horse-teeth and howling. Bartlett could hardly be heard. 'O'Grady – Dr O'Grady –' O'Grady did not respond. Bartlett turned to Dr Greeley, the diastemopsychologist, yelling his head off in the front row and going through the classic parameters of risory near-exhaustion: hand on ribs, finger pointing blindly at the excitatory cause. 'You,' Bartlett said, 'you, damn you,' and he came down from the dais. He hit at tear-blinded Greeley. Then the laughter stopped very abruptly. Greeley hit back. The two men tussled. Bartlett cried: 'O'Grady, put this man under close arrest.' O'Grady got up, straight-faced, and went down and over to the two tusslers without conviction. Then, seeing open mouths and pallor where he had recently seen universal joy, he burst into a huge cackle. This primed Jovian laughter on the back row. 'Put everybody under close arrest,' cried Bartlett. That was the end. Howls and screams and what used to be called hysteria, children. It was all the funnier because of Bartlett's fury.

It was only Bartlett who saw the main door open and Lieutenant

Johnson, head of the residual platoon, come in. Johnson looked in astonishment at the fiftyfold, or nearly, laughter and was forced, by reflex, to relax his own face to a smirk. Then he recollected the apparent seriousness of his mission and said something to Bartlett's ear. Bartlett was hardly able to look grimmer than he already did. 'About two hundred, sir,' Johnson said. 'Some have gloves and wirecutters and are cutting through the electric fence. We're unarmed, that's the trouble. Request permission for arms to be issued, sir.'

'Silence,' Bartlett yelled anew at the wildly laughing. 'Silence. Silence. I have disturbing news. *This* will stop your stupid laughter.' But it didn't, not yet.

Trotsky paces.

Waiting, waiting.
I've done my share of waiting.
But there was always something to do
To beguile
The long while
Of waiting –
Writing a pamphlet or two.
Orating.
But there's nothing I can write now
Right now
To help you, Seryozha, you.
If I had to renounce all I'd taught
To have you safely here,
I'd do it without a thought.
Later, I know, I'd renounce my renouncing.
Men are like that – untrustworthy, untrue.
But the pouncing terror of what I fear
May have happened to you
This night –
Which I put out of mind,
Waiting, just waiting while the 'competent authorities'
Work at seek-and-find,

Puts my priorities
Right.

Trotsky sings.

Family's first.
When I was younger –
Half an hour ago –
I'd a different hunger and thirst.
Now I know
What comes first.
Having a son –
The one ambition
Any man should need –
It's an ancient traditional creed
When all's done,
None of the worst.
Your future,
Your root, your
Fruit, your
All-in-all are in him,
Fruit of your loins.
What is wealth? Coins.
Possessions? Toys.
What is politics? Noise noise noise.
Family's first,
Love is completeness,
Power's a burnt-out star.
To redeem with sweetness the cursed
Things we are,
Family's first,
By far.

As if conjured by Trotsky's own love and pain, Seryozha comes in. Trotsky grabs him and nearly chokes him with relief and affection. He is a very ordinary little Russian boy already turning into an American. He chews gum roundly during his father's embrace. He is accompanied by Dr Goldstein's chauffeur. Trotsky addresses this man, saint, hero.

'You found him, comrade, sir, friend, old buddy – what do I call you? Where was he?'

'It was my guess,' says the chauffeur calmly. 'Mrs Trotsky and Dr Goldstein thought otherwise. Uptown, they said. Down, I said. A question of numbers.'

'Explain yourself. Please.'

'The young gentleman often spoke to me about the logical arrangement of the streets of Manhattan. But he didn't believe there was a *First* Street. I told him there had to be a First Street, but there was no point in going to look for it. You just accepted it like an act of faith. He would not accept it in that way. He went looking for it. I guessed he would. I found him in a very dirty small restaurant. He was playing checkers with an old man.'

'How can I thank you? How can I express my – '

'Start learning about the internal combustion engine. That is where the future lies. This young gentleman will learn. He has the right scientific mind. He was looking for First Street. A very logical thing to do. I will now go back and await the telephone call of my employer. He said he would telephone on the hour. Mrs Trotsky is with him. She will be pleased. Good night.'

'And from me too. And my eternal grat – '

'Good night, Mr Vavasour,' says Seryozha. The chauffeur smiles kindly but loftily and leaves. Father and son look at each other, the father smiling, the son puzzled and even reproachful.

'Dad,' he says, 'you said Mr Marx and Mr Engels were dead. Well, they're not dead. I met them tonight. One keeps an old clothes shop and the other gets drunk. And there was another old man who says that if I'm Trotsky I should know all about dialect something, dialectual something –'

'Dialectical materialism. But we won't talk about that, son. Not tonight. I don't think I can talk any more tonight.' He hugs his son but his son pushes him away sternly, saying:

'Tell me what it is, this dialectual thing.'

Trotsky sighs. 'Well, you see, son – You start off with time, and if you have time you have to have history. But you only get history when you put things inside time. Now what do you put inside it? Thoughts or things? Mind or matter? Matter, things – because without those to think about you can't have thoughts. Do you see that?'

'I think so.'

'Good. You put your first thing in time and you call it a thesis. Wait a minute – don't ask what a thesis is, that's what everybody asks. Listen. A thesis has to have an antithesis – that means an opposite. Like day, night. Sweet, sour. Slave, boss. You see that? Right. Well, thesis and antithesis have to fight. But they don't knock each other out. Oh no. They merge, they become one thing, a new thing, and we call this a synthesis. Now the synthesis is on its own, and we might as well call it a new thesis. And what does it find?'

'A new anti thing. What you said.'

'Right. Good. And this goes on until the last thesis meets the last antithesis. And they make the final synthesis. The proletariat clashes for the last time with the forces of capital, and you get the classless society.'

'And that's the end?'

'The end. History comes to a stop.'

'I don't believe it.'

'You'd better believe it. Peace, justice, the workers' state. There's nothing more for history to do.'

'I can't believe it. There always has to be two.'

'All right,' indulgently. 'And where does the two come from when the Revolution comes?'

Seryozha says promptly: 'A split in the party.'

Reality dawns on Trotsky. 'It *has* come. My God, it's here. I was forgetting. You pushed it out of my mind, son. The Revolution has arrived. Or am I dreaming?'

The door opens, and Vol and Bok and Chud lead in a number of excited New York journalists. They want to know all about the Revolution.

FIRST JOURNALIST: The red flag's flying
On the Winter Palace is
The last word I got
And the password I got
Is: Show your calluses, comrade.
No calluses – you're shot.

SECOND JOURNALIST: The red blood's flowing
Through the Moscow alleys is
Some new news I got.
Is it true news I got?

FIRST JOURNALIST: The red flag's flying
On the Winter Palace is
What I got.
True or not?

THIRD JOURNALIST: I thought the Winter Palace
Was the tunnel that connects
The 34th and Lex-
Ington IRT stop and Penn Station,
That all the bums go inter
To spend their winter
Vacation.

FOURTH JOURNALIST: They're shoving caviar into
The Russian proletariat
Is what I was told,
There's a lot I was told.
Drink your champagne, comrade –
But it gives me a damn pain, comrade.
If you don't lap it up like a real good boy
You're shot.

ALL JOURNALISTS: True or not?

But now Trotsky's wife Natalia comes in with their other son but without Dr Goldstein. There is a joyful reunion, all rancour forgotten. Trotsky, his arms about his family, addresses the journalists:

'Comrades, gentlemen of the press. All I know is that the workers in Russia have seized power. The end of tyranny and the beginning of hope for all the downtrodden of the world. Tomorrow I may say more. But tonight – '

Another journalist has entered, breathless. 'Sorry I'm late,' he says, breathing whisky on Trotsky, who does not mind. 'There's this report just come through about the end of the world. A cable from Valparaiso or somewhere. A planet has swum in from another galaxy or somewhere. It's going to collide with the earth, so they say.'

'Cranks,' says Trotsky. 'Anything to divert human attention from the real issues. The end of the world, indeed. There's only one world coming to an end, and we know which it is. But more of that tomorrow. Tonight, the hell with revolution.' He sings, and everybody joins in:

Family's first,
Love is completeness,
Power's a burnt-out star.
To redeem with sweetness

The cursed
Things we all are,
Family's first –
By far!

Summer 1938, early morning. Freud, Anna and Martha were dozing as the train eased into the station. Anna woke first. She gently woke her parents. Freud came to, opening his eyes in pain, blinking. He tremblingly put on his spectacles, then his hat.

'Paris, mother.'

'We're there?' Other passengers were cramming the corridor, leaving. Somebody had bought a newspaper. There was something on the front page, Freud could see, about the *fin du monde*. Catchpenny nonsense. Anything to divert public attention from the real issues.

W. C. Bullitt was waiting on the platform. So was Princess Marie Bonaparte. She kissed the two women. Bullitt said:

'Dr Freud, welcome to Paris. I'm one of your old patients – Bullitt, United States Ambassador.'

The speaking of a foreign language eased, surprisingly, Freud's pain. 'Ah yes,' he said. 'You got stuck at the anal stage.'

'But I'm all right now, thanks to you. The German Ambassador sends his regrets. It was considered indiscreet for him to come and meet you.'

'A discreet people. They kill their enemies without boasting about it.'

'My car is waiting,' the Princess Bonaparte said, pointing.

'Princess,' Freud said. 'He was taken from the river in a cage of rushes. He lived in the house of the princess . . . '

'The day after tomorrow,' she said, 'London. Everything's prepared.'

An old man, he walked between them towards the resting engine. A new kind of Otto Rank was waiting, fat, prosperous, getting old. He came forward shyly.

'Herr Professor – '

'What are you doing in Paris?' Freud asked in French.

'My practice is here. A flourishing one. May I say how *relieved* I am – '

'Betrayer, traitor,' Freud said promptly in German. 'There's a hell reserved to all you treacherous ingrates – Jung and Adler and Stekel and Ferenczi, and you, Otto Rank – '

'But I *cure* people. Is that betrayal?'

'Traitor, traitor. Out of my sight.' He even raised his stick. Rank cowered. Freud hurried on, without assistance. The Princess and the Ambassador hurried after to support him. Rank stood bewildered, undecided. But Anna gave him a cool smile. Martha did not seem to remember who he was.

He sat in the salon of the Bonaparte mansion, the Princess Bonaparte with him. A footman took away his coat and hat and cane. She said:

'Such a relief – '

'You sound like Rank. No, you don't. The women have never betrayed me. Only the men. One of them is already in hell.'

'Don't, please. This should be a time of rejoicing.'

He chuckled. 'Oh, I'm rejoicing all right.' He had a very bright image of Adler lecturing his last to hard-headed Scottish doctors:

'In conclusion, let me say that my whole endeavour has been to apply the science of psychoanalysis to the service of humanity – not use it to dig into the sewers of the unconscious. The cloacal obsessions of Sigmund Freud, his maniacal preoccupation with filth and fecal matter – these have been, and remain – an inhibiting force – to the – true work – You doctors of Aberdeen – reared in a tradition of Protestant purity which I myself – though a Jew – have embraced – will know what to make of his – pornology – his dabbling – in the dirt – his degradation – of the human – ' Collapsed, gasping for breath, surrounded by hard-headed Scottish doctors who could do nothing for him.

'Even if I die,' Freud said, 'now, at this moment, I've outlived him. Paranoic thief, defector – Yes, Princess – it's only the women who haven't let me down.'

She saw fatigue in the excessive brightness of his eyes. 'Would you like to go to your room – rest a little?'

'I'll rest here,' he said.

Rest there. Strange: he had not expected a congress to be held here, large though the amenities of the mansion were. It was not right either that the dead as well as the living should be present. Thank God for the miracle. He cautiously probed with his tongue point: the prosthesis removed and the hard palate healed. In the great mirror he saw himself probing. Restored to youthful middle age, he could forgive the resurrection of Adler whom he saw there in the background, chatting animatedly with Ferenczi and Jones. Into the mirror leapt a mature woman of astounding beauty, swathed in scarlet silk and white fox, metallic hair, metallic jewels. 'You know who I am?' her reflection said. Freud turned cautiously to meet the reality.

'I observed you. I was naturally – I haven't had the pleasure, no.'

'I am Lou Andreas-Salome.'

'Sigmund Freud.'

She was fierce in her repetition. 'I am Lou Andreas-Salome. I was the mistress of the great poet Rainer Maria Rilke. Before that I was the mistress of Friedrich Nietzsche. You know Nietzsche?'

'His work, of course – '

'I was his mistress. Now I am to be yours.'

'I appreciate – naturally – the honour, that is. My wife, however, might consider that – well, you see, there are certain problems – ' Snake and rabbit. He had heard of this kind of fascination before. He tried to shake himself free. Her eyes and perfume held on like teeth. 'I don't require a mistress, madam – ' (Or should it be 'madam, mistress'?)

'I see. Resistance to women. You're frightened of women. When you spoke of the vagina in your lecture just now I could see the fright in your eyes, it was in your voice. You're scared of being devoured.'

'I am not,' he said stoutly. 'I have a wife. We live happily. It is a companionate marriage – '

'Without sex?'

'Really – that is a most personal – '

She laughed fiercely. 'Oh, you bourgeois Jews. You speak freely of sex on the lecture platform – all theory, little practice. Tell me about a woman's sexual needs.'

'The sexual life of adult woman remains a dark continent. A riddle not to be solved.'

'Now you're quoting some nonsense you put in a book.' He was, too. He had the damned book in his hands. He tried to hide it but it turned into flypaper. 'Why don't you *ask* women?'

'It would be unseemly.' The book turned into a cat and slithered away. 'There are certain decencies.'

'You say also,' she said, now at an ornate dressing table brilliantly lighted, in underwear and negligée, silken legs exposed, delicately painting a lower eyelid, 'that a woman's sexual life lasts only twenty years. Nonsense. The Baroness de Neuchâtel, when ninety-three years of age, was asked when sexual desire died in women, and she said: "I don't know." You say that women's sexual satisfaction is a matter of the vagina, not the clitoris. Of course – you're a man. You want women to be dependent on men. You believe that woman is a breed apart and inferior to man. You know why you hate America?'

'I never said I hated – America treated me with the most – '

'Because their women are free, they've broken their European bondage. You call yourself a psychoanalyst. You know nothing of any psyche except your own.'

'My psyche,' he said, 'may be taken as a kind of model – '

'Not for me, Herr Professor. It is not the same as mine. You will learn. I am to be your mistress.'

'I must respectfully and gratefully – '

'Very well,' in shimmering satin ball gown. 'I must be the mistress of some promising member of your entourage. Your most brilliant disciple. Who would that be?'

'I do not regard it,' stiffly and somewhat oldly now, 'as any part of my responsibility, madam, to choose lovers for you from among my twelve tribes, that is to say apostles, that is to say – '

'I do not ask you to choose,' with perfumed hauteur. 'I merely ask you to evaluate.'

'Well, there's Rank – Jones – No, Jones is married and lives in London – '

'What does that have to do with it? Are there not trains, cross-Channel steamers? Of course, most of them are so ugly.'

'I regret that sincerely. I have always regretted it.'

'You are drawn to masculine beauty? You descry homosexual elements in yourself? That young man over there – he appears to be tortured in spirit, but he is decidedly handsome.'

'Oh, him? Tausk, you mean?'

Tausk was in earnest conversation with Ernest Jones. He was in hussar costume, shako under arm, undeniably darkly handsome.

'Tausk is brilliant,' Freud admitted. 'Tausk is also undeniably ambitious.'

'Good. He shall be my lover. Which means that you and I must be friends.'

'I have no objection. But why? The logic is, shall I say, categorically feminine.'

'He is ambitious. You fear him. He may appropriate your ideas.

He may develop new ideas of his own. You require a spy. I can be that spy. Time for your lecture, dear Sigmund.'

'I object, madam, to this unsolicited familiarity of address, madam.'

'Why? Are we not to be friends? We are also, of course, to be colleagues.'

'But that's im – '

'Possible? All too possible. I propose taking up psychoanalysis myself. Women are better at it than men. They are in touch with reality. They have intuition on their side. But come, your lecture.'

'I've already given one.'

'Ah, but this is an important lecture. And here you learn, not teach. There they all are, waiting.' To Freud's slight surprise a group of women materialized about him. He recognized Hélène Deutsch, Melanie Klein. His mother was there too, very old, with a newspaper in her hands. He approached them shakily, himself old, but not yet stricken with that damnable – His mother said:

'Siggy, this is my ninetieth birthday. Come and give your momma a kiss. Look, there's my picture in the paper – mother of famous man, it says. Terrible picture. It makes me look a hundred.'

'I have to give this lecture, momma. Happy birthday, though.'

'This is my boy, Siggy,' his mother told the assembled ladies. 'My son the doctor. Herr Professor they call him. He speaks beautiful. Just you listen to him now.'

'The subject of my discourse, ladies,' Freud announced, 'is – '

'We know,' said his mother. '*Women*. But ach, bless him, he knows nothing about women. I made sure of that. I don't count that Hamburgerin he married. Watch her cooking. It'll do your stomach no good.'

'Women,' Freud said parsonically, 'are the victims of civilization. Civilization has stultified them. The sexual instincts of women have been artificially retarded and stunted.'

Lou Andreas-Salome did not now appear to be present, but her voice came clear from the crystal chandelier:

'Speak for the women you know. Not me.'

'Women,' Freud said, 'are intellectually inferior to men; they lack the full male libido, they have less energy to sublimate. They have little sense of justice. This is undoubtedly related to the predominance of envy in their mental life. The demand for justice is a modification of envy. It presents the conditions for putting envy aside. Women thrive on envy and hence reject justice. Women are weaker in their social instincts than are men. They have less capacity for sublimating their animal instincts. They have made few contributions to the discoveries and inventions of civilization. They have little sense of humour. Their superego is not so dependent on the impersonal, not so independent of the emotions as with men. Love? Women are there to be loved by men, but love itself may be defined as a sexual overvaluation. It only emerges in full force in relation to a woman who holds herself back and denies her sexuality. So far so good. Is that all right, momma?'

'You speak lovely, Siggy.' The other ladies did not agree. They had listened with amusement, shock, repressed anger. Lou Andreas-Salome spoke again from the chandelier:

'Sit on him, ladies.'

He was sat upon. His mother was not unduly concerned. 'He was,' she said, 'always one for playing games with his sisters.'

'Let me go,' he panted. 'This is undignified. You don't seem to realize who I am. This is intolerable.'

'Is it?' asked Hélène Deutsch.

'Not intolerable, no. Merely unexpected.'

'Unexpected?' repeated Hélène Deutsch. 'But you must always have expected it. Forgetting about the role of the mother, making everything start with the father. The mother is the original love object for women as well as for men. That upsets your Oedipus theory, doesn't it?'

'I'm not well, Siggy,' said his mother. 'My heart. Not so young as I was.'

Freud struggled to free himself from the squatting buttocks. 'Let me get to her. She's not well, she says. She's old.'

'Keep him there, ladies,' said the voice of Lou Andreas-Salome. 'He doesn't have to feel guilty about his mother. Only his father.'

'Ninety-five, Siggy. It's a great age. Nothing to worry about. No regrets. Not enough love, that's all, but who's counting?'

She died. Freud tried to go through certain motions of regret and sorrow, but the buttocks held him down. Hélène Deutsch lectured him.

'You will notice that you have excluded your wife Martha from this dream. And you know why? You wanted from your wife a more mature solace than that which the mother brings to the son. You didn't get it. You resented it. That's why you speak of women as you do.'

'I resent that, this.'

'Of course. You resent women. They worry you. Fear of the female genitalia. Listen to the voice of reason for a change. You said the Oedipus complex comes first. It doesn't. It doesn't for women, anyway. Women love their mothers, idiot. They too want to be fussed and kissed and cuddled.'

'A woman,' Freud tried to shout, 'is a defective man.'

'Oh yes,' Hélène Deutsch coolly said. 'Penis envy. An essential constituent of female psychology, according to the dear doctor. The little girl discovers her genital deficiency when she sees her brother having a bath. She wants a child as a compensation for the penis she can't have. Such nonsense.'

'Why,' asked Melanie Klein, 'don't men have breast envy?'

'Oh they do, they do,' Hélène Deutsch said.

'They don't,' cried Freud. 'I've spent thirty years searching into the female soul, and there's one big question they won't answer. And the question is: WHAT DO WOMEN WANT?'

'Ah,' Melanie Klein said, 'wouldn't you like to know?'

'Yes yes yes. It's the riddle of the Sphinx. You're all a lot of damned sphinxes – '

'Tut tut,' said Melanie Klein. 'Bad language in front of ladies.'

'I haven't answered the riddle. Therefore I'm not Oedipus.'

'Nobody's answered the riddle,' said Hélène Deutsch. 'Therefore there's no Oedipus. Oedipus is only a myth, that is to say a lie. And you can't build a system on a lie.'

Anna came in, shocked. 'What are you doing to my father?'

'Who are you?' asked Hélène Deutsch.

'His daughter.'

'Ah, Antigone to his Oedipus. But Oedipus didn't exist. Ergo, you don't exist.'

'I exist all right. Get these people out of here. He's tired. He has an incurable cancer of the jaw. He's in pain.'

'Agony,' her father groaned. 'Let me up. Let me bury my mother.'

'Oh,' said Melanie Klein, 'that's been done.'

'She was buried,' said Hélène Deutsch, 'while you were otherwise engaged.'

'Where? Where?'

'Does it matter?'

He awoke sweating to find Anna standing over him. 'How's mother?' he said.

'Well. Resting.'

'Oh. Yes. I see. I slept. I dreamed.'

'It's time to take the Monster out. Clean it. Put it back again.'

'It all stems out of the Oedipus complex, doesn't it? Everything?'

'We'll talk about that again. Come on.' She lifted the old man to his feet.

'As they used to say in vaudeville,' Willett grunted, '*this must be the place*.' He made certain adjustments to the controls which kept the thing hovering in the hostile winds – hostile to each other as well as to their craft. Val could still not get over his surprise that Willett, actor, eater, swiller, and praiser of the past, should be so skilful with a helicopter. Something to do with his son George, apparently: Willett did not wish to say too much about it. George, before being transferred to Looncom (Lunar Communications), had done a helicopter course in connection with inspection of high cable laying. He had come home once, illegally, in a company chopper. His father had been charmed by it and insisted on at once going up and then taking over. He had altogether taken to it, a reasonable and at the same time rather poetic machine.

They had picked up this particular helicopter near Sedalia, Missouri. Land transport had by now been thoroughly obstructed by broken roads, folds of upturned earth, perpetual jolting tremors. They had been astonished, near Sedalia, to see in broad midday a patch of air wholly taken up by helicopters engaged in crashing into each other in individual suicide combat. Madness, lyncstatic madness. There was a metal notice, twisted, battered, lying on scorched grass, which said HELIBASE 56. Over an excessively amplified loudspeaker system joyful simple music was being discoursed:

'I scream you scream
We all scream for ice cream
Rah! Rah! Rah!
Tuesdays Mondays
We roar out for sundaes
Siss! Boom! Yah!
Boola boola sasparoola
If you've got chocolate I'll have vanoola . . . '

Val and Willett went cautiously closer, to the thick net periphery. A field day. Drink, fornication, aerial suicide. A tipsy sergeant had welcomed them in to the funeral games. What had begun, apparently, as a helicopter square dance had turned into a dodgem course. Now it was rank joyful suicide. Could anybody play? Well, said the sergeant, Val and Willett were civilians, not really eligible. On furlough, Willett said, both. Meet Colonel Allnut and Major Catastrophe. No trouble, then. And they were zigzaggedly escorted to the helicopter park, bottles of scotch thrust into their hands by a singing corporal. Then they were off and up, not really playing the game.

Over Kansas City they had been bounced up and down by hot air. The town was in flames and ruins. They had a terrifying fascinating view of ant-sized citizens scuttling along buckling streets to avoid collapsing masonry. Over Leavenworth they had a fuel problem. They sailed down to what was clearly a vast deserted filling station, plomped down on thin flat feet, found the pumps out of order but big corrugated drums of polyoctane in the open store. They glugged the volatile gold in and made for Topeka which, by some strange injustice or miracle, seemed virtually intact. They put down outside the town at a big mess that was full of grumbling military – gross stew being ladled out by army orderlies, a fat drunken top sergeant cook. They were fed, sour-facedly, but without real demur.

Val asked about the CAT camp. Nobody knew it. Wait, how about Shorty? Shorty's outfit had broken up, Shorty had been posted to this clear-up battalion, grousing and even tearful about being cut off from his old buddies and full of unbelievable stories about a moonship and a guy in charge called Boss Cat. Shorty was now dragged out of the cookhouse, where he was repairing a portable generator, and said yeah he knew the dump. They was kept in but that was okay, plenty going on, no shortage of puss, no idea really where they was, but when they left they went through a dump called Sloansville, which one guy, Meatball, said he knew of course his dad had worked on the drains there and said gee what a dump, well what do you know, Sloansville.

Up in the air, Willett said:

'You were right, you see, right. Your book probably gave those non-fictitious scientific bastards the idea.'

But Val was depressed. End of the line coming. Better to travel in hope than arrive at hope's fulfilment. Keeping on was the thing, on, on. And now what for him really, what for Willett? It suddenly dawned on him that the world was coming to an end. The fact was slotting into that department of his brain which dealt with real verifiable propositions. More, it was taking on, his mind being fundamentally poetic, the properties of a compressed and instantaneous sense datum. He could smell and taste the end of the world like an apple. He said: 'Why the hell should *we* be saved?'

Willett grunted, busy with his controls, and then said: 'For one simple reason. Because that's not a question those scientific bastards would ever dream of asking. That's why.' Val didn't quite understand. They followed the course of the Smoky Hill River, visibly frothing like a trough of dirty champagne. Seismic immunity, eh? No immunity anywhere now. A very sour apple. His mouth felt dry as after sucking alum.

'As they used to say in vaudeville,' grunted Willett, '*this must be the place*.' Val woke from unpleasant dreams out of which he was, anyway, lucky to be able to wake. He looked down and saw a great neat square, impeccably right-angled, huts, huts, huts, and in the middle *it*, the thing, the end of the known road, big and squat and beautiful. His heart dropped to his gross muddy worn work boots, full of chilled and aching feet. 'So that,' said Willett, with schoolboy's awe, 'is the spaceship. It's true, then. I wondered sometimes. It's real. What do we do now? Land by it? Open its door? Walk in and take a seat?'

'Wait,' said Val, with the caution of a science fiction writer. 'It can't be so easy. They'll shoot us down. There must be warning systems. Or it may be covered with a magnetic repulse shield.' The craft swayed perilously. 'Out, out,' said Val. 'Plenty of time. Nothing impulsive. We'll wait. Land. Behind that clump of elms there.'

'Faint heart,' said Willett, obeying. He dropped down neatly. They sat an instant and sighed at the same time. Willett switched off his engine. 'Food,' he said. It was twilight. They opened up their hamper and pulled out a cold roast joint, a jar of English mustard, bread, an apple pie, potted clotted cream, three bottles of Montrachet chilled by the air passage, and a flask of Meridian cognac (b.o.f.i.). Sad autumn lay all about them. The earth hiccupped.

The earth hiccupped. Just south of Sloansville a man named Elias Howe addressed a crowd through a loud-hailer. The crowd was about two hundred strong – men, women, children, cripples, ancients, frightened Kansans all of them. 'You know the truth of it, friends,' he said. 'I may be no more than a common carpenter, but carpenters have seen the truth before and have had the message sent to them from above. Noah and Jesus Christ are two names that come at once to mind. There's been great silence from the governments of the earth, but some of us can read the signs. The earth,' he said prosaically, 'has had a long run for its money. It had to be finished off some day, and it's going to end as it began, with capitalists on top and working men ground into the dirt beneath. Make no mistake about it, sisters and brothers. At that camp up there, with its electrical wires all around it to keep people out, is a ship that's going off into space, loaded with the wealthy being served with champagne and caviar. All right, some of you will say it's scientists as well, jiggling at switchboards and suchlike, but they're in the pay as they've always been of the capitalists, and it's the capitalists that has the last word. And where are they going, you may ask. Well, I'll tell you, friends and comrades. They're not going anywhere except into space up there, far away from that horrible planet and our moon that it stole to bang at us like a big white rock. They'll live out their lives in a big like space hotel, looking at the stars and drinking and having it off with lovely hostesses they have up there, the best of everything. Not a bad life, is it, the life we've all dreamed of, no work and cruising for ever, watching movies and eating fried chicken till they go off, smiling while they snuff it, saying it's been a good life for them, which it has and will be. Well, I'll tell you what's happening tonight, brothers and mothers and dads and sisters. They're not going. The scientists that run it are going to be in the service of the workers, whether they like it or not. The lovely stewardesses or whatever they call themselves are going to serve champagne and patty dee foy grass and hamburgers to the workers, yes, and serve the workers in other ways which I don't have to specify, you being all thinking people. And I say one last thing to you. If *we* don't go, nobody goes.'

The negative programme seemed to appeal to the crowd more than the positive one. They cheered. A one-eyed man at the front said: 'Who shoots first?'

'Nobody shoots if it can be avoided, friends and comrades. Violence was always the way of the capitalists, they having the money for the violent weapons. Those of you carrying guns, don't fire till the word's given. Those of you with insulating gloves and cutters, don't be afraid of the hard work of cutting their fences down – an outer one and an inner one, as you'll know. The cutting party is to go first. The rest of us will follow quiet and in good order.' The earth hiccupped, the crowd roared. The crowd was made up of decent frightened poeple, but few of them were members of the industrial proletariat. They did not know the word *capitalists*, thinking it perhaps meant crooked politicians from the state capital or the Capitol in Washington. They were farmers and their families mostly, who had lived off the fat of the land. But everybody warmed to the notion of his or her not getting all that democracy entitled him or her to. Howe touched the right nerve.

He was not an American but an Englishman who had led the local strike for higher wages in a spaceship body-building factory in Coventry over a year before. He had helped to ensure that the British ship-building programme was so late as to be unfulfilled when the first shocks came. He was not a carpenter but a skilled metalworker. But he knew the elemental appeal of the carpenter's trade in mob oratory. His true trade, however, had been that of industrial obstruction. Cunning, a reading and listening man, he had got out of England by one of the last transatlantic flights before the destruction of most of the country, except for the tips of the Grampians and the Pennines, where men and women champed helplessly, waiting for the end. He had come to the right place, he knew. And now he, if nobody else, was going, he hoped, to the right place. The working man's dream fulfilled: booze, fucking, and idleness. The earth hiccupped.

Calvin Gropius, his son Dashiel, and the strange girl Edwina, who was now evidently very near her time, drove wearily into the town of Sloansville. It was intact but deserted, except for a small coffee shop with the legend JACK JOE & CURLY above. It was lighted by a couple of oil lamps, and a man who could not be Curly because of his baldness or perhaps was Curly because of it was playing checkers calmly with an old man. They did not at first look up when Calvin Gropius's party wearily shambled in. The old man finished the game with a leaping and demolishing king, then looked up in toothless triumph. 'Got you there, boy,' he said. Gropius asked for coffee.

'Not properly open no more, but I can dredge up a little coffee, I guess, for tired travellers.' A literary touch, noted Edwina distractedly. She was losing faith in Calvin Gropius and gaining it in his son. She felt the child tugging within her. She would soon have to make the choice of a father for it. But a literary touch, she noted. The trade was prevailing at the end. The old man said:

'You folks come a long ways?'

'From Dallas, Texas,' said Dashiel.

'You seen strange sights?' asked the old man.

'A blood sacrifice, God help us, God forgive them, outside Ponca City,' shuddered Calvin Gropius. Losing confidence in him. Dashiel was neat and collected, smiling faintly too.

'That sure is one terrible place, Ponca City. I been there once when I was a kid, no more than knee high to a gracehoper. Good place to keep away from, Ponca City.' The old man cackled. 'You hear talk of the end of the world in Oklahoma?'

'Plenty,' Dashiel said. He gratefully fingered a mug of tepid coffee.

'Believe anything, them Okies will. Still, I figure if it comes then it comes,' said the old man comfortably. He was, Edwina calculated, well into his eighties. 'Earthquakes, volcanoes, and the earth giving up its dead. That's in the good book, mister,' he told Calvin Gropius.

'I know all about the good book,' said Calvin Gropius irritably.

The Tagliaferro brothers now walked in, Gianni wild-eyed but with no gun in hand or at hip. 'Hi, Dash,' said Salvatore. 'You got any coffee behind there?' he asked Jack, Joe or Curly. Gianni had hungry eyes only for Calvin Gropius.

'You fellers come far?' asked the old man.

'Fort Worth, grandad,' said Salvatore.

'That's longer away than these folks a mite. Grandad you say, son. I'm a grandad twelve times over, you know that? No, reckon you don't, not having seen me afore.' The floor trembled. 'You stop that now,' cackled the old man. 'A mite uppish,' he cackled.

'Are you,' said Gianni, 'a minister?'

'Doctor of divinity,' Calvin Gropius said. 'For what it's worth now.' His eyes frowned at Dashiel. He didn't need these two Sicilians explained to him. Dashiel's bosses, colleagues, something, Mafia certainly.

'I gotta confess,' said Gianni. 'I got sins on my soul.'

'I reject auricular confession,' said Calvin Gropius loftily. 'If you want to confess, go and confess in that dark corner there. Why should one man stand between another man and his maker?'

'You don't understand,' said Salvatore, lighting up a tipless cigarette and winking covertly. 'He's gotta confess. It's hell he's worried about.'

'There ain't no hell,' said the old man dogmatically. 'Hell's this world, my old dad used to say. You two guys holy Romans then?'

'Not Roman, no,' said Salvatore. 'And you keep out of it, grandad.'

Calvin Gropius sighed and then said: 'All right. Irregular, but I'll do it. The situation calls for a certain relaxation of – Very well, come.' And he motioned Gianni to follow him to the dark end of the coffee shop. The old man said:

'You folks come for the big rally? Well nigh on two hundred marching to it. That right, boy?' he said to Jack, Joe or Curly.

'What's this?' asked Dashiel sharply.

'Big commie rally. Not seen one of them afore in these parts. No call for comminism this part of the world.' Calvin Gropius could be heard in the near dark crying *Oh God God my God* at occasions during Gianni's purgative mutter. 'Up at the camp up the road. This English feller was in here talking about the workers and the caplists. I knew what he meant. One of my own boys, young Charlie it was, went that way after he'd been in the army. I ain't got nothing against it deep down, mind. It's all folks fighting one for the other, way it was put to me once by this book-learned feller in Anthony. That's South Kansas. Maybe you folks come through it?'

'Orgies,' Edwina said. Then she twitched and felt the child within kick her viciously. The old man was quick to notice. He said:

'I guess you're pretty near your time, little lady. Ain't no doctor in town neither. Ran away with the others like a bunch of jack rabbits. Nearest hospital's at Lossing. Know where that is?' The earth hiccupped twice and then went into violent spasm.

'He's right,' said Edwina. 'I'm near.'

Calvin Gropius came back shivering from Gianni's revelations. Gianni himself was smiling. 'He don't know nothing about *penitenza*,' he said. 'Three Hail Marys should do it. I'll say them on the way. Where's coffee?'

'There's killing to be done,' said Salvatore in dialect. 'You know that, Gianni? Killing.'

Gianni shrugged. 'Self-defence,' he said, following an old Pentagon maxim, 'you do that best when you get in first.' It sounded chilling in Sicilian, but not so chilling, children, as *anticipatory retaliation* used to sound. The old man said:

'You fellers foreigners? You talk kind of foreign.'

'Hundred per cent American,' Gianni said. The earth hiccupped.

The earth hiccupped. 'Is that what that helicopter was about?' O'Grady asked. 'Earlier on, that chopper. Looking at our defences?'

'No problem up there,' Bartlett said. 'As long as our magnetized cover holds.'

'How far can you trust them with weapons?' O'Grady meant the CAT team, himself excluded.

'They'll never get in,' Bartlett said. Still, he gave O'Grady a Hutchinson hipman, with three ammogiros, and took one for himself. He also wound about his torso a casing of gas bomblets.

'And the troops?' said O'Grady.

'Johnson's issuing them with rifles. Blanks, of course Can't risk giving them lives.'

'They're supposed to be here to protect us.'

'We protect ourselves, O'Grady. Abramovitz, Hazard, Vanessa Frame – they're safe, I think. Reliable. I don't know, though. Guns in their hands. I never thought it would come to this.'

'There's a lot you never thought about,' O'Grady said. Bartlett gave the astunomicologist a hard look but said nothing.

Illuminated solely by absurdly amplified moonlight, Lynx being temporarily occluded by his stolen satellite, the two of them went to meet the mob, first looking in on the CAT team, now no longer laughing, and telling them to await instructions where they were. There were instructions, for the moment, only for Hazard and Vanessa. Abramovitz did not look all that trustworthy, despite the course in pacification or selective amnesia or whatever had made him forget all about dissident books. Hazard and Vanessa were taken outside and given, respectively, a hipman and a Lescaz pistol. They handled them unhandily, wide-eyed both. 'I never thought it would come to this,' said Bartlett.

Not really a mob, they saw. There was organization here. A group was concentrating on cutting at the electrified perimeter, one place only, no wasteful hacking all over. A British lower-class voice came with high-pitched clarity over a loud-hailer. 'In the name of the oppressed,' it said, 'we order you to hand over your spacecraft to the workers. We want no violence. We ask you only to see the reasonableness of our demand. You scientists there, stop being the tools of the capitalist oppressors. Come over to our side. You soldiers, you know what's going on. You're going to be left to die while your capitalist exploiters live off the fat of the land up there in space. Drop your weapons, open that gate, let us in. We come in peace. All we ask is what we want, that being what is the workers' rights.' The platoon sergeant, at a nod from his lieutenant, ordered the opening of fire. There was a fine ragged chorus of bangs, a fried bacon smell, but, although the members of the crowd nearest the wire rushed back sending those behind tottering and falling, nobody dropped down dead. Lieutenant Johnson looked round curiously at his civilian masters. The sergeant gave the firing order again, and again there was a blind hash of harmless banging. As in rebuke of such kid's play, growling and crashing from all over the horizon, the adult stuff of real killing, hills falling, cities crashing, resounded crisply.

A voice that disdained the use of an electronic prosthesis was now heard, its possessor unseen. 'This is Calvin Gropius,' it cried. 'I come as the last messenger of the Lord God. I demand the right to bear the Word of the Lord into the wide universe that is the Lord's own creation. Open your gates. I demand it, God demands it.' The voice of the workers loud-hailed in protest:

'The God that's the creation of the bloody capitalists. Open up for the proletariat.' But, because of the nonconformist tradition of British radical oratory, he couldn't help being influenced by the Gropius rhythms. 'The earth is the workers' and the richness thereof. Space for the workers.'

'*Now*, I think,' said Bartlett, and, with a good round aim, he sent a gas bomb flying towards the spot where the cutters cut away, lighted goldenly by high voltage sparks. There was a sudden cloud of immense dirtiness and a loud chorus of curses and desperate coughing. Encouraged, Bartlett sent another, towards where the loud-hailing workers' leader seemed to be placed. The bomb sailed through the air, over the fence, but this time there was no dirty cloud nor coughing. Instead, it was fielded and returned neatly, a British hand at work there. O'Grady pulled Bartlett away with quick policeman's reflexes. Both ran. Gas fumed and then was hurried off by the brisk wind. The earth hiccupped. The earth went into spasm. The Lord's? The workers'?

From the same invisible spot as before Gropius resumed: 'I demand that the bearer of the Lord's Truth be admitted. *I demand*.' As if to back that up, the nervous spattering of what seemed to be autogun bullets started well behind him. And now some of the workers began to go down, many screaming. Others ran. The loud-hailer cried:

'You see what the capitalists are doing, you scientists? Scientists, fellow workers – ' There was no more from him, except a howl, a gurgling, a choking, partially amplified. Then he was, presumably, down, loud-hailer and all.

It is time to change our view and see what was happening outside the CAT camp. Gianni, abetted by Salvatore, was pumping out death into the workers, farmers really, gritting in Sicilian: 'Let them die, why should they live, what right to live do they have, the bastards, when when when – ' But he could not permit bereaved tears to cloud his sight. He pumped away, fine white teeth agleam in the ridiculous skylight, while the ground trembled under him. Salvatore said to Gropius, who came appalled up to their car:

'Gianni, he'll get us all in there, reverend. All we want is the two guys that pilots the plane. The rest don't matter a shit, right? Just us and that broad and Dash and the guys that pilot the thing, and maybe a couple air hostesses.'

'No! No! No! This is murder!'

'Not murder, reverend. Self-defence. Gianni don't have to confess that. Self-defence ain't no sin, reverend.'

Behind a shivering oak, stretched out in the warm night asleep, were, for a time, Val and Willett. They had eaten and drunk heartily, they were very weary after their adventures. They did not respond to noise. They had had nothing but noise since their journey began. They had learned to sleep through noise. It was almost by chance that Dashiel Gropius dragged Edwina Goya to protection behind that same tree. There were not, in fact, many trees around. 'Good God,' said Edwina, forgetting her pains, 'it can't be. It's Dr Brodie.' She shook him. 'Dr Brodie, wake up. There's terrible danger.'

But it was Willett who woke first, grunting, groaning, smacking, very bleary. He did not know these two and he quickly grasped the pistol at his belt. The girl was pregnant, he noticed. Jesus, this was no time for getting pregnant. '*Friends*,' the man said. 'Wait – you're – '

'Willett is the name.'

'I saw you in New York at the Albee in – '

'*Hamlet*. They said I was too fat. But as I pointed out in a letter to the *New York Times* – '

'Edwina,' said Val, now awake. 'What the hell are you doing here?' He had seen her last in the departmental library, glooming over a huge variorum edition of John Donne.

'This,' said Edwina, 'is the end of the world. I presume anybody can join in.'

'What a lot of people,' Willett said in wonder, seeing shrieking Kansans running everywhere. 'The chopper,' he said. 'It's safe?' It was not safe, not with maddened scamperers quite likely to take off from the carnage and the end of the world with it. Willett fired a couple of stray shots and saw people stumble, howling, scattering. Dashiel said:

'Gropius is my name. I'd suggest that – '

'You're too young for Gropius,' Val frowned.

'Dashiel Gropius. My father Calvin Gropius is over there, demanding entrance in God's name. Look, this lady's near her time, as you can see. There must be doctors inside that place – '

'It's all doctors,' Edwina winced, her face clenching on her pain like a fist.

'The only way in,' Dashiel said, 'would be from the air. I'm assuming you know how to drive that thing – '

'Magnetic barrier,' Val said. 'But, Christ, my wife's in there. She ought to be able to let us in. Anyway, I've a right to be in. A duty, in fact.'

'You didn't seem so eager before,' Willett frowned. 'You talked about being shot down.'

'I was thinking of the two of us, if you must know,' Val said. 'I was putting you first, and you have neither right nor duty. And now it strikes me that a man in my presumed position is entitled to a driver or pilot or something – '

'Something,' Willett grunted. Then he said: 'Let's get in and up. At least we can get away from that bastard who's spreading death, whoever he is.'

'One of the Tagliaferro brothers,' Dashiel said. 'He's gone mad. Lost his wife and kids and so has gone mad.' Meanwhile they made their way to the helicopter and got in, Edwina in pain and with difficulty.

Inside the camp most of the CAT team, disobeying orders, had come out to see what was happening. Bartlett was concentrating on his official protectors. 'Out,' he told Lieutenant Johnson. 'Your work's finished in here. Get your men out.' Meanwhile Gianni's bullets glanced whining off the tough metal of the perimeter.

'Out to be killed by that bastard? We're staying with you.'

'An order, lieutenant. Out. Get your men assembled by the transport lines. Take two trucks. Out.' Lightning signed multiple flourishes all over the firmament. Distant townships went tumbling. The hot moon seemed closer than ever.

'We're staying with you.'

The platoon sergeant came puffing towards them. 'For Christ's sake we need ammo. Those was blanks. Some stupid bastard made a mistake.' He looked back sweatily at the writhing bodies felled by Gianni, their lethal car, driven by Salvatore, getting nearer the camp main gate, Gianni bursting away.

'Ammunition's no good to you,' said Bartlett. 'It won't get through that fence either way. You're safe from that gun.'

'Not if we have to go out,' said Lieutenant Johnson reasonably. 'This mad bastard here,' he told his sergeant, 'wants us to take the men away. Christ knows where to.'

'Get your men to the transport lines,' said Bartlett.

'See here, mister,' the sergeant said, 'we don't obey no civilian orders. We're staying.'

'You're not,' Bartlett said.

'You pretending to give me a fucking order, mister?'

'Not you personally,' Bartlett said. 'Not from now on.' He stepped back five paces, put his Hutchinson hipman to his hip, and then fired a brief burst. The sergeant, with a look of utter amazement on his honest broad face, went down. The ground, like a sprung mattress, bounced him up an instant. Then he lay as still as could be expected. The lieutenant and O'Grady looked on Bartlett in awe. Bartlett said: 'I'll shoot your entire platoon, man by man, if I have to. Get them out of this camp.'

'And let the fucking invaders in?' O'Grady said.

'One thing at a time,' calm Bartlett said.

'You're mad, Bartlett. You're fucking mad.'

'Insubordination. I'll have to rehabilitate you myself, won't I? Later, of course. Lieutenant, you heard what I said.' Johnson's eyes were big as though exaggerated by blackface. He looked again at the corpse of his sergeant. He couldn't believe it. 'That corporal of yours would make a reasonable target,' said Bartlett, readying his gun. The lieutenant blew a shrill whistle, again, again, again. Raggedly his men got into three ranks, corporal as marker. Johnson marched them, giving shaky orders. Gianni had apparently done with blasting for a time. Beyond the gate could be seen Calvin Gropius, the Tagliaferro death wagon. Gropius tried again:

'I'm not condoning this man's acts of violence. These two men are not with me. I'm asking you in the name of the Lord to allow only his messenger to enter.'

Gianni, of course, heard that very clearly. 'The bastard,' he said in English. 'After what I done for him, killing those guys. You mean you don't want us in there, reverend?'

'Be reasonable,' Gropius said. 'For God's sake, think. I'm not trying to save people. I'm trying to save the Word of the Lord.'

'*Protestante*,' grinned Gianni terribly.

'Okay, okay,' said Salvatore. 'He just wants in for himself. He don't trust us, Gianni.'

'*Assoluzione, penitenza*,' said Gianni. 'He don't know how to do it. You,' he said rudely to Gropius, 'you sure my sins is forgiven?'

'This is not the time,' began Gropius lamely.

They looked up to the whirring of a low-hovering helicopter. Gianni instinctively raised his heavy autogun towards it.

'Okay, Gianni, you can't kill the whole fucking world,' said his brother.

Two trucks appeared, closed tough-plated monsters with soldiers inside them. They lumbered, nervously it seemed, towards the gate. The gate, however, was electronically locked. Lieutenant Johnson looked nervously out of the passenger seat of the cab of the leading vehicle, making a key-turning gesture, with some diffidence.

'Unlock that gate, O'Grady,' Bartlett ordered.

'And let those bastards in?'

'Unlock it. You know the code. Dolphin E4, night.'

'You're mad,' said scowling O'Grady. But he took out his pocket activator and set it to 7388026. The gate slowly swung open. The trucks started to move out. Some of the troops let out a feeble soldier's cheer. Calvin Gropius, who had always kept himself fit, sprinted to the opening and, crying 'In the name of the Lord', he tried to squeeze himself in. Hipfire resumed on the *bastardo*. He went down, sobbing 'In the name of the'. The first truck went heedlessly over him, then the second. The helicopter hovered very low. It too gave off rapid fire in a blast of filial vengeance. Gianni Tagliaferro, screaming, dropped his gun, clutched his ruined face, and at once knew whether there was a hell or not. Another burst to finish him, quite supererogatory, got Salvatore, who looked up as at the sudden fall of gentle rain. He went down very quietly.

An amplified actor's voice came from the skies:

'How does the damned thing – Ah, yes, thank you. My name is Willett.' The team, including its leader, looked up in wonder. It was all over the camp, that confident histrionic voice, buoyed up by the electromagnetic barrier. 'An actor, now resting indefinitely. I have with me here Dr Valentine Brodie, late in reporting for duty but better late than never, Mr Dashiel Gropius, and Mrs Edwina Goya, who is about to ah parturiate and urgently requires the help of an *accoucheur* or *euse*. Let us come down and land. Remove your piecrust.'

Bartlett said to O'Grady: 'Let them stay out there.'

Vanessa stood, unable to think, even to breathe. Dr Adams was near her. Gently, like taking a toy from a child who has just dropped off, Dr Adams unfolded Vanessa's fingers and let the warm little gun plop gently into her own hand. She released the safety catch. Vanessa came to, shivering. 'Did you hear what I heard?'

'It's your husband, Dr Valentine Brodie.'

'My *husband* – how did you know?'

'You've talked of your husband often enough – before correcting yourself, of course. I think everybody will be delighted to see your husband. Better than being mated to Bartlett, Head of Enterprise.'

'I can see him – he's there, waving – ' And then, fearful, knowing there was much instability about, perhaps even still in sane-seeming Maude Adams: 'Why do you want that gun?'

O'Grady said to Bartlett: 'You heard what he said. There's a woman up there needs help.'

'She won't get it from us. This isn't a maternity hospital.'

'Deactivate the barrier,' said Dr Adams, pointing the gun at O'Grady. O'Grady, only too glad to obey, did a clumsy have-to-don't-I gesture at Bartlett and loped off towards the concrete block that bore the symbol of a sitting cat, back view, with a single thunderbolt at which, as at a fire, the animal seemed to warm itself.

Bartlett pointed his hipgun at O'Grady and shouted: 'I'm warning you, do you hear me?'

'Best get it over,' said Dr Adams. 'We're short of time.' And she very neatly shot Bartlett. Bartlett spun howling, mad eyes looking for something, somebody, then just staring, holding huge twin gibbous moons. He went down very heavily, and the earth, in temporary repose, did not bounce him. O'Grady saw, coming back, agape, going into an ape droop, unable to believe. He saw Dr Adams's smoking gun. Instinctively he went for his own, cold, as yet unused. Dr Adams said:

'Are you going to be a good boy, Dr O'Grady?'

O'Grady licked his lips. Hand went to hipgun. Dr Adams shot very neatly at a point just five centimetres in front of his left boot.

'Are you, O'Grady?'

O'Grady grinned sheepishly, shrugged. Then he threw his weapon down. It was a heavy weapon. 'Not too good,' he said, 'that pacifier.'

'Alcohol, laughter – those help,' said Dr Adams. 'And the odd dose of animal fear.' The earth moved rather urgently. The moon seemed to be breathing on them.

'He was mad,' said O'Grady, looking down on dead Bartlett. 'Clever but mad. Who takes over?'

'Here he comes now,' Vanessa said. The piecrust was off. She ran towards where the helicopter was preparing to touch ground. Val, dirty, leaner than he had been, monstrously unshorn, went straight to her. They embraced, at first awkwardly, then not so awkwardly. Edwina, groaning, appeared, upheld by Dashiel Gropius, at the top of the ladder. Drs Fried and La Farge – her first maieutic assignment of the mission – looked at Vanessa, doubtful. A storm seemed to be blowing in from the moon. The ground felt like a ship deck in storm birth. Hecate, matron of women in childbed, looked down in menace. 'The ship,' said Vanessa. 'The ship from now on.'

'Transportation?'

'A dickeybird hop,' said Willett. 'Back on board, Edwina. Up and in, ladies. I've always wanted to be in a spaceship.' And so he set the blades whirring again. Dashiel Gropius looked down at dead Bartlett and said:

'Who did that?'

Everybody looked at Dr Adams.

'Thank you,' said Dashiel. 'I didn't really want to do it. I'd promised Edwina, but still – ' The corpse heaved gently on its unquiet bed. 'I didn't know him, you see.'

'Yes,' said Dr Adams. 'You have to know him. Have known him,' she corrected herself.

Freud took tea with the Princess Bonaparte. The tea set was embossed silver, swags of laurel, cherubim, bees. From the window he looked on summer Paris with its phallic tower, his monument. Freud said: 'Princess Marie Bonaparte – '

'Such formality.'

'I was savouring the name. I was met at the station this morning by a representative of the greatest of the democracies and by a daughter of the imperial family founded by the greatest of the emperors. I've come far. And yet I've done nothing.'

'Oh, come. You cured my neurosis. And his.'

'It was hardly worth curing, Princess. Neither. I've discovered that boys love their mothers and fear their fathers. Everybody knows that. They've always known it. I've discovered that children have sexual urges. Any nursemaid can tell you the same thing. But I thought I was Oedipus Tyrannos. I thought I'd solved the riddle of the Sphinx. I haven't. Why have you given such devotion to a failure?' His cancer bit. He winced. She did not notice. She said:

'Oh, we're all failures. You failed less than most. You've written the most gorgeous books. They'll always be read. They won't always be *believed*, of course – but does it matter? We read the Bible without believing it. You just asked a question you never asked before. I'll answer it. You remember when you had me on the couch? Analysing me, digging down to the bone – you said something I wouldn't accept.'

'Ah. I said you'd witnessed the sexual act. As a child. You denied it rather tearfully.'

'Oh yes, tearfully. And then I asked one of the gardeners. And he said oh yes I'd seen it. He saw me seeing it. He let me go on seeing it. And I hid the whole experience. But you knew I'd had it. That was why I became your disciple.'

'It's not enough.'

'Not enough? To meet a man who was really a woman? Who knew things that I didn't know? Who had an intuition greater than mine? You don't kill a sphinx: you make a god of it.'

'The Sphinx killed herself, remember. There was nothing to live for when she'd lost her riddle. Are you,' his cancer struck again; in pain he said, 'calling me a sphinx, Princess?'

'Of course. You're part woman and part something else. Lion – eagle – '

'Not eagle, not not eagle.'

She smiled at that. 'Yes, I know what Adler means. Something with wings, anyway.'

'And yet,' he groaned, 'I know nothing at all about women.'

'Nor do women,' she said, and grasped the handle of the teapot in a strong ringed claw.

He had a curious dream that night, lying unwontedly next to Martha in the big double bed decorated with laurel swags and cherubim and bees. He saw his daughter Anna, grown for some reason into a woman of considerable voluptuousness, giving a lesson in a classroom which reverberated with the noise of clashing ancient battle and the surge of the sea. On the blackboard she had written the letters P and V and N and C, and she was patiently trying to explain the inscription. The dreamer could hear nothing of her explanation because of the surge of battle and the howl of the sea. He woke with a start, though neither in pain nor in fear. He woke Martha.

'What is it, dear? Is it the – '

'No no no. P V N C. What does it mean?'

'I don't know, dear. Go back to sleep.'

But he switched on the bedside lamp. There was a whole rampart of books in the bookcase in the great room. He padded towards them and found a volume in English he had not before seen: *Pears' Cyclopedia*. In it he found what was tickling the back of his brain – the placename Pevensey. A coastal town in Sussex. The place where William the Conqueror landed. He smiled, his old triumphant self-confident self. It woke up the cancer.

The music of triumph blared and thudded in him as he got off the train at Victoria Station, London. He had landed. Jones was there, with other distinguished-looking men in pinstripes. Uniformed policemen, and some evident policemen not in uniform. A limousine. A house. A copy of the *Evening Standard* with his photograph. FREUD IN LONDON. Jones was saying: 'The garden, see. And over there Primrose Hill. And just beyond it – Regent's Park – ' But Freud was reading an advertisement in the *Evening Standard*. He read it aloud to Jones:

'How to be a psychoanalyst in twelve easy lessons. Home study. Only sixty-five pounds.'

A gorgeous garden, air full of birdsong, the soil fragrant after London rain, zinnias, roses –

'I think I'll enrol,' Freud said. 'I've just time for twelve easy lesons.'

'There. Your garden. Yours.'

'I've never had a garden. All those years in Vienna I never had a garden. And now Hitler gives me a garden. *Heil Hitler*.'

Two workmen bringing in a crate of books heard that.

'One of them Nazzies.'

'Got the right idea them Nazzies has. Put down the flippin Jews.'

'Do you mind? My brother-in-law's from Whitechapel.'

Freud and Anna took a walk. A policeman tipped his helmet, saying: 'Evenin, miss. Evenin, Dr Freud.'

'Good evening, constable,' Freud said proudly.

The pub at the corner was full. Freud found the corner of a table where men were urgently playing dominoes. Anna went to the counter for two halves of bitter beer. Freud heard two old women talking over their stout.

'So I tells her straight, if you go on like that all the time at him you'll be givin him one of them inferior compresses.' He didn't like that. He frowned over his half of bitter. Traitor, renegade.

'The way he was brought up. Proper mother's boy, scared of the outside world he was. Real Eedy puss complex I call it.'

Ah, that was better. Much better.

And now his London consulting room was ready, and it was almost identical with the old one on the Berggasse. But his patients spoke English. Like this one now, young, brown-haired, not unattractive despite the whine. Sylvia.

'Sylvia. You say that you want to be loved.'

'Yes.'

'You want to be married.'

'Yes.'

'To have a home and children – a normal sex life with your husband. These are the things you want?'

'Of course they are.'

'And yet you shudder at the thought of sexual contact. Why?'

'I don't know why. You tell me why.'

'Take a deep breath. Here's the truth. You won't like it. Nobody likes the truth.'

'I can take it, doctor.'

'Very well, Sylvia. What you really want is to be with your mother. You wish to be a baby, all the time, stuck at the age of one and a half or two – sucking at the breast of your mother. You're caught and fixed at the oral stage – only the mouth can give you gratification.'

'What's that word, gratifi – '

'Ach, it's your language, not mine. Gratification, joy, pleasure. We all go through that phase, but most of us get over it. You don't want to get over it.' She said nothing but looked at him with big brown English eyes. 'You'll take all the kissing you can get. You suck sweets, chew chocolates. But you don't want to thrust the centre of pleasure downwards – to the vagina.'

'You shouldn't say that. It's not nice.'

'Vagina. Genitals. The thing between your legs.'

Sylvia was shocked. All she could say was 'Doctor!'

'You see? You reject it, you want to believe it's not there. Well, it's there all right. What you have to do is to enter the genital stage. Then you'll be ready for sex without going into hysterics. You understand?'

'But I love my mother.'

'She's dead, girl, dead. Dead five years, so you told me. You can't love the dead. All you love is the memory of the sensations you got from her. Oral gratification. Displace it downwards – that's the secret of your cure – '

The door opened and a dog leapt in. It was Martha who had opened the door. Now she closed it again without entering. The chow lunged at Freud, licked his face, then sniffed warily at his cheek.

'Lun, Lun, my darling Lun! Was you kept in horrible quarantine then? But now it's all over, my little darling.'

Sylvia, getting up from the couch, said, with lower-class British perspicacity: 'And how do you explain that – loving a dog? What sort of a displacement would you call that?'

'Dogs,' Freud said, 'are honest. Dogs hide nothing. You don't have to put a dog on a couch, do you, Lun, my darling?'

But Lun struggled and yelped to be freed from his tender grasp. She ran to a corner and cowered, whimpering, looking strangely at him.

'What's the matter with her, then?'

'Nothing. There's something the matter with me. With my mouth, jaw – '

'So your talking funny isn't just because you're a foreigner?'

'No. Same time next week. Good afternoon.'

'Ternoon.' She joined the dog in looking at him strangely. Then she left.

'Come to me, Lun. *Komm', Liebchen.*' But Lun stayed where she was.

Weak, thin, a bandage on his jaw, he lay in bed a few weeks later. Three gentlemen came to see him, one of them carrying a big black-bound book, one of them Sir Albert Seward of the Royal Society. Freud put out a feeble hand. Sir Albert said:

'Don't endeavour to speak, Dr Freud. We heard with distress of your recent operation. We pray for a speedy discovery. We have brought the official Charter Book of the Royal Society, the book of distinguished signatures it keeps and treasures. Here, among others, you will find the names of Sir Isaac Newton and Charles Darwin. I may say that this visit of the Society's officers is the first that has ever been paid – except to the King. Would you add your name?'

Darwin, Huxley, Einstein. Sigmund Freud. Not shaky. PVNC.

Professor Hill handed Freud another book. His eyes lit. It was in English. *Moses and Monotheism.* If he would be good enough to sign this too. Sigmund Freud. A little shaky. At the final *d* his hand wavered in a sudden spasm of agony.

He was back in the Vatican. Horned effigy. Minna said: 'And will you, Dr Moses Freud?' He faced from a rock outcrop the Israelites who had disobeyed him. In his arms rested the tablets of the law. Adler and Stekel, Rank and Jung cowered, hid their faces in the wide sleeves of their dusty robes.

'You have committed abominations. You have denied the libido, which is the Lord your God. You have spat upon the first commandment – thou shalt believe in the sexual aetiology of the neuroses . . . ' He hurled the tablets at them. They struck only the ground. There they fractured into dust. He woke sweating. Anna was there. Anna said:

'Don't talk. Rest. But listen. I think I have a chance of opening a children's clinic here in London. Hampstead. I've been visiting another orphanage today. In Clerkenwell. The children need their mothers. To hold them, protect them. The father – he doesn't enter into their minds at all. The pre-Oedipal phase. Is it perhaps the only phase that matters – deprivation of the warmth of the womb, of the mother's most intimate embrace?'

Her father made hopeless gestures with his gnarled and wasted hands.

'We never,' she said, 'become reconciled to living outside the womb. English is a curiously expressive language. Womb, room, tomb. It sums up living in three words. And the womb and the tomb are the same. The room in between is a kind of prison. Strange. Otto Rank – was there wisdom there after all? All our neuroses spring from the birth trauma – can it be possible after all?'

'No. No. No.' The pain was intense.

'Father – what am I to do? I'm a virgin. I'll remain a virgin, I think. An eternal spinster. Miss Freud. I serve you. I preach the importance of the sexual impulse. But to me, in my own life, sex doesn't seem to be very important. What do I do? Do I push on with the search for a different truth?' He shrugged with great weariness. 'Never mind for now.' She kissed him on the forehead. 'Sleep.'

Dr Pichler was in London also. He presided, wtih an English colleague, over a radiological session. Freud said, with some difficulty:

'Will it do any good?'

'A palliative only. The biopsy shows an unmistakable malignant recurrence. Yesterday's meeting – the unanimous conclusion that no further operation is feasible. You've always faced the truth. Face this – inoperable and incurable carcinoma.'

'Will this treatment – permit me to carry on with my analytical sessions?'

'For a few more weeks.'

Profound irony. The patient on the couch was the very picture of physical health. The doctor was visibly dying.

'Masturbation is *not* a sin. It's a waste of resource, no more.'

'It is, it is,' the patient cried robustly. 'It's a terrible sin. It's forbidden in the Bible. The sin of Onan.' He hit his crotch as though it were an importunate dog.

'The real sin, of course, is the woman you think about while you're masturbating.'

'How do you know what woman I think about?'

'You all think you're the first. You must be, in my experience anyway, about the five thousandth. It's your mother, isn't it?'

'No no no no no.'

'There's nothing to feel guilty about. It happens to all of us. You want to sleep with your mother. And you think your father will come along and find you at it. What's that thing he carries in his hand? A knife, isn't it? And we all know what he's going to do with it.'

'No no no no no no no.'

'It's common. It's universal. It's known as the Oedipus complex.'

'The what?'

'Next time you masturbate read the daily paper. That will take your mind off it.' And he handed his patient a copy of that morning's *Daily Express*, folded open at an article headed WAS HITLER AFRAID OF HIS FATHER?

Near his end, he knew it. And the old Europe near its end. He lay on a chaise-longue in the September garden. Church bells rang some way away. He listened to very trivial music from a portable radio. Jones sat with him, nursing a whisky and soda. Jones said:

'I didn't know you cared for music.'

'I don't. Too much id. Out of the control of the ego. But I'm waiting for a particular announcement.'

'Of course. I'd forgotten. Do you think it's going to happen?'

'Of course it's going to happen. What was the general consensus at the congress?'

'About practitioners? That nobody must practise without a degree in medicine.'

'That means Anna. Who didn't even finish high school. I reject that. I founded psychoanalysis. I've a right to reject it.'

'You can't make an exception for one, not even your own daughter. There has to be medical qualification – otherwise you throw it open to the quacks and charlatans.'

'Dr Adler was a quack. Dr Jung is a charlatan. Do you insist that a painter have a degree in painting before he starts to paint? Should Shakespeare have had a degree in dramatic literature? Psychoanalysis is an art. The subject is now in the controlling hands of my daughter. Ah – ' For he was, *J'aime Berlin*, the umbrella man, now at the microphone, ready to declare war on Germany. They listened. Freud switched the radio off. Jones said:

'They say it will be the last war.'

'It will be *my* last war. Ah – such efficiency.' For the air-raid siren was tritonally wailing.

Jones was not unnervous, but Freud lay impassively, saying: 'War. It breaks all the Freudian rules. The father kills the son but the son wants to be killed by the father. The son doesn't hate the father, doesn't even fear him. He obeys, lovingly. Of course, he also despises him – a little.'

'War,' said Jones, 'may be the only way out of sexual repression. Wars and whores, as Aldous Huxley puts it. Battles and brothels.' The all-clear sounded, high, triumphant, but flavoured with tritonal unease. 'A false alarm.' With some relief. 'You're in pain. Can I get you something?'

'No. I prefer to think in torment than not to be able to think at all. Thank you, no.'

He lay in bed, thinking in torment. Lun whined piteously in the corner of the room. The cancer spoke. 'This is your old enemy, dear Sigmund. I seem to be giving off a most purulent odour. Or rather it's your rotting flesh that does that – I'm alive and strong and healthy. The flies buzzing about you are less fastidious than your little dog.

They long to eat your meat. The pain? Intolerable? Oh, bear it, please, a little longer. I should hate to be parted from you. I'm not a fly, not even a dog. I need living flesh. No corpses for me. Ah, here comes my impotent foe. Do be strong. Don't give in. I don't really want to kill you. And yet, of course, I do. Resolve that paradox, if you can. Unwind the tangled skein, Oedipus, man most mighty, destroyer of the Sphinx. Such nonsense. Nobody destroys the Sphinx.'

Dr Pichler had come in. 'Painful?' he said.

Freud nodded, then spoke in intense discomfort. 'Your promise, Pichler. You said you'd – only when I couldn't – It's only torture now. It no longer has any sense.'

'You're totally unused to morphine. I shall give you a third of a grain. Not a lethal dose. You understand?'

'I understand. Tell Anna – about our arrangement. But not Martha. Realism, eh? To go out realistically.'

Reassuringly Pichler patted his arm.

A wagon-lit, at rest on the rails, work on the line, the flares of the working lights lighting luridly the bare flesh of the young and beautiful mother.

'Come, darling. Come to mamma,' she called. A small naked child crawled out of the light and into the comforting darkness.

The ship kept steady at anchor despite the earth's raging without. In the otherwise unemployed hospital, Edwina sat up, suckling her child, a boy, born somewhat prematurely and no wonder, wondering what he should be called. Calvin? Nathan? Calvin Nathan? Calthan? Nalvin? Dashiel Gropius, sitting at her bedside, admired the upper curve and swell of her slim body. Not erotically, of course. Women who bared a breast for suckling were exempt from the responsibility of provoking desire. 'The name Dashiel,' he said, 'is a good unusual name.'

She looked at him without smiling. 'I've always believed in free will,' she said. 'And yet I seem, more than anyone I've ever known or heard of, to have been – well, drawn, tugged, trascined. Predestination. Have you ever thought that predestination is true and free will false?'

He grinned. 'You forget that I had a father named Calvin.'

'Sorry. You ran a big gambling joint. That sometimes gets in the way of my seeing what you really are. What I was trying to say was – well, I had this idea of your father as a great elemental force – till I got to know him. Really, I suppose, I was being led to you.'

'Perhaps you were really being led to a truth, and it's not a very Calvinistic one. Still, I embody it. God's creation is all number and chance and play. Chance exists, though chance isn't really free will. But if predestination was true, there'd be no point in gambling.'

But she was thinking of something else. 'Poor Nat,' she said. 'He was killed for love of me. Yet he was only a sort of instrument. A premature instrument. I could have waited for you.' She put her free hand in his. The baby sucked blindly away.

'We wouldn't be here,' Dashiel said.

'We *shouldn't* be here,' she said. And then: 'Poor Nat.'

'Poor everybody. You loved this Nat of yours?'

'An interim love. The earthly father of this child who will bring light to the heathen – ' She blushed. 'I don't know why I said that. I don't know what I meant by that. Strange, I still seem to be taken over by – Forget that I said that.'

'Forgotten. An interim love, you said. And now – ?'

'I needn't say it, need I?'

'Whatever you feel for me is returned a thousandfold. But you'll see me more and more as a mere nothing. Among all these ologists. But if I told them that I'm a chartopaigniologist, they might be impressed and give me a laboratory.'

'What's a – whatever it is?'

'It means an expert in gambling.'

She chuckled. 'Write it down for me and I'll learn it off. Then I can tell people that my husband is a – what you said.'

'You said *husband*. Who ties the knot?'

'The captain of the ship, I suppose. Dr Valentine Brodie.'

Dr Valentine Brodie was at that moment addressing the team in the great salon. He spoke diffidently. 'My only qualification,' he said, 'for being in charge is that I'm fit for very little else. I know nothing except a useless trade – the craft of writing science fiction. But now there's no more science fiction to write. The chronicle I propose to commence writing sometime will, I know, be much in the tradition of science fiction, though it will be science fact. I mean the recording of our space journey, a very long record which I will begin but those of our descendants who, like me, lack the *precise* talents of you ladies and gentlemen, must complete. I know only that the first word must be written soon. The earth's last annals have already been written, and we must forget about the earth – as a frail crust of solid matter covering hot water, I mean. The earth that gave us Shakespeare, Beethoven, Leonardo lives with us.' But the words sounded hollow and the hollowness was confirmed by an interruption from Dr Abramovitz.

'No,' he said, 'it does not. Our library contains nothing but the literature of technology. We have no recorded music, no reproductions of the art treasures of the dead world, no drama, philosophy, poetry. This was how Dr Bartlett wanted it. It is too late now to reverse the situation. We take nothing with us except fallible memories which will fade. The reality seems to be one of number and mass and force and gravitational pull. No dreams. No beauty.'

Val heard that not with horror but with a sort of relief. Why? He said: 'Where man is there has to be beauty, there have to be dreams. It seems we must start again from scratch. The man that is to survive must not be some cold steely ideal, all muscle and intellect, but, at least I may hope this, a being warm, wayward, imperfect, adaptable. From such a being dreams and beauty have to emanate. Perhaps,' he grinned, 'I am making man in my own image – or in my friend Willett's. But, if I may say this, you have all had enough of heartless perfection.'

Willett was not happy. He did not much care for the food, which, however imaginatively served up at table, proclaimed all too solidly or unsolidly its artificial origin. He was surprised to find himself full after eating, but it was a cheating kind of fullness. Real fullness was induced by bloody great hunks of beef, partridges, turkeys bursting with forcemeat, plum puddings, apple pies with thick cream, crusty loaves, and there were none of those things here. Nor, after he had finished the bottles he had lugged aboard, would there be any more wine or brandy. Also it would be a non-smoking voyage. He puffed illegally some of the cigars brought on board by Dashiel Gropius, shut away in one of the handsome toilets to puff guiltily and with little satisfaction, but each smoke was a sad farewell to smoking, not an earnest of endless smoking pleasure to come. He recited from a play in which he had once performed a kind of glorification of the dead world of fleshly indulgence:

'Acres of red meat spitting in the ovens,
Hissing and singing to a summer of incredible richness,

With a fat sap of gravy. Turkeys, capons,
Woodcock, stubblegeese – whole roasted aviaries,
And whole hams, pink as innocence. And all the
Junkets, flummeries, fools, syllabubs, ice puddings,
Sharp as a dentist's probe. Think of the wine too –
Rivers of cold sun from all the provinces the sun washes,
Names like a roll of heroes: Cérons and Barsac,
Loupiac, Moulis, Madiran, Blanquette de Limoux,
Jurançon, Fleurie, Montrachet, Cumières –
We'll never see anything like that again.'

Some of the scientists, brought up on a diet of hamburgers and Cokes, found the syntheveg and meat surrogate and artificial milk and juices little inferior to their old earth cuisine, but others remembered more civilized meals and cried. Willett was, Val supposed, at first facetiously, later more gravely, a subversive influence.

Herman A. McGregor, first ploiarch, came to Willett while he was sitting forlornly in a beautifully designed armchair and watching, on the huge screen, the progress of Lynx and his moon. 'You're Willett?' he said.

'None other.'

'Do you know a George Frederick Willett?'

'My son. Why?'

'A message coming through from Lunacap.'

Willett ran, as well as he could, the long distance to the radio cabin. He recognized the voice, young and reedy, but his heart had already sunk to its limit. The voice said, amid static and howls:

' . . . Final communication from Lunacapital, Lunamerica. I say again, all stations now terminating communications. Seismic disturbances on the moon's surface and the prospect of early dissolution render further communication impracticable. I say again, this is George Frederick Willett, head of communications, Lunacap, closing down moon's final message.' There was a pause. 'That seems as banal a farewell as this very banal brain could be expected to contrive. I need better words. My father gave me such words once. If my father is still alive and, by the remotest of chances, receiving this message, perhaps he will forgive my bad accentuation and faulty expression. It is not easy to do anything well at this final moment.' And then, the lines striking at Willett's heart the more for the very unprofessionalism of their utterance, he came out with:

'The cloud-capped towers, the gorgeous palaces,
The solemn temples, the great globe itself,
Yea, all which it inherit, shall dissolve
And, like this insubstantial pageant faded,
Leave not a rack behind. We are such stuff
As dreams are made on, and our little life
Is rounded with a sleep.'

The rest was silence. The two ploiarchs looked in silent sympathy at Willett, who sat for half a minute looking at his worn boots, sniffing. He blew his nose on a dirty handkerchief and said: 'Thank you, gentlemen.'

'No trouble.'

Willett found Val in his office on the lowest deck, busied with a small computer and a lot of papers. Willett said:

'I'm leaving.'

'What?'

'I'm leaving. Going down with the ship. The other ship, I mean. There's nothing for me here.'

Val thought about that, eyes down, tapping a random Morse message with his stylo on the polished steel desk. 'There's nothing much for me, if it comes to that.'

'You've your wife. A delightful girl if I may say so. Less – you know – self-assured than I expected. A sort of *melting* girl.'

'Yes, there's Vanessa. But finally it's her world I join. The world of clean efficiency.'

'You'll change all that. Not too much, of course. There's plenty for you, Val. Duty, for instance.'

'Duty is only duty. Stern daughter of the voice of God. Not very seductive. So. You're leaving. I won't dissuade you, of course. If it weren't for Vanessa and this damned duty I'd be with you. We could at least die drunk. However I die, doing my duty, it won't be drunk. When are you leaving?'

'Now.'

'And where are you going?'

'Just back to earth. It doesn't much matter where.' There seemed to be an unwonted division inside Willett's heart. 'If I leave, am I letting mankind down?'

'You had something to give them. Yourself.'

'I could have acted Falstaff for them. Hamlet too, despite the fatness and scantness of breath. But there's the other mankind out there. Mankind with its feet on earth. Soon to be mixed with earth. My place is out there.'

Val did not say what he knew to be true: that to act Falstaff or Hamlet would be grossly nostalgic, that the past was dead, that Bartlett had, though for the wrong reasons, been right. That culture on this ship was represented by the man with the least pretensions to it, a man who knew all about number and chance. Fate or something had sent the right Gropius.

'You'll find plenty of transport if you want to drive some place.'

'Yes. To some empty bar with bottles as yet unbroken. I shall down whisky and gin and cognac and smoke three cigars at the same time. I may go out singing. Can I get somebody to let me cut in that elevator thing?'

'I'll escort you to the gate.'

And he did. Willett took from his pack a farewell present. 'These are video discs,' he said. 'I am on them, though admittedly in rather small parts. Perhaps they will remind you of me, if you wish to be reminded. You may find them entertaining or even instructive. By chance they sum up the major preoccupations of the race – the nature of the human soul, the problem of right government.' Val looked at the titles: *Freud*; *Trotsky's in New York*. The luxury of revolution and psychoanalytical couches. How remote, how frivolous.

'Thank you, Willett.' And with no other ceremony of farewell, Willett left safe *America* and returned to an America ready, with the rest of the earth, for dissolution. It was an afternoon of high winds, bilious clouds, the gound heaving like boiling porridge. There were corpses about, but the whole world was a graveyard. Val saw Willett waddle towards the transport park. His helicopter had reached its last gasp of fuel. Besides, to travel through air would be to cut himself off from the smell of the dying earth. Val elevated himself back to his office, locked the door, then copiously wept. Natural tears. He wiped them soon, and he composed himself when a knock came at the door. He opened it and welcomed the two ploiarchs in, tough young Scots whose ancestors had fired crankshafts over bitter seas. They wanted instructions.

'Forty days,' Val said, 'to Cat Day. Will we be ready to go?'

McGregor said: 'We can't get out of Lynx's orbit till the work on the G apotha is finished. Dr Jumel still has to complete modifications to the megaproagon.'

Val nodded, not at all out of his depth. This was pure science fiction. 'What has to be done there?'

'Conversion of nuclear energy to jetpush,' said McEntegart. 'There's a thing she calls the epsilon link. She's having trouble.'

'How much trouble?'

'Ye'd best see her yersel.' Val looked sharply up, expecting insolence. No insolence, just a reversion to the speech of his fathers.

'Trouble or not,' Val said, 'our big day must be CAT 35. Five days from now. We can't risk staying on earth much longer. Earth is collapsing. Better to risk a tangential glide even from a turbulent Lynx.'

'There'll be a lot of turbulence,' McGregor said.

'Yes,' Val said. 'I'll announce our sailing date this evening.'

'It's a gamble.'

'Of course it's a gamble,' Val grinned. 'Tonight after dinner we may play a little roulette. Blackjack. Chemin de fer. Monte Carlo night, with Dashiel Gropius in charge. Get people in the gambling mood. Of course it's a gamble. What the hell isn't?'

At that time the Love Field Municipal Airport at Dallas was still serviceable – at least its southeastern half, the northwestern having been overwhelmed by a swollen Bachman Lake. Very little of the city itself was left standing after the last earthquake. Bidu Saarinen and Florenz Zenger were impatient to be gone, along with their President, but Skilling had his own plans. He said:

'You have those orders in writing, stamped with the presidential seal. I want no displays of rugged initiative on your part or on the part of Heyser.' Heyser was the head of the *America IV* project in Richmond, Indiana. The spaceship, nearly identical, following the Frame plan, with its prototype in Kansas, had a feature known as a windstand, superior to the massive foam bed of the ship that Val now ruled: the craft hovered a kilometre over the turbid ground on an air cushion, had to be reached by helicopter (but how did you keep a helicopter safe these days?) and at least those up there already had little to worry about from the convulsive earth. It was to Richmond, Indiana, that Saarinen and Zenger were on their way. At least they were already embarking: they stood doubtful on the steps of their Montfleury 9. Their President should be embarking with them. Instead –

'You don't have to worry about me,' Skilling said. 'Indeed, I order you not to worry. If I'm not there in three days you're to blast off without me. You have that in writing.'

'It's madness, sir,' Zenger said, and he bit his lip.

'A President has a certain duty to the territory he's been responsible for. He has, as it were, to see his country bedded down for the long night.'

Saarinen shuddered at the gallows humour. But he said, mildly: 'See you there then, sir. Good luck.' And he and Zenger got aboard. Skilling watched the little craft take off and then, hands in the pockets of his PotoMac, as it was whimsically named, he strode towards his Phyfe two-seater. Like at least one other former New York City mayor, he had been an aviator. Alas, no airport would be named for him. Not in *this* solar system. The Phyfe bore no presidential insignia: it had been part of Skilling's private life. He loved the little craft – the delicacy of its controls, the thrust that depended on a mere nutshell of nuclear power. It was now the only thing he was able to love. Wifeless and childless now, he could cherish his loneliness, the loneliness that he had previously regretted. But a virtual celibacy, so his Catholic upbringing had induced him to believe, by a natural extension of the conditions for holding the sacerdotal office, was useful if not essential in the ruler of a city, state, country. If he had ever loved any living being passionately, it was the city of New York. He had to revisit New York before it, or he, died.

It was early morning, with a bloody sun struggling against clouds coiling dirtily as oil smoke. He achieved a sweet and birdlike takeoff and then took a bearing from McKinney, north of Dallas. He did not seek overmuch height: he wanted to see his distressed and dying kingdom. All below him lay stricken land, heaving in parts, displaying the open wounds of seismic shock, smoke rising from dead townships. The Red River had broken its banks and spread its own ruin. The Ozark mountains, mounted on their insubstantial base of air and water, leaped towards the sky, were pulled back, leaped again. Hot Springs was nothing but hot springs. He hovered low over Little Rock and saw what seemed a huge neglected stonemason's yard, stony rubbish, the littleness of dead rock. No life in Arkansas, the river towns of Augusta and Pocahontas drowned. And then the Mississippi, father of waters.

The width and rage of the great river was astonishing. He fancied that he could hear its roaring voices even from the height of his hover over Rosedale, even despite the sealed plexiglass of the cabin. And in places the Mississippi leaped high from its bed in a flurry of dirty silver, leaped as a salmon leaps. He flew northeast to Holly Springs and said goodbye to the river's own namestate, crossed into Tennessee and over ruined Nashville ate his frugal lunch – a ham sandwich with English mustard, a Cadbury chocolate bar – and drank from his thermos of strong black sugarless coffee. He took the meal sacramentally, with a special relish. The comfort of the little things men and women would need no more – the silver wrappers of chocolate, yellow pungent mustard in a pot, the leap and plop of percolating coffee.

Kentucky shone no more purple beneath him. A gaping wound, or, he thought less dramatically, a slash like the slash in a baked Idaho stretched, he judged, from Frankfort to Bowling Green. He was not sure of his bearings now, and no known landmarks remained except for a stretch of railroad line, miraculously still lying patiently, with a pulverized town on it: this he took to be Lexington. In the middle of the afternoon he crossed the swollen and deformed line of the Big Sanay River and was in West Virginia. He had once, briefly, courted a girl from Charleston, a lovely coffee-hued dancer named Betsy Domenico. That had been in the days of comparative irresponsibility, when it was all politics, and political competence was expressed through human weakness – like courting a dancer from Charleston, getting drunk at rallies, telling coarse jokes at caucus meetings. Charleston still had a few of its prouder towers standing, which meant perhaps that there was life there. He had an urge to descend, land, embrace, if it were possible, some of those hopeless frightened beings who were still his responsibility and whom he had, perhaps, conceivably, failed.

Failed? Yes, if among his responsibilities had been and still was the responsibility of speaking the truth. He had not spoken the truth. He had not even belatedly apologized for not speaking the truth. There had been a time when he could have spoken on such of the radio and television networks as had still been functioning, and said: 'The end is coming, and I comforted you with false hopes. I lied for the sake of your short-lived happiness. I gave you no time to put your houses in order – meaning to fulfil the need of all men and women to prepare their souls for the end. But I was a man of politics, not of religion. My duty was to keep order, even if to keep order meant keeping you in the dark. Now you know there is an end to all things upon us, and what consolation can I offer? I can say: the world was already ending, though we tried to delude ourselves that this was not so. It was ending because there were too many people in the world and not enough to eat. Because a war was coming whose sole outcome would be to ensure that nobody in the world had anything at all to eat. If God exists, then God has perhaps been merciful. We cannot blame ourselves that the end is coming. We are bidden remember that nature is powerful and man weak. The psalmist was right: all flesh is grass. And now that grass is cast into the oven. Be brave, if you can. Remember that life is not a right but a gift. And now the gift is removed. Be thankful that you have savoured that gift. March into the dark with erect heads, eyes open.'

Nonsense. Cheap useless verbiage. There was nothing to say. There had never been anything to say.

The sun was full on his back as he rose and steered due east. He was over Virginia now, heading for dead Richmond. The James River surged and frothed. Richmond was not only dead but drowned. He made a right-angled turn and sped north. The waters of Chesapeake Bay were rampant over Maryland; Delaware, pincered by two bays, must be under the sea. It was not long before he saw what had once been Washington. He sobbed briefly and then told himself to reserve his tears. He again steered due east and his stomach fell; he knew he was approaching the end. He was coming to the region where it all began – the seaboard where men had kissed the earth and cursed the sea and shaken fists at a Europe that had condemned them to poverty or the tyranny of fools and bigots. They had come seeking a living, peace, tolerance, slow in finding any of the three. New Jersey. And then the city he had ruled, a city he could no longer fully recognize. From universal swirling waters the tallest towers of Manhattan, true, still grotesquely rose. It was pitiable – these proud peaks jutting from the deluge. The Newman Tower's top storeys, the central needle of stone that pierced the heart of the Scotus Complex, the Outride Building and Paternoster Convention City showing roofs bone-white in the bloody sun, the two-hundred-storey Tractarian Folly, as it had been whimsically named, as if the makers had been ashamed of its height or anxious to diminish their achievement in the eye of a God who had shattered the Tower of Babel. 'Mayor of New York City,' said Skilling aloud, 'three terms running.'

God, or something, heard and acted. An audience was needed for the final enactment, and what better audience than the three-times mayor? From the viscera of the universal waters an under-earth fist punched up a segment of a building as neat, save for the ragged edges, as any breakfast waffle. A single swipe from a thick brewis of water, mud, stone, metal smote the remaining towers and sent them under. Then that same hidden fist, then another, hit harder than before, and with each punch came up a fragment of the city as for its mayor's inspection, glowing briefly in the lurid light, hitting the air and going down in a ballet of atoms. Then the earth opened and drank all the waters it could, shutting at once as if to gargle. Skilling, formerly head man of the world's greatest megalopolis, three times running, three terms, saw his ruined boroughs dry as a bone and as dead, preserving here and there by some miracle of irony the configuration of streets and avenues. Then new water galloped in, rusty as the sun, and hid everything. New York was one with all other ancient cities that had gone under the sea. Skilling wept and then wiped his eyes on his sleeve. He nodded goodbye to no one in particular. He put the remains of the chocolate in his mouth, relishing the thick bittersweet bolus, rolling the silver wrapper into a ball he let fall among the pedal controls. Chewing, he turned the nose of his craft earthwards, waterwards, shut off the engine, and dove into New York City, entering the dark with his eyes open.

New York, a pier, a ship sirening imminent departure. Porters, passengers, bustle, luggage, gulls. Trotsky's family is already aboard, but a crowd of workers have detained the great man himself for a reprise of praise. Trotsky, revolutionary goatee raised like a gun, stands at the foot of the gangway. He is sung at:

> Trotsky in New York
> Heard his praises hurled
> Higher than the Woolworth Building.
> Trotsky in New York,
> Stronger than a bull,
> Bellowed of a world worth building.
> Spilling out his wisdom like a corn-
> Ucopia,
> Fiercer than a hurricane,
> Preaching an American-born
> Utopia –

Olga appears, alone.

> Everybody walk
> With his head held high

To the sky the dawn is gilding,
For Trotsky's been in New York!

Trotsky is cheered. He holds out his arms and says: 'Friends, comrades. My necessaries are embarked, and those include my dear wife and children. In a moment the gangway will be raised. I have time only to say to you all, citizens of this city of prose and fantasy – '

But a Mexican appears from nowhere with a guitar. He strums and sings, while Trotsky listens fascinated:

Mexico, Mexico,
A good place to die
Is Mexico,
Under a harsh blue sky
Where the condors fly.
Mexico, Mexico,
An excellent place to die,
Come some day and try
Mexico.

And then he has gone. Trotsky overcomes his bewilderment, saying:

'Our Mexican friend again. Well, I do not think I will either live or die in his country. My work lies east for the moment, the task, with my colleagues Lenin and Stalin, of building a new Russia, first having put an end to the war with Germany. This war, comrades, is wasteful. Refuse, I enjoin you once again, to join it. Make this your final promise to me before I leave you. Fight in an imperialist war and you postpone or even liquidate your opportunity of fighting the true war – against the bloodsucking forces of capitalism And that true war can be won. The glorious news from Russia confirms it. Do you promise me to sabotage the capitalistic preparations for war in Washington, to refuse to take arms against your brothers the workers of Germany, to allow the imperialists to batter themselves to pieces without your help?'

The crowd cheers affirmation, the crowd sings:

Peace, perfect peace –
All the workers beg
And a job with reg-
Ular pay.
Peace to earn

Dollars to burn:
Peace for the –

But newsboys appear, yelling 'War!', bearing posters yelling WAR! The crowd breaks up into individuals buying newspapers. A recruiting sergeant appears with a banner luridly crying UNCLE SAM WANTS YOU. A lone crank bears an ill-lettered placard announcing that the end of the world is imminent. A fat man with a fat cigar, impeccably dressed as a permanent civilian, cries stentorianly:

'As from this moment, the United States of America is at war with Germany. All able-bodied men are invited to join the United States armed forces. The recruiting office is outside the dock gates. Follow the sergeant.'

And the crowd marches off in high patriotic enthusiasm, singing:

We don't want just war,
We want a *just* war.
Let the trumpets roar,
But for a *just* war.
Fight the Germans,
Smite the Germans,
Show them more and more
What a bloody war is for.
Let your voices soar
But for a *just* war.
As we said before,
We want a *just* war.
What is justice? That's a musty sort of thing to ask.
The task
In store
Is fighting in a just just war.
Just war –
Just war –

They can be heard singing the way towards the recruiting office, while Olga and Trotsky are left alone, a little embarrassed.

'Not much of a farewell present, comrade,' says Olga.

'The American workers' stupidity? Ach, they'll learn. Perhaps even you will learn. About the necessity of revolution, I mean.'

'I don't think it matters much. Each of us is finally alone. The real problems aren't political ones.'

'All problems are political ones.'

'You'll learn too.'

The ship's siren blasts. 'There are some things,' Trotsky says, 'I must just close my eyes to. It's the only way to do what has to be done.'

'What has to be done. Note the passive voice.'

'Well, perhaps reality is best defined as the things that are done to us. But but but – I'm not sure any more. And I *have* to be sure. Now.' He sings:

> All through history
> Mind limps after reality.
> And what's reality? Who the hell knows?
> There's no mystery
> In physical causality.
> Matter. Is that as far as reality goes?

A marine officer appears. Trotsky must mount the gangway. A siren hoots again. Mounting backwards he ruminates:

> The truth is without doubt that the root of all human miseries and joys is
> Not to be found in mere political noises.
> It's something any good Marxist is shocked, even to find himself minimally, vestigially thinking of.
> The reality is –

But hooters and the cheers of departure drown the last word. From the taffrail Trotsky blows a kiss. She blows one back. He cries, fist raised:

'Work for the new world.'

'There's no such thing.'

He shrugs, smiles, disappears from view. Olga is alone. She sings:

> The new world coming tomorrow –
> I hailed it again and again.
> And if folk ask me when
> I have to say:
> The day after
> The day after
> The day after
> The day after

* * *

Val switched it off. 'Oh my God,' he groaned. 'So this is what we take into space. And to think I've been dreaming of the world ending in a blast of defiant music. A pit band, untrained voices, banalities. Oh my God.'

'Burn them both,' Vanessa said. 'Better nothing than those.'

'Ah,' Val said, eyes on the wall chronometer in the viewing room. 'It's the moment.'

The crew, or citizens, of *America* were hardly aware of the blast-off. The magnetic gravitation surrogate of the great ship kept steady even the beaker of water that Edwina Gropius put to her lips. It was a three-day trip to growling Lynx. The beast was bellowing, trembling, rippling at the prospect of soon leaping on his prey. What the hell was the thing made of? Pure iron ore? The mass tugged at the craft as it became a new, if diminutive, satellite, circling the hydrogen-misty planet in ninety minutes flat. Instruments took in what they could of Lynx's surface – the scars of ancient wars, pock-holes, a long purplish line that might, to a more credulous group of observers, be taken as an artefact, a Lyngine Great Wall of China. But all instruments squeaked of a dead planet. Dead? It was alive, horribly strong, ready to have its own way, beginning its long or endless sojourn in the solar system in an ellipse that was at a thirty-degree angle to earth's and, of course, most irregularly, trundling round in a direction opposite to earth's. Spinning between Lynx and moon, the crew or citizens saw on the great screen a moon lacking all the features that every schoolboy knew, the seismic disasters having ravaged it like some dreadful disease. Meanwhile, work went on in Dr Jumel's laboratory. She, a pretty fair girl, flushed with effort, her attractive low brow corrugated with thought, worked on the epsilon-link equations. Cybernetics and automation cooperated in turning out successive versions of the tiny complex artefact that would provide the clue to more thrust. Val was with her, but he confessed his impotence to advise, help, even set his SF-writer's fancy to work.

'It has to be soon,' said worried McEntegart. The calendar said CAT 10.

'It *will* be soon,' soothed Val.

But it was not soon. The calendar clicked, at artificial midnight, to CAT 9, then CAT 8 followed. Artificial dawns, artificial noons, artificial nights – their ingenious lighting system clung desperately to the only temporal pattern they knew. But that must change; there must be no buffers against reality. Meanwhile earth grew closer, the moon was huge and blinding, but not so blinding as Lynx. They drank the sun like some strength-giving potion, for attack, for resistance. It was hard, especially for Mr and Mrs Gropius, to believe that a terrible cosmic drama was in progress outside the tough walls of their world. These two cooed at the baby, who yelled in self-centred vigour. He had a name now: Joshua. Edwina crooned an ancient song that her grandfather had heard from his father as a boy:

'Joshua, Joshua;
Sweeter than lemon squash you are,
Oh by Gosh you are,
Joshua, Oshu aaaaah.'

Life was waiting and three meals a day. The food that came from the galley seemed insubstantial, but it filled. It was tastier now, Florence Nesbit and Sven Maximilian Josiah Markelius having proved even more ingenious than the diaitologist Rosalba Opisso in the use of herb and spice surrogates. There seemed to be a great number of amateur cuisiniers aboard. There were even wine substitutes, made by compounding grape flavour with alcohol generated from the still useful waste, recycled, of Professor Frame. Gin? Vodka? No problem at all. Poor Willett should have stayed. No, perhaps not. He was no man for clean aseptic interiors.

CAT 7. Val refused to be desperate. If the job could be done, it could be done by Lilian Jumel. If the job could not be done, then they would all perish. Nobody had any right to life. Life was a free bestowal. Still, as they sailed between the Scylla of moon and the Charybdis of Lynx, between the steam of one and the ravaged face of the other, animal panic grew in those few of them who saw the movement towards cataclysm on the ploiarchal screens. Val refused to think of the velocital demand being made on *America* in order that it might flee the Lyngine orbit: something like half a megakilom an hour. He woke up in the artificial night, sweating. Vanessa slept soundly, beautiful in the artificial old-time lunar light that ingeniously washed gently in from a casement that seemed to give on to a rolling lawn, with a ruined temple. That too would have to go.

Val dredged desperately into memories of the mad books he had written, full of fancy unjustified, undisciplined by the exigencies of scientific fact. He found nothing.

Then, on CAT 6, Lilian Jumel collapsed – overworked, lacking sleep, full of despair. She had colleagues, of course, competent, but mere journeymen compared with her – John Durante, Fred Lopez, Louise Boudinot. The megaproagon was her brainchild. O'Grady, quieter than he had been, diffidently suggested a pacifier. Val said no – a mild hypnotic only. And then he thought: why use drugs? The book he had written so many eons ago – *The White and the Walk of the Morning* – had an amateur hypnotist in it – Jess Hartford or Harvey or somebody. Val had done his homework; he always had. While Lilian Jumel writhed on her bed, in the intervals of waking hysteria, Val brought calm to her bedside, also a swinging gold watch borrowed from Dashiel Gropius, his father's gift to him on graduation. He calmed her with the rhythm of gentle light and a single word. He got her into deep sleep. He spoke to her mind, calmly, always calmly. He said:

'There are many ways out of the problem. The very bounce of Lynx as it eats the earth may provide the jolt needed, the extra split-second boost. There are, apparently, a great number of asteroids spinning about. Who knows whether the pull of one of them, infinitesimal though it may be, may not ease the gravitational problem that faces us? There is nothing to worry about. You have all the time in the world. Things are not really so desperate. Nothing is all that important. We have all known the rich life of earth. This new space life is a mere bonus, a discardable extra. Rest, dear Lilian. Rest as long as you will. Everything is being taken care of.'

On CAT 4 she rose from her bed without a word to anyone, except a demand for surrogate orange juice and coffee. She showered, washed her hair, dressed. She walked calmly to her laboratory, where Durante, Lopez and Louise Boudinot were knotted over equations. 'All right,' she said, and they went to work.

On CAT 3, having achieved a velocity that kept the craft continually retreating from the impending point of collision, Lilian Jumel spoke hopefully. And then all work stopped as they went to the great screen to see the end of the moon.

The moon had been circling its new host in a regular satellitic rhythm. But earth was eventually going to be in the way of one arc of its revolution. This had always been evident, and there had been distracted speculation as to what the moon would do – wobble out of its course, be hurled to the condition of a solar satellite? But what happened now, the obvious, the banal, had always been the prognosis of most of the *America* team. They saw the moon come gracefully wheeling, approach the earth and then, not brutally, not even rapidly, shatter to fragments against it. The point of impact, they adjudged, was the dead heart of Europe. The moon shattered, and they gasped. One of the girls sobbed. Little Joshua Gropius howled, but not for the moon. The moon broke and went into gracefully sailing fragments that slowly changed to sunlit dust and, most beautifully, tried to become a dust-ring around Lynx. But earth was in the way. A ring spun, of most lovely pearly configuration, but, at the point of impact with earth, shattered to amorphous dust, only to re-form when free of that gross body.

On CAT 2, with no large fanfares of triumph, Lilian Jumel announced that they were ready to blast off.

And so, with a desperate-seeming wrenching that even caused a brief dysfunction of the magnetic gravitator, the spaceship *America* broke free of the pull of Lynx and soared into free space, heading in the direction of Mars. What they all had to see now, and yet did not wish to see, was the end of their own planet. As they sped away from Lynx, they saw on the big screen the great hump of the predator, with its ring satellite that had once been the moon of Shakespeare and Shelley and a million banal songs, growing ever more disjunct, ever more something-out-there. Val assembled the team in the salon. He had never yet worn the black gear that was the uniform of the citizens of this new America, and he came in, looking, if anything, scruffier than he had ever been – clad in the worn trousers and sports coat and torn boots of his, and Willett's, anabasis. He said:

'We are, as you know, about to witness the end of the earth. It seems to me that we ought to drink to something – ourselves, our future, perhaps not our past. We have no past, but our future is limitless.' Dashiel Gropius wheeled in a portable cocktail bar that had been very speedily contrived in the util workshop. It bore bottles and glasses and ice. 'Mr Gropius,' Val said, 'will soon be the most important man in *America* or on *America* – we must agree sometime as to the more fitting preposition. In his hands will be the organization of games.' Most of the citizenry looked puzzled, even affronted. 'I mean that all we can reasonably salvage from our past is the game of skill or chance, which is based on the abstraction of number. All else – literature, metaphysics, music – must be accounted mere nostalgia, nothing more. What have we to do with poems about love under the sycamores under the moon?'

'Music,' said Dr Adams, 'we *must* have music.'

'Only if we learn to make it ourselves. What right have we to listen to instruments long dead, scraped or blown in the service of the glorification of a world that no longer exists? No, we must learn to make our own.' Vanessa saw a hardness in him which resurrected the lineaments of Bartlett. But he was a more reasonable Bartlett.

'Let us at least, before earth ends,' said Dr Adams, 'hear some of earth's music.' She took from her shoulder bag a musicassette. Val smiled with unbartlettian indulgence. 'All I have,' she said. 'And after this performance you're at liberty to liquidate it for ever.'

'What is it?'

'Mozart's Jupiter Symphony.'

'The last movement, then. Take this, ladies and gentlemen, as a demonstration of our power, our very human power, to enclose through intelligence and skill the huge but crass and stupid events that are the result of sheer blind celestial mechanics. The earth is dead, or nearly. Long live the human world.' The musicassette was inserted in one of the recording machines. Vanessa's finger pressed a golden lozenge on an instrument panel inlaid in the salon wall. From the four corners of the ceiling music poured – the essence of human divinity or divine humanity made manifest through the gross accidents of bowed catgut and blown reeds. And on the screen they saw what that music diminished and made seem remote, even trivial, or else take on the pattern of choreography – cosmic indeed but seemingly humanly contrived. They saw Lynx and earth meet, and the first patch of earth to catch the blow was the northern Rockies, which must already be leaping with stupid love to the claws of Lynx. They tasted the heartening fire of gin, its little benignant brutality, as earth shattered – core of dancing water, crust of dust – and at once formed an outer ring satellite of its successor in the dizzying annals of the sun dance. The moon was a ring and, a greater ring, pulverized earth spun already in perfect concentricity, luminous dust made of the dust of Skilling and Willett and the Tagliaferro brothers and Calvin Gropius and his family and their cat and millions and millions more, all, indeed, who had scratched that fertile surface and watched the external wonders of mind rear themselves upon it. Mozart, too, was part of that dusty ring, but, miracle, Mozart was also here, tender, triumphant, drowning even the loud howling of a child. The rhythms of Mozart bore them on into space, the beginnings of their, our, journey.

Epilogue

'Their, our, journey. That, boys and girls, ladies and gentlemen, is the story.' Valentine O'Grady stopped and looked quizzically at the twenty facing him in the classroom known as Frame. The story had, of course, taken more than a single session to tell. He had told it at length, dramatically, drawing on his fancy, the long unfinished chronicle that rested in the Brodie Archives, two ancient and fantastic films that were permitted to be seen only by select members of the hierarchy. He had told it to a group of young people who were not quite children, not quite adults, who were in fact hovering in that painful interim of pubescence where *ladies and gentlemen* and *boys and girls* could be used indifferently. 'What,' he asked, 'do you think of the story?' They shrugged, made frog-mouths, pouted. One or two yawned, perhaps with hunger. Maude Abramovitz, a cold and clever girl, said:

'It's not really history, is it? It's – it's –'

'Myth,' said Nat Irving.

'It happened like that,' said Valentine O'Grady, 'more or less. It's good to be reminded of one's origins. That's why I told you the story.'

'Why good?' asked Bill Harrison. 'It's all so – remote, different from what's real. I mean, it's a myth world, full of – what do you call them, buildings, clouds, trees, those things with four legs and things with four wheels. It's not our world. How can they be our people?'

'We sprang from them,' said Valentine O'Grady. 'A long time ago, true.' He looked at them. They were sour, puzzled, sceptical, unresponsive. 'We bear their names, we live in the world they built.'

'Why I said myth,' said Maude Abramovitz, although it was Nat Irving who had said it for her, 'was because this Joshua character we've heard so much about was a myth. I mean, the whole story takes on its myth quality from him. He was supposed to be the son of God.'

'He was the son of Edwina and Dashiel Gropius, though the true father was Nat Goya. He believed he was the son of God. He gave us our first space religion.'

'Which nobody believes in any more,' said Sylvia Ewing.

'Some do,' said Valentine O'Grady lamely.

'It's hard to take in,' George Eidlitz said. 'This business about a journey, for instance.'

'This *is* a journey. This ship was designed for getting somewhere. A place where we can plant trees, erect buildings, feel the wind blowing in our faces.' Some of the class smiled. Sophie Farragut said:

'Your generation talks about a journey. Our generation knows we're just *here*. We've always been here, right back to what they call the mists of myth. I don't believe your story.'

'We'll always be here,' said Bill Harrison. 'It stands to reason. We've always been here, we always will. All that stuff you told us is just lies.'

'Who built the ship?' asked Valentine O'Grady desperately.

'God or somebody,' said Fred Greeley. 'It doesn't matter. It's here, that's what matters.'

'And A. J. Gromrich, who wrote your mathematics book, and the people who invented chess, and the auction bridge masters?'

'They were here too, a long long time ago.' Fred Greeley looked at his wristchron, a new one, straight from the utilab. 'There's nothing but this,' he concluded. 'All the rest is a fairy story.'

Valentine O'Grady pounced then. 'What is a fairy?'

'The thing in your brain that makes you tell lies.'

Maria Brodie had not so far spoken. She spoke now. She said: 'Why aren't we told about the other myth? The myth that makes more sense than the one you've been telling us?'

'What other myth?'

'The one about the bad man called Fred Fraud who kept people strapped to a couch and the good one called Trot Sky who wanted people to do what he did and run through space.'

'That's kiddicrap,' said Fred Greeley. 'That's worse fairy stuff than what we've just been hearing. All about Sike and Pol and the rest of the nonsense.'

'Where did you pick up all this?' asked Valentine O'Grady.

'Oh,' said Fred Greeley, 'it's all supposed to be locked up here somewhere and nobody's allowed to see it. Sike is making people go to bed with their fathers and Pol is singing and dancing. A lot of nonsense. People,' he pronounced sagely, 'ought to keep a hold on reality.'

A sceptical, tough, hard-brained generation. Valentine O'Grady sighed. The end-of-session bell rang. 'All right,' he said. 'Class dismissed.' They went running off for their protein and syntheveg. They had forgotten the story already.